PORTALS IN TIME
THE QUEST FOR UN-OLD-AGE

Winner of Twelve Book Awards:

BEST FANTASY BOOK
1. Winner 2018 Pinnacle Book Achievement Award
2. Winner - 2018 Literary Titan Book Awards
3. Finalist - 2018 (IAN) Book of the Year Awards
4. Finalist - 2018 American Book Fest, Best Book Awards

BEST VISIONARY FICTION BOOK
5. Gold Medal -2018 Readers Favorite Book Awards
6. Winner - 2018 Beverly Hills Book Awards

BEST INSPIRATIONAL FICTION
7. Winner - 2018 American Fiction Awards
8. Finalist – 2018 American Book Fest, Best Book Awards

BEST NEW AGE FICTION
8. Winner - 2018 Book Fest International Book Awards
9. Winner - 2018 Beverly Hills Book Awards
10. Winner - 2017 Author's Circle Novel of Excellence
11. Finalist - 2018 National Indie Excellence Awards

"If you love fantasy, time-travel, and adventure, delivered through inspirational, melodic, and mystical prose, you'd be hard-pressed to find anything more original, satisfying, or motivational than "Portals in Time: The Quest for Un-Old Age" by John Joseph Teressi.

This story is so well-written, it is actually quite beautiful. In addition to the storyline text that flows effortlessly, Teressi's characters often recite poetry and songs, riddles and rhymes, all in an effort to get through to his Gripps. The attention to detail provides readers with vivid imagery and focus. What a wonderful and creative imaginative mind. I thoroughly enjoyed *Portals in Time*. Humorous, inspirational, adventurous, mysterious – it is a complex story full of elements to satisfy a wide spectrum of readers." — Sheri Hoyt, Managing Editor, Reader Views.

If you enjoyed The Alchemist, A Wrinkle in Time, and The Celestine Prophecy, you will love this book. If you thrive in nature and appreciate a spiritual journey leading to wondrous discoveries that can change your life, you will be delighted as you become part of this exciting adventure.

This new, highly original, visionary story is entertaining and at the same time thought-provoking. It is an inspirational adventure that will engage and entertain readers of all ages.

There are few times in our lives when you can become lost in a fantasy that may affect your life in such a meaningful and positive manner. You will not forget the characters and the wonder of nature in this story of love, patience, understanding, and redemption that will enhance your life and live in your heart.

Contact the author at www.Portals in TimeBook.com.
Join our Facebook Page: www.Facebook.com/PortalsinTime.

PORTALS IN TIME
THE QUEST FOR UN-OLD-AGE

JOHN JOSEPH TERESSI

HIGH CASTLE PUBLISHING

PORTALS IN TIME: THE QUEST FOR UN-OLD-AGE

This Book
is dedicated to

All those who are young
at heart and who love nature,
adventure and self-discovery.

Table of Contents

Prologue

FEW KNEW WHAT IT MIGHT FEEL LIKE to make a time jump. Those intrepid explorers who possibly survived were either unable to return or simply chose not to report their location, preferring not to be found. They were simply labeled as WTRs, Waiting to Returns. Yet, there was little incentive to come back from an unsuccessful mission to a failing society on the brink of extinction.

The risk of traveling through time would have its rewards they were told, but secretly those time travelers also held onto the hope that they could possibly escape to a more successful, advanced civilization.

At the beginning of the time travel experiments, human volunteers were very scarce as negative rumors had been spread regarding the many unsuccessful dog trials. However, there were always sufficient volunteers from a more expendable community.

"We've made all the necessary changes to ensure the safety and reliability of the program." So they were told.

Today would be different. The equipment and procedures first initiated in the dog trials were much improved, and scientists had experienced some successes. Most of the time, the test dogs had arrived back from other dimensions, but then again, those results were often suspect, blurred within the haze of scientific reporting.

There was definitely an urgency to make this very critical journey. Grippland was in desperate need of volunteer explorers to bring back answers or any discoveries that might help save their civilization from premature aging.

When the first human trials began, scientists were not able to calculate the probability of success. They had naturally assumed that the volunteers who disappeared were still alive somewhere in time.

It was more likely that the explorers were lost in time. That would be the most hopeful conclusion. Of course, substantial rewards for success were promised to the *volunteers* if and when they ever returned and reported their findings.

The *Grippland Eye of Time Exploration Team* waited anxiously in the laboratory antechamber to enter the time capsule. The four female and six male team members quickly exchanged furtive glances, attempting to allay their fears by monitoring one another for any hopeful facial expressions.

"There is nothing to worry about." They had been assured. "You will simply experience a smooth and seamless transition as if you are moving into a dream."

The exploratory team's training had been rigorous, but brief. Volunteers were hard to come by, especially those with the type of qualifications that could provide all the various scientific services needed at their destination.

Each team member had successfully passed a barrage of mental and physical tests and completed a basic course in survival tactics designed to increase their ability to succeed.

Actually, these tests were programmed by High Command to weed out those prone to weakness or uncontrolled fear.

But there was extreme fear festering in the ten volunteers who were reflecting back on their lives as they entered the foreboding glass and steel time capsule, filled with a labyrinth of twisting wires wrapped around a multitude of the odd-shaped, metallic, and plastic components.

Six shadowy figures, dressed in white lab coats, silently motioned for them to sit with their backs against a blue transparent cylinder. The well-trained, expressionless attendants methodically strapped the ten team members into padded chairs and cross-checked their helmets and breathing gear. There would be no turning back now.

Adrenalin released by fear pulsed through them as they attempted once again to exchange reassuring glances with one another, but that was impossible since now they were locked in place. Within moments, they would be experiencing another reality, so they were told.

Their minds were racing, reviewing all the various details of their training as if that knowledge alone could or would somehow enable them to survive the time jump.

A moment later, the door to the time capsule slammed shut, and a heavy concussion of air echoed and reverberated throughout the chamber.

Outside the capsule, lab technicians carefully observed the streaming data on their various instrument panels, monitoring for signs of excessive stress from the team members and for any possible abnormalities with the functioning of the highly sensitive, magnetic core contained within the cylinder.

A robotic, female voice announced, "Prepare for departure. Breathe deeply. Prepare for departure! You must now control your breathing. Count to four on the in-breath and four again on the out-breath."

Team Captain, Grist #1, took a long deep breath as his mind drifted off to the possibility of his redemption by completing a successful mission. The probability of sudden death would not deter him from the opportunity of clearing his name and reputation as a successful Gripp General.

Unbridled fear coursed through the veins of each team member as extreme pressure built up within the cabin. A powerful vibrational force passed through them as the core was charged to its full capacity.

Within seconds, a high-pitched, whirring sound enveloped the entire chamber. A shock wave from the powerful magnetic field pulsed through their bodies.

And then...there was nothing!

PART ONE

Eye of Time
Exploration Team

A COOL FOG DRIFTED SLOWLY between the stately, evergreen trees in the dense, forest glen that was filled to overflowing with a variety of herbs, flowers, and vines. A large flock of white birds flew effortlessly overhead, unaware of an unusual figure lying partially buried in the tall, wheat-colored grass.

His disheveled and torn gray uniform with black buttons on his jacket bordered a thin, dark gray stripe from collar to waist where a heavy, black, utility belt weighted him down. On his lapels, two gold emblems depicting interlocking G's sparkled when sunlight peaked through the clouds.

He struggled to sit up, removing his helmet emblazoned with the white lettering, G5, and wiped his forehead, trying to gather his thoughts. His hairline had receded over the many stress-filled years when he was calculating and planning complicated engineering projects.

Stare, the engineer, was tall, thin and agile with a long, angular face and small, dark gray eyes that displayed little or no emotion, giving him the appearance of being extremely serious and austere.

Everyone called him "Stare" since he often stared off into the distance or looked up at the sky or down at the ground, never engaging in direct eye-to-eye contact. Others did not comprehend that when they asked him questions, the words became catalysts for a variety of mental images.

He was always searching for ways to describe what he was visualizing, and as such, he usually talked in circles while seeking elusive answers still floating through his mind.

Stare loved technology and problem-solving and found himself studying engineering in school. Grippland was always running low on energy since consumption far outpaced supply. Opportunities became available in the construction of power plants, and he grasped at the chance for personal recognition and advancement.

Everything was working well in his life until he was told to change the calculations on one of the largest facilities. He had considered refusing to make the changes and to report the unethical request, but that would be far too risky. He would lose his job; but more importantly, he was going to be paid tens of thousands of Grippars (dollars) to follow orders. Obviously, "Orders are Orders!" Wasn't that a Prime Directive for a successful Gripp World?

He thought it was well worth the risk. His bosses only wanted a small change, just a simple manipulation of a few numbers that would make the construction cheaper and quicker. That's what they said. "Everything will work out just fine. Grippland needs the energy now, not later."

His prison sentence was longer and harsher than others who had committed similar crimes. How could he possibly have known that by changing a few minor calculations so much could go wrong? Rather…did go wrong!

At the moment, Stare couldn't remember much of the process that had brought him to be among those chosen for the *Eye of Time Exploration Team*. He did know that when time travel research had begun again in earnest, team participants were being selected not from any official research subjects or the scientific community. They came from a more expendable group — those who were considered dangerous to society and a menace to *Gripp Supreme Command*.

Among the members of this unique fraternity of renegades were prisoners who had been convicted of crimes, real or imagined. Since High Command had taken control, the criminal code was greatly expanded, and it was difficult to know what was not against the law.

It was true that there were some among them who had made mistakes and were true opportunists — those notorious for gaining power through exaggerating the truth or neglecting it all together. But Gripp law held to a simple premise: "Always obey or be imprisoned."

However, there were other options available to avoid a life in prison. Scientists were always requesting volunteers, most especially those who would work in the highly classified and experimental *Eye of Time Project*.

While many *non-adaptables* had escaped to the mountains, no one ever returned to tell the tale, since everything beyond the steel and concrete borders of Grippland was reported to be radioactive for thousands of years. So they were told.

The most expedient way to escape prison was through the *Window of Time*. Those who were fortunate enough to arrive home alive and were not mangled by the process of Time Travel were promised pardons as well as the opportunity to establish a new identity.

To be chosen with the slim possibility of survival was considered *The Prize*. Indeed, those volunteers numbered *One* through *Ten* were criminals; but as members of the Exploration Team, they were also potential heroes for a civilization desperately clinging to life.

No one knew why the Gripps were aging faster than usual, only that something dramatic had taken place. There seemed to be no apparent solution. The young had demanded answers amid their constant chanting of "Un-old-age! We want Un-old-age!" At first, the "Law Givers" chose to ignore the demonstrations, but soon they reacted with repression followed by intense and enforced suppression.

High Command then passed laws against forbidden thoughts, and a short while later, the first official *Word Museum* was established to lock away all personal expression.

Words such as *Wishes, Dreams, Aspirations, Beauty,* and *Joy* were all considered treasonous to the overall survival and "Greater Order of Grippland" (The *Greater Good* was now called the *Greater Order* for *Greater Control* by High Command). Most inspiring, hopeful words were labeled ephemeral—words that were without substance or order.

They became *Forbidden Words* to be placed within the *Word Museum*. After a while, no one knew why those forbidden words were treasonous, only that they were. They were considered unacceptable concepts from another time. *Duty, Obedience, Obligation,* and *Sacrifice* now replaced words expressing personal desires.

Few citizens ever questioned the establishment of the *Word Museum*. To object would obviously mean going to trial, and a prosecution guaranteed that you would be declared guilty since everyone was considered to be guilty until proven un-guilty, which was nearly impossible.

Grippland's basic charter stated that everyone was guilty of something. It was only through the passing of time that their lack of innocence would ultimately be revealed.

Suddenly, Stare was gasping for breath. HIs oxygen tube was twisted, and he quickly turned on his side, surprised to feel his hands touching a lush, plant-covered ground. With some effort, he staggered to his feet.

According to landing procedures, he carefully unlocked his breathing apparatus and tested the air while holding the oxygen mask near his face so that he could quickly put it on again if necessary. He let out a sigh of relief. Luckily, the atmosphere was breathable.

"Where am I?" he wondered out loud. He took another deep breath and then gasped at the rush of so much oxygen filling his lungs. The air was fresh and clean, carrying with it the scent of herbs and fragrant flowers.

Images from the past flooded through his mind as he remembered seeing pictures and reading about plants and herbs. That was before the government confiscated those rare books and soon after most of the plant life had died off due to atmospheric pollution.

Stare pulled a small, synthetic, round block from his survival gear, and with a few clicks of a metal rod, a fire began to crackle. He warmed his hands while gazing into the fire and realized that he was finally free of Grippland. He had survived. He was alive, which was all that mattered. The glowing warmth of the fire was comforting, and in a few moments, he fell into a deep sleep.

THE MIDNIGHT RAINBOW

Gripp #2 was lost in consciousness as he desperately tried to reassemble the very last moments of his life in Grippland. He was bruised and battered, but still alive.

Slowly, Twist, the politician, recalled being seated and securely strapped into the time capsule with the other members of The Eye of Time Exploration Team.

"Time travel has its rewards," they had told him. "You will be able to escape your past, and if you are fortunate enough to come back with the answer to Un-Old-Age, you'll be free again. All of your crimes will be wiped clean. Your life will be renewed!"

Those thoughts and more were flowing through his mind as he stared motionless into the night sky. He had survived, but what of the others? He wondered if he would be the lone survivor of the mission.

As he regained his strength and tried to move, Twist became aware that standing on his feet would require all his effort since the aches and pains in his punished body now protested even the smallest movements.

Would there be no solace for Twist, he thought. "I am bigger than all of this," he stammered out loud, pushing himself to his feet to gaze out at an unknown landscape that would be his home for an indeterminate amount of time.

"Yes, I am on my feet again, but there are no crowds to hear my words. There is no one to be mesmerized by my speech and flowing verbiage about all the benefits to be showered upon those who might vote for me!"

He was second in command on this expedition for good reason. As the Politician, he would be the one to negotiate treaties or bargain with anyone they might encounter. After all, his nickname, Twist, was not given to him without due cause. He succeeded at out-negotiating and tricking his opponents and was considered the best of the best.

He was also good-looking by Gripp standards with a strong jaw, bright blue eyes and a welcoming expression on his face. Yes, he was always ready to meet his supporters no matter what the circumstances.

And now, those very same bright blue eyes that formerly welcomed his adoring fans were searching for answers in the midst of what appeared to be a very dense and inhospitable wilderness.

He began to wonder if he would now be truly alone for the first time in his life.

This expert politician had successfully constructed his life with words upon words, and the meticulous twisting of those words. That is how he had become successful in Grippland.

But if he were to survive now, he would most certainly need far more than words. He would need the expertise of #5, Stare, the Engineer, who would be the one to analyze and predict the odds of their survival. As for all the rest of the team, well, they were most likely…unnecessary.

Once more, Twist's attention quickly shifted back to his current reality. He attempted to focus upon the faintest glow of what appeared to be a Midnight Rainbow. As he gazed upward, he could see undulating streams of light creating ribbons of color gently moving across the night sky and wondered what kind of reality would emerge when that midnight rainbow vanished into the light of day.

Reality was the last thing he wanted to consider. The only real-world view he enjoyed was the one he created in an endless web of lies.

In fact, it was his last devious plan that landed him in prison. *I did what everyone else was doing,* he thought. *I just wasn't supposed to get caught!*

But a new, unknown reality was now staring him in the face, and he found himself immersed in the very surreal, and yet, harsh reality of his aloneness.

"Where are the crowds, now?" he jested out loud, trying to maintain a sense of connectedness. "Yes. Yes. Yes! Where are all those Gripps who were so excited to hear me speak about living their dreams and were so eager to hear words such as *Hope, Opportunity, and Success!*

"Well, one out of three is not so bad," he laughed, as he remembered that the words *Hope* and *Success* had been labeled as *Treasonous to Grippland!*

"Yes, those words were now in the Word Museum," he mused. "On the other hand, *Opportunity* had been elevated to the designation: *Words that serve the greatest good of all Grippland!* The statement really meant: *the Opportunity to serve the most Powerful in Grippland!*

"And, now, here I am…right in the middle of a great *Opportunity!*" He chuckled to himself.

Slowly climbing up the hillside, he could see an unusual sequence of lights begin flashing in a series of colors: violet, blue, red and gold, all the colors of the rainbow, were moving randomly across the night sky.

He stopped abruptly when a shaft of pure red light illuminated the ground, creating a pathway for him to follow. In the far distance there was a distinctive and familiar humming. It was a sound he had heard before, the slow, steady, comforting drone of electric motors. Indeed, that continuous pulse was the very heartbeat of Grippland.

He quickened his pace with anticipation as visions of becoming the mission savior were racing through his mind. Suddenly, his thoughts were interrupted by strange, unspoken words drifting the night, "Follow the light beam. Follow the light stream. Follow the changing colors. What a marvelous scheme!"

The politician shook his head and laughed. "Perhaps others have become victims of this...this...this trick, whatever this is!" he stammered, trying to embolden himself to surmount his fear. "It will not be so easy to fool old Twist!"

He cautiously maneuvered up the steep, rocky trail with his mind signaling alarms that this could be a deadly trap. Still, he pushed on, stretching out his arms to pull himself up and over the rocky precipice.

His large fingers inched slowly along the face of the cliff, moving him ever closer to his rendezvous with the unknown. He held his breath and was unnerved to discover that he no longer felt the bravado of his meaningless words, which were now silently drifting away into the star-filled, heavens above.

What *was* real, however, was his shortness of breath and a wide-eyed expression of terror. There before him and projecting far out beyond the hills around him were more intense colors of purples, violets, and blues.

"Why risk it all?" he moaned, looking back down the steep trail. "The other team members could be dead. I should turn back. I will pretend that I reached the crest of the hill, and there was nothing to see...nothing at all."

The humming and movement of the light intensified as if a strange force field was aware of his presence. The patterns of light seemed to be calling him, "Come to us. You have nothing to fear. We have been waiting for you!"

MOMENTS SUSPENDED IN TIME

A grove of trees with wide, spreading branches, in a field of dark green grass, had served as a landing site for another team member. Perhaps, it was his quest for success and fame or simply his desperation to escape prison that brought Gripp #3, Scheme, the businessman, to this particular place in time.

He was barely awake when he noticed colorful, light streams moving across the night sky, shining like a welcoming beacon or as a silent messenger calling him. He had gathered the strength to follow that night vision; but soon after setting off to discover the source of the light exhaustion set in, and he felt the need to rest.

Scheme was taller and heavier than most Gripps, which he believed was part of his success formula. He knew that big always wins in business. Bushy eyebrows nearly covered his squinty, brown eyes, and with his slightly tilted, angular mouth, he looked as though he was scheming even when he was not.

While resting near the top of the hill, he fell into a deep sleep and dreamed of following the light stream. Mysteriously, after what seemed like only a few moments, he awoke and found himself sitting in the center of an overwhelming structure glowing with light.

Above and around him was a triangular construction consisting of three, transparent, multifaceted crystals standing over thirty-feet tall, pulsing with intense colors of various hues. They towered over him like silent sentinels in the night.

Scheme heard no voices, and yet he was confident that the crystals were sending out some form of communication. He looked up and was shocked to see eight ghost-like forms spinning high above him in the center of the formation of crystals.

His mouth dropped open as he cried out in disbelief, "Those are my teammates!"

Above him, eight phantom figures, his fellow Gripps, were circling in the air like birds caught in an updraft. They were turning in spirals seemingly activated by an invisible current of energy. Their faces were distorted, yet they seemed unaware of their condition. It appeared as if they were sound asleep while suspended in mid-air by an invisible force-field.

A moment later, he began to feel weightless and gasped as he floated upward, struggling defiantly to resist the pulling force but soon found himself tumbling and spinning with his teammates in the midst of the crystals.

The humming of crystals increased as their powerful resonance moved through his body until his bones and teeth were vibrating at such a rate of speed that he could do nothing more to resist.

Still conscious and attempting to speak, he gathered his strength and called out, "I am Scheme, third in command! Who are you? Have you no face to show me? Do you have no other presence than these crystalline towers protecting you? Reveal yourself! Who are you?"

His broad, round face flushed red with anguish. His demands and commands rang out sharply into the stillness of the clear night air. And then his words came back to him in the form of an echo: "Who are you? Who are you?"

A grimace moved across his face as he heard his words returning to him, haunting him, and taunting him even more. *I get it,* he thought. *We are playing a game. It's always a game. I know games. I play games. My whole scheming life has been a game!"* His head throbbed and the veins in his neck and forehead pulsed with rage as he struggled for words.

"So.....so, so, what do you want? Have you no words to speak, nothing to say? What do you want?"

The echo grew even louder and far more intense: "What do you want? What do you want?"

Scheme vigorously fought to free himself as he continued to tumble round and round, but the strength of the force field was overwhelming. His fellow team members were still unconscious, asleep within its grasp. "When will it end?" he shouted out to whoever might hear him.

The echo responded by repeating, "When will it end? When will it end?"

He searched for something to hold on to...some way to escape the rhythmic waves holding him captive and called out again, "We seek knowledge! We need more time!"

"More time! More time!" came the echo.

He waited a moment and yelled, "We mean no harm...no harm!"

There was no response! There were no more echoes. For the first time in his scheming life, words were failing him. His ability to talk his way out had failed; and now, not even his echo would come back to him. He wondered if there was anyone or anything to hear him.

Watching in despair as the light beams engulfed him, he felt the energy vibrations drowning away his thoughts. He was immersed in silence, suspended in a pause within the very framework of Time.

*He was immersed in silence, suspended in a pause
within the very framework of Time.*

It seemed as though he had been spinning forever when suddenly, the energy stream stopped moving. The businessman, now explorer, was grateful to once again be on solid ground.

He began to tremble. A cold chill ran up his spine as he remembered being trapped in a powerful, swirling energy. Slowly, his mind began to clear.

He looked around and realized that the crystal towers were nowhere in sight. Breathing a sigh of relief, he thought, *Was it just a dream, a horrendous nightmare?* He only knew for certain that he had awakened feeling refreshed and was lying in tall grass under a large, flowering tree.

There were voices nearby, and a moment later he heard, "Scheme, we thought we lost you. Where have you been? Did you see that electrical storm last night?"

He looked up to see Gripp #4, Babble, the young, woman publicist, hovering over him. A short distance away, he watched his team gathering their equipment and beginning to prepare their rafts for departure.

"Did you know we are on an island, Scheme?" asked Babble, pushing her short, blond hair away from her eyes. "I was the first one to see the shoreline. By the way, where have you been? Where's Stare? We thought he was with you. Have you seen the engineer?"

THE DELPHOS ENCOUNTER

It was almost the break of dawn when the first ripples of energy moved over the island. A gentle wind had pushed away the early morning fog to reveal Stare still curled up near his campfire fast asleep. His half-closed eyes were staring blankly into the orange glow of the dying embers.

The second and third waves of energy came more swiftly. The movement around him turned in circles as if some invisible force was examining him, seeking information about his identity from every possible angle. The motion was not random, and the probing energy was driven and controlled by an intense curiosity.

If he had been awake instead of dreaming, the engineer might have felt a strange and sudden coolness move over his body. He might have thought it was coming from the fog bank that was now hugging the shoreline.

He was lost in a dream, but not even his most unusual dreams would have prepared him for his next encounter.

Hovering near him was an extraordinary being who possessed the gift of *trans-dimensional* sight. This Cosmic visitor had followed a signal indicating a sudden shift within the *Harmonic Resonance* while cruising through Level Seven on his standard patrol.

The multidimensional traveler's words moved effortlessly into Stare's consciousness. "Ah, yes, what dreams may soon come? How is it that you've ventured so very far from home?"

The voice was heard and not heard, yet the vibrational frequency quickly penetrated into the very core of his dream, causing him to begin to breathe more rapidly as if he were seeking escape. And he was.

Stare was running for his life through empty and ruined streets where buildings were on fire and bridges and roads were collapsing. The further he ran the more devastation he could see stretching out before him.

The only vestiges of society still operational were the large, luminous message signs flashing on and off, alerting Grippland: *Stare, the Engineer Wanted for Treason! Wanted for Treason! Wanted for Treason!*

"It wasn't my idea!" he sobbed in his dream. "They told me to lie. They said I need not worry! Not to worry!"

He continued to run; but in his panic, he was unaware that no one was running after him, no one at all, except — well, perhaps there was one exception.

There was someone or something capable of pursuing anyone, anywhere, even into the depths of their dreams.

In the midst of his unconscious state, Stare took refuge in an abandoned warehouse where he sank into a corner of what once must have been the shipping area. The barren interior was covered in debris and filled with billowing clouds of gray-black smoke. He could see nothing.

"I am not guilty!" Stare cried out to whoever might be listening. "It was them. They gave the orders!"

He struggled to his feet, ready to run again when his legs folded, and he staggered and stumbled onto the wooden floor. He lifted his gaze, trying to see in which direction to escape when he caught a glimpse of something moving in and out of the billowing clouds of smoke.

At first, it was impossible to determine what it was. The phantom was there, but not there. The engineer knew that if you want to see something that doesn't want to be seen, you need to look away and quickly look back again. You shift your vision and look at it from the corner of your eye.

That's when he saw it, staring back at him with eyes so black you could see the entire universe in them. Azure blue rings rimmed the pupils that moved in and out as the creature fixed his piercing gaze upon the shaking Gripp crouching on the warehouse floor.

Stare was shocked to see an enormous head and a long, undulating body floating just above him. The filtered light reflected upon the creature's iridescent skin of green, blue, violet, and red.

Gasping for breath, the engineer began coughing, trying to clear his throat and rubbed his eyes, which were stinging from the dense smoke of the fire. And then Stare awoke! His entire body shuddered, and his mind raced, trying to grasp where he was. *Could this be a dream? Which scene was real?* He doubted them both.

Shaking his head and focusing on the campfire, he sighed in relief. "That vision must have been in a dream, a terrible nightmare. It was the smoke from this campfire that caused me to see the burning buildings and that terrifying creature with such alarming eyes!"

"Hmmm…Am I truly so frightening?" came a voice from an invisible speaker.

Stare sat straight up, rubbed his eyes again, and directed his attention toward the sound. "It's you again! Are you real? Why don't you show yourself, or do you only torment the innocent in their dreams?"

"The innocent? That is doubtful!" the voice's responded. "Hmmm…let me look at you." There was a pause. Only a few crackles from the fire filled the silence.

The melodious, yet penetrating voice, spoke again. "In your dream, I learned that you are terrified of your crimes, and you are fearful to the core. Your heart is dense, and there is no direction in your life. You have lost your way, and you don't know who you are."

"I know who I am!" argued the frightened Gripp. "I'm #5, a scientist, well, actually, an engineer, on a critical mission to save our society. I am...I am...almost a hero." He took a deep breath and asked, "Why not show yourself?"

"You are a disbeliever in the invisible...that I perceive," stated the voice. "The fact is that I was lured here by my overwhelming curiosity, and I rarely make an appearance to *strangers!*" The deep, resonant voice placed a long, drawn-out emphasis on the word *strange*.

"After all, trans-dimensional travelers rarely make their presence known," he explained, "but since you are stuck in your mind, dense in your heart and have no imagination, *for you*...I shall make an exception."

Stare's eyes grew wide as he witnessed the shimmering film of light increasing in intensity. The unknown presence suddenly appeared in form.

"My name is Delphos," said the enormous creature as he came into view. "As you can perceive, my head is large, my eyes are the deepest black, and my body is long and undulating since I have no feet or arms to encumber me."

"B-b-but, you're a f-fish!" stammered #5, staring blankly into the face of an immense, fish-shaped creature at least ten Gripp bodies long floating effortlessly overhead. His bulbous eyes moved back and forth, and its large, pouting mouth was opening and closing as if continually testing the atmosphere.

"Well, yes, you might say I am a fish by shape and size, but I am shaped for adventure, not just for surviving, although I do swim so very, very well; and I do love floating upon the *Cosmic Sea*."

"You are not real! I am dreaming a terrible nightmare!"

"Well, in a way you are still dreaming. Some might say, 'Life is just a dream!'

"Perhaps a song will brighten up your very dense and dark heart." Delphos spun entirely around from tail to head and back again, and then began to sing:

> *I swim on tides of dimensionality,*
> *expressing my complex personality.*
> *I'm a curious fish chasing endless dreams*
> *following clues on intuitive streams.*
> *My journey takes me far and wide,*
> *seeing what I can see as I glide.*

Gripp #5 stared in disbelief when a golden saxophone appeared out of thin air. The creature stopped singing and began blowing the horn, playing a lovely, haunting tune. And after finishing with that instrument, a beautiful polished wooden guitar floated past him. The giant fish grabbed it and plucked the strings with his fins as he sang:

> *Delphos observes the by and by.*
> *A very rare creature indeed am I.*
> *Inspiration leads me where I should go,*
> *seeking out those who need to know*
> *the answers hiding in the endless flow*
> *as I swim with ease in the Cosmic Sea,*
> *singing my songs in perfect harmony.*

Stare sat with his mouth open, and his narrow, deep-set, gray eyes widened as the creature bowed his head as if he was waiting for applause. There was none.

Yet, Delphos glanced up with a bright smile and said, "Ah, yes, now my performance and appearance are complete. I have seen what my curiosity has led me to see. And as for you, strange and dense creature, you have just begun your adventure into multidimensionality. Welcome to Level Seven. There is much for you to learn here in the land of Acronos. Now, I must say adieu."

With that last statement, Delphos simply disappeared into the nothingness.

THE CROSSING

The amber glow of morning washed over the surrounding hills and illuminated the thick, gray fog hugging the shoreline, creating ghost-like shadows of the Gripps on the white sand as they silently gathered up their equipment for the crossing. Lost in both time and space, the ten intrepid explorers were now also lost deep within their own thoughts, thoughts of their survival.

A solitary figure paced slowly up and down the shore as if he could or would locate evidence of civilization somewhere on those stretches of pure white sand. But there was nothing to be found.

#1, Commander Grist stood watching the continuous ebb and flow of the translucent waves quietly washing ashore from the sea surrounding the island. He was of average height and stocky, standing straight with his shoulders back and his head held tall. He was dressed in a gray uniform, and his jacket was adorned with the medals he had received from the many Gripp wars in which he led his troops to victory.

Stopping for a moment, the Commander reviewed his small, unseasoned team as they came into view. He had walked most of the distance around the small island alone only to discover the extreme severity of their predicament. They had just one choice: head out to sea.

He was certain that this group would follow his orders; they had been trained since childhood to obey any high-ranking member of Command without questioning. Since he was Number One, they would have no choice.

A slight grin crossed his face as he looked down at his black, high-topped, combat boots and then gazed far out to sea. He turned and walked toward his team members who were methodically stacking equipment into two inflated Gripp, long rafts.

His solo walk around the island shoreline had produced nothing but more questions…questions regarding the possible success or failure of their mission.

Is this to be my decision? Should I be the one to choose? He thought. *I could possibly be condemning these Gripps who are so desperate for a chance at a new life to experience a premature demise in those small boats on an unpredictable ocean.*

"Where is the enemy we seek?" he asked of the wind and sea. "Is Time the enemy…only Time, or is it our race against the Tock, that ever-present ticking, always measuring our fear against our persistence to succeed? What will we achieve before that ticking of the Tock finally stops?"

Grist walked toward Babble and watched her speaking into her recording device. As #4 on this mission, she was ordered to file as many detailed reports as possible for High Command. Those statements would later be used to analyze how to make future explorations more successful.

Babble was the youngest of the Exploration Team; and by Gripp standards, she was the most beautiful, trim and fit, with large, bright, blue-green eyes and blond hair.

Her personality seemed out of place since she was undoubtedly the most energetic and outgoing member of the team. Grist questioned if that enthusiasm was only due to her youth. He decided her unusual behavior would require greater scrutiny.

He turned his attention to the others and wondered which ones would be weak links in the chain of command. Number Two, known as Twist, certainly had no combat experience, except for his unique ability as a politician to use a war of words and deception. He was always making promises that were impossible to fulfill.

Number Three in command, Scheme, was promoted by High Command to his position because he possessed an extreme ability to negotiate or rather out-negotiate anyone he encountered. Those qualities were considered essential to the mission, and yet his ability to cut a deal would only be valid if they found an advanced civilization.

Indeed, the rest of the team numbered Five through Ten, belonged to the medical and scientific community and perhaps, more than all the others, would prove themselves worthy of this expedition.

Grist gazed back toward the sea and wondered what might be lying beyond that vast stretch of azure nearly hidden by the rolling, thick swirl of fog that had greeted them at the first light of dawn.

What enemy slips and slides within the tides and within itself is now beckoning us to enter and explore? He wondered as he crouched down to grab a handful of sand and let it slowly flow through his fingers.

Explore what…the open sea? Indeed, those unfathomable depths of fluid deception either existed to propel them forward to fulfill promises of a new future, or it was luring them into their watery graves. What strange fate made them land on this lonely, uninhabited island surrounded by water with no sign of life…no evidence of civilization?

From a distance, he surveyed his fellow explorers who were making final preparations for the launch of the Gripp rafts when he suddenly grasped the futility of continuing.

He knew that they were all tortured souls—these explorers ready to cast off into an abyss—that vast, undulating, mass of water that might lead them nowhere. How could he possibly ask his team to proceed over that glistening surface without end or definition?

He knew that most certainly this unexpected body of water was calling them. He could feel it. The sea was demanding their presence. He wondered what might lurk below the waves that could be so anxious to consume them.

Indeed, should he try to live within the parameters of the incessant *Ticking of the Tock?* He knew that this foreboding ocean would soon surround them, and there would be only fear to guide them.

Yes, I am #1! I am the Commander of men and materiel! What irony it would be to take my Last Grasp (my death) and leave behind all that I know and have experienced! What wisdom from my previous victories might I successfully bring to this pivotal moment beckoning us forward?

He pondered whether the decision to head out to sea should be made only by the one in Command, or should he adhere to a type of democracy? Who should best determine whether to proceed into what could be an end to their most hopeful explorations?

The team members, busily preparing the rafts, were not thinking about the peril awaiting them once they set off on an uncharted course without maps or equipment to guide them.

Grist was well aware that he needed to make his critical decision now, and he motioned for his team members to form a circle around him.

He began walking slowly around the circle, particularly observing Gripps Five through Ten. He knew #5, Stare, the engineer, was loyal and dedicated, serving well as a monitor of technical equipment and *Keeper of the Tock*.

#6, Doctor Grouse was there to maintain the health and welfare of the team, but she also had the responsibility, along with Grimm, #9, the female psychologist, to determine whether any of the high-ranking Gripps were mentally capable of handling their responsibilities.

#7, Grubb, the biologist, would identify plants that might provide an answer to the Secret of Un-Old-Age.

#8, Gritt, the geologist, was offered up by High Command as a necessary addition to help secure the Mission's success. His job was to search for minerals and especially to find everyone's favorite substance – Grold.

And then, there was #10, Grind, the anthropologist. He wondered why she had been chosen for this mission since they hoped to find an advanced civilization. They wouldn't have time to study some extinct, ancient society.

He stopped pacing and asked the assembled group, "Do you know why you are here on this mission?"

There was no immediate reply! Their only response was silent stares and exchanged glances.

"We are here to capture *The Prize!*"!" he exclaimed, answering his own question. "We are here to win our freedom and discover the Secret of Un-Old-Age!"

The team members nodded in silent agreement.

"You understand, of course, that you all are expendable, which is one of the reasons why High Command chose each of you for this mission." Several Gripps shifted nervously from side-to-side while others continued staring at the ground.

It was apparent that #1 was attempting to talk himself into feeling confident enough to decide to cast off. But to where? Nothing had changed.

Whatever was compelling him forward, whatever was challenging him to move from the safety of the island and enter into the vast unknown was seemingly not real. It was only a hidden wish that perhaps a real enemy, or more hopefully, an advanced civilization with knowledge of maintaining Un-Old-Age existed on a not too distant shore.

"I cannot ask you to proceed," #1 declared reluctantly. "As your Mission Commander, I could order you to launch the boats, but under current circumstances, I feel compelled to allow you to decide your fate!

"Take a moment to reflect on the challenges and intense dangers we face and decide if you are ready to head out to sea. If you wish to proceed, please take one step forward."

After waiting several moments, not one Gripp took that step. A few inaudible words were mumbled amongst them, and then there was only silence.

Grist took a deep breath and said reluctantly, "Very well. You wish to remain here and wait out the seven Grabbons (days) before returning to Grippland. I can understand your choice. That is why I allowed you to choose."

Before he could give his order to reassemble their equipment and drag the boats back on shore, the team let out a sudden gasp of surprise, all except one.

Standing in the center of the circle was #4, Babble, the team's communications expert. She held a determined stance of fearless abandon, and on her face was an expression of defiance, a willingness to meet any danger that might be lurking in the unknown.

Grist could not believe his eyes. It was disturbing to see the youngest and least experienced member of the team displaying the most courage. He had not noticed that Babble evidently possessed a unique quality that none of the others were able to demonstrate.

It was clear that she did not step forward due only to her youthful ambition. She was demonstrating a profound strength from deep within her that appeared to be fueled by a desire to win and a willingness to move beyond her fears.

A moment later, another Gripp stepped forward into the center. #8, Gritt, the geologist also demonstrated his strength, courage and resolve.

Soon, all team members reluctantly followed the lead of the two brave Gripps and walked into the center of the circle as they shared glances of trepidation with one another.

Without hesitation, Grist gave the command, "Prepare the boats for launch!" He walked over to Babble and nodded approvingly. He was preparing to say something when she noticed the corner of his mouth starting to break into a smile. She smiled back in acknowledgment and silently walked beside him toward the boats.

WHAT LIES BELOW?

A strong breeze was blowing a thick spray against the two rafts, gliding side-by-side, oars in the water, rowing. Still, the fog persisted. Only the faintest outline of the island could be seen as a point of reference, and it was fast fading from view.

Each raft was crewed by five team members, One through Five in the first boat and Six through Ten in the second. The well-constructed rubber rafts were designed to carry heavy equipment if by chance they encountered rivers or lakes on their journey. No one had considered that they might need to travel over a vast expanse of open sea.

Grist decided that the two rafts should remain close together for safety and ease of communication. The necessary survival supplies, such as food and water, were divided equally between the two rafts, just in case. Just in case? In case of what? That question raced through the minds of each team member pulling hard on their oars. They were attempting to find what could be termed their *opportunity*.

As Commander of the mission, he was more aware than any of the others that there was little chance of returning to the island without proper navigational equipment...of which they had none. On board were weapons, medical supplies, coms, laboratory tech for mineral and plant analysis, and equipment to monitor movement on land...not out to sea.

Was I wrong to allow them to decide our course of action? He thought as he watched his team now falling into a comfortable rhythm of working the oars they had never before experienced. Gazing blankly at the fog-covered sea, he felt the chill of a cold mist moving around and through him and stared at the glass-like surface, wondering about the watery deep that supports no life except that which lurks far below.

Grist felt the urge to start pacing. Walking in circles had always provided him with a sense of space that allowed a clarity of vision to make proper decisions. How ironic it would be if instead of walking around in circles they were to find themselves rowing in circles. How would they know? The island had already disappeared from view.

Was this voyage through Time some form of ongoing, cruel justice? Hadn't they already served enough time locked away in that high-security prison? Wasn't this mission to be their opportunity to gain a chance at freedom?

To occupy his mind, Grist turned his attention to Scheme, the businessman, or so he was labeled. None of the team members actually knew one another. They had all been given nicknames while in prison. It was much easier to identify them that way.

Scheme was nervously looking from side-to-side as if he would be able to discover what he most desired to see...land. And naturally so. Everyone's attention focused on that one hopeful expectation, but after another Grippon (hour) out at sea, there was not even the slightest hint of solid ground.

Had they reached the point of no return? The Commander's original idea of instructing his team and turning them into a formidable fighting force now made him laugh at the absurdity of that notion, considering their current surroundings.

As they continued rowing on and on, #1 decided to lash the two boats together, bow to stern. That precaution would allow a greater latitude of freedom if a sudden swell were to hit them.

"Preparation provides its own reward under all circumstances!" he reminded the weary explorers. And yet, he knew that even the best planning could not provide what they now needed most: the sight of land.

The wind and water quieted, and he issued the order to ship oars and take a much-needed break. After so many years in prison, no team member could be considered physically fit enough to make such a voyage, and yet they had no choice. They had decided to push on.

The mirror-like surface of the water supporting the rafts also seemed to be moving within each of them, reflecting back thoughts they held deep inside.

Grist would admit only to himself that he knew nothing of navigation on the open sea, and he had heard very little of the ancient, seafaring folklore handed down over the centuries by word-of-mouth.

He was aware that certain historic sailing vessels contained something termed *The Charm*. That *Charm* was a type of magical spell enveloping a ship, and it protected the ship from dark forces and evils, or so it was said. Gazing over at Babble, Grist wondered if by some strange act of fate she was, indeed, that *Charm*.

The Gripps had drifted into a stupor from the continuous rolling of the raft back-and-forth when suddenly they were awakened by Babble shouting, "I have movement! There can be no doubt! We are no longer alone!"

Grist felt a surge of adrenaline erasing his prior misgivings, including his fear of merely drifting away on a course to nowhere. Babble had saved him once before and had given him a chance to take command, even though the others thought the mission was lost. Perhaps, now she could direct their course to discover other sailing vessels or maybe the movement came from land.

The dense fog was clearing, allowing some visibility into the far distance. Team members gazed through telescopes and scoured the horizon for any signs of movement.

After many Grippings (minutes), the rowers' excitement transformed into only a faint hope that Babble's instruments had indeed shown movement, rather than just malfunctioning. The Commander was certain Babble was onto something. He sensed that she had a unique quality none of the others possessed, and he was positive her equipment did not malfunction. She had recorded movement, and it must be real.

On the second boat, #10, Grind, the anthropologist, was caught up in contemplating the mystery of the sea and entertaining her imaginings of what might lie below.

The eerie, gray fog surrounding her melted into the gray water, forming a seamless curtain that created a feeling of floating into another world, a world beyond the veil that she had read about so long ago.

Grind looked like a normal, Grippland citizen. She was of average height, muscular and physically fit with an angular face and dark brown eyes. Yet, she was a very unusual and well-educated character.

Her crime was collecting, hiding, and reading forbidden books to learn about ancient cultures and former civilizations. Studying mythology and spirituality had provided her with a much-needed escape from the *Tone-Drone-Drift* of robotic, *Gripp Speak* and *Gripp Logic*—a form of thinking that eliminated curiosity and imagination.

This logic had been designed to interrupt extraneous thought processes. In other words, stopping any concepts that might lead to the *truth* or that might provide possibilities for an alternate future.

There was always a double and triple standard in Grippland. And the idea of "The Truth" provided a wide variety of interpretations, depending upon which of the many *Truths* High Command determined were the most beneficial for *The Greater Order*.

Grind's profession as an anthropologist was rarely in demand in a society that was erasing history and replacing it with the *New Historical Narrative*, a falsified version of history to enhance the power and order of Grippland.

Her studies of previous civilizations were viewed as a significant threat to *The Greater Order*. And yet, it was her unique knowledge that Gripp Command reluctantly surmised could be important if the exploration team were to encounter an advanced or even a primitive civilization.

High Command had approved her volunteer status and released her from prison at the very last minute. Even though she carried the lowest rank on the mission team, they thought she might piece together clues along the way.

So, here she was on a raft, imprisoned on a course to nowhere, slowly spinning around as if she were riding on one of those mythological carousels where children had once played.

Just like the others, Grind volunteered, and her motivation was the concept that *Chance* would set her free — the idea that an unknown event could and would intervene somehow to provide her with a new life. And what was *Chance* delivering now? It was making both rafts slowly, ever so slowly, spin around in circles.

Grist shouted, "Oars in the water! Keep them deep! Counteract the spin! We are in the midst of a strange current! If the undertow increases, we will need to cut the ropes between the rafts so we don't lose equipment if we ram into each other!"

As if on cue for perfect timing, both Twist and Scheme declared simultaneously, "It's time to turn back!"

Twist called out, trying to be heard over the thunderous sound of wind and waves, "This spin is a warning! We are where we shouldn't be! We need to take another vote!"

"Yes, another vote!" shouted Scheme, desperately holding onto the ropes to prevent himself from being swept overboard in the midst of the increased intensity of the churning water.

Grist ignored their complaints. He commanded all ropes be cut, allowing each raft to go free to survive on its own. A knowing grin crossed his face as he looked at Twist and Scheme and remembered hearing the old adage:

> *The most significant threat is when*
> *you do not know where or when*
> *the next danger will surround you.*

"Secure all equipment! Lash yourself to the boat's mooring rings! We are in a storm that appears to be driven by some mysterious force!" exclaimed Grist.

The first high waves hit the boat and violently rocked it back-and-forth and side-to-side. Twist and Scheme were nearly thrown from the raft by the force of the swells, but instead, they were slammed against the waterproof, equipment cases. Only the well-strapped ropes held them securely on the raft.

So, this is the storm that ends it all, thought Grist as he held tight to the side of the boat. *Here is the moment we all signed up for...to survive or not to survive upon this foreboding nightmare of undulating desolation that was designed only to swallow everything upon its surface!*

What miracle could intervene to save the explorers now? Only their courage would allow them to testify to the truth that they had survived.

How could they possibly turn back? They had lost sight of the island at least a Grippon (hour) ago, and the sun was also hiding somewhere in the density of the ever-present fog, which denied them even sight navigation.

To all appearances, they were in the midst of a perfect storm: a set of events, a final test of courage similar to those faced by lonely, ancient mariners who sang about their many battles upon the sea in such sad and haunting songs.

"Keep those oars deep in the water!" called Grist.

"Our only hope is to ride through this!"

His voice was immediately drowned out by the sound of the waves striking both rafts with tremendous force. If he had not ordered lashing themselves to the boat, every Gripp would have been quickly swept away.

"This is our moment!" he declared. "This is the test we signed up for when we volunteered to grasp our freedom in exchange for prison!"

His defiant words were welcomed by all struggling to survive. They needed those words...words that would give them that extra impetus never to surrender.

"Get your grips into it!" commanded Grist to his crew. "This is your moment! Pull, stroke, pull!" his booming voice rang out so loudly that those very sounds seemed to be penetrating into the sea, accelerating the boats that were no longer spinning. Instead, they were speeding forward across the heaving surface of what had become a rolling, foaming monster without end. "Prepare your flares!" #1 shouted. "Prepare your flares! Red flare for distress! Blue for the sight of land!"

At that moment, Grist had no way of knowing whether Dr. Grouse heard his instructions. The second boat had disappeared, carrying with it Dr. Grouse; Grubb, the biologist; Gritt, the geologist; Grimm, the psychologist; and lastly, Grind, the anthropologist.

They were most likely expendable, thought Grist. After all, they were the lower numbered members of the exploration team. He paused and considered that perhaps in the grand scheme of things, they would all be nonessential. Who was he to judge? He straightened his shoulders and pulled himself together to face the inevitable.

Dr. Grouse, #6, held command of the second boat. She was soaking wet like all the others struggling to pull the oars. What little strength she once had was gone. Her expertise had been as a researcher and surgeon, skills that required deep thought and precise movements of her hands, not the brutal force necessary to pull oars against ocean waves demanding surrender into the deep.

Sitting at the far end of the second raft, Grind was the first to see them. It was as if she had attracted a vision from the pages of one of her forbidden books. They were not visible at first, but they were there. She could feel it. She felt the same way as when reading pages of fantasy books in which authors described eyes that could see other eyes when least expected.

Luminous yellow lights were floating in the distance just above the highest waves that were continuously rolling towards them. She felt an eerie sense of déjà vu as she remembered mythology that explained in great detail how ancient Mariners experienced strange lights just before their ships disappeared into the sea.

And now we are separated from the other boat! she thought, beginning to panic as the wind howled around her. *How can I warn them of the imminent danger those glowing yellow lights represent. I fear it is too late, too late for all of us!*

It seemed as if it had been only moments before, barely a few Grippers (minutes), since they had launched their rafts from that small, uninhabited, and isolated island. The truth was that those Grippers had turned into Grippons (hours) of torment. What was to be a simple exploration seeking landfall had quickly turned into a battle of life and death, a struggle that was continuing seemingly without end, but it would end!

In the first raft, Babble was trying to communicate with the second boat, but her Gripp-Com device indicated no connection was possible. It was receiving only static. She turned to Stare requesting his expertise to fix the device. But there was no time for that analysis.

Their raft started spinning out of control, turning around and around. They could do nothing but hang on for the ride. The Gripps shipped oars lest they be lost in the depths while treacherous waves intensified to the point that only their will against the storm and sea allowed them to remain on board.

Twist and Scheme were pale as ghosts as they clutched onto the ropes binding them to the mooring rings on the raft, but that did not prevent them from experiencing the horror of their discovery.

Straight above them, looming high overhead were luminous, glowing, yellow lights.

Twist instinctively grabbed a metal oar in self-defense.

Scheme shouted out, "D-do-do you see them? Yellow lights… there… above us…within the swirl of fog!"

The others searched skyward, straining to see the lights, but there was only the endless fog, the rocking motion of the boat, and the icy cold spray washing over them.

"There is nothing to see," commented Stare. "It's the illusion of the sea and the desperation of desperate men wishing to see that which does not exist!"

Grist and Babble exchanged glances. They had never heard Stare speak a complete sentence, especially not at a moment of imminent peril. Twist and Scheme did not reply. They were disturbed by the engineer's statement and cast their eyes down as if they had been scolded by someone they least expected to attack them.

Grist did not think that Twist and Scheme were lying or reporting an illusion. Even though they were professional deceivers, charlatans, and thieves, it sounded to him as if they had seen something. Perhaps there were yellow lights in the sky. What did they have to gain by that deception?

He did not bother to offer his opinion since the raft was quickly filling with water, and all hands were needed to bail out the constant inflow just to stay afloat a little longer.

So, this is how it all ends! He thought, looking over at Babble who was still struggling with her Gripp-com device, which was only generating a static buzz.

They were managing to stay afloat, but for how long? The incessant battering by the massive waves abated somewhat, but the current was now delivering them into the most profound darkness they had yet encountered.

We can survive this! He paused to take a deep breath and then continuing to bail out the boat. *Perhaps, we have seen the worst of it. Those illusions of moving lights might be only reflections. Most likely they were a play of light trailing in and out with the rolling motion of the fog.*

The wind and water settled down again as the thick fog shrouded them, creating a sense of foreboding. The dense, gray clouds allowed only the faintest shadows of the rafts to appear on the surface of the sea.

Recalling his experience of only moments before, Twist wondered if the vision he had seen was real. *Maybe, I just imagined those ominous lights above us. Perhaps, there was nothing there at all.*

Twist glanced over at Scheme and considered suggesting that the illumination was just their imagination, but that reconstruction of events would need to be postponed. For some reason, the oars he struggled with only moments before now seemed to be lighter in his hands. With minimal effort, the raft was now skimming over the waves much faster than before.

Is this also my imagination? There was no time for questions. The large, heavily laden, rubber raft was swaying back-and-forth and then started turning ever so slowly. Within moments, they were spinning in a powerful rotating current that wasn't created by the ocean alone or at least it didn't appear that way.

Grist's gruff voice rang out, "Maintain the rudder against the spin! We are in another intense, unpredictable current. Hold your oars against the spin!" He was almost invisible now, completely enveloped in the swirling, thick, wet fog.

Peering over the bow of the boat and searching the depths of that undulating and menacing, charcoal gray sea, he hoped to discover rational clues to the mystery now overtaking them. In response, the vessel shuddered shook violently as if under the control of an invisible, force field.

Strangely enough, in the midst of all the frightful confusion, Grist saw this chaotic situation as his chance to truly command once more! It was invigorating!

Not only did he have an opportunity to prove himself to himself, but more importantly he could prove his worth to all those whose lives depended upon his well-honed, decision-making skills. He felt a surge of adrenaline that more than verified his need and quest for command. Whatever the challenge, it could never be a match for Grist, Commander of three successful Gripp Wars and veteran of many more.

"Put your backs into it! Keep your oars always at the ready! The shuddering of this vessel can only be due to rocks just below the surface!"

But there were no rocks. They could only feel rhythmic, thumping sounds continuing to hit the bottom of the raft.

"We must be caught on shifting sand. Prepare to push off! Get those oars back into the water! We can't afford to be trapped in the sand!"

He had barely issued his last command, when Babble shouted out, "Gripp-Com Two is sending a message! It sounds like Grind is attempting to warn us, but her message is garbled and fading in and out!"

Babble looked up and caught sight of a barely visible, red flare and heard the distant echoes of Gripp voices lost within the density of the fog.

They must be in trouble, thought Twist. *Otherwise, why would they be shouting!*

"Ship oars," commanded #1. "Ship all oars! We should be lifting off from the sand as soon as the current changes direction again."

His voice trailed as the first shock wave hit the raft, almost throwing Grist head first into the water. Only the power of his over-sized hands allowed him to hold onto the ropes of the violently shaking boat as he heard the shouts of his team.

"Look in the water...in the water!" yelled Twist. "The water is glowing with unusual colors!"

Stare's mind was filled with images of bizarre, life forms when out of the corner of his eye he caught the sight of other eyes. They were huge, yellow eyes rimmed with red, glowing with an inner light, looming over Twist, ready to strike. "Watch out!" Stare warned.

Twist swerved quickly to one side as the massive creature hovered above him and then violently hit the raft, narrowly missing his shoulder. Its razor-sharp teeth sank into the thick ropes holding the equipment in place. "T-they look like s-sea s-s-serpents," stammered Twist.

Th-they must be Spinners!" stuttered Stare, remembering stories about menacing, sea creatures in folklore, but he hadn't believed such creatures ever existed.

Fast and agile, the twenty-foot long, slithering Spinners possessed extraordinary sight, allowing them to quickly prey upon all who would venture into their domain, above and below the surface of the sea. Their blue-green, snake-like heads were shaped wide at the top and narrowed to a mouth that displayed several rows of fearsome teeth.

The Sea Serpents attacked from all directions, turning the raft around and around, ramming into the bottom, leaping out of the water, and striking on all sides as the Gripps valiantly beat them back with their oars.

The more fear generated by the Gripps, the more violent and intense were the attacks. The Spinners, who were usually docile creatures, had become activated into a frenzy in reaction to the Gripp's fear, and now they were protecting themselves from that fear the only way they knew how.

"Prepare your weapons! Prepare to fire at my command!" shouted Grist as the Spinners circled the boat.

"Here they come again!" screamed Twist, grasping a heavy, metal oar tightly as he continued to strike back at the spinning creatures attacking them from every side until the Explorers in Time were overwhelmed by the sea.

PART TWO

The Valley of Acronos

A MOVING COLLAGE OF SOFT PINK and white clouds floated in the sky above, casting soft gray shadows on the glimmering landscape below, covered in an array of colorful flowers and foliage.

A clear sparkling stream carved its way down from the majestic mountains, through canyons and across grassy plains into the forests, flowering fields and glens of the Valley of Acronos before ultimately moving on to the sea.

There was a crispness in the early morning air as Filloloper felt herself floating in the midst of a joyful dream. Her physical body was relaxed and asleep in the comfortable, soft moss growing under a spreading Morraya tree covered with bright yellow blossoms and thick, green leaves.

Lost in her dream, Filloloper had no thoughts of her recent transition to Level Seven where she found herself embodying an energetic, golden-haired dog with long ears and a white muzzle. The transition had been shocking at first, but soon she became accustomed to her new strengths and abilities and found herself enjoying her new embodiment as she shared exploration of Acronos with her dear companion, Fabius.

In her dream, she felt herself floating up toward a brilliant white, billowing cloud moving slowly over the valley. She relished the view of her new home below. There was so much to see and learn, especially since she and Fabius had been appointed Guardians of Acronos.

Suddenly, without warning, her dream cloud was disappearing, and she was tumbling like a leaf blowing in the wind, turning over and over again. On the verge of panic, the strong and normally fearless dog attempted to control her thoughts. Moments seemed like hours of tossing and turning in the turbulence of what felt like a powerful, magnetic storm.

The wind then stopped just as suddenly as it began. There was no movement. It was quiet...almost too quiet. She let out a sigh of relief, shaking her head, trying to free herself from the dream state.

What was that? What is happening in Acronos? She wondered as a dense fog slid stealthily over the shoreline and out toward the island. Under those billowing, gray clouds, Filloloper could see dark objects slowly spinning around and around on the surface of the sea.

Her body twitched as she desperately struggled to awaken. *I must remember this dream. I need to recall these visions.*

REFLECTIONS IN TIME

The coolness of an early morning breeze ruffled the hair on Filloloper's long ears and moved across her silky, golden hair. Sparkles of bright light reflected the first glimmers of the sunrise now illuminating the branches of the tallest trees.

Fabius could sense Filloloper was in a deep sleep. He lay nearby, nestled in the leaves and moss. He was larger than his dear friend and had a long, thick, shiny black and white coat with a white muzzle and black ears.

How it came to be that Filloloper had become his companion in time was an event that Fabius was obsessed to ponder. It was as if by remembering the minutest details, he would be able to understand how each moment was woven from their past and now into the present.

Yes, he and Filloloper had been *Time Companions* for many years. Once again they were on assignment, but now their task was to be very different, or so it seemed. From what he could recall, they had both earned the unique opportunity to be the Guardians of Level Seven and were now able to live a peaceful existence in a land called Acronos.

Through the centuries, Fabius had always found a way to resist the memory veil—that infamous curtain that quickly closes at the end of each life. The closing of the curtain between lifetimes usually prevented memories from moving forward into the next adventure.

Time? What is Time? He asked himself. *Is Time a spiral...a simple thread of energy that is wound around and around itself? Or is Time attempting to reveal to us who we are, again and again, in each new, distinct manifestation of flesh and bone?*

Is Time a spiral...a simple thread of energy that is wound around and around itself?

He knew that there was always the next journey, but to where and even more importantly to when? Is life just a game—a series of lives, following lives, yielding memories upon memories, and then nothing?

Fabius smiled as he glanced again over at Filloloper still lost in sleep! We are all asleep, he thought. Perhaps, even when we are wide awake, we are all actually trying to remember our true identities!

He wondered why it would be wrong to remember our past lives and to contemplate all those days and nights. Could we not revel anew in our moments of achievement, and yes, even our triumphs?

Fabius was absorbed in his musings, contemplating that there must be guidelines for the game—rules that one could break, perhaps just a little.

He often heard sounds and witnessed persistent visions of another time and place—distant echoes of voices, commanding voices calling out orders: "Hold that line. Tight formation! Shields up! Prepare to engage!"

Vivid images of soldiers often appeared in his mind. Proud and powerful men in formation, preparing to march, and then quickly turning into ghost-like figures, becoming more like shadows moving through his mind.

He could hear sounds of past events, distant whispers moving within the winds of time.

Was that the sole purpose of life's design...to live and forget? Are we here only to continue experiencing the same life lessons over and over again, never remembering all that we have learned?

There must be other reasons for the way our memory is designed. Perhaps there is an invisible knowingness which travels with us and is there to guide us in the next lifetime.

Fabius breathed out a long sigh. It was indeed a significant transformation from being human and then changing into animal form. *I am amazed by my unlimited senses – the ability to see and hear so clearly,* he thought, *and to feel the power of creation under my four feet as I run!*

I mean the power of my four paws, he corrected himself as he marveled at the incredible balance that four legs provided rather than just two. *So, this was our reward: to be transformed into dogs and to live in a land of harmony at total peace within itself!*

He wondered if his Level Seven Assignment would be different. It certainly felt different.

What if all those echoes of the past remained only as whispers from the *Before Time* and those words, "Hold that line!" were now to be transformed into adventures far more meaningful and beautiful?

Fabius glanced over at Filloloper and noticed that she was rolling back and forth in the soft moss, pawing the air at what seemed to be an invisible force. He hurried over to her and softly nuzzled her warm neck covered in perspiration.

"Filloloper! Wake up! You're having a nightmare."

Slowly, she struggled to awaken and felt the warmth of the new day flooding over her as the unusual images in her dream soon began to fade from view.

Fabius looked lovingly into the depth of her large, amber eyes and gently kissed her forehead. "You'll be all right. Dreams can seem so very real. They can take us to places and events we would rather not experience."

Filloloper appeared very worried and Fabius became concerned, wondering what she had experienced in her dream and asked, "What did you see?"

Pausing for a moment, she took a long, deep breath. "In my dream, there was a disturbance, a major shifting of energy moving throughout the Valley of Acronos. It was as though another presence, a foreboding presence from another world had entered uninvited!"

Fabius spoke softly, "It was just a dream or perhaps a vision, but only that and nothing more." He was well aware of the truths, and often the prophecy, revealed in dreams and preferred to cast away those thoughts to allay her fears.

"So, let's put our concerns aside, and enjoy this day of celebration. It is the beginning of another Synchronicity!"

THE SYNCHRONICITY

The golden rays of the rising sun were moving gently across the rolling hills and valleys of Acronos. In the distance, the sound of a unique and rhythmic humming grew louder and louder. At first, it was almost impossible to see the low-flying creatures that were reflecting the brilliant sun, but their impression and presence became quickly evident on the landscape below.

Flying in perfect formation like a flock of large birds, a swarm of ancient, flying insects, the Vibrium, were gliding over the Valley of Acronos. Their colorful, twelve-foot-wide, translucent wings with delicate lace-like patterns were filtering the intense rays of the morning sun. The wings were becoming a kaleidoscope of vibrant blues, violets, red and gold. The Vibrium's sweeping flight patterns created a magical wash of moving color across the landscape below, mixing with the many hues of flowering plants and trees.

Their long, tubular, iridescent bodies and enormous wings gave them the ability to fly low and fast over the rolling fields of the valley. The speed and smooth pace of their flight combined with the powerful, steady vibrations of their wings effortlessly lifted pollen from the plants and spread it far and wide, seeding the valley.

The giant insects were flying in precise formations only a few yards above the ground. The graceful movement of their wings gently infused the currents of air with a perfumed fragrance from thousands upon thousands of flowers blooming in *Synchronicity*.

Fabius gazed in wonder at the sight of the Vibrium. The colors in their wings filtered by the sun were reflecting off star-shaped, white blossoms nestled in the shrubs along the pathway. It was as if the flowers were being painted in pastels by an unseen artist in the sky.

The companions watched in silent awe, touched by the intensely emotional experience of watching such a brilliant spectacle of living color as flowers began opening, preparing for the synchronized blooming.

The meadow below was filled to overflowing with an amazing collection of flowering plants and trees, creating a shimmering sea of blossoms pulsing and quivering with energy and life.

As Guardians of Acronos, Filloloper and Fabius felt an extreme sense of responsibility to ensure that the beauty and harmony of the *Synchronicity* in this magical land would continue far into the future. They would enjoy living in the wonder of a natural environment.

"Look, over there, some of the Trillia have fallen from the force of the Vibrium passing overhead," observed Fabius as he carefully lifted the vibrating, flower laden, silvery vines and placed them on the bushes beside the trail.

The white flowers and green leaves of the Trillia vines wound their way throughout the forest, growing over the rocks, wrapping around trunks of trees and climbing high into the tallest branches.

These amazing psychogenic vines were the very nerve center of Acronos. They provided a continuous background humming, which changed tones according to the messages they carried, alerting inhabitants to any disturbances or unusual events. The Trillia flowers could quickly change color from white to yellow to orange, and then vibrant red, depending upon the level of danger detected.

At that moment, the Guardians became very aware that the vines were in the process of communicating and the humming was becoming louder. The tall, flowering trees above them began swaying back and forth. The dogs felt a slight vibration, followed by a stronger force moving through them. The Trillia tuned yellow and then orange, reporting a significant disturbance near the shoreline.

Filloloper caught her breath, turning to Fabius with a worried expression as she remembered her nightmare in which strange, shadowy creatures were violently spinning on the surface of the water. Without further hesitation, they quickly headed toward the shore following the ominous, warning signals of the Trillia vines.

PART THREE

Is This a Dream?

STARE, THE ENGINEER, FELT LOST somewhere in Time as he struggled to regain consciousness. Was this all only an illusion? He certainly could feel the icy water of the ocean swirling around him, and the extreme cold made him acutely aware that, indeed, he must still be alive.

His eyes sprung wide open. "Where am I?" he gasped, trying to orient himself to his surroundings, but all he could see were ominous, rolling ocean waves with no shore in sight. Visions raced through his mind, and he panicked, remembering the continuous spinning of the boats and the vicious, serpent-like creatures attacking his raft.

They must still be here! He exclaimed to himself anxiously. *They're waiting to attack again!* His eyes darted frantically in all directions as overwhelming terror paralyzed his ability to think beyond the moment.

And then, his worst fear came upon him. The water began to churn faster and faster as if he were caught in a whirlpool, but instead of being pulled down, he was being pushed up higher in the water. Before he knew what was happening, a massive wave thrust him into the air. Then something hit him...hard, very hard.

Stare tried to move, but he was being held tightly around his head and shoulders. He was choking and fighting back as bravely and courageously as only a true Gripp could fight, down to his very *Last Grasp (to his death).*

There was no time to search for weapons. It was a struggle of life or death with an unknown creature wrapping itself around him, tighter and tighter.

The harder he fought, the more entangled he became. Exhausted, Stare stopped fighting momentarily to gather strength. He struck back against his attacker trying to loosen the coils around his neck and upper body.

A moment later, he realized that his attacker was nothing more than a large mass of tangled seaweed that had twisted tightly around him. He shuddered and breathed a sigh of relief as he pulled off the tangled coils that were binding him.

"Yes, I am, indeed, alive," he muttered to himself as he staggered to his feet, looking around to see if any of his other teammates had also survived. "I can't be the only one to have escaped the Spinners!" he thought. An overwhelming fear of being left alone swept over him like the waves that had just washed him to shore. Could he be the only surviving member of the *Eye of Time Exploration Team*?

Stare slowly and cautiously turned around in circles, trying to catch a glimpse of the other team members. He peered through the shoulder-high, gray-green grass surrounding him. There was no one in sight. "They must have been...," he paused for a moment trying to push the idea out of his mind. Could they have been devoured by those sea creatures that suddenly emerged from the deep?

"No! They are Gripps, after all. Some of them must have survived!" he stated while trudging down the shoreline anxiously looking for any evidence of rafts and the critical gear that would be necessary for a successful mission. All he could see were towering trees, bushes, and thick grass covering a sloping hillside and beyond.

"I-I am an engineer," he stammered, "I was trained to interact with civilization. What an irony to be abandoned here in this foreboding wilderness all alone and completely without resources."

His voice trailed off as he frantically checked to see if his Gripp survival belt was still attached to his waist. It was. He would need that equipment with him: fire starters, emergency food packets, a water canteen, and most important of all, his Gripp survival knife and Gripp gun.

But Stare was not alone. Other eyes were watching him, eyes that were trained to observe and not be seen. Stare could not possibly understand that a very strange creature was now fixating on his every move. It was impossible to see that a giant Oswitch, over seven feet tall, was only a few feet away.

Phelan stood quietly, camouflaging himself in the foliage around him. *I have to report every detail of my observations to Filloloper and Fabius*, thought the Zigalot Oswitch, who loved to spy unseen. Yes, he was the last of the Kolourians, the mythical birds who could instantly change the colors of their feathers and blend into any surroundings. This unique ability provided him with the courage he needed to follow his overwhelming curiosity.

Bright blue irises trimmed in yellow highlighted Phelan's bulging eyes, each moving independently so that he could quickly see in both directions simultaneously. His long, flexible neck enabled him to easily move his head to look around obstacles and glance behind him even when running.

Taking a deep breath, Phelan silently watched and waited for Filloloper and Fabius to arrive.

Stare stopped moving. Did he hear something? Was there movement in those trees or just beyond? The adrenalin rush of fear surged through him as he tightened his grip on his survival knife and cautiously pushed his way through the nearly head tall, wheat-colored grass.

But there was no time for thought...no time to prepare. He was grabbed, pulled down and was being dragged backward into the underbrush.

He screamed, "No good Gripp dies without a fight!"

Shockingly, as soon as those words left his mouth, the attacker released him.

"Stare you're alive! I couldn't see you. I only saw a form moving through the grass. Glad you yelled out just in time!" Stare spun around to see Grubb, the Biologist.

"We've been looking for you," explained Grubb. "We thought you were dead! You are the only one who was missing. We have all the equipment. Without your expertise, it would be useless!"

The two Gripps quickly recovered from their strange reunion and made their way to join the surviving team members gathered on the beach.

As they walked through the tall, marshy grass, Grubb asked, "Did you see anything...anything unusual?" He cast a curious look into Stare's deep-set, gray eyes.

"I thought I heard something moving. That's when you found me, or rather attacked me."

"The other team members found no signs of anything unusual either," continued Grubb, "but we did see some movement in the grass. Perhaps, it was just the wind."

"There is a lot of atmospheric activity here, wherever we are," suggested Stare. "That mysterious fog seemed to come out of nowhere; and after the Spinners attack, there was that strong wind and current that swept us to shore."

"Somehow we all survived! Isn't that all we need to know," answered Grubb nervously.

Stare nodded his silent reply as if to say, "It's obvious that we're no longer in Grippland."

Just ahead, a familiar voice was speaking as they entered a small clearing overlooking the shore. The team members were assembled in a half-circle around Grist, the Commander. He was trying to convince them that they had won the battle of the Spinners.

"We will not be defeated, and why have we survived, fellow Gripps?" #1 taunted with a wry and twisted smile on his craggy, wrinkled face.

The team shouted out in unison, "Because we grab on! We grip on! We grind on! That is our way!"

"Never forget it," responded Grist. "Never forget it!"

He turned and pointed, "We will make camp there on that rise under the trees. When the fog eventually clears we will begin our exploration of this land."

SECURING THE BEACH

When Fabius and Filloloper arrived at the shore, they immediately sensed a change in the energy field. It was as if something or someone was watching them. In fact, they could hear the sound of shallow breathing nearby.

Looking around, the dogs noticed that the red and yellow leaves were moving ever so slightly on the tall bushes a few feet away.

Alerted to that movement and sound, they heard a very hushed voice whisper.

> *I had to see what I could see*
> *that is intruding upon our territory.*
> *Creatures of neither fur nor feather*
> *were standing there, alone and together.*

"It's you, Phelan," Fabius greeted him in a hushed tone. "We know you're here. Please show yourself."

A moment later, Phelan stepped away from the bushes and revealed himself in his natural, light gold and white feathers. He had been invisibly observing them all along. Once more, the Zigalot's ability to camouflage himself and match his surroundings had enabled him to see and not be seen.

Phelan's wide, saucer-shaped eyes seemed even more prominent than when the Guardians had last met with him. His long, yellow beak made clicking sounds when he spoke, and the feathered crest on top of his head was now fluttering rapidly in a very agitated manner.

The oversized bird began to anxiously describe all the details of the strange creatures he had witnessed on the shore, but the dogs were doubtful since Phelan loved to exaggerate from time to time, which was most of the time.

Phelan spoke in his favorite, poetic style:

> *Strange strangers have washed ashore.*
> *Will there be many more?*
> *Acronos may never be as before.*

Fabius motioned to be quiet. There should be no conversation, not even whispers. Most importantly, Phelan needed to refrain from expressing himself in his normally loud and poetic manner. The trio could only exchange glances, expressions and body language to communicate. They continued cautiously forward, careful to be as quiet as possible so no one would be alerted to their position.

What has Phelan witnessed that could provoke such fear in this great bird? Filloloper wondered as she reached the top of the steep ridge.

From her vantage point there appeared to be four strange, gray beings walking along the beach. Then she saw three more and three after that! "I count ten," she murmured, pressing her nose into Fabius' ear, so as not to let even the faintest sound escape her breath. Fabius nodded his reply, his eyes showing the shock that, indeed, Phelan's report was accurate! This time the danger was real!

Filloloper cocked her head to one side and listened. She heard a voice shouting, "Secure the beach!" Within seconds, she witnessed the ten strangers pulling rafts onto shore and gathering equipment. They stood on two legs like Phelan, but they were much shorter. They dressed in identical gray uniforms with unusual markings and numbers on their lapels and on their round helmets.

The shock of the encounter seemed to be transporting Filloloper far away from Acronos. It felt as though she was viewing another time while she silently watched the ten strangers moving around a warming fire on the shore. Their movements seemed far too familiar as she watched them stacking what appeared to be containers nearby.

Had she witnessed such a scene before? If so, where and when? She wondered if this was only her imagination. The harder she tried to push back thoughts of a similar encounter, the clearer her memory became as it penetrated to the very core of her being.

Fabius was with me, she thought. *I'm beginning to remember it all!* Short of breath, she cautiously inched her way back from the line of sight. She recalled not only the presence of men and equipment; but more importantly, in her memory, she saw armed warriors from a lifetime when she was not Filloloper but was instead a young woman named Filloperna, a Warrior Princess from another time and place.

Her mind continued to drift into emotional scenes from her distant past as she watched Fabius also observing the strangers below.

Phelan shook nervously and declared,

> *Strange beings suddenly appear*
> *all grim and gray and marked with fear!*
> *Danger is lurking in the air!*
> *Danger's here and everywhere!*

The Zigalot held his breath as he inched backward into a clump of bushes, completely hiding him from view. Fabius and Filloloper nodded to him as they also concealed themselves deep within the tall grass.

One of the invaders ran toward the group gathered by the fire and stated, "Beach secured, #1! We find no evidence of any traps or inhabitants!"

"Don't just stand there! Check the hillsides," snapped the stranger with a distorted grimace on his face.

Scouring the hillside, Stare whispered to Grubb, "I thought I saw something moving...moving over there." He motioned toward a grouping of boulders and trees about ten yards away. "I saw something. There is no doubt about it. Tell

Grouse and Gritt to circle around those trees with their net guns. Take the enemy alive for interrogation."

Filloloper inched backward away from the Gripps who were moving closer; their shadows grew larger on the sand. She glanced over her shoulder to see three of the strangers only a few yards away.

"Look...there! Dogs! Wild dogs!" yelled Grubb.

Filloloper and Fabius were frozen in shocked confusion. One of the Gripps was running toward them. "Fire the net guns at the target!" commanded Twist who was sprinting over the sandy shore.

Fabius nudged Filloloper who followed him, running as quickly as possible toward the safety of bushes growing at the tree line.

"Keep them together! Now! Fire the net-gun!"

Two shrill, metallic, popping sounds filled the air and continued to echo through the crisp wind sweeping up from the shoreline below.

"We have wild dogs!" boasted Grubb. "We've got them!" he shouted triumphantly. "Take them to #1!"

Filloloper and Fabius felt their world turning upside down as the Gripps pulled the heavy net along the ground, tumbling the dogs over and over as they twisted and turned. Their eyes were burning from the wind-blown sand, and tears began streaming down Filloloper's cheeks.

Another hard jerk, and then a thump! The dogs landed in a heap in front of #1, Grist, the Commander, the only intruder who had rows of medals pinned to his jacket.

Filloloper lay exhausted, aching with cuts and bruises, looking frantically toward Fabius who had fallen from the net. His body was trembling and shaking. His eyes were dilated with fear as he extended his right paw toward her. Speaking without words, he was projecting his thoughts to Filloloper: *Remember who you truly are. Never forget all that you know.* He stared into the distance. His eyes went blank.

"Excellent work! Dr. Grouse, examine the dogs!" ordered #1, grinning and rhythmically stomping his black, Gripp boots in the sand. A satisfied twinkle sparkled in his gray eyes.

"I wonder if these dogs could be ours?" mumbled Doctor Grouse as she slowly bent over Fabius. "They might be dogs from our earlier Gripp Time Trials," she explained.

Grouse turned to the others and asked, "Who has the codes? We need to check their ears to see if they have the codes, so we can cut them open and examine the recorders that should be in their chests. These recordings would be very valuable to the success of our mission!"

#1 immediately looked over at Babble, "You have all the codes, don't you? You're in charge of mission data!"

Without hesitation, Babble started pressing the keyboard on her electronic data monitor. She searched for codes starting with GC-TT (Gripp Command — Time Trials). The numbers of the trial sequence and time stamp would appear tattooed on their ears.

"Very well, subdue the animals!" commanded Grist. "Dr. Grouse, do you have all the necessary equipment to remove the recorders from the dogs?"

She nodded as he continued, "This could be a critical moment for your career, Grouse, a very significant operation indeed! High Command will be grateful to hear that we'll be the first to extract information from the dog trials. Obviously, we will also need any information that you can carve out of these beasts that might enable the success of my mission."

#1 hesitated for a moment and then said, "I mean the success of OUR mission...for all members of the Eye of Time Exploration Team!"

ANOTHER PLACE AND TIME

Filloloper desperately tried to reach out to Fabius through her thoughts. *Fabius, Fabius! I know you can hear me. Wake up, Fabius, please come back!*

He didn't respond. The reality of his passing away began to strike fear into her heart as tears of sorrow fell from her eyes and washed over her face. Moments passed by, and then minutes. There was no response. Nothing.

Filloloper's world was spinning out of control. How could it end this way? She struggled to her feet pushing hard against the net. Her emotions reached a peak as she screamed out loud, "Fabius, wake up! Please wake up!"

Her words pierced the silence with penetrating anguish, "Fabius, please come back! Show me a sign that you are still here...still with me! Don't leave. Please don't go."

The Gripps quickly exchanged startled glances and were puzzled by what they had just witnessed.

"Did you hear that?" asked Twist. The others stood in silence. Twist repeated, "That dog was speaking words!"

"Th-the-the dog can talk!" stuttered Scheme as he backed away from Fabius. "Th...That's impossible!"

Never one to question the unknown, Grist stared at Filloloper and motioned to Doctor Grouse. "Check the dogs!"

Grouse examined the ears of Fabius and Filloloper, looking for the codes. "They have no Gripp codes on them. I'm certain they aren't our dogs," she reported. "They were not a part of the Time Trials."

The doctor quickly grabbed a strange instrument out of her bag and knelt down, holding a type of wand-like device over Fabius' body. It made a soft buzzing sound as she moved it over his heart. She quickly read the data from the instrument and glanced over at Filloloper.

"You can't reach your friend with words," Dr. Grouse said curtly. "He's taken his Last Grasp."

Filloloper could see that Fabius' eyes were blank. They looked like black mirrors, reflecting only the twisted faces and confused expressions of the Gripps now glaring at him.

Even though his eyes were transfixed deep within himself, Fabius could hear. The sounds were faint at first, like a strange wind that was now accelerating his consciousness into a more familiar sense of being.

As the wind died down, he could hear the clash of metal, the sounds of sword upon sword and the crash of shield against shield. He heard the pounding of horses' hooves racing across the hard earth.

There were shrill voices loudly calling, "Hold the line! Keep formations tight! Push forward! Push forward!" Those words began to echo repeatedly in his mind, sweeping over him like the warm embrace of power.

He heard a voice saying, "Remember…Strength and Honor! No retreat!" They were his words, and the men were his men. And yet, he could not even lift his head to utter the weakest of commands. Only the distant clash of steel upon steel kept him from ignoring his thoughts.

The words began to echo in his mind, sweeping over him like the warm embrace of power.

"Who am I? Who am I?" He demanded in desperation. The wind was his only reply. A powerful current of air rushed over him, lifting him, accelerating him forward as if his lifeless body was falling, tumbling into a dark, never-ending void.

And then he entered a silence he had never experienced before, except in the depth of his dreams. Perhaps he was dreaming, but then again, maybe this was the way of all those who passed on to the other side.

Fabius rested for a moment in reverie with no thoughts, no feelings, just peace. And then that peace was broken by a flash of light, bright white light, and upon opening his eyes, he found himself standing in a glorious hall of mirrors.

He looked into the mirrored surfaces, angled in such a way that they reflected into one another, creating an ever-expanding collage of images. Reflected in the mirrors were scenes of his many lives, and he could observe events in those lives from many different angles and points of view.

He looked into the mirrored surfaces, which were angled in such a way that they reflected into one another, creating an ever-expanding collage of images.

He looked again from one mirror to another and another, seeming to stretch into infinity, each showing images of who he had been, but not who he remembered himself to be. He saw himself as a man — an ocean voyager, a teacher, a trader, and a researcher, and a warrior.

"Those are all d-different manifestations of who I have been," he stammered out loud while watching spell-bound as the images began moving slowly in time, and then he began travelling *through* time.

As the visions became more and more animated, he saw a warrior on a horse fighting against overwhelming odds. He remembered that battle. It was a time when he was being attacked by a band of barbarians when he was valiantly trying to save the life of a princess.

In the vision, he was turning his mighty, white stallion, Majestic, around and around, courageously swinging his sword from side-to-side to ward off the attackers.

In a clearing not far from him, he could see Filloperna, a beautiful, young princess with long auburn hair and bright green eyes. Seated upon her golden horse, she quickly glanced over her shoulder at him as she managed to escape from the barbarian warriors.

She's safe! He thought to himself.

The scene in the mirror continued. Fabius could feel himself in the heat of battle, while at the same time, he seemed to be watching everything from a distance.

He increased the pressure with his legs even tighter on Majestic's ribs, turning his faithful horse around and around to evade his attackers.

It was a dance of life and death. He and his beloved stallion had experienced a great many battles before, always fighting bravely together.

And at this moment in time, the man was attempting to save his horse. The horse was protecting the man.

From far off in the distance, he could hear the whirring, whistling sound of a spear flying through the air. Fabius swerved, trying to avoid a direct hit, while reaching out to block another sword.

Suddenly, the shock and pain of that sharp projectile raced through him like lightning entering the right side of his lower back.

He took a deep breath and pressed his knees tighter into the flank of his horse, kicking and turning. The magnificent steed reared up on his hind legs, instinctively trying to push away every blow from the attackers.

It was all too much. Fabius lost his grip on the reins. He felt weightless as he flew through the air, and then he was falling, falling. At the very last moment, while still in midair, he saw all the mirrors become dim, except for the mirror that was directly in front of him.

In the remaining mirror, he found himself staring at the image of a large dog. When he turned sideways, the dog in the mirror turned in the same direction.

He moved closer to the mirror and saw that the dog had black ears and bright, amber eyes rimmed with deep brown, and his muzzle was pure white. His head and back were covered in a thick, shiny black and white fur.

"Th-that must be me," he stammered to himself. "I am a dog. I am now manifesting as a dog. I have become an animal. And look at me. I don't even have arms to bear arms! I can't even carry a sword!" His thoughts became confused as his mind filled with questions.

Finally, he told himself to stop. He breathed deeply.

An answer came softly in a warm, comforting voice. "Fabius, your act of courage led you to an act of self-sacrifice. You saved the life of Princess Filloperna by sacrificing your own life in exchange. Yes, Fabius, in the heat of battle you saved another's life from certain death. You have received an exemption for your act of selflessness."

Fabius felt tears moving down his cheeks as the voice continued speaking slowly and methodically. "You have a higher destiny now, Fabius. You have been granted a new command and entry into Level Seven as the protectorate of a land called Acronos and all of its inhabitants."

Somehow, deep within his being, Fabius recognized this voice, but he could not remember where he had heard it or when. And then, it was quiet.

Fabius felt compelled to speak to this unseen entity. Words poured out of his mouth. At first, his statements were almost inaudible, and then he grew more determined as he grasped the awareness of who he had become.

"How can I be a protectorate of anything? I have no men at my command. I can't carry a sword, nor do I have a horse to ride. I am...I have...I mean...I am only a dog...an animal with four paws!" His voice was impassioned as he watched his image—the image of a large dog with black ears trimmed in silver—reflecting back to him as he spoke.

And in response, that same calm voice began again. It was a voice that Fabius somehow knew he could trust just by the sound of its tone. "Nothing has changed, Fabius. You are still the same animating persona—the entity from the past that you remember.

"You have only altered your form of manifestation, which I might add may take some adjusting to now that you are aware of the changes. Remember, you are still Fabius, and your responsibilities are even more valuable now. You will experience many more tests of courage, but then again, that seems to be the way it has always been."

The familiar voice continued calmly. "Remember, Fabius; you have a new adventure unfolding in front of you. And yes, you saved the life of Princess Filloperna who is now your companion, Filloloper, here in Acronos. She will staunchly remain by your side; although, she may not remember her former identity immediately.

"As you know, Fabius, Level Seven is at Filloloper's and your command. You are on a higher level of existence now. The clash of armies, the destruction of cultures, and the wasting of lives is all behind you. Even though you may still feel that memory in your veins, the impulse to aggressive, violent action must change.

You are on a much higher level of existence now.
The clash of armies, the destruction of cultures,
the wasting of lives is all behind you.

"You have earned an exemption from all that has passed, Fabius. It is your choice. You will not be alone. The Seven Harmonies are there to protect you against all those who would trespass against you and Filloloper."

"But I can see the reflection of the present time in the mirror. My body is lifeless. The ones known as Gripps have captured Filloloper. What can I do?"

"Remember your words: "*Strength and honor. On Level 7 you need not kill or destroy the enemy any longer. They will learn as you have learned. The choice is yours."

"But what do I do? How do I...?"

The voice answered:

Remember your words...and breathe, Fabius. Breathe deeply! Let that fire in you become vibrant again!

Know that the Harmonies will be there for you! And remember to enjoy the adventure!

Life is always about the Now and not the Then or When. Power is ONLY available to you in each moment and all those extended moments, becoming more moments, ultimately becoming the Powerful Momentum of Time moving through all things!

Fabius could feel the voice penetrating every fiber of his being, filling him with warmth and courage. It seemed as if he had always known and trusted the voice that was speaking, even though he didn't know from where or when.

The phrase, "You are still the being known as Fabius," continued to echo in his mind. He took a deep breath and stared in awe and reverie, transfixed by the images of his past lives reflected in the unending Hall of Mirrors.

"Wait. What was that?" Fabius questioned. Out of the corner of his eye, he noticed that in the mirror nearest to him, the image of Fabius, the dog, moved ever so slightly. Yet, he was standing completely motionless.

And then the mirrors started changing form. The images from the past were turning and twisting. Fabius watched the reflecting sheets of glass being whisked away like thousands of shining, silvery leaves caught up in a sudden gust of a summer's breeze.

Fabius was no longer aware of who he was, nor who he had become. The images reflected in the Hall of Mirrors were gone, spirited away by an unseen force field. He felt as if he were sinking further and further into an endless void that seemed to be consuming his thoughts, his past, and his future.

He was falling, unable to control his body, which felt as though it was being moved ever so gently by an invisible hand, and then a shock of pain flashed through him as the dark void transformed into flickers of light.

RETURN OF FABIUS

Fabius could hear voices again…unfamiliar voices. There was no love or warmth in these tones, only the cold, harsh words of commands: "Drag the dog's body off the trail. Tag it, and wrap it. We may need to examine it later for testing."

Dr. Grouse retrieved a large, metallic collar with the design of two hands gripping one another. She snapped the collar around Fabius' limp neck and then pushed his head back down onto the sand.

Was it that last, painful insult or Filloloper's piercing cry of anguish that filled Fabius' lungs with life, reanimating his physical Being?

His body shuddered, and his legs shook. Quickly, with one rolling turn, Fabius regained his full height and using all his power he rammed into Grouse and sent her tumbling hard to the ground.

"Not on my watch, you won't!" He declared, standing over her. With renewed life and energy, he ripped the leash from Dr. Grouse's grasp and ran to stand next to Filloloper.

There was no response from the huddled Gripps as they stood motionless with their eyes and mouths opened wide in astonishment.

The staring continued. Not one team member even blinked as Fabius stared back, piercing into the very recesses of the darkness that lived at the core of every good Gripp mercenary. Held by a form of fear they had never experienced, their deep-set eyes and lined faces transformed into a perpetual gaze. Looking as if they had turned to stone.

When will they attack? Thought Fabius as his eyes darted from one strange being to another, expecting them to become even more violent and outraged. Instead, they only stared back at him in total disbelief, stunned and transfixed by seeing something that never should have occurred.

Seizing the moment, Fabius turned and moved quickly. He pulled at the net holding Filloloper until she was free and quickly glanced over at Grist, whose face was ashen; his eyes narrowed as he moved toward the dogs. He started to speak but stopped only a few feet away.

Fabius looked up at the strange creatures and spoke, "Welcome to Acronos. Welcome to Level Seven."

Fabius was shocked to hear his own words. Yes, they were his words, but not the words he had imagined he would say after being tagged and left for dead only moments before. And he was speaking a different language—the language of the Gripps.

Scheme looked at Grist and then at the two dogs and stammered, 'Th...That dog said, 'Welcome to Level Seven. Welcome to Acronos.' What does that mean?"

Filloloper and Fabius stood close together and stared defiantly at the ominous strangers from another world.

Grist raised his eyebrows and twisted his lips back and forth as if he was being forced to swallow a strange reality that he refused to recognize for fear of disturbing his established mindset.

"The dog said welcome to Level Seven," repeated Babble. "And he said it in plain Grippish."

"I know what he said!" snapped Grist angrily.

Babble moved closer to Fabius with her camera to catch an image of the dog who was dead only minutes before as Grist hurried over to Dr. Grouse and asked. "What is your report, Grouse? You said you examined the dog!"

"Well, yes. You see, this dog was obviously dead," explained Dr. Grouse. "His neck was broken. I felt broken bones when I put the Gripp collar around his neck. This animal was dead. He wasn't moving."

"So, fellow Gripps," began Grist. "We have encountered the enemy. We have seen the enemy. We have killed the enemy. And now the enemy is here staring back at us!"

He looked down the sandy shoreline, lifted his head, cleared his throat, and continued, "Fellow Gripps, know this: we never retreat in the face of the enemy! Don't you get it? They even speak Grippish, our national language. They are setting a trap, but you just can't see it!" He glared at Filloloper and Fabius and then turned toward Stare.

"I know what you're saying, #1," ventured Stare. "But, uh, look at them. They don't appear to be vicious. I mean, they just seem to be...you know...dogs. I mean...dogs that can talk. Well, uh, evidently two, wild dogs that can speak perfect Grippish."

Grist didn't reply. He shrugged his shoulders and then turned to his fellow Gripps and ordered, "Prepare to make camp on the hillside under that large, twisted tree with wide, spreading branches, the one with roots protruding high above the ground. It will serve as a defensible position.

"Gather your equipment and secure the dogs! Move out!" He picked up his gear and trudged silently up the hill to establish his command.

Pausing for a moment, Grist looked back and could see the dogs resting next to each other and wondered what their welcome to *Level Seven* really meant.

A brilliant shaft of sunlight was moving through the parting clouds onto the beach where the dogs were sitting. Grist watched in surprise and amazement as that bright beacon of light made it appear as though the dogs were wearing shining coats of silvery armor.

A DEFENSIBLE POSITION

Babble quietly settled herself near enough to Grist, Twist, and Scheme to listen in on their conversation. Silhouetted against the darkening sky, their bodies seemed to merge into one animated, solid mass with arms moving and fingers pointing.

Babble could hear their whispers echoing around the tall boulders. "We need a defensible position! We must be ready for attack! How can we trust these animals?"

They must not know the first thing about strategy, she thought, moving to a more secluded area where she carefully unpacked her recording instruments. Satisfied that no one could hear her, Babble opened a small rectangular device with a recording screen, which she pulled close to her face. *These mission reports are my ticket to amnesty,* she thought, an *amnesty promised by High Command.*

Babble's official position on the team was to provide an ongoing record of all activities and to film the Gripp team in the most favorable ways possible. These documentations and recordings would be used by High Command to influence the funding of future Time Portal missions.

That was her official reason for being chosen for the team, but there was another, a perhaps more sinister reason why she was being granted amnesty and given status as #4 in command.

She had been officially ordered to spy for High Command and to create reports on the other team members in a series of secret recordings. Thus, there were to be two versions of Gripp Log reports.

The first would be the official report, and the other, a top secret document. She would describe all events as they happened and how the others handled those situations.

Amnesty is amnesty, she thought and proceeded to log on to *Gripp Encryption Level 5* and began recording.

GRIPP LOG 1: 47643-A
Official Report to Gripp High Command

The following entry marks the end of the first full Grabbon (day) since our arrival through the *Eye of Time Portal*, leaving six Grabbons until the Portal re-opens for our return to Grippland.

All team members were successfully transported to a landing zone on a deserted island during what seemed to be an intense electrical storm, which must have altered our projected course destination.

Several team members became separated and suffered extreme disorientation from the shock of the dimensional reactivation. However, all members were examined and found to be in optimum gripping and grasping condition.

After spending the night at our transport destination, we awoke to find the island covered in fog. When conducting surveillance, we discovered our landing zone was a desolate island with no signs of civilization. Team members discussed the options available to us, and after Grist, the Commander took a consensus, we decided to leave the island and explore the open sea that surrounded us, hoping to discover new landfall.

During the crossing, underwater creatures attacked our boats. Resembling mythological, sea serpents in the folklore of extinct ocean animals, they were merciless in their attacks by continuously striking the bottom and sides of our rafts while spinning their undulating bodies around and around, but we heroically beat them back with our oars.

There was no way to accurately judge the size of those monsters, save to say that each measured at least three times the length of a Gripp raft. Defending ourselves in a prolonged battle, our team bravely fought off the creatures, now designated as "Spinners."

The overwhelming motion of the waves capsized our rafts and sent us into the sea. We made landfall after swimming in dangerous waters for what seemed to be many Grippons (hours).

After finding landfall, we secured the beachhead and began exploring inland where we encountered dozens of strange beasts resembling wild dogs. Although those vicious animals outnumbered us, we managed to capture two of the creatures and collar them.

The other rabid animals were beaten back by our fearless team members, and we proceeded to challenge the seized dogs that possess unusually long, protruding canines and razor-sharp claws, resembling those of extinct, savage predators.

Our biologist, Grubb, and team doctor, Grouse, agreed that no animals resembling those beasts were ever seen before and certainly should not be confused with the experimental dogs first sent through the time portal by High Command Labs.

We have made camp on a hillside under a large tree with an unusual root system growing high above the ground and spreading out in all directions. Hoping for a peaceful night. We will leave tomorrow before sunrise. *End of Official Report.*

Babble jerked her head as a twig snapped nearby. She abruptly stopped, crouched down, and peered out through a crack in the rock formation, making certain that no one had noticed her.

Returning to her recording device again, she signed off on the Official Report. (If the recorder were to be lost or stolen, the Official Report on Level 5 could be easily accessed by any team member.)

She carefully inserted Encryption Code Level 10, Top Secret Report (accessible only by members of High Command) and spoke in a hushed tone of voice.

GRIPP LOG 1: 47643-B
TOP SECRET REPORT

This Top-Secret Unofficial Report marks the end of the first full Grabbon (day) after arrival at our destination. We are currently camping under a large tree near the shoreline where we landed a short time ago after a harrowing experience while out at sea.

We made a successful transfer through the time portal and arrived last night, landing in the midst of a large formation of natural crystals, which may have been responsible for saving the entire team from becoming nothing more than a swarm of scattered electrons.

Gripp Stare, our engineer, mentioned that crystals could receive and direct energy through their structure. The three crystalline towers equally spaced in a triangular formation, may have magnified their power, enabling us to survive the transport. Although many team members experienced memory lapses possibly due to the severe electrical discharges at the landing zone.

This morning when we awoke, we found that we had landed on a desolate island exhibiting no signs of civilization. This small island is composed of natural phenomena such as sandy soil, various trees, flowers, and bushes. (See enclosed video)

When Commander Grist questioned the team regarding our experiences upon landing, it seemed that some of the team members were withholding valuable information. Scheme, Stare, and Gritt were asked what they had encountered. They answered, "No unusual activity." I am monitoring all their behaviors and conversations as High Command requested.

There was a strange sense of foreboding on that small island as if it was continuously questioning who and what we are. Perhaps, this was the principal reason why Grist allowed us to decide whether to proceed onto the open sea in our Gripp rafts or to wait out our remaining six Grabbons (days) on the island until the portal reopens.

No one stepped forward in the initial vote to explore the sea surrounding us, but after hesitating, I understood that the only possibility of success was to take advantage of this rare opportunity. I was the first to step forward into the circle followed by Gritt #8, our Geologist. After that, all other team members reluctantly stepped forward, thus confirming their decision to explore the open sea with the hope of discovering another, more productive landfall.

A mysterious fog had surrounded the island ever since our arrival, and this morning when we launched our rafts was no exception. After a little more than one Grippon (hour) at sea, we were struck by an unexpected storm. The storm at long last subsided, and we entered into an ominous calm; the surrounding sea became like a lake reflecting everything upon its mirror-like surface.

And then the winds came up again, the waves began swirling, and the rafts were spinning like tops in the water. Something was thumping rhythmically against the bottom of the boat.

That's when we first saw them, those monstrous, snake-like creatures, which had somehow sensed our presence. Without warning, the sea serpents, possessing enormous strength, mercilessly attacked our rafts. The more we fought back, the more they were activated, swirling around our boats. Their bodies became luminous, filling the dark waters with a multicolored glow.

The creatures seemed to be activated by our level of fear. We fought on, trying to push the *Spinners* away with our oars, but they continued spinning us. Their violent attacks capsized our boats. We lost recall of what happened next, awakening on a sandy beach, not knowing if we were back on the island or another shore.

The entire team miraculously survived the encounter, even though we were thrown into the depths of those dark waters wearing all of our heavy gear, which should have dragged us down into that treacherous sea. How we managed to escape the deadly Spinners is a mystery, unless those vicious predators aided our survival for some unknown reason.

Shortly after our arrival on a desolate beach, we encountered two dogs watching us from a distance. We were able to capture them and were amazed to learn that they spoke Grippish, which made no sense.

Even more disturbing is the fact that according to our instruments, the male dog died after accidentally hitting his head and breaking his neck when he was dragged in our nets. In a short time, the dog returned to life. He underwent a miraculously healing, for which we have no explanation. Neither dog appears vicious, but instead, they welcomed us to what they call, "Level 7, Acronos," and seem to be willing to answer any questions we put forward.

There is a very real sense of foreboding in this version of reality they call *Level Seven*. We should not have survived the crossing, and I fear that nothing here is as it seems! *End of Top Secret Report.*

Babble checked the Encryption Code on her unofficial report, and quickly closed her recorder when she heard the sound of approaching Gripp boots moving across the sand.

She thought to herself, *I didn't finish my comments about the dogs. But who knows if High Command will ever receive these reports anyway? But never mind, I remain hopeful we will survive this mission and return to Grippland triumphantly.*

Scheme approached her and suggested, "Babble, we need some photos of our camp and the captured beasts. We want you to show that we heroically survived the time portal transport and all those life-threatening attacks!"

"Yes, of course, #3," she replied, as they walked silently up the hillside to the camp. She overheard Grist ordering Stare, Grubb, and Gritt to head back to the beach to secure their equipment and return before nightfall.

Grist glared and mumbled, "Remember, there are no excuses for failure!"

TIME WAVES

The faintest glimmer of evening stars began to appear just above the outline of the distant island as the dense fog slowly retreated from view. Grubb, Stare, and Gritt were anxious to retrieve the remaining equipment that had been scattered across hundreds of yards along the expansive, sandy beach.

As the Eye of Time Explorers silently trudged along the shore, they each were lost deep in thought, wondering how they had managed to survive. There were so many unanswered questions regarding their miraculous salvation from certain death after being attacked by the vicious predators known to them only as *Spinners*. And yet, the three Gripps chose not to speak about their experience, nor did they dare to verbalize that which could not be analyzed or explained.

Instead, they remained stoic and expressionless, silently pondering their fate as they gazed across the sandy shoreline out to the calm of the sea. It was the very same sea, which only a few hours before had demanded they forfeit their mission as well as their lives.

Gritt was the first to sense that something had changed. He was usually acutely aware and alert to any shifts in the environment, and it was now apparent that the appearance of the landscape before him was dramatically different.

He had been named Gritt because of his endless drive and determination, but there was something else about him, some unknown quality that made him stand out from all the rest.

His tall, powerful physique, bright, blue-green eyes, well-proportioned, unlined face and sandy-colored hair, presented a handsome image by Gripp standards. Equipped with a razor-sharp mind, he was able to solve problems very quickly, but at this moment, Gritt couldn't believe his eyes as he stared in amazement at where they had landed a short time ago.

He mentally retraced their steps over and over, and yet, came to the shocking conclusion that even though this was the exact location where their boats and equipment had washed ashore, it was no longer the same beach.

Tall, gray-green grass, swaying in the soft, ocean breeze, along with rolling dunes had replaced what was sand and rock a short time before. As a Geologist, Gritt knew that this was not possible but preferred to remain silent waiting to hear the reactions of his team members.

Stare, the engineer was deemed the most logical member of the Gripp team. He was quick to process information but very slow in speaking his opinion or venturing his analysis of any situation.

Gazing at the dunes, which had replaced the flat sandy beach they had walked upon only two Grippons (hours) before, he carefully examined the shoreline. "I-It's not the s-same beach and not the s-same bay. It has become more curved, forming a half-moon," he stammered.

Grubb, the biologist, noticed the different pattern of the shoreline and changes to the landscape, but he did not respond. He preferred to remain silent, knowing there was no reason to implicate himself. As a specialist in botany, he would be the one to analyze any life-enhancing plant material they might discover, and he did not want to risk his reputation by speculating about the impossible.

Standing at an average Gripp height of five-feet, five-inches with a round face, Grubb was stockier than most. Although the others considered him to be weak-willed, he possessed a hidden, inner strength that was only apparent to a few. He was also usually more secretive than most, perhaps due to the nature of his work; but then again, he typically kept to himself, rarely offering his opinion unless someone specifically requested him to speak.

"What do you think has happened here, Grubb?" asked Gritt as he pointed toward the landscape.

"Well, uh, everything has apparently changed," he answered. "The general shapes are the same, but these plants could not have manifested within two Grippons (hours)."

Perplexed silence overcame the three explorers as they anxiously scoured the beach, hoping to discover any explanation or clues to avert the realization that their equipment had vanished into some unknown void. Was their mission doomed to failure? Would they be the messengers of that disaster to Grist, the Commander?

"This simply cannot be!" exclaimed Gritt in an exasperated tone of voice. "We are all scientists. There must be an explanation for what has happened here."

It seemed evident that as an engineer, Stare should have some answers. Serving as #5 in command, he would be the one responsible for filing a report indicating that their mission-critical equipment had disappeared.

However, he was certain that his analysis of the situation would never be acceptable to the logic of the Gripp mind. He mumbled a few words to himself, trying to form a statement that would somehow evade expressing the total absurdity of their dilemma. Taking a deep breath, he murmured in a nearly inaudible voice, "The *Eye of Time* is looking back at us!"

"What do you mean?" questioned Grubb, turning to his left and right, hoping to catch a glimpse of the *Eye of Time*, whatever that was, while Stare seemed transfixed by something in the far distance.

Gritt dismissed Stare's *Eye of Time* statement, took a deep breath, and suggested there were three possibilities. "We are either in the past or in the future, or we're lost somewhere in between. It's like those waves lapping onto the shore. They rise and fall. When they disappear, there is a hidden energy stream moving through the water forming new waves. Now you see them rising and now you don't."

"I don't understand? Are you saying that we don't really exist or that we are moving in and out of reality like the ocean waves?" questioned Grubb.

Stare shook his head and blinked his eyes, appearing to awaken from his trance-like state. "M-m-maybe we don't exist the way we were, but we are alive because we are still breathing and consuming energy."

Gritt thought about Stare's statement. Perhaps he spoke some truth even though it sounded too simple to be scientific.

He began to pace back and forth thinking out loud. "We came through the Portal, and we never looked back. We set up camp, and we have returned looking for our past, and it's gone," he paused momentarily to look around him. "That's it! Time is erasing Time! We have to go! We have to leave here now!"

"How is that even possible?" asked Grubb.

"Don't you see? The events of the future are accelerating into the present. Time is speeding up! We have to distance ourselves from this Time Wave as fast as possible! Follow me!" Gritt ran toward the trail that would lead them back to base camp with Stare and Grubb close behind.

TIME ERASING TIME

Gritt was the first to reach the trail entrance. It had not yet changed. He called to Stare and Grubb to hurry and follow him. Dark shadows cast by the trees made it more difficult to see clearly, and they abruptly stopped when noticing that the impressions their thick-soled boots had made in the sand only moments before were fast disappearing.

"Those were our boot prints!" exclaimed Grubb as he glanced back down the trail. All evidence of their presence was vanishing before his eyes, and the pathway was overgrown with new grass. Out of breath and in disbelief, he hesitated for a moment to search for something, anything, he could comprehend.

Without further thought, the three Gripps dramatically increased their pace up the hillside. Gritt's mind was racing with questions. How, but more importantly, why was time accelerating? It appeared as though nature was eliminating all traces of their existence, and everything they had touched might soon disappear.

They paused to look back at the shoreline. "We are out of phase with where we are!" exclaimed Stare anxiously. "Our energy doesn't match the energy animating this level of reality. It would take a miracle to get out of this alive!"

"What are you trying to say, Stare?" questioned Grubb, anxiously seeking any information that might help solve their fateful dilemma.

Stare desperately sought any logical answer to offer a reply. He glanced off into the distance before stumbling over his words. "I-I-It's only about us! We are triggering this entire event sequence because we are the anomaly in this place and time! I cannot say it more simply than that!

"Our resonating electromagnetic field is creating an intense *Time Dilation*, a *Time Wave*, which is accelerating future events into our present!"

Grubb rubbed his hands back-and-forth over his face as if he could wash away the full meaning of the engineer's reply. Looking directly into Stare's gray eyes, he exclaimed, "What you mean is that we're going to die! We've survived prison, time travel, storms, and we even battled sea monsters, and now it's all over! Isn't that what you are saying?"

Gritt stepped forward and spoke emphatically, attempting to break the paralysis of fear overtaking his teammates, "We took a chance. We all volunteered to seek our freedom and a chance for amnesty. Success seemed possible. And it isn't over yet! Not yet!

"We are Gripps. We were born to grab on, grip on and grind on when others do not dare!"

It was apparent that there was an alteration in the magnetic field protecting Acronos. Everything around them was bristling with energy, and the power of that force was now passing through their bodies and out of their hands, creating painful surges of electricity moving through them. There was nowhere to run, nowhere to hide.

"So this is it!" declared Gritt. "This is the moment when our current reality merges into the unknown, and unfortunately, we will merge with it as well!"

The three scientists could never have imagined that their journey would end this way. Stare was horrified at the thought of being swept away into oblivion. "How ironic it is to be defeated by an invisible enemy, called *Time*, which we have been chasing all of our lives.

"We may have only a few Grippings (seconds) left to contemplate why we ever thought it possible to slow down time's steady pace."

Gritt interjected his thoughts, hoping to come up with a solution, "It's all about resonating fields! Every one of us has a matching resonating field that corresponds to where we are or where we should be! Obviously, we cannot outrun who we are, even though that might be a solution."

"It's time! It's time for your miracle now, Stare!" exclaimed Grubb, not knowing whether to run or simply resign himself to his ultimate fate.

With those words, the energy surge slowed down, and then, amazingly, it stopped altogether. The three Gripp explorers peered down the sandy pathway they had just traversed and caught a glimpse of a light blue, electrically-charged haze moving quickly toward them.

"It appears the future is fast approaching, or shall I say our future…?" said Gritt while staring directly into a mystical, energy field now only a few yards from their position.

To their surprise, they heard a voice saying, "Miracle? Is someone looking for a miracle? Well, yes, I am known by many names, but Miracle is certainly one name that I do find acceptable!" The soft, lilting tones of the invisible speaker drifted just over their heads as if he had been listening to their entire conversation.

The voice continued, "Indeed, you do need a miracle! And I might add, that miracles are usually most appreciated when they're least expected!" Those startling words seemed to reverberate into the very center of their being.

"Did you hear that? Did you hear that voice?" repeated Stare, jerking, twisting, and turning his body around trying to locate the source of the sound.

"I heard it," replied Gritt, "unless I am hallucinating!"

"That voice must be coming from somewhere behind us! No, I think….I mean, it seems to be all around us!" declared Grubb, frightened by the possibility of another far more dangerous encounter.

They could hear him. They could feel him. But they could not see him. They were afraid to stop moving, but the plants were no longer growing as fast as before. It was as if Time was being held in suspension.

Your response is not what I had intended.
Your hearts and minds must be extended.

It was evident that the invisible speaker was not enjoying the encounter as much as he had anticipated, so he decided to make himself visible…perhaps not completely visible, but just enough to alter those unconscious travelers' tedious and boring concepts of reality.

With that thought in mind, he partially manifested his most magnificent form. His large, radiant and iridescent body could be seen swimming effortlessly in the air, back and forth and around the huddled Gripps.

"Great Grasping Grippdom! D-D-do you see that?" stammered Grubb, backing up several yards and looking for a place to hide.

"Yes, I see it!" replied Gritt. "And you, Stare?"

The engineer looked uneasy and slightly embarrassed. He pretended not to see the vision floating through the air in front of them. "What do I see? I do not know! Uh, tell me what are YOU seeing," he responded, shuffling his feet and looking off into the bushes that lined both sides of the steep trail.

Delphos asked, "Is it so difficult to say hello, Stare? Why don't you introduce me to your friends?"

"Do you know him?" questioned Gritt. "How can you know this, this enormous fish?"

"Well, I mean, ah, all I can say is that…"

"Never mind, allow me to introduce myself," answered Delphos, and with that simple statement, he materialized into his full majestic form, shining brilliantly with radiant, glowing colors. This time the Cosmic Traveler appeared to be even bigger than when Stare first encountered him on the island.

"What a monstrous creature!" exclaimed Grubb as he and Gritt took cover behind tall bushes.

"It is not easy to find an appreciative audience...not easy at all," lamented Delphos sadly. "There was a time when I was not a fish. I was a lead singer and a very gifted, guitar player in a once-famous rock and roll band. Alas, that was many eons ago. Now, I am often traveling more inter-dimensionally. You do understand; we are ALL really in show business," continued Delphos, smiling. "Everything depends on how you manifest and perform on the stage of life."

Stare looked up at the giant fish and turned to where Gritt and Grubb were hiding in the bushes. "Please come out," he beckoned. "I know this fish...I mean Delphos. He will not harm us. I met him just after we landed," He grimaced wiping his forehead, "I thought he or it was just an illusion. I was certain he was only a distortion of reality caused by time travel, but now you can see him, too.

"It's all right. Come out. You don't need to be afraid."

Grubb and Gritt stood up slowly, moving cautiously toward the pathway, positioning themselves so they could quickly escape if necessary.

"Thank you, Gripp Stare, for that less than wonderful introduction. I am pleased that you are so willing to save yourselves from what might have appeared to be your imminent destruction by one as large as I am."

The great fish seemed to be thinking as he swam slowly around the Gripps in an ever wider circle, creating ripples within the energy field.

He then continued speaking, "Ah, yes, a rhyme about Time for Three Gray Gripps so very lost in Time and who are constantly seeking more and more Time to lose," he chuckled and then spontaneously began to create a poem just for them.

> *I see that you are out of place,*
> *lost in both time and space,*
> *still chasing your dreams*
> *with outlandish schemes.*
>
> *Time, you will discover,*
> *you can never recover*
> *or will it allow you to rest*
> *from your perpetual quest.*
>
> *Even though your intention*
> *is to keep Time in suspension,*
> *you are still seeking the prize,*
> *searching with those vacant eyes.*
>
> *You have always been chasing,*
> *but never replacing*
> *the full strength and measure*
> *of your most valuable treasure.*
>
> *Time cannot be embraced*
> *or soon you'll be displaced*
> *as you awaken to the paradigm:*
> *Time is indeed erasing Time.*

Delphos drifted from side-to-side, sending currents of energy around and through each of the Gripps whose minds were lost in confusion as they tried to comprehend that such an outrageous being could even exist.

"Now then, *Three Gray Gripps*, you've much to learn during your trespass upon Level Seven. I have most generously intervened on your behalf and slowed the rapid acceleration of Time, so that you may experience your journey at a pace that reflects your concept of reality. May you open your hearts and minds when you encounter the Seven Harmonies, which you will undoubtedly experience along your way, and now, my friends, I must say adieu."

The iridescent shape of Delphos slowly faded away. A soft, blue-violet haze enveloped the enormous fish, and he disappeared into a cloud of silvery blue.

"Was that real?" pondered Grubb, visibly shaken.

The three Gripps looked skyward, searching the remnants of the silvery fog that still lingered above them.

"Well, you heard him, didn't you? You saw him reciting his poem," stated Stare, wishing he were back in the predictable chaos of Grippland. "Did you think it was real?" He glared at Grubb briefly and then gazed into the sky, wondering if Delphos might reappear for an encore performance.

"We all saw him," stated Gritt. "What should we do?"

"We do nothing," responded Grubb, wiping the sweat from the back of his neck.

"Yes, I agree," affirmed Stare. "We do nothing. We say nothing! We report nothing!" He knew that as #5, he was in charge of all the lower ranking Gripps and needed to exert his authority. "Are you going to believe in the words of a singing fish or the grasp of your grips? What is real? What is true?"

A golden moon was slowly rising above the sea, and the sky was scattered with brilliant stars when the three bedraggled and dismayed teammates reluctantly returned to the base camp. They found their fellow Gripps standing around a small wood fire listening to Grist review the events of the mission thus far.

"We have found ourselves challenged, team," stated Grist. "We were confronted by circumstance and by chance, and we have survived using our ability to grab on, grip on and grind on, because that is our way!

"Now, it is time to strategize and develop our plan for the rest of our mission," Grist continued. "According to Stare's calculations, we have six revolutions of the *Eye of Time* remaining until the portal reactivates, so we must find an advanced civilization before it is time to depart."

Grist hesitated for a moment before acknowledging the returning threesome. "So, you have finally returned. Stare, is the equipment secure?"

Stare, Grubb, and Gritt exchanged quick glances as they warmed themselves by the fire. They stood before Grist with their mouths slightly open, shoulders slumped, and eyes lowered to the ground. After a long pause, Stare began to speak, "We, we... I mean the discovery was that...ah...there were..." His voice trailed off.

"Is there a problem? Did you retrieve our valuable equipment or not?" demanded Grist impatiently, pacing back and forth in front of them. His eyes darted from one expressionless face to another. "What is the matter with you? Stand at attention! Make your report!"

"The Equipment is gone! All gone!" blurted out Grubb, rubbing his hand over his forehead. "We scoured the entire length of the beach and found nothing."

"We found no rafts," added Stare. "We found nothing but dunes...and there were plants growing everywhere, covering the shoreline." His voice cracked under the strain of delivering the worst possible news.

"So, then, that's it! This is where it all ends!" exclaimed Grist, realizing that Stare's words could represent the total failure of their mission.

"Perhaps they are mistaken," offered Grimm, the psychologist. "They may be suffering from severe mental stress disorder," she stated warily. "Maybe the equipment is there, and they just couldn't see it."

Grist jabbed his finger into Stare's chest, "Do you have stress disorder? Are you delirious?"

"N-n-no, #1, we are not delirious...not at all," answered Stare nervously. "We saw the *Eye of Time* accelerating time! *Waves of Time* from the future were overtaking our current time. I mean to say...uh...that..." Stare stopped in mid-sentence, realizing that he was trapping himself into explaining what happened on the beach.

"Is that your last word?" growled Grist as he looked deep into Stare's eyes, hoping that their report was a joke.

Stare, Grubb and Gritt nodded silently, continuing to gaze blankly at the ground.

Grist slammed his fist into the palm of his hand and declared, "Know this! Some of us will survive! Some of us will not. We are all explorers, adventurers seeking answers, but never forget we are at the mercy of the *Power of Time*.

THE POWER OF TIME

Grist continued to contemplate his next move as he sat by the fire when he glanced over at the two captured dogs who were secured with metal collars around their necks and tethered to a large tree.

"Scheme, go and see what you can learn from those dogs. Interrogate them. Find out what they know about Time Waves or anything else for that matter! I'm sure those dogs know more than they are revealing!"

Scheme sauntered over to the dogs and said, "You heard the questions. What do you know?"

Filloloper looked up at Scheme and answered, "We don't understand the concept of *Time Waves*."

"So, do you know the meaning of Time?" Scheme couldn't believe he was even bothering to talk to an animal.

"Watching time is not part of our lives in Acronos," answered Fabius.

Grouse, Grimm, Gritt, and Stare had left the campfire and joined Scheme in front of Filloloper and Fabius. Dr. Grouse was rather stout and stiff from her many years of sitting as a researcher. Even though she was only in her late thirties, her dark hair was turning gray, and deep lines were visible under her eyes.

"Maybe I can help extract some information from these dogs," she suggested, pushing past Scheme and pacing back and forth with her hands in her pockets.

She spoke in a commanding voice, "Where is the rest of your pack? How many more dogs are here like you?"

"We don't know of any other dogs here in Acronos," answered Filloloper."

Dr. Grouse looked surprised, and then said, "Well, then, let's get back to our subject of time. You need to understand that in Grippland we measure time according to the cycle of the sun and by the pace of our ever-increasing heartbeats. Over several generations, the beats of our hearts have been accelerating, aging us prematurely!"

Psychologist Grimm who appeared weary and confused by all that had happened, interrupted Grouse and stated, "In Grippland, time is not just a measurement of celestial movements in space.

"It is the psychological state of our entire being. We feel that time is moving too fast...eating away at our lives. Even with all our technology, we find ourselves aging long before our time!"

Filloloper and Fabius stared at these explorers from another world who were nodding their heads up and down in agreement with her statement. The Gripps appeared to be sinking further into their bodies, and they were looking older as each moment passed.

"The beat of our heart is how we measure time," continued Dr. Grouse. "Too many beats mean less and less time! How do you measure time?"

Filloloper reflected on the peaceful Valley of Acronos and answered in a quiet tone of voice, "It's easy. We follow the movement of the sun. We enjoy the daylight, and sleep by moonlight."

The Gripps stared in disbelief, unable to imagine such a stress-free life. Stare, the engineer, stopped peering into the far distance and added, "Well, that's not how we look at life! We measure everything! Absolutely everything!

"We measure life in increments. The smallest measure of time is a *Half Gripping*," Stare explained, snapping his fingers together to demonstrate. "Such a small increment of time makes our day seem somewhat longer." He listed the measurements of time in Grippland:

- A full *Gripping* (a second)

- 60 Grippings is a *Gripper* (a minute)
- 60 Grippers is a *Grippon* (an hour)
- 24 Grippons equals a *Grabbon* (a day)
- 365 Grabbons equals a *Grind* (a year)

Stare retreated into his cave of thought, rubbing his forehead and adding, "Yes, sadly we describe an entire lifetime as a *Grasp*. When we pass away, we simply say it was our *Last Grasp*." Stare choked on his words for a moment and then slumped down into his uniform, appearing to be almost half his normal size.

Gritt declared, "Time shouldn't be accelerating faster!"

Scheme took a deep breath and interrupted Gritt, exclaiming, "We have no idea of how to live in the moment. We feel like we are sliding down a never-ending tunnel, a slide we have found impossible to stop!"

Filloloper and Fabius were distressed by the tone and extreme sadness that the strangers were sharing.

Scheme shook his head as if to clear his thoughts and began to speak again, "We seek to stop the Ticking. That is the reason we are searching for the Secret of Un-Old-Age. Even younger Gripps now have the diseases of the old.

"They look and act as if they are sick, confused, tired and weary." Scheme continued. "They move slowly and have become heavy in their bodies and dull in their minds. We are here to find the answer to Un-Old-Age so we can save our fellow Gripps from themselves!" he exclaimed in a heroic tone of voice.

The businessman straightened his posture and continued, "If you do not know about Un-Old-Age, then, perhaps, you are aware of Grold—that golden, glittering, wonderful, shining metal that reflects the sun. With Grold we do not grow old so quickly. Those who possess large quantities of Grold can purchase a life away from the pollution and hardships of our tedious lives. Everyone knows that with Grold you can slow the process of growing old, but first and foremost we are seeking the Secret of Un-Old-Age!"

Fabius remained silent. He knew too well the type of power Scheme was describing. He was aware of the quest for "gold," the name he remembered from the *Before Time.*

Looking up at the strangers, he replied, "Time is not what you measure in Grippings, Grippons, and Grabbons! Un-Old-Age is a state of mind.

"You can feel old at any age," Fabius continued. "How you feel is important, not what you measure. During your exploration here in Acronos, you will encounter the Seven Harmonies, and they will reveal to you what I mean."

Gritt listened intently. His eyes grew wide as if he possessed a secret he might be willing to share with Fabius and Filloloper if the right circumstances would allow. Turning to walk with the others in the direction of the campsite, he paused and looked back at the dogs with a knowing smile.

PART FOUR

The Tower Tree

T HE FLICKER AND GLOW from the campfire created an eerie collage of silhouettes, shapes and shadows moving against the backdrop of the soaring Tower Tree. Its unusual roots rose to over four feet above the ground and then spread out thirty to forty feet in all directions. The base of the towering tree resembled the twisted tentacles of an enormous, gray octopus crawling across the land.

Grist had decided there would be no need to post security guards since he felt confident that the unusual structure of the tree would provide more than enough security.

Each team member carefully selected their sleeping positions within the massive root system of the Towering Tree before returning to the campfire. They quietly devoured their Gripp rations and gathered in small groups.

"Why do they continue walking around the fire," Filloloper asked Fabius, both still shackled and staked to the ground on a small hillside not far from the campsite.

Fabius did not respond. He was watching the movement of the explorers by the campfire and felt himself being transported back to the *Time before Time* when another fire surrounded by soldiers was a prelude to military action.

Filloloper crept cautiously toward him, pulling against her heavy chains until the collar, designed with the Gripp power symbol of two interlocking hands, tightened too painfully around her neck. She could see the campfire reflected in his eyes and became aware that he was studying the precise movements of the strangers.

He was observing the way the Gripps held their heads and the cadence of their walk. These details were vital information to be stored and analyzed for future reference.

Out of the corner of her eye, Filloloper caught sight of dark shadows being cast by two approaching Gripps growing larger and more ominous.

"So, you can speak Grippish? How is that possible?" asked Grind, whose mission as the team anthropologist was to study and investigate all life forms, living or dead.

"Excellent question, Grind," commented Grimm who then spoke directly to Fabius. "Dog, why don't you explain how you know our language? Go ahead…speak! Tell us what you are staring at?"

"Let him be!" responded Filloloper, straining against her collar as she pulled herself next to Fabius who was deep in thought viewing another life he knew so well—a lifetime of conflict and war when he was a soldier in command.

"Go ahead…speak Grippish!" demanded Grimm as she forcefully kicked the chain binding Fabius to the ground.

Past visions of the *Before Time* were still racing through his head as he felt a swift, hard jerk to his neck. He instinctively lunged forward, rising to his full height, paws clawing the air.

Shocked by his sudden response, Grimm and Grind lost their footing and stumbled backward, tumbling down the grassy embankment. They landed only a few feet away from Gritt the Geologist, who had been watching from the outer perimeter of the camp.

"So, the chains holding those dogs were not enough to protect you?" jested Gritt, looking directly at the two women lying prostrate on the ground. "

"Those dogs certainly look vicious to me!" A wry smile crossed Gritt's face while helping them to their feet. "It's been a long day, why don't you two relax by the fire, and I will guard those beasts," offered Gritt, looking up toward the hillside where the dogs were resting peacefully.

Fabius continued to observe the Gripps as they moved around the campsite. He seemed lost in deep concentration, when he spoked quietly to Filloloper, "There's something different about him. It's the way he moves."

"What do you mean?" asked Filloloper.

"#8, the one they call Gritt, the Geologist. He doesn't move like the others.

"What are you saying?"

"I am saying that every being has a different walk. We all speak in a variety of ways, and we carry ourselves in our own particular manner. How we move is the way we interpret the space around us. Gritt occupies more space than the others. He shows a unique self-confidence in his movement and gestures. That information is important to know on the field of battle. He definitely has a secret he's hiding from the others."

Every being has a different walk. We all speak in a variety of ways, and we carry ourselves in our own particular manner. It's the way we interpret the space around us.

Filloloper was intrigued and answered, "The right time will reveal all," she mused, gazing into the amber glow reflected in Fabius' eyes.

She paused and asked, "Do you have a secret, Fabius?"

"Do I?" He hesitated, blinking back the tears in his eyes. "Some secrets are best kept secret until they reveal themselves naturally. You will know soon enough."

"We must be patient and trust in the Seven Harmonies," he continued. "The Gripps may soon discover far more than the Secret of Un-Old-Age. So, yes, we must be patient and also vigilant and very aware."

They watched as Gritt moved cautiously away from the others without being noticed. He made his way over to the fire and pulled out a glowing piece of charcoal with his bare hand and crushed it between his fingers and then threw the fragmented embers high over his head. They floated like stardust in the night sky, and as the red glow of a thousand sparks slowly disappeared into the darkness, a smile of recognition crept over his face.

Gritt hesitated and then turned to look directly at the dogs, as if to say, *I know what you know.*

THE TREE OF MEMORIES

There were reasons to fear them. They were strangers lost in another world, confused, desperate, obviously violent, and definitely unstable. Their demeanor was gray and grim, matching the color and severity of their uniforms; and yet, there was something about the lost explorers that inspired hope and the possibility of a more promising future.

Perhaps, it was the Gripps' potential to experience a different future in Acronos that made Fabius and Filloloper realize there is always a greater learning to be discovered beyond our immediate understanding.

However, it was difficult to imagine a positive outcome since the Guardians of Acronos found themselves chained to a small rise of rocks overlooking the Gripp campsite.

They considered attempting to escape from those trespassers on Level Seven, but the heavy, Gripp chains and tight metal collars made it impossible.

Filloloper and Fabius watched in silence as the flicker of the Gripp campsite slowly began to fade. They closed their eyes, hopeful that tomorrow would be far more rewarding for all concerned.

Grist, the Commander, had chosen to make camp at the base of the Tower Tree since its vast, root system rose high above the ground, creating secure shelter. He felt confident that the unique structure would provide enough protection against any surprise attack during the night.

Perhaps it was the Gripps' pure exhaustion or the rhythmic sound of the waves on the shore below that quickly carried them into the dream state where memories of memories and nightmares also reside. No matter, the team felt more than confident that the night would offer up no surprises or at least none that they could imagine.

It was soon after the last flickers of light from the campfire had faded away that gradual changes began to occur within and around the Tower Tree.

Fabius was the first to feel a vibration moving through the ground. It was subtle at first, but when the intensity of the movement increased, his large, amber eyes sprung wide open. Startled by the scene unfolding below them, he nudged Filloloper to awaken.

"Listen, can you hear it....do you feel it? A humming sound is resonating through the ground."

Filloloper listened intently and replied, "Yes, but I also hear something else. There are rustling and clicking sounds in the bushes behind us or perhaps it's just to the right of us, I can't be certain."

Fabius turned his head, trying to locate the source of the sounds, when a familiar voice whispered, "Quiet, be very quiet. I am here for you to attempt a speedy rescue."

The staccato sentences of Phelan were undeniable. The tall, gangly bird with a large bulbous body, covered in gray and white feathers, stepped away from his perfect camouflage and immediately released the chains holding them hostage.

Using his clawed feet and sharp beak, he managed to unshackle the tight collars around their necks. "You're free now!" announced Phelan, exuding great pride in his ability to rescue his dear friends.

Even before Filloloper and Fabius could thank him or consider in which direction to run, they were amazed to witness the tallest branches of the Tower Tree glistening and glowing with colors of varying intensity.

Phelan's saucer-shaped, blue eyes grew larger and larger as he turned his head in all directions, seeking clues as to what was happening. After a moment of hesitation, he spoke in rhyme:

> *The tree you see is not a tree*
> *when it is fed by curiosity.*
> *Spinning into a magnetic field*
> *delving deep it soon will yield*
> *memories shifting through time and space*
> *manifesting here in this very place!*

When fearful memories start to flow,
the tree turns bright and begins to glow!

"What are you trying to say?" asked Fabius, wondering whether or not Phelan was exaggerating as was his custom.

The dogs were trying to analyze Phelan's cryptic and rhyming responses when it became apparent that his warning was far more real than they could have imagined.

The Tower Tree was changing before their eyes. Its wide, spreading branches glowed with a strange luminescence and then began rising higher and higher into the night sky. Illuminated strands fell from the tallest limbs and floated softly down and around the sleeping strangers, forming an ever-widening circle of glowing light.

Phelan spoke again:

Time filaments falling to the ground
encircling all memories to be found!
For those who sleep within its sphere
dreams transform into all they fear!

Phelan's words were still drifting in the coolness of the night air when other lights with focused beams suddenly appeared, moving high above the Tower Tree. The shafts of light shifted from side-to-side as if searching for something or someone. The Gripps had been right to be fearful. The enemy they most feared was very present; and at this moment in time, they were completely surrounded.

There is no time for indecision
the tree doesn't allow suspensions
once it shifts through dimensions!

With that last utterance, surprisingly, Phelan quickly disappeared into the darkness of the night. Normally, his overwhelming curiosity would have enticed him to remain to see what he would call: "The Show!"

And a show it would be. It was beyond imagining that a tree could possess the power and ability to bring forth strange visions — mysterious revelations that would surprise the intrepid explorers resting unwittingly at its base.

The Tower Tree had begun a magical transformation and was in the process of accessing the emotional memories hidden within the recesses of the sleeping Gripps' consciousness.

Multicolored lights glimmered on its branches as thousands of images were received, processed, and passed through the tree's central core like a massive brain forming new neural networks. The Tower Tree was becoming the *Tree of Memories*.

Gritt, the geologist, was the first to be startled awake by the sights and sounds of bright searchlights and the familiar wailing of Gripp sirens now piercing the once silent night. *Is this even possible?* he thought. *A dream can turn into a nightmare or perhaps even a hallucination, but nothing more!*

Stumbling to his feet, Gritt quickly determined that the horrifying sights and sounds of Grippland were not mere tricks of the mind.

"Hallucinations are not composed of concrete!" he exclaimed looking skyward at a city now looming over the campsite. The once clear, star-filled sky was hidden by streaming clouds of gray…a gray familiar to all Gripps.

What is real? He questioned. *Or does it even matter? What matters now is how we react! Gripps don't run from adversity, not even adversity as bizarre as this.*

By some cruel trick of fate or an outrageous manipulation of Time, the Tower Tree was now surrounded by what at first appeared to be holographic images of tall, glass and steel buildings of Grippland. High above the streets were large signs displaying the illuminated faces of the ten members of the *Eye of Time Exploration Team* with the words, "Wanted for Treason...Dead or Alive!"

Gritt was struggling with the absurdity of what he was seeing and hearing, preferring to believe he was still dreaming. *How real are our dreams*? He wondered, looking up at the searchlights moving back-and-forth just above the Tower Tree. The intensely focused beams, shining brightly in the night sky, were now moving ever closer to his position.

"Stare was right!" Gritt exclaimed. "We are in the midst of a Time Trap, or maybe it's a dream trapped in Time! And now, at this moment, it is our reality!"

Thoughts tumbled through Gritt's mind as he struggled to comprehend what his senses were showing him. It seemed as though the past was alive again, or was it? How could that be? The team had not returned through the Time Portal back to Grippland, so how could they possibly be in Grippland and wanted for treason?

He was quite confident that Time was not shifting them back into their past. It was more likely that Time was showing an alternate reality that was being created by their fears, their most terrifying fears!

Gritt was astounded to note that he was the only team member aware of the changes happening around them. The others were still lost in a trance-like sleep, even though the shrill, wailing sounds of Gripp sirens continued to penetrate what only moments before had been the stillness of the night.

Asleep? How could they possibly be asleep? Could this be Gritt's very own hallucination...his alone? He found himself running to awaken the others. "We are under attack! We are under attack!" he shouted.

Grist was immediately startled awake and bewildered by Gritt's shouts. "What do you mean...under attack?"

"There is no time to explain! We need to seek shelter and prepare for a counterattack if that is possible!" Gritt anxiously responded, becoming aware of someone moving just beyond the tree line. "We are all wanted for treason against Gripp High Command!"

"Treason? How is that possible?" Grist's voice drifted overhead before dissipating in the rumble and roar surrounding them. He looked up and witnessed three-dimensional images of Grippland materializing into reality.

Only the illuminated Tower Tree remained as evidence of their arrival in Acronos. The entire perimeter around the tree was now devoid of shrubs, flowers, plants, and trees. A huge variety of gray, concrete structures had replaced every aspect of nature.

Filloloper and Fabius were bewildered by the terrifying scenes manifesting below them, but they were also well aware of Phelan's last words of warning:

> *For those who sleep within its sphere*
> *dreams transform into all they fear!*

Deep in sleep, Grind, the anthropologist, could not hear the banging on the door of her small, basement apartment where she slept in a single bed in the corner of the room surrounded by tall bookshelves stacked with hundreds of illegal books. These volumes were her only treasure.

Grind loved all the novels and dramas, the histories and scientific discoveries, the how-to books, the poetry, and the metaphysical and spiritual writings that warmed her heart and filled her mind with new concepts and ideas.

She had read hundreds of the contraband books and enjoyed stories in which the authors described in wonderful detail what it was like to live in the midst of beauty and peace. They had written about natural environments, which could provide a plentiful food source and abundance for all. Other books listed the many freedoms that no longer existed in Grippland and the ability to speak freely about any subject without fear of assault or imprisonment.

If authorities were to discover that she possessed hundreds of banned books, they would prosecute Grind for treason. The writings considered most unlawful were those that encouraged personal expression and liberty, as well as individual thought and creativity. All such activities were deemed to be destructive to the *Greater Order of Grippland*.

High Command had destroyed all public libraries, and the media was censored and monitored since they represented a genuine threat to the "New History," which was always being updated and rewritten according to current policies of the *Greater Order of Grippland*.

In her dream, the sound of pounding on Grind's door became more and more intense, as was the voice of her dear friend, Psychologist Grimm, who was desperately trying to warn her that the G.R.A.B. Team was on their way to search her apartment for illegal books. Those precious books would send her to prison.

Grind suddenly felt someone grabbing her arm. She tried to fight them off and attempted to run, but there was no escape from her basement apartment. She was trapped, struggling to get free; but her assailant seemed to be stronger and more persistent. She heard her name being called, echoing deep within the very center of her dream.

"Wake up! Wake up! The G.R.A.B Team is here! They are coming for you! They are coming for all of us!" Grimm was shaking her, forcing her to awaken from her dream. "They are here now! There is little time to escape!" she shouted over the wailing of sirens.

The loud, rumbling sounds of fast-approaching, armored vehicles at last awakened Grind, and she looked around in confusion. "What do you mean escape? I was in a dream. Wasn't I?"

"Look around you," insisted the psychologist. "Look around you! What do you see?"

Grind could not immediately respond. Caught between two worlds—the world of her dreams and her world in a dream, she had no idea which was real.

"We have to escape!" declared Grimm empathetically. "We have to run now!"

In a state of shock and incapable of deciphering the reality of the moment, Grind and Grimm took shelter behind large boulders but immediately were spotted by the G.R.A.B. Team.

"There is no escape! You are under arrest! You have violated the laws imposed by Supreme High Command!" A metallic voice continued to repeat the same phrase over and over again. "You are under arrest! There is no escape!"

Watching from the hillside, Fabius heard the distant sound of machines moving across the forest floor, accompanied by the loud echoes of voices yelling commands.

"They're here now! Look below! Those mechanical beasts are moving directly towards the Gripps!" He nudged Filloloper to follow him further up the hill, moving out of harm's way.

The metallic voice continued, "This is G.R.A.B. Team One to G.R.A.B. Team Two. We have located the fugitive Gripps! Repeat, we have located the fugitive Gripps! Over!"

From out of nowhere, two, armored, Gripp Command vehicles appeared, crashing through the forest on metal tracks and crushing everything in their path. They stopped suddenly only a few yards away from where the Gripps were hiding. Each vehicle was marked with large capital letters: G.R.A.B., the acronym for Gripp Reconnaissance Armored Battalion.

Twenty, armed, Gripp High Command Soldiers trained in search, seize, and destroy missions, rushed out of their vehicles with only one objective: capture Gripps numbered One through Ten and bring them back alive or dead.

Grist was the first to fire on the approaching soldiers who were closing in on his position. Blaring speakers continued warning: "Your escape is futile! You're under arrest! Surrender your weapons! You're under arrest!"

The heavy, armored vehicles were blocking the Gripp team's escape, and they were out-numbered. The surprise attack had taken them completely off-guard—all, except for Commander Grist.

He had always believed there would be an ambush somehow, somewhere, and now his deepest fears were happening before his eyes. He was outraged that for some reason this assault was organized by High Command and carried out by official G.R.A.B team soldiers.

Quickly surveying the area, he noted that none of the other team members were visible. *Did they take cover and escape from the menacing G.R.A.B team attackers?* He had his doubts, fearing that they had been captured, or worse!

Running as fast as he could to find shelter, Grist's mind was full of questions: *Will I survive? Why are we being attacked? Is this real?*

His thoughts tumbled onward as he stopped to catch his breath behind a large boulder several yards from the approaching troops. *They won't get old Grist so easily! Not this time! No, not this time!* he swore to himself before disappearing into the darkness of the forest.

It was only moments later that the sky was clearing, and the glow from the Tower Tree dimmed. Once again, time had crossed time, merging one reality into another. The piercing shafts of light from the search beacons were disappearing into the night sky.

The long, undulating branches, which had been alive with the glimmer of multicolored lights began to close down like an umbrella folds in upon itself. The sharp, elongated leaves were fading back to the dark olive and brown colors of their original appearance.

The memories in the explorers' dreams had appeared like waves of emotion, emerging into awareness and out again, flowing like the endless waves of the ocean rolling on shore, crashing, and receding again into the sea.

From their safe position on the hill, the dogs observed the Gripps reappearing from behind boulders and trees and then collapsing on the ground, exhausted from the intense fear, noise, and confusion of the attack.

"It must be over," said Filloloper hopefully.

Fabius gazed into the night sky. "No, not yet. Look, there, just above the tallest branches of the Koa trees."

In stunned silence, the battle-weary, time travelers witnessed two objects floating in the sky, single file in a silent procession. They gasped when they realized that they were watching their missing rafts floating overhead, carrying their critical supplies and equipment.

In the second boat, seated in the back, was a shadowy figure with the shape of a Gripp. He was staring straight ahead, and his right arm was moving back and forth and in and out as if he were taunting the Gripps to follow him.

Twist stepped forward and was the first to speak, "That's not one of us. All ten of us are present and accounted for!" he stated emphatically, trying to put a good spin on the sinister, ghostly vision.

"If that phantom is not one of us, then why is he wearing a Gripp uniform and motioning for us to follow him?" questioned Scheme.

"Well, Scheme," replied Babble, "It's quite simple. Perhaps the Gripp in the last boat is the sole survivor of our ordeal with the Spinners, and maybe we have already met our Last Grasp, and we just don't know it...yet!"

Several of the Gripps let out a deep breath and distanced themselves from Babble. She looked at them in disgust and continued to speak, "Or maybe it is a future ghost Gripp, and one of us will soon be gone."

TIME HELD IN SUSPENSION

A rush of fresh, night air carried with it the strong scent of herbs and flowers moving through the forest. The soft breeze pushed its way through a small outcropping of rock where

Filloloper and Fabius had witnessed what could only be described as a shift in dimensions.

They managed to exchange questioning glances but remained silent and immobile, lost within their shock while attempting to process what they had both experienced. For the Guardians of Acronos, there was so much to ponder that the collision of questions in their minds divided and broke apart until their thoughts dissolved into a haze of confusion.

Was it real? It appeared that they had caught glimpses of another place and time — a very detailed and realistic world that had manifested through a trans-dimensional shift of energy and emotion. The intense pulsating and penetrating patterns of energy from that other world continued to linger in the atmosphere and remained suspended in the electrical field surrounding the perimeter of the Tower Tree.

Fabius was the first to speak. "We have just witnessed another reality — a different dimension that is completely devoid of a natural environment. It appears that the Gripps have traveled from a world in which they have no opportunity to experience the beauty, harmony, and peace nature provides."

"It seemed very real!" replied Filloloper, shaking her head in disbelief as if she could shake away the brutality they had witnessed. "No wonder the Gripps have been sent through time to seek out solutions for the desperation in their lives!"

Fabius nodded in agreement. His attention was fixated on the movement below as he watched the Gripp team assemble under the Tower Tree they had so carefully chosen as protection from any unknown enemy.

There were reasons enough for Filloloper and Fabius to run. Most certainly the Guardians of Acronos now had the opportunity to escape. Phelan had freed them and had warned them, but how could he possibly have known the extreme danger that would manifest so quickly?

Grist noticed that the dogs were looking down at the camp from the ridge above, he could see that the Gripp collars and chains were no longer holding them prisoner. He stared intently at them and thought to himself, *Leave them be. They evidently want to stay with us for now.*

He turned his attention to the team and began to speak: "We have survived again. It was a slim victory to be sure, but a victory nevertheless," said Grist while kicking the grass that had replaced what was concrete only a few moments before.

"There is no longer room for error! We need not discuss what may or may not have just occurred, or shall I say what we may have experienced? All of that is irrelevant! Survival is all that matters! Don't you agree?"

Twist and Scheme were acutely aware that they and the other members of the team were caught on the edge of reality, peering down into an unknown and uncharted abyss.

Indeed, it seemed that there would be no benefit in discussing the events of their near capture at the hands of Gripp Command soldiers or questioning whether the attackers were real or imagined.

Grimm and Grind were huddled together in an intense conversation, oblivious to the others who were gathering their equipment preparing to push on at first light.

"I know that I brought those soldiers forward into this time!" explained Grind anxiously. "I am to blame! You were the one to save us. If you hadn't awakened me from my dream, who knows what even more tragic events could have unfolded! It seemed so real!"

Grimm, the psychologist, was well aware that Grind was still in a state of shock. She was visibly shaken and unable to compose her thoughts.

"It will take a while to recover from what you have experienced. We are all responsible for what happened, not you alone. It is not up to us to determine how it happened or why it happened. We need only recognize it did happen and tomorrow we will have to grind on as before. After all, you are named Grind, aren't you?"

PART FIVE

The Forest of Tones

THE MORNING LIGHT FILTERING through the spreading branches of the Tower Tree revealed the battered Gripps who were awakening to a new day. Babble was up and working with her equipment, testing the frequencies to determine which direction they should go.

This doesn't make sense, thought Babble, fiddling with the radio again, taking it apart and putting it back together until the device began receiving sounds that were much stronger and clearer.

She turned to Grist who was standing over her shoulder and announced, "I just discovered a universal signal that is originating from within or just beyond that forest."

Grist gazed at the vast darkness of trees before them and murmured. "Yes, it's always like this! You do know what's waiting for us in that forest, don't you? It's a trap! It's always a trap! That's what!"

Babble responded, "A trap...but perhaps, it is essential to our mission to find out who's sending that signal!'

"Nothing is ever as it appears to be." Grist spoke loud enough for the gathering team to hear him. "Is someone playing with us and our time? Grippons (hours) are slipping away, and the Portal in Time waits for no Gripp! There can be no delay! Our arrival means survival!"

Grind, the anthropologist, timidly spoke up. "I've heard of such forests mentioned in myths and fairytales. In the forbidden books, I learned that there were forests such as these where people disappeared in mysterious ways."

Grist ignored her comment and rubbed his face and shook his shoulders as if trying to dismiss any concept of magic. "Well, what say you? Shall we meander around the forest like Grippless wanderers, or do we grind on?"

"Grind on!" they shouted in unison as they packed their equipment and moved into formation for their advance into the darkness of the forest.

AN OMINOUS JOURNEY

The explorers hadn't traveled far into the dense forest when Babble, watching the lights on her monitor, exclaimed, "We have movement! Something is moving in a zigzag pattern. It's coming from the north! No, it's from the south. They're coming from the east, the west! We're surrounded!"

"Take cover," commanded Grist running to shelter.

The team dispersed behind boulders and trees, and the dogs hurried into tall grass beside the pathway and turned to one another with a knowing nod.

"What moves in a zigzag pattern and cannot be seen?" asked Fabius.

"It's Phelan! What is he doing? He could be in great danger if the Gripps capture him."

"He is doing what Phelan does best — trying to warn and ward off the trespassers. He considers this to be part of his domain, which he imagines includes all of Acronos."

Racing through the forest, Phelan was sending out his echo, playing his favorite game of zigzagging unseen and bouncing his voice off different objects so that his words seemed to be coming from every direction. The sound of his voice became louder, creating an eerie echo:

> *Trees standing in formation*
> *ever seeking information.*
> *Knowing thoughts that are hidden*
> *are thoughts forbidden*
> *within the Forest zone.*
> *The best time to run is long before*
> *the forest begins to tone.*

The words were ricocheting through the trees, moving in and out and around the intrepid explorers.

Grist stood unflinching in the midst of the confused Gripps. "So, now we have a ghost for an enemy? What is this spirit saying, exactly?"

"It's a code!" shouted Babble. "They've issued a warning! We need to retreat!" She quickly picked up her equipment and started to retrace her steps back down the trail. And then it was quiet...very quiet.

"Come back here, Babble!" called Grist, shaking his fist. "We'll fight if we have to." He removed his helmet and rubbed his head in exasperation. "Proceed! We're going through this forest."

He looked up at the spreading branches and flowering trees and grumbled to himself, "Everything looks the same! How I miss concrete and steel!"

THE TONING BEGINS

The play of light and shadow flickered through the trees, creating moving shapes on the boulders lining the path. Large-leafed ferns arched gracefully overhead, but when fronds brushed against the Gripps' faces and the backs of their necks, they jumped, suspecting an ambush.

The air had chilled slightly, carrying with it slender fingers of fog moving silently through the dark stands of trees that seemed to be watching vigilantly as the strangers pushed ever deeper into the very center of the forest.

The Trillia vines growing across the land, covering the boulders, and climbing up into the trees began to hum ever so slightly as the Trillia flowers changed from white to yellow, signifying danger.

No Gripp would have dreamed that another consciousness was observing and examining their thoughts and feelings. They could not have guessed that a forest of trees could be questioning them. Thus, they did not heed the warnings from the invisible presence, which they named the "Forest Ghost," who was calling out to them:

> *Torn by Tones,*
> *vibrating the body to the bones.*
> *No secrets concealed.*
> *All must be revealed.*
> *Showing thoughts hidden from view,*
> *you cannot hide those parts of you*
> *which seek to be untrue!*

The members of the exploration team were not aware that the grass was vibrating ever so slightly and that the smaller trees were emitting a faint tone.

Babble stopped abruptly. The usual static and squeals from the radio had ceased. She listened carefully and heard only the shuffling sound of Gripp boots behind her. Something had definitely changed.

She motioned for the team to stop when an audible toning sound broke the silence. Distinct vibrations spread out from the trees in all directions as the branches started to sway ever so slightly, and the grass began twisting and turning in strange patterns between and around them.

"It's happening now!" declared Fabius. "The toning of the forest has begun!"

Grist hesitated and then stared in disbelief at the phenomena unfolding before his eyes. "Is this the toning the Forest Ghost warned us about?"

Fabius looked up at Grist and said quietly, "Yes, we should have asked permission."

"Are you suggesting that even though we are in a zone where no one lives, we should have asked permission to enter?" asked Grist. "Who should we have asked?"

"You need to ask the trees." answered Fabius. "When you request entry, there is always a door to enter."

Rubbing his chin and looking around at the trees, Grist exclaimed, "I don't understand! Trees can't think!"

"This forest is very aware and has been alive longer than you can imagine. The trees and other plants are a family. They are always communicating with one another. And now they want to know who and what you are and why you are here. It is a simple request. Don't you agree?"

Grubb, the biologist/botanist, was thinking about the concept of trees in a forest being a family when suddenly the land began shifting and undulating under his feet. He was amazed to see Twist and Scheme rise off the ground and then quickly fall back to earth again.

"It's a quake tearing the land apart!" exclaimed Grubb.

"No, it's not a quake," replied Fabius, glancing down the trail at Filloloper to determine that she was in no danger. "This movement is caused by the root bases of the larger trees extending their reach through the land. They are hoping to gather more information.

"The trees are aware that you are not grounded." Fabius continued. "You have forgotten that you are part of nature. You don't understand that you made of the same energy as the trees."

Grist opened his eyes wide, and the lines on his forehead deepened. "What do mean?"

"You have arrived in the trees' domain, and now they want answers," answered Fabius. "Once you are inside the Forest of Tones, you cannot just turn around. The exit is never the same as the entrance. I have found that to be true for every event we experience in life."

Grist glared at Fabius and was abruptly interrupted by a commotion on the pathway behind them. A tangled mass of vibrating branches and Trillia vines had trapped Twist and Scheme. Grimm and Grind were struggling to unravel the limbs of the trees that were covering them. Filloloper was attempting to communicate with the trees to release the Gripps.

In the midst of all the confusion, Babble hurried to Grist asking, "What is going on? Our locator beacon is showing movement everywhere. But we know that's impossible!"

"We forgot to knock," responded Grubb ironically with a wry smile on his face. "And we didn't ask permission when we entered the door."

"What door? Where is the door?" Babble turned around in circles looking for a door.

"Does anyone here have a logical explanation?" asked Grist who turned to look down at the innocent face of Filloloper. "Just what are you holding back? What information do you have about the trees?'

Filloloper gathered her courage and answered, "What you are experiencing is the way the plants, trees, and, yes, animals speak to one another. They don't communicate in words. They speak in harmonics—a particular frequency. They are in the process of searching for your inner harmony so they can enter into a conversation with you."

SUBTLE ENERGIES EVERYWHERE

Stare held his hands tightly over his ears, attempting to stop the resonating tones from penetrating deep within him. His dark gray eyes were focused on the ground as he walked around in circles and then paused to pace back-and-forth.

He was trying to determine a simple, scientific hypothesis or mathematical equation that would enable him to understand what they were experiencing in the midst of this forest.

"This will never work," Stare muttered as he glanced over at the dogs. His look implied that they were to blame for all that was happening. "There's nothing to discover here, only the vibrations of these ghastly trees. We came to learn about Un-Old-Age, and now, now," he stammered, "we find ourselves in this vast, unending *Nothingness!*"

Fabius was appalled and perplexed as to why an engineer such as Stare did not comprehend the opportunity that was before him.

"You speak of age?" answered Fabius. "Why are you not curious to learn more about this beautiful forest, which you refer to as *Nothingness?* These trees have been alive for many thousands of years! They are very old souls!"

Stare shook his head as if he wasn't interested in what Fabius had to say. But the Guardian of Acronos continued his explanation while Grist and the rest of the team listened.

"These *ghastly trees*, as you refer to them, are trying to communicate with you the only way they know how: through their vibrational frequencies. Each tree is a different age, and each has a distinct vibrational tone. The trees capture Time during every year of their growth, and all details are recorded and locked away within their circumference.

"These trees are old; indeed, they are ancient, and yet they are always expanding and listening as they grow and are curious about those who enter the forest. The trees are eager to record each visitor's presence within their yearly rings of life."

For a moment, the toning quieted and Fabius took a deep breath, gazing directly at the engineer. "You call yourself a scientist, Stare, and you most certainly should know more than any of your fellow team members that energy permeates all animate and inanimate. Energy and mass are interchangeable. That is basic science."

This forest, this vast *Nothingness* of which you speak, is an energetically connected system, which has its own unique and complex consciousness."

Stare looked at Fabius with annoyance and replied, "No one understands or studies consciousness in Grippland. We know chemicals in our brains determine everything we think and they manipulate our actions."

Fabius held his ground and replied, "Perhaps, you do not wish to accept the basic concept that consciousness is energy, but this forest only wants to know who you are, and the way the trees learn about you is by discovering your vibrational frequency, your tone.

"When the trees match your tonal frequency, they will be able to communicate with you. As you are experiencing, the forest is continuously toning and vibrating; because, quite simply, it cannot find your tone. It doesn't know who you are!

When the trees match your tonal frequency,
the forest will be able to communicate with you.

Stare gazed directly at Fabius and then Filloloper, "I have no idea what you are saying," he grimaced. "Yes, these trees may be old, but that's all they are! They're old! They might be useful for making wooden boards to put nails into. That's it! Nothing more!"

Filloloper shuddered and asked, "Indeed, Stare, what are your expectations? Do you see *nothing* in the Universe? If you observe and listen, nature and the unseen will give you answers when you are open to discovery. You should know that there are subtle energies everywhere waiting to communicate without the benefit of using words."

Stare became more and more annoyed at the ideas he was hearing. In Grippland everything was black and white; there were no shades of gray. "The concept of communicating with trees, plants, or bushes or any other inanimate object is utter and complete nonsense, nothing more! I have nothing to learn here," he mumbled and again cupped his hands over his ears.

You should know that there are subtle energies everywhere, waiting to communicate without the benefit of using words.

The forest resonance resumed in earnest, and the Gripps struggled to maintain their balance as the vibrations increased in intensity. A moment later, the first, large boulders, loosened by the powerful ground movement, were now tumbling down the trail directly towards them.

"Find the enemy before it is too late!" commanded Grist, quickly dodging a boulder and jumping out of the way of broken limbs of trees that were flying toward them.

The toning forest was now focusing intently on their location and the sound was becoming louder and louder.

"The trees only want to share information," shouted Fabius, trying to be heard over the increasing volume of the humming. "They are keepers of knowledge. They are the record keepers of all living creatures who have ever visited their domain. There is no need to attack. There is no one to attack, except yourselves."

Crazed and enraged, Grist commanded, "Prepare to fire weapons upon my command!" He was blinded by his obsession to engage an enemy, even an invisible enemy. He ran toward the trees with the highest resonance, followed by Twist and Scheme, and quickly vanished into the forest.

All the plants and trees were slowly and deliberately practicing their tone, like musicians in an orchestra tuning up their instruments before a performance. Since everything in the grand vista of creation is vibrating at its own unique frequency, each of the plants took turns adding their distinct tonal value to the harmony of the forest.

First, the shorter grasses vibrated at a high-pitched tone, followed by the younger trees harmonizing at a slightly lower key, and then the older trees began complimenting the harmony with even more profound depths of tonality.

Filloloper and Fabius listened joyfully to the awesome splendor of nature's symphony. Altogether in unison, the entire Forest of Tones was creating beautiful music—a harmonic resonance that perfectly matched the majestic, tonal quality of the Universe.

Little did the Gripps grasp or care to understand that the Forest had only wanted to say, "Hello!"

REVEALING IMAGES

The toning and the Forest symphony had ended. Grist, Twist, and Scheme were lost in the midst of the trees, searching for an enemy. Therefore, Babble as #4 in command was in charge of the remaining team members now moving cautiously forward, vigilant for a surprise attack.

Following the line of explorers, Fabius was walking next to Gritt. He was aware that the geologist didn't seem to be phased by the danger around them. It was evident that #8 was not an ordinary Gripp. He always seemed to be detached from the events around him and was not affected by fear like the other time travelers.

Fabius was pondering these perplexing thoughts when out of the corner of his eye he caught a fleeting glimpse of a familiar, tall figure moving in his usual zigzag patterns and then quickly disappearing into the forest again.

Gritt slowed his pace for a moment, looking in the direction of the unknown creature who had crossed their path. "You know, those words keep echoing in my mind." He repeated the warning:

> *Thoughts that are hidden*
> *are thoughts forbidden*
> *within the Forest zone.*
> *The best time to run*
> *is long before*
> *the Forest begins to tone.*

Gritt paused and took a deep breath. "I guess we are on a similar mission," he continued. "It is strange how fate moves through space and time. You are here in your world, and I was in mine. And yet, we are both visitors here in Acronos. Aren't we, Commander Fabius?"

The word *Commander* had not been spoken in Fabius' presence since the time of his transformation. How could this one called Gritt, a geologist, from another world, possibly know who he was?

"What are you suggesting? I am not a Commander. Filloloper and I are just dogs serving as your guides in Acronos...Nothing more."

"Oh, but there is more, isn't there, Commander Fabius? There is more to you, and much more to Filloloper and Acronos. Is that not true?"

Fabius hesitated, and then stopped to look directly at Gritt who possessed a strange calm about him. His long, angular face was different from the rounder faces of the other Gripps, and his blue-green eyes seemed to portray a knowing awareness

Gritt continued, "I guess that is why your friend, that strange bird, issued the warning. He was trying to stop us from being harmed. Wasn't he?

"I understand that we all try to keep our thoughts hidden, and we all have our secrets. Don't we, Commander? You are holding secrets as well as the Princess Filloperna."

"How is it possible that you can see so much?" Fabius asked, astounded by the accuracy of Gritt's revelation.

"See so much? Do you mean that I know you were a valiant Commander who died saving a life, the life of the one known as Princess Filloperna? I am aware that you now call your companion, Filloloper."

Noticing that the toning had quieted, Fabius gazed at the forest in wonder, observing the radiant beauty of the colorful energy, the auric field surrounding the trees.

Gritt broke the silence between them. "You see, Fabius, I also have a secret. I am only half of what I appear to be. In fact, I am what is termed a *Half-Synth*. I am half-Gripp and half-synthetic, a partial robot, if you will, or in my particular case a War-Bot."

Fabius' eyes grew wide as Gritt explained that among the many technical features of a *Half-Synth* was his ability to monitor and decipher electromagnetic fields.

"You would be amazed at how much information is encoded and broadcast around us. I can see the images of your past lives in the auric field around you and Filloperna.

"Sorry, I meant to say Princess Filloperna. As you can imagine, I have found it quite difficult to keep all this knowledge and my abilities a secret."

Gritt explained that no one on the team knew that he was a Half-Synth or War-Bot. Some team members may have been suspicious of him, noticing that he was different. But it was evident that most of the Gripps were very self-centered and had little awareness or interest in anyone or anything other than themselves.

He said that this type of selfish behavior hadn't always been so prevalent in Grippland. The displaying of intense emotions and the tendency to react violently had accelerated when the population increased in size, natural resources became scarce, and the water supply had been polluted.

When the people became uncontrollable, that's when High Command announced the *New Gripp Doctrine* and increased surveillance to stop the erratic behavior. Laws and regulations were enforced to remedy the failure to work together. Unfortunately, the Gripps didn't know how to stop their selfish behavior until there was no one else to steal from — not even the environment.

"I am the first of my kind," continued Gritt. "As a *Half-Synth*. I am designed to survive if Gripp Society collapses. I was programmed with the knowledge of chemistry and biology so that I could create a new race of Gripps if we cannot find the Secret of Un-old-Age."

Fabius listened intently. He was well aware that his own past had also been filled with struggle and strife in an endless quest to dominate others and the natural world.

"I understand what you are saying, Gritt. There are reasons why our paths have crossed. The source of our learning is to be discovered here in Acronos. In the wonder of this natural world, there are great teachings if we are sensitive enough to be aware of them."

Fabius explained that the Forest of Tones taught the first of the Seven Harmonies, *Knowing Your Inner Tone*. The forest was looking for the strangers' inner tones. It was searching for their unique identity.

"When you know your inner tone, you know who you are," continued Fabius. "You are at ease with yourself, alive with curiosity and able to fulfill your purpose in life. The cells in your body vibrate harmoniously, maintaining your health and vitality, thus delaying the aging process."

"Yes, I agree with everything you have said," replied Gritt quietly. "But learning the information is one thing. Living the teaching is another."

Knowing Your Inner Tone

Your inner tone reflects your dominant feeling nature and acts as a resonant, guiding beacon that can indicate which events and circumstances are in harmony with your life.

Just as there are no two fingerprints or snowflakes exactly alike, this unique vibrational frequency signifies your true nature, character and manner of being that define personal motivations and the decisions that are most beneficial for you.

Your ever-present, inner tone influences your responses, attitude, and interactions with people and events. When you are aware of your inner tone, you will be able to make choices that are more in Harmony with your heart and soul.

BABBLE REPORTS

Babble noticed out of the corner of her eye that Gritt was talking to Fabius. She wondered what information they might be sharing as they emerged from the forest.

I must hurry, she thought as she led the team into a clearing covered with thick grass resembling a lush, dark-green carpet. Babble commanded the remaining team members, Gripps Five through Ten to take a thirty-Gripper (minute) break. She wanted to record an official report while events were still fresh in her mind.

Taking cover in in a small grove of trees, she settled behind an outcropping of rocks and began to speak into her recorder.

GRIPP LOG 2: 47644-A
Official Report to Gripp High Command

This entry marks the second morning since our arrival through the Eye of Time portal. At this moment, all Gripps are alive and accounted for, even though we have endured shocking encounters with strange phenomena and unseen forces that are intruding upon us as we journey further away from our landing site. These startling events appear to be malevolent. They deny our presence and limit our access to information here in this zone known as Acronos.

All Gripp team members have witnessed strange visions and mind-altering experiences that are slowing down our exploration. These illusions seem to be manifested by the plant life, even though Grubb our Biologist, believes there is no connection between what we have experienced and the trees, bushes, and flowers we encounter on our passage through this vast wilderness. We have successfully and most heroically traversed a dark and ominous forest, known as the *Forest of Tones*, while our equipment continues to register moving patterns of an elusive enemy hiding in the trees.

Gripps #1, 2, and 3 have rushed ahead to engage the enemy, displaying great courage. I have led the remaining team members into a clearing, following the radio frequencies and periodic signals that seem to be a form of music.

We have not gathered any information or evidence to document our quest for the Secret of Un-Old-Age. All Gripps have performed admirably, and they continue to Grab-on, Gripp-on, and Grind-on, as our mission statement commands. *End of Official Report.*

GRIPP LOG 2: 47644-B
TOP SECRET REPORT

There are only six Grabbons (days) left before the Eye of Time portal is reactivated, and there is no evidence that there is a civilization here in this vast wilderness. We have all experienced terrifying events, which both Doctor Grouse and Psychologist Grimm believe are designed to drive us all into sheer madness.

In the middle of the night, we were camping under a huge tree and were startled awake by a merging of realities. Glowing colors illuminated the tree, and Gripp sirens were wailing. G.R.A.B. soldiers surrounded us and demanded that we surrender, charging us with treason. We were led to believe we were back in

Grippland and were subject to immediate arrest. All team members survived this strange, illusionary attack.

When we thought it was all over, two illuminated rafts floated overhead, carrying our lost equipment. In the last raft was a vision of a solitary, ghostly Gripp beckoning us to follow, and then the horrifying illusion was over.

This morning I received signals that indicated some form of life was lurking beyond a large stand of trees. There were unknown, echoing voices warning us about the forest toning, and soon the trees were humming and vibrating. We were nearly crushed by boulders as they came tumbling toward us when the ground quaked.

The dogs said we should have asked permission to enter an invisible door into the forest and that the trees only wanted to know who we are. We are dealing with this type of nonsense while trying to survive.

There is no doubt that there seems to be an enemy lurking everywhere. We are always preparing for a surprise attack. But Grist, Twist, and Scheme are apparently losing their grip on reality. They have vanished into the forest, following a suspected enemy force that Grist thinks is hiding there. I have serious concerns regarding his ability to command the expedition in his current state of hysteria.

Some evidence, however, does indicate that the dogs are withholding information. It appears that they might be guiding us into a trap from which we may not escape. Filloloper, the female dog, seems to have an innocent nature, but that is doubtful since she is very loyal to the male dog who seems very secretive and cunning.

It appears that Filloloper is motivated by what only can be called a *Secret Force*. She lives in a fantasy world and fabricates stories about trees talking to trees and speaks of doorways that do not exist. She is undoubtedly working with an invisible enemy and is using an unknown means of communication.

Our equipment is beginning to fail. It works intermittently; and Stare, the engineer, thinks that it will soon stop due to strange electrical surges that pervade this entire zone.

In conclusion, we have lost our way in a land without civilization and our equipment is failing. It is conceivable that we may be doomed to exist in this world of treachery and bizarre illusions. We will continue to follow the radio signals, and perhaps, we may encounter a civilization. *End of Top Secret Report.*

EMERGING FROM THE FOREST

Babble started packing her equipment when she heard a loud burst of sound coming from the last known location of Gripps 1, 2 and 3. At the same time, her radio crackled and began to broadcast a rhythmic beat. She gasped as she heard the sound of forbidden music!

The locator beacon confirmed that something was moving ahead of them. It was just beyond the clearing where the terrain became more uneven, leading to what appeared to be a plateau with rocky ledges.

Babble, serving as #4 in command, was well aware that according to Gripp Law, she was now technically in control, at least until the reappearance of Gripp #1 and his teammates, Scheme, and Twist.

In addition to her duties as a journalist and keeper of the mission's Gripp Log Reports, Babble was assigned to handle routine functions, take photos, and document her observations, but now she was forced to make command decisions by virtue of her assumed importance.

Her ability to gather information and sense her surroundings had served her well in Grippland, but now those skills hardly qualified her for the role of team leader. This would be a tremendous test of her ingenuity and resourcefulness. The ultimate success or failure of the mission now rested on her narrow shoulders.

Venturing forth into the clearing just beyond the last growth of trees, Babble paused, looking out at the vast expanse of open terrain. She was startled by another loud, cracking sound in the distance and quickly motioned for her team to take cover. In less than a second, she saw a sharp blast of reflected light burst forth from a position further up the tree line and took cover behind a rocky ledge.

"It's an ambush!" exclaimed Babble as #5 through #10 gathered around her. Peering into her monitoring device, she saw moving objects, confirming her suspicions that an enemy was waiting for them to emerge from the forest.

Gritt stepped forward and stood next to Babble who was breathing heavily. He pointed to a position behind the suspected enemy and motioned that he and Grubb could circle behind the shooters, attempting to capture them alive.

Dr. Grouse shook her head. She felt her rank as #6 should carry almost equal importance to #4, Babble, who knew virtually nothing about military strategy. #5, Stare, seemed to be in a trance-like state, so Grouse decided to assert her authority. "You are out of your league, Babble," announced Grouse. "I should take control! I know more about military campaigns than you do since I served as a doctor in several Gripp wars."

Gritt began to speak, but quickly caught himself when he remembered that as a Half-Synth, he was not allowed to reveal his true identity. He stood back and listened as Babble and Grouse huddled together in a private conversation.

UNDER ATTACK

Fabius instinctively turned and looked toward the forest. He caught sight of another a bright flash and heard a sharp snapping sound. He glanced over his shoulder to see Gritt fall backward onto the ground.

A moment later, something whizzed past his head, and he watched Babble spin around and drop to her side, still clutching her recording device. Dr. Grouse and Grubb rushed to her aid as the others hid behind trees.

"We need to take cover," warned Fabius as he nudged Filloloper who was distressed by the sight of the motionless teammates lying on the ground near her.

"Return fire! Fire at will," shouted Grouse.

Fabius motioned for Filloloper to move cautiously away from the blaze of gunfire echoing just within the tree line. "It must be the enemy they have been searching for, and now their enemy has become a reality!"

Dr. Grouse crawled quickly along the ground to check the wounds sustained by Babble and Gritt and to confirm their suspected demise.

"The enemy has killed Gritt and Babble!" she exclaimed, without the performing a thorough examination, having only given a quick glance at their motionless forms and checked Babble's pulse.

With that news, Stare seemed to awaken from his stupor. He shook his head and called out, "Return fire," in a less than convincing voice.

Grouse grabbed her gun and then positioned herself behind a large boulder next to Grimm and Grind. They were both hesitant to use a weapon since they had little training; and as a psychologist and anthropologist, they believed that killing was immoral. Nonetheless, they joined the Gripps in firing their weapons blindly in the direction of the attackers, no longer considering Gritt's plan to capture the enemy alive.

"Cease fire," called out Stare. The last burst came from Dr. Grouse. "Listen! The enemy is silent!" exclaimed Stare with the most enthusiasm he had displayed since arriving in Acronos. "We have stopped them! We have engaged the enemy, and we have won!" he declared triumphantly.

The dogs ran to the edge of the clearing. They were curious to see the enemy emerge from hiding. Instead, they witnessed a rolling ball of bright, blue light rising into the sky. "Look, Filloloper. What is that strange light hovering above the enemy position?"

Grubb sauntered up behind the dogs and gasped as he looked up at the blue light. He shouted over his shoulder to the other Gripps, "We have a flare! It's ours! The enemy we just fired upon must be none other than our lost team members: Grist, Twist, and Scheme!"

Fabius shook his head and slowly walked back to look at the body of Gritt, arriving just in time to witness the Half-

Synth's eyes begin to flutter, and his body shook. Gritt took a deep breath, and his eyes flickered open.

"You're alive!" exclaimed Fabius happily as he moved closer to Gritt's face.

Gritt managed a weak smile, "I guess being a Half-Synth has its advantages." He pointed at his chest, tapping it lightly, and explained, "Bullet proof. It is very efficient." He rubbed his face and asked, "How many casualties did we take?"

Fabius replied softly, "It appears that Babble was killed instantly, just after you fell to the ground."

Gritt stared in disbelief for a moment, and then rushed to Babble's side, displaying an uncommon sense of Gripp anguish and remorse as he lifted her lifeless form and held her close to his heart. "Babble, I-I will miss you," he stammered, holding her tightly.

Dr. Grouse and the other Gripps stood in amazement as they watched Gritt stroke Babble's face and sadly repeat, "I am so sorry. I shall truly miss you."

"Look," exclaimed Filloloper, pointing at the twisted and deformed recorder that Babble was still holding. No one paid attention to what she was saying since they were too busy watching Gritt.

Filloloper could not contain her distress any longer. She bent down and quickly administered a well-placed nip on Babble's lower leg. The limp form jerked, and Babble suddenly came back to life, opening her eyes to find herself face to face with Gritt...wrapped in his strong embrace.

"Wha-what happened?" she stuttered as she rested in the comfort of Gritt's strong arms.

"You'll be okay now," replied Gritt happily. "The bullet must have hit your recorder and knocked you unconscious from the force of the impact."

As the other team members turned away from such an embarrassing show of affection, they noticed a white flag with interlocking G's—the symbol of Grippland—waving in the distance. Grist, Scheme, and Twist were walking toward them, looking from side-to-side.

Gritt mumbled under his breath, "We have seen the enemy, and the enemy is us!" He was thinking about his particular advantage—he could survive almost any attack with his durable, synthetic, bullet-proof skin protecting his body. But he was very disturbed to consider that Babble's survival was based on sheer luck. The two, high-powered munition rounds had pierced deep into her radio equipment instead of her heart.

Commander Grist approached the team with bravado. "We almost got them!" he boasted as he recalled the battle again in his mind. "Sorry, you got in the way. We could have made the enemy pay for what they tried to do to us in that forest. Something was moving between those trees. It was right there in our sights! Wasn't it, Twist?"

Grist nudged Twist who didn't reply. Instead, he turned to look back into the forest.

"Well, I'm certain we almost got the enemy!" Grist continued. "But I didn't get a good look at them. They were moving too fast! Weren't they, Scheme?"

Scheme looked away for a moment as if to recall what he hadn't seen, and replied, "Yes, #1, you almost got them!"

We'll make camp here," Commanded Grist. "It looks safe, and there's been enough excitement for one day."

Babble moved cautiously to stand next to Stare and Grubb. Her body was aching from the severe blow when the recorder slammed against the right side of her torso, bruising her ribs. *I should be dead*, she thought, remembering the strange sensation of regaining consciousness and finding herself within Gritt's strong embrace.

She could still recall the warmth of his gaze, and the intensity of his blue-green eyes fixed upon her.

He is the only one who cared whether I lived or died, she mused. *Even mercenaries, such as we, should have feelings, but not this Gripp team. Babble let out a deep sigh. I was right about #1. He is dangerous and unfit for command.*

PART SIX

The Crossroads of Time

A SOFT, ROLLING MIST SWEPT ACROSS green fields that were sparkling like diamonds, stretching out into the far distance as the Gripp team emerged from the Forest of Tones. Only the slightest whisper of the wind could be heard rustling softly through the tall grass, which was swaying like the waves of a gentle sea.

Grist was well aware that entering into such an open field could expose them to a possible attack. He motioned for the team to stop and for Babble and Stare to take readings for any suspicious movement ahead. Nothing was reported that would indicate danger.

Fabius and Filloloper lagged behind, preferring to be out of sight since Grist was suspected that they were somehow responsible for the illusionary attack at the Tower Tree and the bizarre occurrences in the Forest of Tones.

"If only these explorers could understand that their answers to their quest for Un-Old-Age is all around them," suggested Filloloper.

"Yes, but first they must be willing to learn from the wisdom of Nature," replied Fabius. "As the Guardians of Acronos, we can only serve as their guides, not as their instructors. Perhaps, during their encounters with the Seven

Harmonies, they will understand more about their quest and who they are."

Filloloper nodded her agreement as they quickened their pace so as not to fall too far behind.

Acronos had always been a place of refuge, a transition destination for those who had progressed beyond the need for confrontation and aggressive action. Each element, every blade of grass was in tune with the very essence of a *Universal Harmony* shared by everyone and everything on *Level Seven*.

Acronos had always been a place
of refuge, a transition destination for those who had
progressed beyond the need
for confrontation and aggressive action.

And yet, this beautiful valley was not without its defenses or communication systems. The Trillia vines, twisting and winding their way throughout the valley, were indeed the very nerve center of that system. They carried messages and warnings that were only apparent to those who were most sensitive to the natural world around them.

The vines were capable of different levels of subtle vibrations, and their small blossoms changed color from white to yellow to orange, and then to bright red to warn of ultimate danger. The Trillia had first sounded the alert of the stranger's unexpected arrival and were continuously monitoring their movement with increasing sensitivity.

Lost in thought and barely aware of their surroundings, the Gripp team continued their silent procession forward. They were extremely grateful that every step was taking them further away from the dangerous Forest of Tones.

More importantly, they had also escaped the Tree of Memories and the frightening, illusory appearance of Grippland and the G.R.A.B. team from the previous night. But the memory of those images generated by their greatest fears were still haunting them.

They had all witnessed the Tower Tree's transformation and the merging of one reality into another. But, how could they possibly imagine that the dramatic visions the tree produced might have been an opportunity for them to experience joy and wonder? The Memory Tree was capable of bringing forth any emotion that a visitor held within their hearts.

Unfortunately, their deep-set feelings were fear-based, and the tree manifested the terrorizing reality of Grippland, a land where obligation, duty, and foreboding had long ago replaced freedom, love, and joy.

Is any of what we have experienced real? Grimm asked herself. As a psychologist, she found it somewhat ironic to question reality and to wonder if anything in Acronos was real, anything at all.

The signal Babble was receiving on her tracking device indicated activity on the other side of a rocky outcropping. "There is rapid movement. I hear an unusual language," declared Babble, checking and rechecking her equipment to be certain. "It's coming from just over that ridge. We must proceed with extreme caution!"

A NATURAL AMPHITHEATER

Without encountering any resistance, the team reached the top of the rise to witness an incomprehensible scene in the canyon below. Was it the movement, the music or the lyrics that created such a shocking spectacle now unfolding before them?

Gritt, the Half-Synth, was the first to see the creatures from his position on the ridge. He was able to calculate their height at more than seven-feet tall, and they were birds, two enormous birds.

They were moving back and forth on what appeared to be a stage sculpted out of solid stone by the forces of water and wind, creating a smooth and flat surface. This natural amphitheater was the perfect setting for any performance, no matter how outlandish the performers might be!

The oversized, singing and dancing duo were prancing across the stage creating a dazzling appearance. They were taller than the tallest Gripp with blue eyes, yellow beaks, and large, golden, webbed feet designed for balance and agility.

Their ensemble included coats of blue feathers that looked like tuxedos with pure white feathered vests, and on their heads were tall crests of black feathers that seemed to resemble top hats. Indeed, they were larger than life in more ways than one.

Sensing no immediate danger, Commander Grist motioned for the team to approach the amphitheater. He was ready to interrogate and thoroughly investigate these unusual, bird-like performers who seemed to have emerged from a bizarre and twisted dream.

With weapons drawn the team proceeded with caution toward the two birds on center stage. "Nothing here is ever what it seems," Grist groaned. He was aware that the two outrageous characters in the form of birds could soon change into something else, perhaps, something even far more ominous.

WELCOME TO YOUR SHOW

As the time travelers approached center stage and before Grist could even begin to formulate questions to interrogate these absurd, yet majestic creatures, the birds stepped forward, bowed slightly, and peered down at the strange beings assembled before them.

"Greetings! Greetings! Greetings to one and all! "What a wondrous day! We are so happy to have you in our audience! Welcome! Welcome! I am Bo, and this is my brother, Ben. Together we call ourselves the Rockin' BoBens, or if you prefer, we are also well known as Rhythm and Rhyme." Without hesitation Bo and Ben began to do a slow dance routine accompanied by a song:

> *There were bright lights!*
> *All those opening nights.*
>
> *Adoring fans were rushing the door!*
> *It was Bo and Ben taking the floor!*
> *A dazzling, dancing sensation are we!*
> *A Broadway Duo entertaining so brilliantly!*

"Well, that was then, and this is now!" Bo and Ben exclaimed in unison. "There's no need for tickets or advanced reservations. Open seating is now available for one and all. The show is about to begin!"

"Whose show? You might ask. Our show!" exclaimed Bo. "But most importantly, since you have appeared on time, and just in time, this is also YOUR show! Indeed, welcome to our humble stage, which just happens to be located most strategically upon...the *Crossroads of Time!*"

"The Crossroads of Time? What kind of Gripperish is this?" questioned Grist. "You're not real birds! Birds neither dance nor do they sing. Well, they don't sing in words, that is," he stated, correcting himself.

Without hesitation, the Bash Birds begin to croon a little tune and started gliding across the stage, dancing effortlessly in perfect synchrony with one another. Bobbing, weaving and turning, and then moving back and forth, each step was executed with precision.

Disregarding the lack of audience reaction or participation, they launched themselves into another flurry of musical medleys. Their powerful lyrical phrases drifted far out over the expansive amphitheater and echoed back again:

> *Welcome to the Crossroads of Time*
> *where you can relax and simply unwind.*
> *You've traveled here through time and space,*
> *seeking answers in an endless race.*
>
> *Chasing, not replacing your measure,*
> *searching for an elusive treasure,*
> *you're wishing to escape the shock*
> *of the constant ticking of your clock.*
>
> *Within the depths of your wandering,*
> *your decisions have left you pondering.*

It's time to shine a glowing light
on all your deeply hidden fright!

When Time and you are aligned
you'll be in the "now" you hope to find.
Your creativity will begin to soar
escaping dark thoughts forevermore.

Open you hearts to rhythm and rhyme,
and you'll discover your natural design.
Welcome to the Crossroads of Time
where you can relax and simply unwind.

The large birds danced faster and faster, trying to create a profound, emotional impact on their audience who were sitting perfectly still and appeared to be in a dream-like state. Their eyes were open wide, but they didn't seem to understand what they were hearing or seeing.

Bo and Ben knew they had given their best, presenting a spontaneous creation of lyrics uniquely designed for these time travelers. And yet, there was no applause and no reaction, just the dazed expressions of the audience.

"Well then, how about another special song?" They smiled their large Bash Bird smiles and burst into a loud, boisterous, upbeat song, using their feet as well as their wings to tap out the rhythm.

Dreams and schemes and changing faces
take you to new and unusual places.
Each event mirroring your point of view
as lessons learned while passing through.

When you discover your inner tone,
energy flows from a powerful zone
and whatever you desire to find
will always arrive right on time!

The Bash Birds bowed low and waited for applause, but none came. The Gripps had never witnessed such a strange event. They sat transfixed in an altered state of being, motionless and unable to comprehend the meaning of the words they had just heard from such unusual performers. It was as if their consciousness had been transported out of their bodies.

Only when Filloloper and Fabius began applauding did the team members appear to awaken from their trance.

Bo leaned forward, looking sympathetic, and said in a gentle voice, "I hope you enjoyed the show. We believe we performed quite well! Indeed, it may have been one of our greatest performances ever."

SPONTANEITY IN TIME

The Gripp team could not respond. They had no idea what it meant to find their natural design. They had tempted fate to regain their freedom from their former lives as prisoners in Grippland. They were willing to risk the uncertain perils of time travel to discover the Secret of Un-Old Age. Yet, they had never been allowed to develop genuine, deep emotions in Grippland.

Joyful entertainments were considered illegal. No Gripp could possibly imagine the meaning of being in tune with their inner tone or opening their hearts to rhythm and rhyme. Those words meant nothing to them.

Fabius and Filloloper were well aware that the explorers could not grasp the meaning of the Bash Birds' songs. "I guess they just need more time," commented Fabius. "They need a lot more time."

"Ah, time...everyone is looking for time," suggested Ben Bash. "But time is the beat under your feet. Living in time requires spontaneity. Being spontaneous is the only way *you* can catch *the real you* in Time."

Being spontaneous is the only way
you can catch the real you in Time.

Bo smiled broadly and added, "Time is what you wish to explore. Time is always presenting a door, an opening to here or there, to now or then, or even before. Now is your time to choose. Would you prefer to go back into your past, remain in the present or progress into your future? The choice is yours, but not to ignore."

Time is what you wish to explore. Time is
always presenting a door, an opening to here
or there, to now or then, or even before.

Ben paused to do a quick shuffle and hop-step with an expansive sweeping gesture of his right wing, a flourish that ended with him pointing upward as if portraying a hand on an invisible clock.

Grist drew in a deep breath. His eyes narrowed as he looked menacingly at the strange birds. "This is nothing more than another sinister plot, a trap, a well-carried out plan to mesmerize our minds," he responded in a condescending voice. "Bash Birds, Rockin' BoBens, as you call yourselves. You are nothing more than super-sized, dancing, prancing, bags of feathers; and you are here for one reason, and one reason alone...to deceive us!"

"Deceive you?" questioned Fabius. "The Bash Birds are only presenting you the opportunity to choose one of the crossroads of time. They want to know if you will you decide to travel back into the past, remain in the present, or attempt to go forward into an unknown future?"

Grist looked extremely bewildered as Ben said, "You know that everything in life is related to timing."

And with a flourish the Bash Birds sang another tune:

> *Without timing, you would swirl*
> *like a wave without its curl.*
> *You'd live in a lingering daze*
> *like the moon without its phase.*
> *You'd be a boat without its sail*
> *or a dog without its tail.*
> *Isn't it exciting?*
> *Everything has its timing!*

"Timing? Is that what you call it? I believe you're a Time Trap!" exclaimed Grist. "Your show is nothing more than a complicated deception designed to steal our time by wasting our time, while we are apparently running out of time. How can we possibly choose between past, present, and future? We are lost in the present. Our future appears to be a constant repeat of the past, which means that we may never know where we are once we arrive. If we ever do arrive at all!"

The Bash Birds were now clear that Grist was incapable of making any decisions, and since all Gripps were required to follow his command, they were also incapable of change. Bo and Ben spun around full circle to face the Gripps, and announced, "We will leave you with one last song:

> *Feeling the rhythm of your inner tone*
> *is discovering your beat like a metronome.*
> *Your inner vibration and frequency*
> *will carry you forward effortlessly.*
>
> *Know yourself in words and visions,*
> *trust your feelings when making decisions,*
> *use your powers to consider choices,*
> *don't be a victim of worldly voices.*
>
> *Letting go of the constant race*
> *will bring you to a magical place*
> *where each moment will become sublime*
> *as you stand at the Crossroads of Time!*

Babble, Grouse, Grimm, and Grind remained perplexed, barely moving, and unable to grasp the meaning of the Bash Birds' song. Grist, Twist, and Scheme moved their heads quickly from side-to-side as if trying to shake off the information they were hearing. Only Gritt seemed to welcome the meaning of their words.

Ben Bash smiled and added. "Gripps from Grippland, remember, please remember that there are many ways to learn the lessons of life. Some are difficult, and others are grand, most grand, indeed!"

The two outstanding performers executed one last twirl on stage and then raised their wings high. "It was wonderful for you to stop by; but now, well, it's time to fly."

With that last declaration, Bo and Ben started to flap their enormous wings and slowly lifted their large, bulky bodies high into the cloudless, bright blue sky.

Rhythm and Rhyme

Rhythm and Rhyme are your heart, mind and body connection creating the musical harmony you feel inside. This harmony enables you to make the very best choices every moment at the Crossroads of Time and serves as your harmonic guide to those events which most closely match your true identity.

Rhythm is your inner tempo or beat that helps form and define how you relate to the world. Do you feel comfortable in upbeat, high stress situations or are you more productive in low stress environments?

Rhyme is the melody, the flow of your feeling nature, which is alert to all matching events, people and activities that will create the desired harmony in your life.

Acknowledging your life's unique Rhythm and Rhyme helps to determine the tone, tempo and flow of your natural rhythm, which frees your mind and heart to become the true you in all aspects of life.

PART SEVEN

Crystal Falls

A S THE BASH BIRDS PERFORMED their very last song, Gritt, the half-synth, who possessed extrasensory abilities, was able to see mysterious, multi-colored lights streaming from the cliff behind the stage.

Moments after Bo and Ben flew away, the beams of light began sweeping back and forth across the amphitheater. It was as if an unknown energy force was seeking to find the intruders who had entered its space.

Fabius and Filloloper were also aware that the continuously moving streams of colorful illumination could in fact be *Ripples in Time*.

The Bash Birds had explicitly told their audience that this was no ordinary stage. In fact, they had declared that their amphitheater was located directly at the *Crossroads of Time*. And now it appeared that *Time* itself was determined to take Center Stage.

"Why is this happening?" asked Filloloper softly.

"Time has shifted again," responded Fabius. "Grist would not decide whether to live in the past, present, or future. He refused to make a choice; and now, Time is in the process of deciding for him."

Pausing to consider his words carefully, Fabius continued, "The Gripps don't understand that time is moving in spirals, bringing forth events that match their inner rhythm.

"Time does not judge which events are positive or negative. Each of the occurrences the Gripps have experienced are slightly different, but the result is a clear demonstration of how their thoughts, emotions, and actions combine to create their reality."

Filloloper remained silent, listening intently to Fabius' words and asked, "You mean those who refuse to listen and learn will experience the 'Time Spiral' bringing forth similar and possibly even more shocking events?"

You mean those who refuse to listen and learn will experience the 'Time Spiral' bringing forth similar and possibly even more shocking events?"

Fabius was about to reply when a strong, vibrational force passed through him accompanied by a rumbling tone and a powerful, tumbling sensation. He was the first to hear the sound of rushing water.

"It's a *Time Wave*! Time is accelerating all events at this very moment!" he exclaimed as he ran toward higher ground with Filloloper following close behind.

"Yes, I knew it was true," cried out Grist, as he climbed onto a rocky ledge overlooking the flowing water. "From the first moment we landed in Acronos, I knew that everything here would be part of an ingenious deception. Everyone knows there is always a grand and most devious trap waiting to grab a great Gripp."

Time had indeed created the Gripps' next event sequence. Rushing over the Bash Bird's stage was a torrential river. A raging current was pouring over the stage and flooding the canyon, carrying with it an abundance of debris from the surrounding forest along with an unusual surprise.

The startled Gripps gasped when they saw their two missing rafts speeding past them in the turbulent river. "That's our equipment!" exclaimed Stare in a near hysterical tone of voice, pointing as he ran.

"Yes, and there is something else!" declared Dr. Grouse, gesturing further up the river.

Indeed, in the second raft was a ghost-like figure sitting in the back of the boat, staring straight ahead.

"Jump now!" commanded Grist, "Grab on! Grip on!"

Without further hesitation, Grist flung himself directly into the torrent, desperately trying to grab onto one of the rafts now speeding by the stage where the Bash Birds had been performing only moments before.

Reluctantly, the others jumped into the river, trying to grip onto the rafts, and were quickly swept away by the unrelenting current.

In the distance, the dogs could hear only one voice, "We will survive. We will survive!" It was Grist's voice echoing through the canyon as the *Time Wave* carried them through an opening in the cliff to an unknown destination.

Astounded and amazed, Fabius and Filloloper could see that the power of Time was moving the explorers to yet another unplanned rendezvous. If they survived the turbulent current, it would take them directly to Crystal Falls where the flowing Time Stream would pause before moving on again.

In their hearts, the Guardians of Acronos felt that no matter how devious and cruel these strangers had been, it was difficult not to be sympathetic to their cause.

Ever since the Gripps arrival in Acronos, they were desperate to capture Time. If only they had chosen to remain in the present, they might easily have avoided their collision with the Time Wave. But now their survival depended upon whatever knowledge they might have gained since their arrival on Level Seven.

Filloloper and Fabius wound their way through the thick underbrush, following the rough waters of the Time Stream on its way to Crystal Falls. They hoped to find the team safely deposited somewhere within the small canyon surrounding the falls.

Fabius recalled that the Gripps had talked about losing time and wasting time and now all those precious moments were slipping away. The constant challenges and tribulations the team experienced always seemed to be lingering just ahead. Events that matched their erratic rhythm and rhyme were patiently waiting for them to arrive, no matter how hard they tried to escape.

The design of the 7th Level was to allow a feedback loop for thoughts fueled by emotions to become reality. This beautiful and bountiful, natural valley of Acronos acted as a reflector that served to manifest one's heart's desires and was activated by powerful emotions such as joy and love.

But those same reflective patterns of energy could also reveal, magnify, and portray negative thoughts, feelings, and attitudes. Whatever was abiding in consciousness would eventually be revealed.

THE TIME POOL

It was not just a cruel twist of fate that had intervened to sweep the Gripp team out of the amphitheater into a torrent of rushing water. They were asked to make a choice by a very entertaining pair of former Broadway stars. Did the explorers wish to return to the past, remain in the present, or move forward into the future?

Was it fear or a stubborn refusal to receive the information being presented that allowed Time to take center stage and ultimately choose for them? Perhaps it was both. Regardless, they were heading to a new point of departure, a unique event that would be entirely out of their control.

Fabius and Filloloper cautiously followed a narrow, overgrown trail above the river rapids, arriving at a long, flat outcropping of rock overlooking Crystal Falls. Rushing water poured down from the high cliffs, causing icy cold blasts of spray to wash over them.

The river had widened and was flowing across large boulders and cascading down into the canyon. The continuous shower of sunlit water glistened with rainbows in colors of violet and blue and hints of sparkling gold. The magnificent display of water was tumbling over rocky outcroppings and through crevices, creating mini-waterfalls before becoming a powerful stream.

Moving to the edge of the cliff, they gazed down into Crystal Canyon. It was difficult to see through the cold spray and clouds of water vapor, but it was clear enough to see there was no one in sight.

"Few beings could survive this force of nature," remarked Filloloper sadly. They quickly turned and followed a winding pathway down the steep hillside through a maze of jagged, slippery rocks and twisted, uprooted trees.

At the base of the falls was a large, deep, irregularly-shaped Time Pool reflecting the clouds in the sky. It displayed the effects of Time in its whirling patterns moving in a spiral, pulling everything into its central core.

Fabius turned around slowly, searching for any remaining signs of the team. Unfortunately, the Gripp's journey appeared to be over. There were no equipment or clothing; nothing remained as evidence that they had ever arrived in Acronos. Yet, Fabius still had hope. He would not give up the possibility that at least a few of the Gripp team members had managed to survive.

Approaching the *Time Pool* cautiously to avoid sliding off the slippery, moss-covered rocks, Filloloper paused for a moment to observe the magical reflections glistening on the surface of the *Time Pool*. "This scene is so beautiful," she remarked. "The Gripps always seemed to be oblivious to the beauty of nature around them."

"I know," replied Fabius. "But I think there was a greater motivation compelling them to risk it all."

Filloloper hesitated and took a deep breath as she gazed into the reflecting water of the *Time Pool*. She gasped and exclaimed, "Look! Do you see it?" She pointed at the water. "Something is swimming in the pool!"

Fabius stretched and stared into the pool. "I don't see anything but rippling patterns of water."

"There it is again!" she exclaimed while balancing precariously on a rocky ledge. "Those radiant colors are now manifesting into an iridescent form."

"I think you are seeing reflections from sunlight refracting on the water, or maybe you are seeing ghosts of the lost Gripps," he said in a joking manner.

He was well aware that her observations were usually very accurate. As a former Warrior Princess, she was hyper-aware of her environment. Her life, as well as the lives of her soldiers, depended upon her ability to perceive what others could not see. He needed to give her the benefit of the doubt.

But before questioning her further, he caught sight of something strange. There was an outline of a form in the pool. Those were definitely not random light patterns nor were they ghosts. There, just below the surface of the water, was a large, unusually-shaped, nearly invisible creature swimming around and around.

As Fabius was trying to comprehend what he was seeing, the shadowy form emerged from the powerful pull and swirl of the Time Pool. It floated effortlessly through the air, stopping for a moment to hover overhead; and then, it glided under the cascading water of Crystal Falls into a large opening in the cliff wall.

Both mesmerized and confused, the two dogs exchanged glances and hurried to follow the unknown phenomena under the falls and into a large cave complex. The phantom seemed to be looking for something or someone as it floated above the underground stream that wound its way deep into the cavern.

DARK CRYSTALS

In just a few moments, the large, wavering light form stopped in front of a cluster of towering, dark crystals, which were projecting upward at different angles from the cave floor. The creature floated around and over the dark crystals, forming an ever-widening spiral and returning back again.

"It's searching for something," observed Fabius quietly, concerned that it might be attracted to their position. He knew this was not a ghost, but it was enormous and very ominous. He moved closer to Filloloper and attempted to direct her away from whatever was about to transpire when an unusual murmuring sound began to reverberate and then echo through the cave.

As they moved further away from the crystals, the tonal vibration intensified and transformed into words that rhymed:

> *Here I am just passing through*
> *and thought I'd get a glimpse of you.*
> *I see you here caught in Time*
> *like frightened fish upon a line.*
>
> *Pulled from a waking dream,*
> *created within a perfect scheme,*
> *you've found what you were looking for:*
> *to be suspended in time forevermore.*
>
> *Traveling with sight that couldn't see,*
> *refusing your gifts of harmony,*
> *now you have your perpetual prize,*
> *you will never age with crystal eyes.*

"It knows...it knows who they are!" Fabius' voice trailed off as he looked into the darkened depths of the gray towers. There, held within the crystals, were the twisted and tangled forms of the Eye of Time Exploration Team.

Fabius counted nine of the missing explorers trapped within the crystalline shapes, like ancient fossils petrified in amber. Somehow, their very last moments and movements were captured and magnified inside the crystals. The Gripps were suspended in Time.

Grist was standing with his hand pressing against the inside surface of a crystal in his very last attempt to push his way out. Twist and Scheme had tortured expressions on their faces with their eyes and mouths wide open as if they were shouting. Babble was still clutching her communications device close to her chest. Stare, Grouse, Gritt, Grimm, and Grind were each frozen in different, twisted poses within their own crystal. Only Grubb was missing.

Fabius and Filloloper were barely able to process the scene before them. It was difficult to believe that the entire Gripp team were now frozen forever within the towering, dark crystals. Only the last few phrases of the creature's song helped them to comprehend that the scene they were witnessing was actually real.

> *Traveling with sight that couldn't see,*
> *refusing your gifts of harmony,*
> *now you have your perpetual prize,*
> *you will never age with crystal eyes.*

Fabius moved closer to Filloloper who had tears rolling down her cheeks. "We were trying to be their guides! Do you think we are in any way responsible for what has happened to them?" she asked, her voice filled with sadness.

"There was nothing we could do to change their fate," answered Fabius as he stood strong beside her.

There were no words to explain the tragic event they were witnessing. Time had chosen the next experience for the Gripps when they had refused to decide if they wanted to be in the past, present, or future. Their lack of trust in the unseen forces of nature had brought them to their ultimate destiny and final destination.

The invisible forces of the event matrix — the fabric of the Universe which listens intently to all thoughts spoken or unspoken — had delivered the Gripps their ultimate request: the answer to the Secret of Un-Old-Age. They would never age when crystallized.

Their inability to affirm or subscribe to the full meaning of their journey had created a distortion field in the space- time continuum. Thus, they now found themselves trapped in the closest approximation and manifestation of their hearts' desires.

Fear replaced trust; and as a result, discord replaced harmony. Their words betrayed them, and their thoughts secretly and irretrievably stole their future.

Fear replaced trust; and as a result, discord
replaced harmony. Their words betrayed them,
and their thoughts secretly and irretrievably
stole their future.

Fabius looked deep into Filloloper's golden-brown eyes and replied, "In some ways, we may have failed to save the Gripps; but then again, we must remember they could have made different choices. It appears that they didn't know how to save themselves!"

He had just finished uttering his statement when a cool blast of wind pushed past him almost knocking him off-balance. An unseen voice spoke to them,

> *Is it really so terrible*
> *that these creatures so unbearable*
> *so very difficult to advise*
> *have met their ultimate demise?*
>
> *You are not responsible for the fear*
> *of these beings without charm or cheer!*
> *Perhaps, they'll serve as lessons learned*
> *for all those who may be concerned.*
>
> *I came to say hello and then goodbye.*
> *A busy Cosmic Traveler am I.*

They could hear the creature's warm, melodic voice as though he were in front of them, but they could not see him, at least not immediately.

After a moment of hesitation, Filloloper exclaimed, "Look, there are reflected images of us in the midst of that shining, mirror-like darkness just ahead."

"Why does no one see what they see?" the voice asked in a frustrated tone. "Well, there are those who have described me in far less favorable terms. I shall accept your description. 'That shining, mirror-like darkness' you mention, is actually my most magnificent eye!"

"Your eye?" questioned Fabius, trying to see more of the creature speaking to them.

A wave of cold air moved over and around the dogs as the ghost-like image became slightly more visible.

"So it is, and so it was!" answered the unknown creature floating in the air. "What can I say, other than to mention that the Gripps' inevitable was most justifiable since they created a *Ripple in Time.* As for me, the shift in energy helped to pique my curiosity, and I truly am most grateful for the diversity!"

"Are you so very cruel?" questioned Filloloper defiantly, acting fearless in her reply and demeanor. "Why not show yourself? Certainly, you are not afraid of us!"

Suddenly, without warning, a creature of enormous size manifested in front of them. A glowing monster from another world was now on full display. Its huge, black eyes focused intently on them, and it's pouting, oversized mouth was opening and closing as if searching for more words to expel into the atmosphere.

"Greetings! My name is Delphos. A multidimensional traveler am I, swimming effortlessly upon the Cosmic Sea."

The two dogs stared in disbelief and amazement at the magnificent form of an enormous, radiant fish over twenty-feet-long (including his tail) with a head that was at least four-feet tall and equally wide. His six-foot, dorsal fin appeared to serve as balance; and his over-sized, pectoral fins were used as wings as he floated in the air. His giant tail acted as a rudder to facilitate changing directions.

He floated in a large circle around the dogs, preparing to answer Filloloper's question. "Hmm, cruel, you say? Am I so cruel? As you may or may not know, it is not my obligation to intervene on Level Seven. I have only followed my curiosity. Does that qualify for such a charge as cruelty?" questioned Delphos in a very detached and unemotional tone of voice.

He glanced over at the crystals containing the distorted and twisted forms of the Gripp team and said:

They were more than foolish
and always rather brutish;
and as you can plainly see,
they have simply reached
a new level of absurdity.

Delphos swayed and grinned, appearing to be very pleased with his simple retort in rhyme.

"Is that all there is? Is that all you can say? Is there no hope...no way of reaching them?" pleaded Filloloper as she peered into the crystal containing Babble who had an innocent expression upon her face.

"Well, the answer to your question is yes and no!" he quickly replied, rolling his large eyes and taking a deep breath. He tested the air repeatedly with his large gills opening and closing rapidly.

"You see, it's all about qualifications. I swim in the air, rather than the sea. I did make a few modifications to my form, but I'm a certified, multidimensional traveler, unlimited, if you will, and certainly not confined to Level Seven.

"I really do wish you well, and I must admit, I did enjoy the visit!" With that last exclamation, Delphos was becoming more transparent as he prepared to depart.

"Wait, wait....don't go!" declared Filloloper

"Hmm, those words would make great lyrics for a new song. Now then, how would the music sound?" He started singing with a beat, "Wait, wait...don't go! Wait, wait..."

"Stop! Please, Delphos, we need your help!" Fabius knew that he needed to step forward to assist Filloloper who was very upset and shaken by the trauma of seeing the lifeless Gripps trapped within the dark crystals.

He looked up at Delphos and asked, "Do you have the power to free them?"

Delphos looked surprised by Fabius' question. "Why, do you feel responsible for them?" he asked. "Do you want them to escape to freedom only to become trapped again down the line somewhere in time?

"As I recall they had three choices!" he continued, not waiting for a response from Fabius. "They chose not to choose, and that, obviously, was not one of the choices! Do you see how very simple this game really is?"

It was apparent that Delphos was enjoying himself since he was beginning to manifest more fully and was floating back-and-forth propelled by his massive blue tale, creating waves of cool air around him.

He turned and looked back at the Gripps caught in their different poses, each trying to escape from the crystal that encased them. "Well, well, well...I have met some of these characters. That is before they became crystallized."

Delphos stopped speaking and looked more closely at the two dogs who stood staring at him in amazement.

"As I mentioned, my name is Delphos. And your names are Commander Fabius of many battles won, and this would be the lovely, Princess Filloperna from Aranthia. What a beautiful princess you are, indeed! Greetings to you, Brave Ones!"

The energy of those last words instantly flooded through Fabius, creating an energetic field of such intense power that the vibration resonated to the very core of his being and almost overpowered him. He centered himself and managed to maintain his balance.

He felt as though he was falling. He was tumbling through space-time and arriving back again within a matter of moments. In the mirror-like surfaces of the crystals, he was astounded to see his reflection did not reveal Fabius, the dog. Instead, there stood Commander Fabius, a leader of the Roman Legions. Standing next to him was the stunning, Warrior Princess Filloperna.

His reflection revealed the handsome figure of a young warrior with broad shoulders wearing a blue cloak. On his left arm was a small, round shield engraved with the symbol of an Eagle.

Fabius looked in amazement at his reflection and experienced a new feeling of strength. He stood proudly on two sturdy legs, and he comfortably supported the heavy weight of a long sword within its leather sheath. On his right side was a short jeweled sword — the very last implement of battle he remembered holding before the time-shift.

The reflected image next to him was Princess Filloperna, an auburn-haired beauty with bright emerald eyes. As they turned to look at each other, face-to-face, the shock wave of remembrance of their meeting at that last battle instantly moved through them, and without hesitation, they fell into a loving embrace.

Filloperna's appearance was exactly as Fabius remembered. She was a tall, powerful, radiant, young woman, a leader of her army. She was dressed in a beaded, embossed leather tunic and a short leather skirt. Over her shoulders were a longbow and a quiver full of arrows.

She was the warrior who had lived in his memory, the very same woman he had given his life to save.

At that moment, they merged into each other's eyes, sharing tears...forever locked away in time!

Delphos circled the two young warriors, wrapping them in a glowing circle of light. After a few moments, he spoke in a caring voice, "Hmmm...well, so there you are. I hope you enjoy seeing each other again as you once were."

Fabius and Filloperna nodded and silently gazed at each other, remembering another time and place.

Delphos paused and waited for them to come back from their remembering and return to the present. He cleared his throat and pointed one large fin towards the captured team.

"Here you are...and there they are! My song was for them, but then again, how could they hear...frozen in time. They never did enjoy the genius of my rhyme."

Filloperna smiled slightly and responded, "I guess they couldn't hear much even before becoming trapped inside the crystals. And now it seems their fate is sealed. I guess you would say, sealed in time forever."

"Indeed," replied Delphos. "Forever is what they were looking for, and now they are perfectly preserved, just as they desired. The Gripps will never age. Their forms are suspended in time."

"But they never learned nor could seem to understand the essence of harmony or the rhythm of life that the Bash Birds were singing about," said Fabius in a deeper voice.

"Hmmm...the Bash Birds. I knew them well. I have heard them sing. I watched from a discreet, non-visible location," commented Delphos, and then he asked, "Who do you think sings better...The Bash Birds or me?"

"Well, you are bigger," suggested Fabius. "It's hard to say that one or the other is better. After all, they do put on a whole show at their…"

Delphos interrupted, "I know, at their theater. It's not their stage, you know. I practiced there long ago. That is to say, before I moved on to other assignments."

He started to move his tail and began to fade from view, ready to bid adieu. "Nice to see you again, Princess and you Fabius. And now, I must be on my way. I must follow my curiosity without further delay."

"No, wait!" called Filloperna. "Don't leave just yet. Can't you help them?

"Help who?" replied Delphos with a slight annoyance.

"Help the visitors in the crystals!" replied Fabius, pointing to the Gripps in the Dark Crystals that were now vibrating with a low humming sound.

"Oh, they'll be alright. Those explorers in time have found their heart's design!" Delphos chuckled.

"Isn't that the Bash Birds song?" asked Filloperna.

"Well, you know, lyrics and songs…they do float on by, in time and out of time, don't they?"

"You just can't leave them to die, or are they already dead?" she asked.

"Well, technically, yes, they're mostly dead, but then again, the Gripp team was almost dead when they arrived," replied Delphos. "They were not alive in their hearts and minds, and now they are just a little less alive." He smiled and then laughed as only an enormous, blue-green fish could laugh, with his whole, illuminated body vibrating the air around him.

Filloperna bravely moved closer to Delphos and stared up at him with a pleading look in her eyes. "Please help them? Can you give them another chance?" she begged as tears streamed down her cheeks. "Don't you feel we all need a second chance?"

"Hmmm, perhaps that's true," replied Delphos. His resolve softened as he watched sweet Filloperna making her plea. "I remember once when I was a young wannabe rock star. There was a special day when my band didn't show up for an important audition. I was very disturbed, and the club owner told me he'd give me a second chance if I came back with the band the next day. We got the gig, and it was the beginning of my exciting career! I mean…okay. I see your point."

Delphos hesitated for a moment and then spun around three times, generating a tremendous surge of energy that set the crystals humming. He was glowing with such brilliance that when Filloperna and Fabius closed their eyes, the light still penetrated into the center of their being.

"So nice to see you again," echoed Delphos' voice.

In less than a minute, the cave seemed to darken, and Filloperna and Fabius once more transformed into dogs. They opened their eyes and saw that Delphos had disappeared.

Standing before them were nine Gripps, free of the crystals, shaking their heads, and breathing once again.

NOW THERE ARE NINE

As the Gripps staggered toward the exit of the Crystal Falls cave complex, they were dazed and disorientated. All memories of the events leading to their entrapment within the crystals were gone.

They had struggled bravely to survive after being swept over the cliff by the enormous waterfall and had fought against the spinning within the Time Pool, but to no avail.

Babble was the first to notice that there were only nine team members present. Grubb was missing. Her report would need to indicate that he had either died or disappeared. She hesitated for a moment, and then mentioned to her fellow team members that the biologist was gone.

Grist would ultimately be accountable for the death or disappearance of any team member. But in the end, he knew that any official responsibility would be expediently handed down to the lowest numbered Gripps on the mission team. Naturally, Grimm and Grind would be equally blamed and then prosecuted for Grubb's untimely death.

Grist, however, was lost within the incessant calculations of his military mind. He did not seem to comprehend that Grubb's knowledge of botany and the healing properties of plants were crucial to the discovery of any treatments or cures to sustain Un-Old-Age.

Now, that Grubb was missing, the nine remaining members would have far less opportunity to achieve success, and more importantly, less chance for them to receive amnesty and freedom in Grippland.

Stepping forward, Grist announced in a cold and detached manner that Grubb was missing and presumed dead. "It is essential to understand that any of us may meet the same unfortunate fate. Nevertheless, we have an important mission ahead of us, and for that reason, we will not waste any precious Grippons (hours) searching for Grubb. We must assume that he has grabbed his Last Grasp! So then, what say you?"

The team chanted in unison: Good Grubb has grabbed his Last Grasp! Good Grubb has grabbed his Last Grasp! (He's at the end of his lifetime.)

Having repeated their quick farewell to Grubb, the nine tired and battered team members and the two dogs proceeded to follow Grist as he climbed the steep hill beside Crystal Falls.

The pathway winding precariously along the cliff face brought them ever closer to the precipice. They passed jagged rocks and boulders as icy blasts of cold spray from the waterfall made the trail especially dangerous. They knew that any sudden slip would result in their Last Grasp.

Exhausted and psychologically stunned by the presumed death of Grubb, the Gripps eventually reached the high plateau where they began to make camp for the night. Their Gripp logic indicated that this would be the safest location, providing them with a vantage point whereby they could defend themselves from any sudden attack.

Fabius and Filloloper silently watched from a safe distance, as the Gripps assembled around a large campfire. Grist, Twist, and Scheme attempted to describe the strange and confusing events they had experienced thus far. Each believed their version of what had happened was correct.

In reality, all they could remember were bits and pieces of their traumatic odyssey, which ultimately led to being encapsulated in solid, rock crystal.

Strangely, they didn't discuss their bizarre encounter with the Bash Birds who had emphasized the extreme importance of discovering their inner rhythm and rhyme, nor did they mention being washed away in the flash flood that sent them to Crystal Falls.

The leaders of the team seemed to have no remembrance of those events and acted as though they had never happened. Their contrary opinions very quickly turned into accusations and blame. Shouts and threats echoed through the darkness of the surrounding forest.

Meanwhile, team members Four through Seven condemned and accused the lower numbered Gripps of being incompetent, not fit for duty, and responsible for all the terrifying events that had occurred since their arrival.

Fabius was appalled by their vicious threats and accusations. "They do not want to take any responsibility for their actions, nor do they even recall their interactions with Bo and Ben, who specifically warned them that they had ventured onto the Crossroads of Time. It seems as if somehow their memories have been blocked."

"Yes, and they are acting even more cynical since being trapped in the crystals," suggested Filloloper. "It's as though the worst parts of them are gaining strength and their fears are increasing. Their Gripp logic was evidently lost somewhere within the depths of those dark crystals."

"The crystals were not dark before the Gripps washed into the Time Pool," responded Fabius. "It was their energy which created the darkness, and it was that very same energy which trapped each of them within a Crystal."

Filloloper nodded her agreement. "The power contained within those crystalline forms has somehow expanded their most extreme behavior and negative beliefs."

She thought for a moment and then looked into Fabius' eyes, "You know, we just couldn't leave them trapped inside the crystals. No matter how ungrateful they are, I still believe there is hope. I know they sound more menacing and extreme than ever before, but perhaps, they will gain more awareness as they proceed."

Fabius was very sympathetic to Filloloper's brave optimism, but he had his doubts. "It is true that we cannot just abandon them since they would never find their way back to the island; but at the same time, we must be well aware that they are also in the process of losing their most precious possession — their Gripp logic. But then again, it was by using only their logic that led to their entanglements with nature and the Crossroads of Time."

The dogs retreated into the high grass to escape the constant banter, shouts, and accusations. It was late in the night when the exhausted team relaxed into sleep. A blanket of dark gray smoke from their dying campfire washed over them like a menacing cloud.

The break of dawn came quickly. With only a few hours' sleep, Babble arose before the others. She secluded herself behind a large tree and began to write her reports, official and unofficial, to High Command.

GRIPP LOG 3: 47645-A
Official Report to Gripp High Command

This entry marks the morning of the fourth Grabbon (day) since our arrival through the Portal of the Eye of Time. The two dogs, who for some reason speak perfect Grippish, are still with us; and although we have our suspicions as to their real intentions, they do not appear to mean us harm.

We know we cannot trust them, but they are familiar with the terrain and the very bizarre behavior of nature here in Acronos that continues to slow and sometimes stop our progress.

In my last report, I mentioned we had followed an unusual sound, similar to music, into a heavily forested area, known as the *Forest of Tones*, an expansive growth of trees and shrubs, which seemed to be aware of our presence.

The entire forest was alive with energy, and after a few Grippings, the trees were apparently attempting to communicate with us. The dogs explained that the trees could not identify who we were. As we tried to continue through the forest, we experienced an overwhelming density of tones and vibrational currents.

In an attempt to escape moving rocks and boulders, #1 Grist, Twist and Scheme became separated from the rest of the team and commenced firing erratically into the trees. Grist believed that hostile forces were hiding within the forest, and in his confused state of mind (thinking we were the enemy), he mistakenly targeted the remaining team members.

The first shot struck my recording equipment, which acted as a shield, and it fortunately saved my life. A glancing bullet hit Grit, the Geologist, who for some reason was not severely wounded.

It was apparent to all team members that the trees in this forest were aware of our presence and that their probing energy was destabilizing us physically and emotionally.

After surviving our dangerous and foreboding exploration of the forest, the unusual, musical sounds we had been following became louder. After a brief rest near a meadow, the team decided to pursue the source of the sounds, hoping we might encounter some version of a civilized community.

We continued to follow the indicators until we arrived at a large, natural amphitheater with a stage, upon which two entertainers, appearing as seven-foot tall, dancing and singing birds, beckoned us to enjoy their show! They called themselves Bo and Ben and referred to some unknown location, called Broadway, where they said they were stars.

No team members believed even for one Gripping that these were real birds. However, we reluctantly listened to their songs and tried to determine any possible hidden information that they might accidently reveal regarding their actual identity.

The Bash Birds continued to talk and sing in riddles and rhymes, suggesting the absurd idea that somehow we had arrived at the *Crossroads of Time*. They sang about harmony and synchronicity, which they said creates ideal timing in one's life. We quickly realized that their message was total Gripperish and their "show" was designed to confuse and overpower our Gripp logic.

After their bizarre performance, the "birds" insisted that because we were at the *Crossroads of Time*, we were required to choose whether to stay in the present, return to the past, or enter into some unknown future. It was apparent that this was yet another trap, and Commander Grist bravely refused to choose.

Within a flash, the two performers disappeared and a torrent of water washed through the amphitheater carrying our long rafts and necessary survival equipment. In the second boat was a Gripp-like ghost, beckoning us to follow.

Commander Grist made a valiant effort to seize one raft but was swept away along with the rest of the team members who quickly followed close behind him into the raging river.

None of us recall the next series of events. However, we do remember regaining consciousness in an enormous cave where we were standing next to towering crystals. There in front of us were Fabius and Filloloper with delighted expressions on their faces, which seemed to imply that they were somehow responsible for saving our lives.

It is evident that the land of Acronos is not what it appears to be; yet, the constant assault upon our mission will not deter us. Our objective is to find the *Secret of Un-Old-Age.*

We successfully survived the flash flood and the mystery of the cave. All team members are alive and well, save for one, #7, Gripp Grubb, who went missing sometime during our experience at Crystal Falls. Sadly, we fear the worst. After an exhaustive search for our valuable team biologist, Commander Grist made the difficult decision to continue on without him. *End of Official Report.*

GRIPP LOG 3: 47645-B
TOP SECRET REPORT

This is early in the morning of the fourth Grabbon (day) since our arrival in Acronos, leaving little time to return to the island for the scheduled reopening of the Portal in Time. We have endured every manner of illusion and trickery since our brief sojourn here. It's apparent that the animals we encountered are most probably not animals at all, but rather some other life forms appearing as dogs or birds, etc.

Most team members are doing well under these extreme circumstances, except for Commander Grist and the second and third in command, Twist and Scheme. The three of them have become agitated and angered, because they have not accomplished their mission objectives nor are they succeeding in their obsessive search for Grold.

As mentioned in my last report, on the morning of Grippon three, we endured a nearly disastrous journey through the *Forest of Tones*. I believe that the forest was an elaborate illusion created by a mysterious energy force, which demanded to know who we were as intruders into its domain.

When the source behind that vision could not comprehend our identity, it began vibrating at an extreme rate, sending out overwhelming tones that created an immediate madness in all team members, but for some reason Grist, Twist, and Scheme were showing the most adverse effects.

Commander Grist was hallucinating, believing that he had seen enemy forces hiding deep within the forest and started shooting randomly at shadowy forms almost killing Gritt our geologist and me.

After barely surviving the *Forest of Tones* it became apparent that the threat to our safety is everywhere, but especially from our three leaders, whose lack of leadership and balanced judgment now jeopardize the rest of our team.

Escaping the forest episode, we cautiously headed toward what sounded like music. We soon found ourselves in front of two, seven-foot tall, blue and white birds who were dancing and singing what they called "show tunes." Those enormous birds invited us to enjoy their show. Immediately after they stopped singing, they insisted that we must choose between the past, present, and future since we had entered into their domain, located at the *Crossroads of Time*.

Realizing that we were not falling into their trap, the Bash Birds quickly disappeared. A Gripper (minute) later, they unleashed a torrent of water washing all concerned downriver into a vast cave complex.

We have no direct memory of any events leading up to our escape from the cave complex, only that we managed to survive. When we emerged from wherever we had been, we were greeted by the two dogs speaking Grippish and acting as though they had saved us.

Sadly, our Biologist is missing and is now presumed dead. When Grist was informed, he quickly decided to continue on, saying he didn't want to waste time searching for him.

From the numerous obstacles, strange illusions, and bizarre events that continue to unfold, there is little hope any of us will survive this mission. It is now becoming more and more apparent that Grist is losing control of his senses and represents a real danger to the success of the mission as well as to all remaining team members. *End of Top Secret Report.*

PART EIGHT

The Unraveling

B ABBLE QUICKLY PACKED UP HER EQUIPMENT as the Gripp team rose to their feet, awakened by the gruff, staccato voice of Grist commanding, "Prepare your gear! Break camp! Thirty Grippings before departure! No time to lose!"

Fabius and Filloloper were also jarred awake by Grist's harsh commands. "They're always rushing," observed Filloloper. "These strangers act as though they know where they are going. The truth is they have lost their way!"

"Unless they are making explicit maps of their explorations." responded Fabius, well aware that military maps were crucial to his success as a Commander in his past life. "It's hard to imagine how they will find their way back to the island before the Eye of Time closes."

Grind, the anthropologist, was moving far slower than the others. She was staring into the smoldering campfire when she caught sight of Grimm walking nearby.

"Grimm! I want to talk to you!" called Grind who was visibly shaking. She whispered with a quivering voice and a worried expression, "Grimm! I need your help! I saw something strange, very strange!" She looked around to be certain no one was listening. "You're a psychologist, Grimm.

You know how to analyze information, all types of information. Isn't that why you're here? Aren't you supposed to help sort out what's real from what's unreal?"

Grimm smiled weakly and looked directly into Grind's gray-green eyes and answered reassuringly, "I'm sure that whatever it is, there is no need to worry. You're just tired."

"You're not listening," continued Grind, gesturing with her hands. "I've seen strange visions! I awoke and found myself in a many-sided, glass house. A large bird was pecking at the windows. It was trying to break in and attack me!"

"It was probably a dream...a nightmare," counseled Grimm, looking at the archaeologist, whose short, dark brown hair was hanging around her face like a shredded curtain, and her left eye was starting to twitch spasmodically as she continued gazing blankly into the smoke rising from the campfire.

Grind suddenly looked up and spoke in a desperate tone of voice, "It was real! I know it was real! I tried to run! I tried to escape! But I was paralyzed! And this giant bird kept watching me from every angle of the house. It was glaring at me through those windows, waiting to attack!"

"You've had a terrible dream, nothing more," declared Grimm, trying to be patient, but feeling unsympathetic to Grind's dramatic behavior. "You're under a lot of stress from all that has happened since we arrived here. It's been a long journey, and it affects each of us in different ways.

Grind shook her head and replied, "You don't understand! There's a problem here! You are the psychologist, Grimm. Can't you see what's going on? Something terrible happened at Crystal Falls, and we don't know what it was! We can't remember!"

"We'll talk about this later, Grind," said Grimm, shrugging her shoulders as she turned away from the disturbed archeologist to prepare for departure.

Grimm began packing for the long hike ahead, but she stopped abruptly as her mind flashed back to Grind. She knew that something was wrong. Few Gripps had ever displayed such intense anguish and frustration, nor did they usually seek help from her as a psychologist.

An uneasy feeling moved over Grimm as she remembered the depth of emotion displayed by Grind when she described her strange dream in great detail. Her upset and fearful reaction were unusually extreme.

More importantly, she wondered about her own unprofessional behavior. Why, as a trained psychologist, did she immediately dismiss Grind's traumatic dream as if it were meaningless?

What could those images about being trapped in a house of glass mean? Why did she show no sympathy when Grind was desperately seeking answers? Was there a hidden meaning locked away in that dream?

In Grippland, any emotional response was considered a weakness. All Gripps were trained not to show emotion since displaying your feelings could ultimately lead to chaos, thus disrupting the perfected logic of the Gripp mind and the organized structure of society.

Psychologist Grimm knew Grind was a well-educated anthropologist who had studied hundreds of forbidden books and was probably more knowledgeable and possibly even more intelligent than most of her peers. What could she have encountered in that cave complex to unbalance her Gripp logic? *Perhaps, everyone has been changed in some unknown manner*, she thought.

A moment later, she was disturbed to catch a fleeting, refracted image of a large fish in her mind's eye. It appeared to be a type of reflection, as if it was bouncing off a mirror or perhaps a multi-faceted crystal. Could this strange vision be similar to the glass house Grind was describing? She wondered if this was the beginning of the team's unraveling.

GRIMM'S REVERIE

Grimm watched in silence as her fellow team members prepared their equipment for the long march ahead. Their faces portrayed the heavy psychological burdens they had experienced during the expedition.

There would be little time for conjecture or remorse regarding their current state of mind as each had a mission to complete. Even though it had been only a few Grabbons since their arrival, it was obvious that their encounter with this *very intelligent wilderness* was becoming far more demanding than they could ever imagine.

Grimm sat down on her Gripp-pack and took a moment to reflect upon their journey. Her mind became flooded with images from her past when she was more than capable of helping all those who had desperately sought out her advice and counsel.

So, here we are and here I am, she thought. *I am the one they know as Grimm. It seems as though they have called me Grimm for such a very long time that I can barely remember when it all began.*

Grimm was remembering: In the past, I had another view of my reality—a far more optimistic view. I would have preferred to call myself Glow, because once upon a time, I really was in the know. She laughed at the current absurdity of that outdated notion.

When High Command created the concept of what they called *The New Order* for the greater benefit of all, they also eliminated my ability to help my fellow Gripps.

My words were censored and my thoughts were monitored by the *Thought Police*. Even if I were to escape their oversight, there always were the *Thought Stalkers* who would quickly turn me in for *Reward Grippars* (money). My outlook became dim; and soon thereafter, I became known as Grimm.

So, now in this current Gripper (minute) of my reality, here in this bizarre unknown land, I can only look back and know that I tried. I was a very successful psychologist, dedicated to rescuing as many lost souls as I could, attempting to save all those who were suffering under the *New Orders of Control* from High Command.

What did High Command know besides control? What, indeed, would they be able to control here in this land of Acronos where trees want to say "Hello," and you are supposed to knock at some invisible door before entering a forest's private domain?

How does the invisible become visible? she wondered. Is it when thoughts and words begin to manifest our reality? High Command knows about words, especially inspiring words that empower individual expression, such as creativity, hope and aspiration — the forbidden words.

Grimm smiled as she reflected back upon the very moment she became an undeclared and secret revolutionary against High Command's twisted and distorted view of the *Greater Order of Grippland.*

It was one ordinary Grabbon (day) when suddenly the golden rays of the sun broke through the heavy, grey pollution normally hanging over Grippland, revealing a beautiful patch of blue sky. That singular moment of inspiration awakened me from the hypnosis of Gripp speak.

That was the patch of blue I needed to heal myself and my fellow Gripps. I knew that if I could just transform the feeling of seeing that patch of blue into healing words, words which could open their hearts and minds, I just might be able to help them change their lives.

Grimm glanced around the campsite and watched her teammates sitting patiently, awaiting their orders.

Orders, indeed! She thought. How could I save souls or redeem anyone's life by imploring them to follow orders? That's a laugh!

Oh, I just used the word *laugh,* implying joy and spontaneous self-expression! No wonder I was imprisoned for using forbidden words....*Museum Words.* Words such as *honor, dignity, gallantry, trust, harmony, hope, joy* and *love* were certainly treasonous and forbidden to be spoken out loud or written.

Yes, all those words are now quietly resting upon the walls of the *Word Museum* with detailed explanations regarding why independent thoughts leading to dreams are destructive to the Greater Order of Grippland.

Soon after initiating the *Greater Order*, High Command began to secretly monitor our conversations through all Gripp-Com. Only much later were we told that the rule would be: "No expectation of privacy can be assumed." Every word was recorded, and everything you said could and would be used against you.

No wonder those poor souls are looking and feeling old much faster than normal. What do they have to look forward to? More orders to follow? More surveillance? More confinement within our own minds, fearful of the *Thought Stalkers* constantly seeking their rewards?

Hidden away were all the concepts that had once helped the Gripps' dream of a brighter future, and the loss of those ideas had created mass depression, increased use of drugs, and suicides.

But the changes didn't stop there. The leaders of our *Great Society* then confiscated all the books, denigrated and banned classical and harmonic music and all uplifting songs about love and romance.

Walks in the forest, gardening, cooking, child-rearing, conversing face-to-face with other Gripps were all replaced by some sort of computer or other *technological advancements*. Gripp-coms and other digital equipment replaced all forms of communication. No one took the time to interact with others or to commune with nature.

High Command proceeded to tear down beautiful buildings and monuments while applauding ugliness, distortion, and war. The physical arts, music, and film focused on chaos and death. The opposing, independent thinkers were silenced. And then High Command systematically rewrote history!

My assignment was to convince the disturbed citizens to forget who they were and who they might want to become. The slogan of Greater Grippland was that each Gripp must be ready to "*Grab on with their hands, Grasp with their minds, Grip with their eyes, and Grind on until they captured the prize!*" for the benefit of all Grippland.

So, here I am lost in this unknown land looking for the Secret of Un-Old-Age with two dogs who for some unknown reason speak fluent Grippish along with nine other criminals whom I call my teammates.

Yes, I am Grimm, and I paid the price for treason against *The Greater Order,* in whatever way they chose to interpret their *Order* on any given day. Prosecuted as a revolutionary, I have no shame for trying to help others.

As for my fellow team members, their names were also chosen to appropriately describe their unique personalities and life experiences.

There is Grist, the Commander. He lives up to the description of his name: a hardened substance used for grinding. He's tough, unrelenting, impersonal, calculating and obsessed with his obsession. The *Quest for Glory* has blinded him! And victory, any victory is what fuels his very reason for existence!

It was an event in one of the Gripp wars that landed Grist in prison. Against orders from High Command, he refused to fall back to a more defensible position. The word retreat was not in Grist's vocabulary. He pushed on, deep into enemy territory, without sufficient back-up. He won the battle, but unfortunately paid the ultimate price in both men and materiel.

Is he mad? Is he psychologically disturbed? Aren't all Gripps disturbed? Indeed, Grist is #1 on this mission for a reason. Yes, for a very, very good reason!

Then there is Twist, the Politician, who became #2 for reasons utterly unknown to me! As a student of the mind, I would find it impossible to help him regain his mental balance and well-being, knowing full well that his entire life has been a virtual lie. Twisting facts and inventing the truth along the way has been his endless game, and thus he was given Twist for his name.

I believe his prison sentence was far too short since he was sent away for the treachery he perpetrated on innocent Gripps who desperately wanted to believe in the impossible. Apparently, High Command thought he was valuable enough to rank him as #2 on this mission, hoping his trickery would give him the edge in any negotiations, *if,* by chance, we were to find civilization in this forsaken land.

I believe he even twisted his way around High Command, promising them the impossible as well. But then again, it is easy for Twist to distort the truth, because, frankly, I don't think he knows the difference.

Naturally, it's important to review Scheme, ranked #3 in the mission. He committed fraud on multiple counts and was sentenced to ten Grinds (years) in prison, but was granted volunteer status when he persuaded High Command of his invaluable talents of persuasion.

He claims that he is a businessman, but the truth is he a just a very busy man who is continuously working on deals to satisfy his obsessive greed and his calculating mind.

High Command obviously fell under the spell of his devious schemes, woven with words, and selling dreams of mission success. Scheme is a master at manipulating others and convincing his targets to suspend logic so he can gain control over them.

How could I possibly work my way through his never-ending world of make-believe?

Of course, we must mention Babble, the Publicist, ranking as #4 on this mission. She is a fascinating study from a psychological point of view. The question is how could anyone ever begin to unravel the constant stream of words flowing out of her mouth? She continuously babbles on and on like a brook bubbling its way downstream. I would never have enough time to help her unravel all those conflicting thoughts.

She lives in a maze of words like the rest of us. However, she just may be using her jumble of words to hide the fact that she is brilliant. For some reason, she was imprisoned for a far lesser crime than all the others, being sentenced to five Grinds (years) for the theft of High Command secret documents. I believe she received volunteer status because she is intelligent and healthy.

There is a mystery, however, as to why Babble would receive the rank of #4. I believe she is hiding something and that her membership on this team involves far more than just recording mission notes!

Stare, the engineer is not a complicated study. He is socially stunted, blunted, and entirely unaware of himself and others. I understand his importance to our mission's success, and perhaps, his rank as #5 may be justified, if and when we encounter an advanced civilization.

He did receive a very long prison sentence due to his involvement in the power plant explosion, but he was granted volunteer status since there were no other engineers imprisoned at the time.

Stare is obsessed with Time, and it is only logical that he should be the *Keeper of the Tock*. His constant staring into instruments of various descriptions seems to be another reason that Stare became his name.

I could say his logic has destroyed any chance that he might lead a normal life; as if any Gripp could ever lead a normal life! From the perspective of those ranked above him, Stare is the most trustworthy since he has dedicated his entire life to science and usually doesn't think in terms of trickery or deceit. There might be hope for him if he became aware that he is not a machine.

Grimm hesitated for a moment. Her inner dialogue was interrupted by a loud snap as Stare walked by while gathering his gear for departure. He paid no attention to Grimm who was sitting quietly, reviewing the team.

These are supposed to be the best choices for the team, she thought, *but the best hasn't gotten us very far.* How could it? The secret of Un-Old-Age seems to have eluded us in this endless "Natural Environment."

None of us could have imagined being stranded in a vast wilderness with no population or advanced civilization to offer any clues as to why we have become the way we are — a technologically advanced society on the brink of extinction. And yet, here we are continuing to grind on!

And then, there is the notorious Dr. Grouse, the medical doctor and researcher, who appears to be much older than her thirty-five Grinds (years). She probably aged due to the stress she encountered during her trial for treason and subsequent imprisonment. Yet, there is an inner strength to Grouse that is imperceptible to most.

She is a survivor who would be invaluable to any mission. If only there were an opportunity for us to use her skills to help unravel the mystery of our quest!

Yes, yes, the accomplished Dr. Grouse, is a brilliant medical researcher whose career was cut far too short. High Command arrested Grouse when her research company was shut down for fraud after being found guilty of perpetrating false claims regarding a youth-enhancing serum.

She tried to blame it on the rats! Those poor laboratory rats always do seem to get the blame when things go wrong, and they did go very wrong!

The lab technicians had tried a variety of combinations of drugs and other concoctions, and their last effort seemed to work for nearly one Grind (year). And then it didn't work at all. That was the end of the laboratory rats, and also the end of Dr. Grouse who was sentenced to ten Grinds to Grasp (life).

And who can forget #7, Grubb, the biologist, who is no longer with us **and the enigma called Gritt, #8**, the geologist. He is difficult to read and his background is a mystery.

It's true that High Command decreed that my mission statement was to "Ensure the mental health and welfare of the team to guarantee our best efforts to succeed."

Why did I volunteer for this impossible quest? I wonder. Probably for the same reason as the others. Hope! But we don't call it *hope* any longer. Now, it is: *Mission Objectives* written into *Mission Statements*.

The concept of hope and optimism has nothing to do with our quest...at least not for now. Those are museum words!

So, here we are. Volunteers, one and all, still racing against the *Tick of the Tock*!

Grimm returned to the moment and stared out at the sunrise coloring the sky in hues of soft gold and rose, as she remembered her original question: *Is this the beginning of the team's unraveling?*

The answer to her question became more apparent as she observed Twist and Scheme standing nearby, locked in a heated argument. Moving closer, Grimm overheard them accusing one another of trickery, deceit, and fraud (usually considered to be necessary traits in Gripp society). But this was different. The argument was personal.

Scheme was speaking. "You promised that this trip through the portal was going to be easy, Twist! You told me to volunteer, saying that you would use all your political skills and experience to take advantage of any civilization that we might find. Meanwhile, I would be able to exploit the citizens for substantial profits!"

Twist did not respond immediately. Instead, he turned around slowly, gazing out at the landscape that revealed nothing but forests and rocky trails leading somewhere, and yet apparently to nowhere.

"How can I respond to you, Scheme? You are obviously only concerned with making profits and are unaware that we are lost...hopelessly lost! And yet, we are continuing to follow this deranged leader who is only seeking to gain personal triumph and glory!"

Grimm's suspicions were validated. Apparently, the mental unraveling of the Gripp team had already begun. It would only be a matter of time before their chaotic emotions would prove dangerous to all concerned.

PART NINE

Lost Between Worlds

I T SEEMED TO BE CALLING HIM from a distance, almost like a voice in a dream. The sound continued on and on, repeating over and over again, calling his name.

But it wasn't a dream. He was lost between worlds… the worlds of the conscious and unconscious. That distant voice, echoing in his mind, was not calling with words, but with the rumble and roar of cascading water. It was the strong and powerful voice of Crystal Falls.

Barely alive in an underground world, Grubb wasn't aware that his body had been battered, beaten, and overpowered by the tremendous forces of the raging torrent. He had been swept against boulders and hurled over the falls until the river ultimately deposited him beneath a craggy outcropping of rocks. He was unconscious, resting against dark green moss growing at the water's edge. The soft cushion of the moss had truly saved his life.

The choppy current of the underground river was shaking him like a boat in a turbulent sea. Eventually, he awakened and became aware of his very painful body.

Grubb was of average Gripp height with a round face and a strong and vigorous body. He had always enjoyed exploring, hiking, and collecting various plant specimens in Grippland, but that was before the environment changed. The flowers, trees, and crops disappeared in the extreme weather conditions and the ever-increasing air, water, and ground pollution.

That was then and this is now, he thought, struggling to gain his footing against the force of the current. He crawled on his hands and knees to reach a rocky ledge located just above the fast-moving stream and found himself in the midst of what appeared to be a narrow cavern.

Looking down at the underground, grey-green river, he saw the faintest rays of golden light illuminating a narrow ledge that he could follow. He breathed a sigh of relief. *I am alive,* he thought, *at least for the moment.*

Yes, Grubb was bruised, but not broken. He would walk or crawl if necessary. After all, he was a Gripp. He could grab on, grip on, and grind on because that was his way!

Peering into the depths of the cavern, he noticed that the ceiling was becoming taller, allowing him to stand erect. Supporting himself against the boulders on the shoreline, he managed to move further into the cave. After only a few yards, he felt his head spinning, and he fell to the ground. Anxiously, he touched his forehead and discovered he was bleeding.

Grubb instinctively reached for his Gripp survival belt and was relieved to discover it was still securely fastened around his waist. He reached inside the medical kit, located the bandages, and wrapped his head to cover the wound.

Dizzy and disorientated and barely able to walk, he realized that he must have been knocked unconscious. He paused for a moment to regain his balance and thought, *I know it's important to rest, but there's no time to stop. I need to find my team."*

The light in the cave was growing dimmer, indicating nightfall, and Grubb knew that if he could find his way out of this cave complex, it would need to be now, not later.

As he pushed himself forward, slowly walking along the shoreline of the now placid stream, a bizarre image was moving around in his head. In his mind's eye, he saw his fellow teammates desperately calling for help.

They were struggling to survive the fast-moving river that swept them against a large grouping of towering, pure white crystals rising at different angles from the floor of the cave.

He tried to clear his mind of the vision, but instead he heard his teammates crying out, calling his name, "Grubb, help us! Come and help us!" Grubb could not block out the images any longer. He finally remembered that when the current was carrying him deeper into the cave, he had turned and witnessed his team members disappearing into the very center of those giant crystals.

That couldn't be! It's all a surreal illusion; a terrible dream turned into a nightmare, he thought, attempting to push away all the shocking images and bizarre recollections of shouts and screams for help. But he could still hear them. They continued echoing louder and louder in his head, haunting him.

None of this could be a reality, he thought, but the pain was moving around and through his aching muscles giving testimony to the fact that at least his body was real. In fact, all that he remembered, and all that was yet to come, would be far more surprising than he could ever imagine.

SURPRISES IN THE UNDER-EARTH

As the cave widened, Grubb entered a large, cavernous room with an opening in the ceiling allowing the late afternoon sunlight to filter through, lighting his way. He paused for a precious moment to gaze at the grandeur of nature.

There were no longer any churches or temples in Grippland, but Grubb had seen pictures of such places in old magazines from the past. The immensity of this domed cavern resembled those ancient, majestic, inspirational cathedrals with stained glass windows.

The peacefulness of the room and the pain in his aching body were urging him to lay down, close his eyes and sleep, but he knew it was essential to keep moving.

The last rays of filtered light streamed through the cave opening, and Grubb began to panic, realizing it would soon be dark. He hurried forward, at first unaware that the ground was soft and starting to shift beneath his feet.

Before he could change his position or grab onto anything to catch his fall, he fell through an opening in the cave floor, turning over and over as he tumbled past rocky cliffs on either side, and then even further down, and further down after that.

He landed with a thud and found himself sprawled out on a spongy bed of moss in a dark, cavernous hole. Miraculously, he had survived, but just barely.

He moved his arms and legs and stretched his back to be certain he wasn't injured. Before he could reach for the small flashlight strapped to his belt, he heard a voice echoing around him.

"Welcome to the Under-Earth, beneath the land and sea. Know that you are no longer alone. I hope you will enjoy our hospitality." The words seemed to be coming from far away, and yet they sounded so very near, echoing on a dense current of humid air in the depths of the cave.

One of Grubb's worst fears had come upon him. He was unable to see anything or anyone in the total darkness. *Who can that be?* He wondered, rubbing his forehead, trying to release his confusion while pressing himself tightly into a narrow crevice in the cold, wet cave wall.

"Please, please do not be fearful. We are your hosts," droned the deep, resonant voice. "The Grundells are we…Stumble, Bumble, Tumble, and Wise. And, indeed, who may you be?" The voice was louder and coming closer.

A strange, musky smell filled the air as Grubb heard a shuffling sound on the stone floor.

They are getting nearer, and there's nowhere to run! he thought as fear and panic overcame him. He felt a rush of adrenaline moving through his body; his heart was racing, and he gasped for air.

The Grundell cleared his throat, and in a melodious voice stated, "An extremely, strange creature you are, indeed, to have fallen so far…so very far into the underflow."

Grubb did not reply. Slowly, he adjusted to the limited light and could see that there was only an eight-foot-wide ledge supporting him above a treacherously deep canyon.

Staring into the semi-darkness in disbelief, he tried to focus on the mysterious creatures emerging from the shadows into the soft, filtered light.

There before him were four mammoth animals who looked like giant, furry opossums standing on their hind legs and wearing yellow vests over thick, gray fur. Large, slanted, black eyes stared at him from narrow, white faces with long, protruding black snouts and bulbous black noses continuously sniffing the air.

The strange beasts shuffled closer to Grubb who shrank back against the wall. The largest said, "Welcome. We are the Grundells. I am Grundell Wise," stated the bizarre creature as he stared at Grubb. "Come now, who may you be?"

Grubb tried to control his thoughts and decided to reply with the standard Gripp protocol.

"I am #7 of the *Gripp Command Eye of Time Exploration Team* sent to retrieve information," said Grubb, and then he abruptly stopped speaking. It was important not to reveal too much about the mission.

"Indeed, and it appears that you are now alone in your quest, eh?" suggested Wise, leaning over the fearful Gripp, trying to get a closer look at the disheveled stranger who was breathing heavily.

"And what exactly are you looking for that you would dare to tumble, stumble and bumble your way here into the underflow of energy?" Wise laughed with a deep, hollow tone, similar to the rumblings of the earth. "Are you seeking wisdom from the Wise?" He began to roar with laughter at his parody of Grundell names.

Grubb tightened his jaw and repeated, "I am #7 of the *Gripp Command Eye of Time Exploration Team*." His voice quivered. "We are on a q-q-quest."

"Yes, we are aware of your quest, and it is evident from your concerns that you know nothing about anything," answered Wise. "But we admire your ability to continue struggling on to gain your potential knowingness!" He tried to stifle his laughter and started coughing until his large body shook. He wiped the laughing tears from his face and continued, "So, then, let's take a look at you."

Tumble, Stumble, Bumble and Wise shuffled slowly around and in front of the trembling Gripp. Still fearful, but pretending bravery, Grubb rose to his full height, adjusted his helmet and brushed the dirt off his lapel, revealing the bright red number 7 and the team's official emblem.

"You are not here to hear, are you, #7?" inquired Stumble. "You are here to see what you can see, which I perceive is revealed in the insignia on your jacket. It is obviously your special *Eye of Time*."

Bumble approached Grubb cautiously, his long and narrow head was continuously bobbing up and down as he viewed the stranger more intently and asked, "To know the flow of time…is that your seeking?"

"Well, no, I mean yes, I mean, well, not exactly…"

"Perhaps that is your problem," pondered Tumble.

"I...I...uh, don't have a problem. I am a Botanist. I look for plants. I mean, I like plants and other growing things. It's the others. They are the ones seeking the Secret. I only came to see what there was and…" His voice trailed off as it became clear to him that he was entirely alone in the darkness with the strangest creatures he could ever imagine.

"Indeed, you might find us strange," said Wise, seeming to read Grubb's mind. "But understand that we are the keepers of the underflow where energy begets energy, which moves in and out and into time, beyond time, and then back again. You just might think of it as magnetic magic!" he exclaimed, chuckling to himself.

"Do you know about such things?" asked Tumble.

"I am Gripp Grubb, #7. I am a Biologist seeking plants to use as medicine to hopefully slow the *Tick of the Tock*."

The Grundells laughed in unison, and asked, "*The Tick of the Tock*? And what be this ticking of which you speak?"

"Time...The time...the time! It's all about time moving away from us, taking us away!" Grubb's voice cracked. He felt desperate, realizing that he was making no sense at all.

"These unique plants and this *Ticking of a Tock*? This is your quest?" asked Stumble quietly.

"Well, yes. I mean, not exactly, but yes, probably yes!"

"Then let us see what we can see, #7," mused Stumble thoughtfully. "What is to see can be seen in time and beyond time. Now follow me."

PART TEN

Hedges of Hedora

F ILLOLOPER AND FABIUS FOLLOWED closely behind the nine remaining Gripp team members who were seeking some semblance of civilization. The weary travelers were desperate to validate their quest for the Secret of Un-Old-Age or at least to find Grold.

Gritt, the geologist, was lost in thought, reexamining the sequence of recent events since their arrival in Acronos that made no sense at all. *There are so many missing facts*, he thought. *This uncharted land is full of mysteries and surprises that make it impossible for us to calculate a successful outcome.*

It seemed to him that there were also underlying plots, intrigue, and treachery festering within the Gripp team. He wondered why neither he nor any of the others seemed to recall what happened after being swept into the Time Pool.

What happened to Grubb? Why didn't anyone discuss or even worry about his disappearance? How could he just evaporate without a trace?

Gritt could not stop the whirling flow of his inner dialogue as he searched for answers and considered possible motives. *Perhaps, for some reason, Commander Grist had disposed of Grubb*, he thought. *If so, any one of us could be next, anyone at all.*

As he mechanically followed the cadence of the Gripps, suddenly, someone or something slammed into his back, sending him stumbling off the pathway. He stopped himself from falling, recoiled instantly, whirled around and punched the attacker, knocking him to the ground.

To his surprise, he found himself looking down at Babble who quickly scrambled to her feet.

Gritt and Babble were both surprised, shaken, and suspicious of the other's actions. Admittedly, the hillside was not steep enough to cause him any severe damage if she had tried to knock him off the trail.

Staring into her eyes, he didn't see any anger or grievous intent. Instead, the corners of her mouth turned up, betraying a slight sense of amusement. "I'm sorry, I accidentally slipped on the trail and fell against you," explained Babble. "But you hit me hard."

"I didn't know it was you," answered Gritt apologetically, dusting the dirt off her jacket. "I hit you in self-defense. For a moment, I thought you might be the unknown attacker who was responsible for Grubb's disappearance. After all, a good Gripp is always vigilant and watchful of other Gripps, wouldn't you say?"

Babble's smile disappeared. "What do you mean?"

"Can I trust you with my thoughts?" he asked. "Can you keep a secret?" He moved closer and gently held her arm. He wanted to share his deepest concerns with her, but he also had been programmed not to divulge classified technical information to anyone.

He continued, "Perhaps you aren't allowed to keep secrets. You do work for High Command, don't you? You're the one writing the reports and noting all the events that happen to us. But then again, you were convicted of passing secrets, government secrets to the revolutionaries hiding in the mountains. Weren't you?"

Babble didn't answer as she rubbed her cheek, which had turned red from the hard punch from Gritt's large, half-Synth hands. She looked into his bright, blue-green eyes and thought: *There is something there. There's something unknown and intriguing behind those eyes.*

She instinctively knew that Gritt was different from the others. He was almost a head taller than most Gripps with a healthy physique and was good looking in a sculpted sort of way, and he was more considerate and refined than any Gripp she had ever known.

His features blended evenly into his face with a smooth forehead, high cheekbones and a pleasant mouth, which turned up slightly at the ends, unlike most Gripps' faces, which usually expressed anger or sadness.

But she also was aware that his criminal past was not available in any government documents she had researched. In fact, information about Gritt's history did not appear in the *Eye of Time Mission* reports. Gritt was listed merely as *The Geologist* with the necessary documented education and experience for the mission.

Babble turned to look at Gritt again, this time hoping to catch some inner reflection from any underlying thoughts hidden beneath his smooth exterior.

She took a long, deep breath before replying quietly, "Gripps don't trust. You know that, Gritt. Non-trust is the foundation of our Great Gripp society. We were taught to believe in no one and nothing, but instead, we are to follow orders and laws created for the *Greater Order.*"

Babble suddenly realized that her words were precisely parroting government propaganda. In fact, she heard herself repeating the state protocol that she had memorized to gain her position with the Exploration Team. It was the only way she could ever escape from her very lengthy prison sentence.

In reality, she didn't trust anyone, and certainly not someone as different as Gritt. She quickly pushed aside her feelings that might lead to a possible infatuation for this secretive team member.

He was apparently hiding something, she thought, but what? Everyone on the team certainly had a lengthy, criminal record, and yet Gritt had no history at all, or at least the information about his past had been eliminated by someone much higher up in High Command.

Gritt was looking out at the mountain scenery as Babble searched his face for clues to his true identity and wondered if he could be a partner to her, someone to share information and maybe more. She knew alliances were forming between other team members. Could this reclusive Gripp become her ally and share classified information that only she possessed?

Her role as a publicist was to write the official reports, but her unofficial assignment was to spy for High Command. Her job was to determine which Gripps were conspiring and what they might be hiding; and for those secretive efforts, she would earn amnesty and regain her freedom.

"We need to catch up with the others," said Babble as she turned her back on Gritt and hurried up the trail.

MEETING HEDORA

Babble and Gritt followed the trail around a large boulder and were bewildered to see that there was no longer a pathway.

The open view of the mountains that had existed moments before had disappeared. Three members of the Gripp team were staring at a barrier of tightly woven vines standing over fifteen-feet tall.

It was a massive, green wall of hedges—a beautiful, living tapestry of interwoven, evergreen branches, interspersed with red and gold foliage stretching out to the horizon. There was no visible way around this incredibly dense obstruction and little evidence as to how they might pass through it.

As Babble and Gritt approached the hedges, they heard Grimm mumbling barely audible words, as if she were trying to recall a memory or vision she did not want to comprehend.

"I am certain that I heard laughter," she said. "Not the kind of laughter you might expect in an amusing situation, but rather something like a chuckle that sounded like it was taunting or teasing us as we approached this wall."

Grimm's face tightened as her gray eyes focused intently on the hedges. "I am positive they were directly in front of us. I saw them. I know I saw them! They were right there. And then, I felt something, something strange. At least, I thought I did. And then they disappeared. They're gone!"

Babble and Gritt exchanged suspicious glances as Grimm continued. Her voice seemed much weaker than before, barely audible, more like a whisper. "All of them...gone."

"Who's gone?" demanded Babble. "What happened?"

Grimm did not respond. She knew her job was to be in charge of the mental health of the team members, and she should be the very last one to lose her grip on reality. Her mind was spinning out of control as she gazed at the massive green barrier, which appeared out of nowhere and had absorbed four of the Gripps without warning.

Doctor Grouse stepped forward. "I also heard the sound of laughter," she stated matter-of-factly. "And I saw a female face. At first, I wasn't certain, but now I am. The eyes were large, and the mouth...yes, those lips were tilted up at the ends, as if it was smiling."

Grind, the archaeologist, objected, "That is not what I saw, and that's not what I heard!" She was one of the three remaining Gripps who had witnessed the event. "There was a door, a tall, narrow door, and it opened into a very dark and seemingly endless corridor. Can't you remember? Just ahead of us on the trail were Grist, Twist, Scheme, and Stare. They stopped for a moment, a door opened, and they walked through it."

"And then what happened?" demanded Gritt, in a frustrated tone of voice. "Tell me what happened after that?"

"The door just closed behind them, and they...they were gone! They simply disappeared." Grind mumbled.

Babble glanced over at Gritt, hoping to catch his expression. She was puzzled by his showing far more concern than he'd ever done during the many unexplainable events they had previously experienced in Acronos.

"I remember now," replied Grimm, staring blankly at the immense barrier confronting them. "There was a door, a massive door. It opened and closed! Nothing more."

"That's ridiculous!" exclaimed Babble. "This is simply a hedge. Yes, it's a huge wall, but it's just a hedge. How could there be a door, and then no door?"

Gritt paced slowly back and forth, staring at Dr. Grouse, Grimm, and Grind and then again at the wall. "What you are saying, Grind, is that the leaders of our team walked through a doorway that opened in this wall, and the door closed behind them. Is that correct?"

"Yes, they all seemed to, well, just disappear," explained Grind with a strained expression on her face.

Gritt, as a Half-Synth with his advanced sensors, was very capable of gathering more information than the other Gripps. He had been specifically designed to survive any mission. Yet, for the first time, he began to feel something he had never experienced: a surge of adrenaline initiated by a response to fear and confusion, which he quickly managed to push aside.

Fabius and Filloloper had positioned themselves far enough away to witness the entire scene. They could see, but not be seen. They could speak and not be heard. They were in the midst of discussing if they should reveal what they knew about this grand, natural impediment with a unique name from ancient times: *The Hedges of Hedora.*

"The Gripps came to this location seeking a point of view," suggested Fabius. "Hedora is only helping them to find it. It's not up to us to reveal what we know."

"But, Fabius, they were looking for a physical not a psychological point of view," corrected Filloloper. "The team became lost, and they traveled to this higher location on the plateau to see what was ahead and to determine how far away they are from the Time Portal."

"I know," sighed Fabius. "Hedora is just doing what she loves to do. We can't help them make their choices."

Filloloper did not respond. While listening to Fabius, she was watching the scene unfolding. The five remaining team members were trying to decide what to do next. Although hearing only parts of their discussion, Filloloper knew that their logic would not help them find the missing members of the team.

It was essential for them to acknowledge the presence of Hedora who was again in the process of creating yet another surprise. There was a subtle shift of energy. A slight current of wind wafted past the living wall of green, creating a rustling sound as it moved along the hedges' broad expanse. A barely perceptible ripple of energy silently surrounded the Gripps as if someone or something was examining them.

A moment later, two large doors appeared in the wall of hedges. They were twice the height of an average Gripp and stood equidistant from each other.

"Hedora is teasing them again. What should we do?" implored Filloloper anxiously.

"She is offering them a passageway," Fabius replied nonchalantly as he casually rested on the grass.

"But you know they will be lost. They will never be able to find their way out of the maze of hedges without our help. They will be retracing the same steps and making the same mistakes. How can they learn to communicate with Hedora if we don't tell them who she is?"

Doctor Grouse was the first to see that Hedora was now presenting them with two choices. Only a few steps away were open doorways, new opportunities to explore. As a practical, medical doctor, Grouse, was fundamentally grounded in what was considered accepted reality.

She was now becoming more accustomed to the illusions of Acronos, and no longer believed that anything she witnessed was real. But, she sensed that these two doors were somehow beckoning her to enter.

The Gripps huddled together, discussing their choices, trying to arrive at a solution. They needed a logical plan of action. Unfortunately, the more they attempted to develop a strategy, the more complicated their choices seemed to be.

Ultimately, they agreed that no matter which door they chose, it would surely lead to another unknown destination.

Psychologist Grimm welcomed the opportunity to use her Gripp logic and was busy contemplating the phenomenon manifesting before them.

"I have studied the Gripp mind most of my life, and I am very aware of how we maneuver our way through events," explained Grimm. "I know that we can grab on with our hands. We can grasp using the power of our minds, and we know how to grind on to find a solution. Look around you, what do you see?"

Babble answered. "We see hedges, and we see doors and dark corridors twisting back and forth inside. And yet, our team members have disappeared in there. That's my response," she stated in exasperation while peering through one of the doorways into the depths of Hedora's mystery.

"It is undoubtedly a trap," she continued. "There is no reason to enter into any of these doors; and besides, and we should be aware by now that those two dogs are holding back what they know," she sighed, motioning in the direction of Fabius and Filloloper.

UNDERSTANDING HEDORA

Fabius did not have a chance to react. He could only stare in disbelief as Filloloper ran toward the Gripps at full speed. He closed his eyes as if not wanting to know the outcome, but he was not the only one startled by Filloloper's sudden action.

Gritt, the Half-Synth, also felt the shift in energy around him and watched Filloloper bolting toward them. He was able to observe far more than the others, and his extrasensory vision provided him with an entirely different image than that of the dog known as Filloloper.

The vision he perceived was a tall, toned, and strikingly beautiful young woman with a lovely face and long legs sprinting effortlessly. Her lean, bronzed arms rippled with muscles formed from carrying a heavy shield and sword into the heat of battle. She projected a powerful image of strength and beauty.

As she ran, Filloperna's green eyes became transfixed upon Grimm, whose face was contorted in anger. Filloloper, the dog, would not have understood such negative emotions, but as Princess Filloperna, she certainly knew animosity and jealousy all too well.

No Filloloper! Fabius called to her silently. *You mustn't reveal who you are!* His mind continued to swirl with thoughts of the *Before Time* and the hard-won battles that had propelled them to this land of peace and harmony.

But Fabius was not the only one concerned. Gritt, the half-synth, was now recording in his sensors the real image of Filloloper as the Warrior Princess, Filloperna, leader of her people from another time.

Gritt had seen her briefly before when he became aware of the past life image of Fabius. Awestruck by Filloperna's radiance and strength, Gritt was certain she was about to release the power of her words.

The female Gripps didn't notice Filloloper running toward them. Only Gritt saw Filloperna. The others perceived the dog, Filloloper.

She spoke to them as if every word were a powerful mantra, "Babble, you stated we are holding back information and not revealing information to you. How can we share what we know if you do not listen? How can you feel what we feel if you do not open your hearts to receive nature's wisdom?

"The Hedges of Hedora are a special manifestation from ancient times, and Hedora is offering you a choice," continued Filloloper. "She is giving you the opportunity to know and to experience trust by transforming the fear that lives within you.

"Fabius and I cannot hand you the information we know," she continued. "You must learn to trust entirely to understand the truth completely. Trust is one of the keys to living your life in harmony."

You must learn to trust entirely to understand the truth completely. Trust is one of the keys to living your life in harmony.

Fabius ran to her side, hoping to intervene and prevent the startled Gripps from directing their upset and confusion at Filloloper. Something had shifted in her. A dominant force of power and righteousness was now manifesting through her, revealing her true warrior nature.

Babble, Grouse, Grimm, and Grind glared menacingly at Filloloper. They were insulted by her words that rang so true. "You must learn to live in trust entirely to understand it completely." They felt offended by what appeared to be a dog speaking so forcefully to them.

Only Gritt remained composed. He continued to appreciate the striking image of Filloperna who was standing proudly in front of them, and he could feel a smile crossing his lips, a smile of knowingness and wonderment.

"Let her speak," suggested Gritt. "Let her say what she needs to say. After all, what do we Gripps have to fear from these animals?" He nodded at Fabius and silently conveyed the message, "*Don't worry, I will protect Filloloper.*"

Gritt continued, "After all, Filloloper is only a dog, and she's probably as lost as we are. We can never forget that we are Gripps. We have survived so much, and nothing can stop us now, certainly not a row of Hedges called Hedora."

Fabius was pleased that Gritt had successfully defused the situation. The four female Gripps quickly turned their attention to the phenomenon still confronting them: how could they rescue their team members from the depths of this twisted maze of dark green vines. Most certainly, they would not neglect their duty and dedication as the result of a few insulting words or a dog's bravado.

"We have no more time to lose. We can't play any more games," stated Grimm defiantly. "And we don't have the luxury of listening to more words from animals who obviously know nothing more than we do.

"The reality is that we must either walk around these hedges to find our way back to the time portal or attempt to rescue our team members by choosing one of the two doors standing before us." Grimm was using her best mental skills to increase the enthusiasm of the five lost explorers so they could actually make a critical decision. But, the others seemed even more confused.

Babble responded, "We are going nowhere to find that somewhere we left behind, but the truth is…time is not going to wait for us to find our way back to the portal."

"Babble is right," agreed Dr. Grouse. "I suggest we quickly choose one of these doors. It doesn't matter which door because somewhere within the Hedges of Hedora we will find our team members. In case you hadn't noticed, there is no way to maneuver around this never-ending maze!"

The others nodded final approval of their choice in unison. All except for Gritt who along with Fabius already knew that Hedora had changed her game during the time the Gripps were standing with their backs to the doors. Only Gritt and Fabius could see the two large doors leading into long, dark hallways of Hedora had now become one.

AN UNSUSPECTING ENCOUNTER

There was no further discussion among the Gripps as they cautiously entered the one remaining door Hedora offered to them. Once inside the corridor, they sensed a strange magnetic pull that was indescribable at first. The magnetic resonance was like a tone that one can feel, but not hear, and that force was beckoning them forward.

As they walked through the dim, shadowy, long and narrow hallway with towering hedgerows on either side, Dr. Grouse suggested they needed a strategy to overcome this living maze of green walls woven with branches.

It was impossible to determine how thick or dense the walls might be; but it was evident that no matter the size of the hedges, it would be unreasonable to think they could cut through them. Even if they were successful in burrowing through one row, there was no way to determine what would be beyond the first or even the second or third rows they might encounter.

The dogs walked a short distance behind the others while listening to Hedora's quiet and amusing whispers. Fabius' thoughts were elsewhere. He remembered there had been no discussion about Filloloper's confrontation with the Gripps.

He sent a silent transfer of thoughts to her, expressing his admiration for her bravery and the power of her words. She smiled when she heard him congratulate her for helping the explorers understand that they were paralyzed by their inability to decide, and her actions had ultimately prompted them to move forward.

The path was straight and narrow through the hedges, and it was impossible to determine what lay ahead. Only muffled tones, sounding like distant words could be heard. The Gripps stopped abruptly, waiting for Filloloper and Fabius to catch up to them. They wore expressions of anxiety, worry and frustration.

"How much further do we need to go?" Babble asked. "How long must we wait before we can find our missing team members? Is there a secret behind this unending maze?"

"There is no secret to Hedora," responded Fabius. "She only wants to play."

His words turned Grimm's face even grimmer. She peered down the seemingly unending corridor of hedges without any curves or openings. "What do you mean, she only wants to play? Don't you understand that she is stealing our time...our precious time? We have no time to waste on games. I think you know where the others are! I demand to know what has happened to the leaders of our team!"

"Don't be concerned, Grimm," interrupted Gritt with a conciliatory expression on his face. "I don't believe these dogs know any more than we do."

Grimm looked at Gritt suspiciously and wondered if he was trying to protect the dogs, but she answered politely, "I understand what you're saying, Gritt. Yes, I suppose you're right. We all came up the hill together. They could not know what happened to the other Gripps." She looked down the unending row of hedges and thought to herself, *There are games being played in Acronos, and Hedora isn't the only one playing them.*

Fabius was also beginning to wonder what had happened to Grist, Twist, Scheme and Stare. Had they willingly entered the hedges to satisfy their curiosity? Or were they chasing something or someone they had seen moving inside?

At that moment, a voice could be heard rhyming a message that rippled through the corridors of the hedges

> *Better to know than not to know.*
> *Better to run and follow the flow.*
> *Better to listen beyond confusion,*
> *following your feelings, not delusion.*
>
> *Moving beyond the mental mind*
> *that only knows what is defined,*
> *you are looking for a future,*
> *you will perhaps never find.*

The startled team stopped, and the voice repeated:

Better to know than not to know.
Better to run and follow the flow.

Just as quickly as it had begun, the voice stopped. Fabius and Filloloper now knew their friend, Phelan, was ready to help them whenever they called.

CLOSED DOORS OF THE MIND

Something is not right, thought Fabius. He wondered why Hedora hadn't offered any choices. Where were all the twists and turns this mysterious being usually presented to them when they came to play?

He soon began to comprehend that the time travelers could not feel Hedora even though Hedora could sense them. It was apparent that she was not offering any choices because they had no idea who, what or where she is, and most importantly: *when* she is. Suddenly, the corridor came to an abrupt end.

"So this is the finale'!" declared Grimm. "This is the end of the road! And now we need to hurry back…back to where we entered the hedges and set up camp outside the perimeter of Hedora."

As she spoke, Grimm and the others had not bothered to turn around, but when they did so, they found Hedora had other ideas. Only a short distance behind them she had manifested another wall. They were expertly trapped in a single room, caged within a living maze of green.

Babble turned around and around, moving her hands up and down and across the hedges. Exhausted, she slumped to her knees and started banging against the vines with her fists. Tears filled her eyes, as she cried out, "You know we are trapped, Hedora, why can't you just open a door? I'm waiting for a door...any door!"

Babble did not have to wait long for a response. Within an instant, she was no longer beating against Hedora's Hedges. Instead, her arms were flailing in the air. Hedora had instantly granted her wish.

There before her was an expansive door that opened into a large, circular room. The others watched in amazement as Babble silently walked through the open doorway asking, "Why? Why did she at last offer me a door?"

Filloloper followed Babble into the room and replied, "You acknowledged her existence. You touched Hedora with emotion. She was always waiting... waiting for you to say, 'Hello.' She wanted you to contact her from the first moment you encountered her outside the perimeter, but you never even tried."

"And what about our missing team members? What happened to them? Why did they disappear?"

"We may never know," answered Fabius who had entered the room. "However, I am certain that no one can command Hedora. She will do what she wants, and it is essential for you to listen. She likes to whisper, you know," he commented, looking directly into Babble's eyes. Her expression displayed confusion and wonderment.

Grimm spoke in a hushed tone of voice, "I can hear something moving, but I can't see what it is. Suddenly, the rustling sound in the corridor ceased, and the same staccato voice spoke in rhyme:

> *Lost far from home in another dimension,*
> *seeking time beyond comprehension,*
> *never viewing valuable clues to be seen*

or sensing what lies behind the scene.

Crashing through time and space,
escaping the 'Tick of the Tock' is their race,
not knowing that energy lost can be found
when the mental mind is clearly unbound.
Inner guidance flows and always knows
when you truly trust what intuition shows.

Fabius and Filloloper nodded to each other knowingly, aware that Phelan was warning them not to hesitate.

Babble stared into the distance and said, I have no idea what that voice is saying. What does it all mean?"

"Well, the meaning is evidently not what it seems! Is it? I don't believe any of this is real," said Grimm in a tired and frustrated voice.

"This is all very real!" exclaimed Fabius. "If Hedora were not a reality, you would have been on your way by now! You would be with the other members of your team."

"Whether it is real or unreal, it doesn't matter. The truth is that we will find a way out even if we have to hack our way through these hedges," Grimm responded angrily.

"You don't have to do that!" exclaimed Filloloper. "The one known as Hedora always offers two doors, one to enter and one to exit. She doesn't want to trap you. She only wants you to listen."

"Hedora wants us to listen? Listen to what? I don't hear a thing. I don't hear anything at all. Does anyone hear anything? Anything...?" ranted Doctor Grouse.

"This is nonsense," added Grind, disgusted by all the arguing. "It's obvious that these two dogs are here for a reason. They have been guiding us, so they say, but to where?"

Trapped in a circular room within living walls, Babble, Grouse, Grimm and Grind were seething with anger and frustration. They became lost in a sea of words—words of blame and accusations of trickery.

Fabius and Filloloper were the only ones aware that slowly and mysteriously twelve equally spaced portals were opening around the room. Hedora was offering them their hearts' desire. There were now multiple doorways through which they could escape to freedom.

Gritt glanced up and was the first of the five to become aware that their prison of hedges was transforming.

Dr. Grouse's face turned crimson with embarrassment over her outburst. She remained silent, waiting for any of the others to offer their opinion.

"Hedora now wants you to make a choice," suggested Fabius. "She knows that you are aware of her presence, and she is offering the opportunity for you to show her what you may have learned thus far in the game."

The team's bluster turned into confusion when it became apparent that Hedora was presenting them with yet another unusual challenge. Here was an opponent they could neither see, feel, or sense, and the irony was that repeatedly they were paralyzed by indecision. This time there were twelve choices confronting them, and they acted as though they had no options at all!

"Perhaps each of you might choose a door, and the one who successfully makes it out of Hedora can return to lead the others to their freedom," offered Filloloper.

Babble started chuckling to herself hysterically until Gritt gently shook her to stop. "Don't you see? We are all going to die here!" she exclaimed. "We only know how to obey. We don't know how to make spontaneous decisions. We are going to be lost in here forever!"

Grind had been silently observing the events within the maze. She stepped forward and offered her opinion. "There were legends about formations such as these...circular walls with doors. Ancient mythologies tell about strange powers and rituals and even more incredible energies. They described a kind of consciousness inhabiting a structure, forming its size and shape."

Babble, Grouse, Gritt, and Grimm gasped at such a wildly bizarre concept. They turned in unison to stare at Fabius and Filloloper, appearing to plead for help.

Help came in another form.

It arrived with a blur of feathers and the staccato sound of chanting words that were becoming very familiar to the beleaguered captives of Hedora.

Babble was the first to catch a glimpse of what she thought was an unusual presence standing in one of the corridors. She was almost positive something was there, but then again, maybe not. She remembered feeling a strange vibration when they had first entered the hedges, and since then her thoughts were no longer her own. In fact, the ideas floating through her mind were very unsettling.

Could it be true that an unseen consciousness manifested these hedges? Is it possible that a living awareness created this massive structure? *From where do those ideas come?* She questioned, fearing that she was the first of her team to slip her grip on reality.

A feeling swept over Babble as she sensed something moving from one corridor to another. But how could that be? Were doors being created as it traveled through the vines? All she remembered was seeing something whiz past her.

What's happening? She wondered, rubbing her forehead. Her logical mind no longer seemed to be gripping on to what she was experiencing. For the first time in her life, she was sensing the unknown, rather than just being aware of words flowing through her mind. *I am certain there is a presence here,* she thought. *I'm beginning to feel it.*

The first blast seemed very far away. It came only as a concussion of sound rippling through Hedora's thick walls. The second and third bursts seemed much closer, and then the explosions stopped altogether.

"Did you hear that?" asked Grimm, breathing heavily.

No one responded. Instead, the Gripps fixated on a glimpse of feathers and the words that followed:

> *Moving through closed doors of the mind,*
> *neither blocked nor stopped...freedom I find.*
> *Following only the sense sensations,*
> *doors open quickly without hesitation.*

"It's Phelan," Filloloper whispered to Fabius. "What do you think he is doing?"

"He's doing what Phelan does best...what he always loves to do, which is to be aware of everything that is going on in Acronos," Fabius replied in a hushed tone of voice, They listened as Phelan continued his rhythmic song:

> *Here, there, and everywhere,*
> *seeking and finding…no need to prepare.*
> *Running sideways to my destinations,*
> *I have no doubts nor calculations.*

Filloloper took a deep breath and sighed, "Phelan could be in grave danger if these explorers capture him."

"Those sounds we heard were blasts of real explosives," said Fabius. "I don't know if Phelan is trying to help or is simply escaping to save himself."

> *There is no real explanation*
> *of the mind's need for examination*
> *or the need to know the why of when,*
> *or why the when won't return again.*

Phelan happily finished his poem, knowing he spoke the phrases with clipped precision.

"He must be testing himself again," suggested Filloloper. "He's a master of the games of Hedora, always pushing his unique senses to the limit. He can twist, turn and stop in an instant and completely disappear in his camouflage. But he is playing a perilous game with these strangers."

Filloloper stopped talking and turned to look in the direction of strange chanting, growing louder and louder.

> *No matter where we go or how far,*
> *we always are the way we are!*

Fabius nodded in silent recognition. Phelan had, indeed, either by accident or by design, led the lost visitors to their exact location within the very heart of Hedora.

Grimm turned to Fabius and said in a surly voice, "I guess you heard what we heard. Our fellow team members are only a short distance away, and soon we will be gladly depart his nonsensical maze as though it never existed!"

It is always easier to believe that what you know is all you need to know, thought Fabius, shaking his head slightly back and forth. *Lessons learned are lessons earned,* he recalled looking back at his own experiences. *These strangers will eventually learn that they will never blast their way out of Hedora.*

It is always easier to believe that what you know is all you need to know. Lessons learned are lessons earned.

HEDORA IS NOT A PRISON

Gritt stared silently in the direction of the last blast, hoping to catch a glimpse of the team leaders who might soon emerge from Hedora's grasp. As a Half-Gripp he could see nothing, but as a Half-Synth, he sensed that the missing explorers were only a short distance away.

A pale gray, acrid, rolling cloud of smoke and dust from the last blast drifted overhead and lingered momentarily before dissipating into the bright blue sky above Acronos.

Filloloper could no longer contain her frustration with the stubborn explorers' refusal to learn. "You need to understand that Hedora is aware of you and is responding to your energy. She expects you to mirror her ability to sense and feel."

"You mean these plants know our thoughts and feelings?" asked Dr. Grouse, trying to understand such an outrageous concept. "Do you mean that these bushes will move when you give the command?"

"No, you cannot command Hedora, but you can move when she moves. All she requires is that you ask quietly and let her whisper back to you. It's a game we love to play when we visit Hedora."

"So, who is she? Why doesn't she show herself?"

"You can't see Hedora," answered Fabius. "I don't think you understand. Hedora is always present, even though it seems as if nothing is here. You can only hear, sense or feel Hedora by tapping into the flow of synchronicity. Then you can move with her effortlessly. It is all part of process of understanding and learning the Seven Harmonies."

"This makes no sense at all!?" snapped Grimm who could no longer tolerate such ridiculous ideas. "Grind, you've read all those forbidden books. What are these animals saying?"

"Well, yes, I think, I mean, I believe that I understand what they are trying to say," stammered Grind in reply. "What Fabius is saying is that you have to listen to the nothingness. And when that nothingness speaks back to you, it will tell you when to turn right or left or go straight ahead if you are willing to listen and trust in that nothingness." A satisfied grin appeared on Grind's face as she glanced over at Grimm for confirmation.

Psychologist Grimm closed her eyes as if she wanted to block out all that was happening.

Dr. Grouse was unnerved by the garbled nonsense of Grind's response, and yet, she tried to repeat the concepts she had heard. "What you seem to be saying is that we have to learn to listen to the nothingness, and then when you hear nothing speaking to you, you are to become aware of what that nothing has said? Is that what you mean?"

FOLLOWING INNER GUIDANCE

Fabius could no longer contain his amusement at the seriousness of Dr. Grouse's sarcastic analysis. "Hedora is not about 'hearing nothing,'" he explained. "We are talking about your learning to hear the quiet whispers beyond your conscious mind — listening to the subtle voice of Hedora. She will most willingly show you the right way to go or will indicate the right choice when you feel her presence."

"She will direct you effortlessly," enthused Filloloper. "We love to see how fast we can run through Hedora's Hedges! It's an adventure, a great game that we love to play, and Hedora loves to play it with us!"

The five Gripps were stunned into total silence as they thought about the unusual words: *joy, fun, and adventure.* They could not imagine that their upset and frustration might be someone else's enjoyment. After all, those "positive" words were forbidden long ago and locked away in the *Word Museum*.

"Who is Hedora really?" demanded Grimm, "Why does she refuse to show herself?"

"We thought you would understand what was happening," answered Fabius. "Hedora is not a person. Hedora is your Intuition. She is your inner guidance system."

Hedora isn't a person.
Hedora is your Intuition.
She is your inner guidance system.

"Are you saying that those whispers, which give you directions, are coming from somewhere inside your mind?" asked Grimm, bewildered by the concept of intuition and inner guidance.

Fabius was amazed at the Gripps' inability to understand or grasp the most basic of the Seven Harmonies. He immediately sent a silent communication to Filloloper, *We will need to rescue them from Hedora.*

Within moments, the circular room began shaking, and the five teammates gasped in astonishment and fear as the walls slowly started spinning around them as if they were in the center of a rotating wheel.

"There is no more time to wait!" called Fabius, and without hesitation, he moved to the center of the room, facing one of the twelve openings surrounding them.

"Follow close behind us," cautioned Fabius. "Move when we move, or if you prefer you can remain behind."

The Gripps exchanged quick glances, and blurted out in unison, "We will follow you!"

The dogs approached one of the doors and crouched low to the ground.

"Take a deep breath," suggested Filloloper.

The dogs closed their eyes and silently acknowledged the *Total Unity* that was continuously forming and reforming the barriers in Hedora's maze.

They readied themselves, and Fabius commanded, "Stay close behind us," "Do not hesitate! Run when we run! Turn when we turn! Understand?"

The five Gripps silently nodded their agreement and moved into position close behind Fabius and Filloloper.

Filloloper and Fabius waited patiently as the room rotated around them…one opening moved past them, then two, three, four, five, six, and then seven.

As the eighth door rotated in front of them, Fabius was running full speed with Filloloper and the Gripps following close behind. Without any hesitation, they hurried through the narrow passageway before the door closed behind them.

The faster they ran, the more aware the dogs were of when and where to move as doors quickly opened in the walls ahead and immediately closed behind them.

Soon, other voices and commands could be heard ringing through the Hedges. Fabius caught sight of the flag of Grippland with its interlocking G's waving back and forth above the wall.

Before the Gripps could blink, they were reunited with the four missing members of their team in a room three times as large as the one they had just departed.

From his angle of vision, Grist did not to notice that Fabius and Filloloper and the remainder of his team members were standing directly behind him.

He was once again in the midst of another non-stop discourse as to why his team should have mastered the ability to grab on, grip on, and grind on to the situation they were in, and thus, overcome the circumstances confronting them.

Grist continued, "It's painfully clear that you most certainly might die here, murdered by these tall bushes! Is that what you want? Is that your desire…to live out your very Last Grasp caught within the clutches of some shrubs?

"Have you forgotten that we still have our knives, our ropes, our Gripp logic, and most importantly, our cunning?"

encouraged Grist. "Eventually we will escape, even if it means we must hack our way out of here piece by piece!"

"That won't be necessary, Commander Grist," suggested Fabius quietly.

Grist immediately spun around to witness Fabius and Filloloper and his fellow team members standing before him. His face turned a ghostly white as if he had seen an apparition appear from out of the nowhere.

"H-h-how did you do that?" he stuttered.

"They know the way out," answered Grimm quietly. "Don't even bother asking them how!"

"We can lead you to safety," suggested Filloloper, standing confidently next to Fabius. "If you follow close behind us, we will open all the doors to your freedom."

"Lies, more trickery, isn't that what you mean?"

"They are telling the truth, #1, Sir" answered Babble. "Truth is rare in Grippland, but they are not lying, Sir."

Grist looked down at the ground to hide his frustration and mumbled under his breath, "Let's follow the dogs."

Exchanging glances and without further conversation, the Gripps lined up behind the Guardians of Acronos who quickly reconnected with Hedora.

A door opened immediately in front of them, and the dogs easily led the tired team through the complex maze of Hedora. It was smooth and effortless. Each opening in the wall responded as if they had an invisible magnetic key that could unlock any door with words unspoken.

The Gripp team dutifully followed Fabius' every move. They ran when he ran and turned when he turned. They began to sense and understand the concepts of intuition and synchronicity.

After only a few more complicated twists and turns, the tormented explorers climatically emerged free of Hedora's grasp. They fell to the ground exhausted from running and the tension of being trapped within the unrelenting, energy force field named Hedora.

Filloloper and Fabius quietly rested in a grassy clearing surrounded by green, leafy trees and a variety of colorful flowers. In the distance were tall, rugged mountains silhouetted against a light blue sky.

Standing on a flat rock at the top of a grassy hill, Grist cleared his throat and said. "This is a great moment, fellow Gripps! We have overcome still another obstacle designed to make us fail. But we did not fail, nor will we ever fail! Victory is ours again! So, what say you?

The Gripps chanted in unison: We grab on! We grasp on! We grind on! Because that is our way!

Intuition and Trust

Intuition is your inner knowingness. It is an instinctive feeling, which protects and enhances your life experiences. Your inner guidance comes through quiet words, dreams, visions or feelings.

Monitoring all aspects of life, intuition is your sixth sense alerting you to events in the present as well as in the future, providing information that is beyond your conscious reasoning.

As you begin to hear, sense or feel your inner guidance, you will develop trust in the information. When that trust grows stronger, you will be able to respond immediately to warnings of danger and also to follow specific pathways to your success.

Using your intuition, you will become more aware of people, places and experiences, and you will expand your ability to perceive information beyond the physical world around you.

PART ELEVEN

Meeting the Enemy

G RIST AWOKE EARLY AND RETREATED to be alone, resting under a large, Amarra tree that was covered in bright orange blossoms. Rarely did he take the time to be introspective or to consider profound ideas. He was a Gripp of action with a trained military mind who was always ready to fight the next battle. But here he was, after so many challenges, sitting quietly under a blossoming tree.

It's always about time, he thought. *So little time. And for all our efforts, we have found only this vast wilderness. There is not even a trace or a sign of civilization.*

How ironic it was that a brilliant, military strategist such as he would find himself unable to use his talents, abilities, and experience as a commander. He was beginning to think that the only option available to him was to turn back and admit mission failure.

What's the sense of this mission? He asked himself. *There is nothing here in this never-ending wasteland, completely devoid of concrete and steel! How can we gain the Secret of Un-old-Age, or any secret for that matter, from this emptiness and two talking dogs who have absolutely nothing to say? The time has come to retreat.*

These thoughts and more were racing through Grist's mind as he motioned for Twist and Scheme to join him. "I need to make a decision, fellow Gripps, and I am going to include you in the process."

"What kind of decision, #1? What do you mean?" they asked almost in unison.

Grist pondered what to say. He witnessed the anxious expressions on the faces of #2 and #3 when he declared, "I believe it's time to cancel the mission. I believe we need to turn back and admit defeat. I am asking you as second and third in command for your opinion. Please consider your response carefully."

The politician and businessman had counted on this mission for fame, fortune, and freedom. The idea of returning to Grippland as failures would only mean imprisonment at best.

"We still have time," replied Twist. "We still have three Grabbons (days) left before we need to return. Why are you suggesting we turn back now?"

"And you, Scheme? What do you have to say?"

In Scheme's typical fashion, he pretended not to understand what Grist was asking and began to answer the question with questions, "Turn back? Is that what you mean? Pack up and leave now?"

Grist knew very well that returning as failures to Grippland would be unacceptable to his team, but remaining in this wilderness would mean that his reputation as a great general would never be redeemed. "It's time to decide," he said. "I will allow you a few Grippers (minutes) for your final word."

Twist and Scheme could not believe Grist was uttering those words: *Mission Failure!* How could they possibly return to Grippland without anything to show for their near-death experiences in Acronos?

Something dramatic had changed within Grist. Why was he asking them to quit the mission, accept failure, and return defeated to Grippland to become prisoners once more? The two Gripps exchanged glances, knowing that somehow they must convince Grist to continue grinding on. There just might still be a chance to succeed.

Scheme whispered into Twist's ear, "We cannot turn back now. There's still some ticking on the Tock. We will challenge him to complete the mission. We have no choice."

Twist was ready to reply when Stare came running towards them.

"We have a sighting! We have a sighting!" exclaimed the unusually excited and animated engineer. "We've discovered a clearing. I think it is a Gripp-made clearing. Gripp-like hands must have made it!"

Grist's expression immediately brightened. He turned to Twist and Scheme and stated enthusiastically, "I knew we were close to a major discovery, a significant breakthrough! I just knew it!"

The Gripp team followed Stare to a vast, grassy plain surrounded by a thick stand of trees.

"It's perfectly flat! There is not a rock or a pebble in sight," explained Stare. "I am confident that someone cleared this area for a very particular reason, perhaps as a staging ground for assembling troops."

"Well done, #5, well done!" exclaimed Grist, rubbing his right hand over his face, as if to wash away all of his former doubts and thoughts of canceling the mission.

He had thankfully escaped failure, but that memory lingered long enough to make him pause to consider that perhaps he was losing his grip. Maybe they all slipped their grips.

"We have lost our edge," he mumbled to himself. "Is it possible that we are simply unworthy of finding the enemy guarding the Secret to Un-Old-Age? Or worse, perhaps the enemy truly believes we are incapable of fighting them."

Grist continued to mumble on to himself as he scanned the flat, grassy meadow stretching out before him. He felt it was important to act decisively and reverse the damage to morale caused by engaging in so many battles since their arrival. How could he possibly admit that nature was beating them at every turn?

"Eye of Time Explorers," announced Grist, "It is evident that we are now deep in enemy territory, and as such, without fear, we now claim this land until the enemy decides to show themselves on the field of battle!

"Some of you will remember your specialized training at the GATW, the *Gripp Academy for Total Warfare*. As you know, our lessons were learned the Gripp way—through hand-to-hand combat. We seized land from the enemy and held tight to their territory. At this turning point we can't afford to lose our grips. We can't lose our edge. The success of this mission depends upon our ability to maintain our grasps at all costs!"

Gripp cleared his throat and continued, "You may recall that there was a game at the War Academy that we played to improve our skills in Gripp warfare."

Grist smiled, remembering his Grabbons (days) at the Academy, and said, "This particular game was designed to demonstrate our cunning, deceit, and trickery — all the most admirable traits to be found in any true Gripp warrior."

Even though none of the team members had attended the War Academy, they nodded their heads as if they, too, remembered the game.

Moving his arms to encompass the entirety of the meadow, Grist stood straight and proud. "Hereupon this very field, which appears to be a Gripp-made staging ground for the assembly of troops, we will play that game!

"We will form two teams, a red team, and a blue team. Each team member will wear their appropriate colored flags that are in your utility belts. The simple object of the game is to seize territory."

"It's time to play! It's time to play Gripp-War-Ball," exclaimed Grist, in a nearly hysterical tone of voice.

The confused and frustrated team members began to stretch a long and narrow net across the flat, grassy plain. The net was approximately five Gripp strides (five yards) in length and had a large circular hole in the center.

"Now, I need your full attention," demanded Grist. "This is a game, but it is far more than just a game. This contest is will test your ability in warfare as you compete against the other team with a different colored flag in their belts.

"The objective is simple. When a team member throws the ball above the net, another player will grab the ball and proceed to maneuver around to the opposite side of the net...not under the net," he chuckled.

"When you manage to shove, push and prod your way through enemy territory, you must throw the ball through the opening in the net, striking your ground. When the ball hits the ground, it's called a strike. Five strikes by any team equals a victory. Do you understand the rules? Any questions?"

Not one of the eight team members had a clue as to how to play the game. So, rather than respond to Grist's question, they fixated on his facial expressions, hoping somehow to catch a glimpse of his motive for playing this type of game in the middle of nowhere. They wondered why they were not continuing to seek the answers to Un-Old-Age or engaging with a real enemy.

Noticing their bewilderment, Grist clarified, "Very well, I will explain the game in slightly more detail. You will be wearing either a red or blue flag on your belts that will signify your team membership. The objective is to remove the other team's flags before they have the opportunity of grabbing the ball and scoring a strike through the center of the net."

He explained that this ancient game of Gripp-War-Ball was initially designed to determine who was more physically fit on the field of battle. In the past, it was acceptable to injure, maim and or physically incapacitate a fellow team member, including breaking their ribs, arms, and legs.

"We cannot afford to lose anyone. Therefore I suggest, even though you may wish to cause injury to the opposite team for the cause of victory, I recommend you adhere to the rules of the game.

"I will serve as judge and referee. There will be four on each team. Two through five, you will be the blue team. Six through ten, the red team, minus #7, Good Old Grubb, of course." Grist quickly inflated the colorful ball emblazoned with the interlocking "G's" of Grippland.

"You will use this ball to taunt all those who would take it from you. Agility, speed, and trickery will aid you in achieving victory. Good luck! Play Gripp-War-Ball!"

Grist tossed the ball toward the center of the net. Members of each team bumped into each other as they scrambled to catch it.

Gritt moved quicker than the others, grabbing the ball mid-air, running around the net, and invading enemy territory. He passed the ball to Babble who scored a victory by throwing it through the center opening.

Watching from a safe distance, Filloloper and Fabius could not help but ponder the Gripp's unusual behavior now playing out before their eyes.

"They seem to think that this meadow represents enemy territory and that a foreign military is using it as a camp or assembly area," suggested Filloloper.

Aware that this bizarre game was nothing more than an escape from reality, Fabius replied, "They are grasping at illusions to maintain their sanity. They are trying to create the feeling of battling an enemy they are always seeking!"

"Their illusions seem real enough to them," suggested Filloloper, watching the Gripps battling on the field.

Fabius was very impressed with each team member's intense determination to win at all costs. They were pushing, shoving, and throwing each other to the ground while trying to grab the ball tossed from one to the other.

"It's sad that they are desperately trying to become something that they cannot be," commented Filloloper, "They play battle games rather than seeking out another level of wisdom and understanding."

"It's not up to us to judge," replied Fabius. "They believe they're lost because they've lost their grip on reality."

INTRUDING ON THE DREAM TIME

It was apparent that Grist truly believed his troops could regain their powers by creating confusion and chaos on the field below. As a warrior, he feared that a lack of training for war threatened their existence, and he was desperate for an encounter with an enemy, any enemy.

"Maybe they are succeeding," suggested Filloloper, pointing at a filmy curtain of light encircling the teams below. "Do you see that pattern of energy creating a distortion field? Those branches and leaves wavering slightly."

"Perhaps, it's another Time Wave," conjectured Fabius, transfixed by the phenomena unfolding before them. "It appears to be a subtle energy stream," he continued. "It's as if the Gripps' physical and mental density have intruded on the lighter energy field of Level 7, which is responding the only way it knows how, by protecting itself."

"What are you saying?" asked Filloloper, watching intently as the curtain of light slowly surrounded the two mock armies who were fully immersed in their make-believe war.

Fabius did not respond. Instead, he pointed to the center of the field where the ball had bounced free from the team members' grasps. It was suspended in mid-air and was slowly rotating above their heads as if to taunt them.

Fabius closed his eyes ever so slightly, and after a long pause, he looked directly at Filloloper and replied, "It's the Startlings! Soldiers in some phantom army did not create this grassy plain. I remember. This is the home of the Startlings.

This open meadow is their nighttime refuge. It is where they feel safe surrounded by all these magnificent, towering trees."

"I don't understand. What do the Startlings have to do with this curtain of energy around the Gripps?"

"Their warrior energy has intruded upon the dreamtime of the Startlings who are using subtle energy to oppose the Gripps' aggressive, vibrational frequency. It is the war Grist so desperately desired; and so, now it begins."

"You mean the Startlings can see this location in their dreams? They can see the intruders who invaded their home?"

"Look!" exclaimed Fabius. "Watch the ball!"

The ball, which only moments before was spinning so effortlessly in a stationary orbit above the Gripps' heads, was now bouncing back-and-forth, hitting each of them squarely in the face, knocking several to the ground.

"They wanted war, and now they have found it," laughed Fabius. "Only this time their enemy is invisible. The sleeping Startlings are sharing one compelling dream. They must protect their homeland."

"Where are they?" asked Filloloper, her large golden-brown eyes darted to and fro trying to see the Startlings.

"They cannot be far away. When the sun begins to set, the Startlings will most likely return. Hopefully, these warriors will not attempt to engage them."

As soon as Fabius uttered his last remarks, Filloloper felt a trembling sensation moving through her paws. "I think the Startlings are coming home. I believe they are on their way here!" She pointed to a cloud of dust growing larger beyond the tree line.

The two dogs were amazed to see the hundreds of large, brown and gray, flightless birds with sturdy legs and large feet running with overwhelming speed and agility.

Usually, these docile birds were not aggressive; however, at this moment, they were using their incredible herding instinct to form a wall of beaks and feathers moving forward with powerful momentum.

Grist was the first to see the dust cloud from his slightly elevated position above the playing field. "It's the enemy!" he shouted, his voice filled with excitement and anticipation. "They're coming! Prepare for combat! The battle is about to begin!" Grist was in a state of delirium.

"Follow me! Three-by-three formation! They are about to meet a General capable of immediate response on the field of battle!" He continued to shout commands, detailing last-minute methods and means of engaging the enemy.

And then, the Starlings appeared. The first wave of birds hit them like a tsunami, instantly flipping all nine Gripps high into the air.

The second and third wave swarmed over the land, occupying the entire, grassy meadow that was their home. The war that Grist so desperately wanted was over in a matter of Grippers (minutes).

"So, those are the Startlings," mused Filloloper, trying not to laugh. "But where are the Gripps? I don't see them."

Fabius hesitated for a moment scanning the battleground that was supposed to be the true test of the Gripps' ability to engage the enemy. "There, over there...! And also over there!" He pointed to all the various positions where the Gripp team members had ultimately landed.

"Yes, I see them, "responded Filloloper, "Isn't that Grist clutching desperately onto that large tree? The others seem to have been scattered just about everywhere else."

"Evidently, these Gripp warriors were simply not prepared for this type of warfare," Filloloper mused, trying desperately not to ridicule their best efforts, knowing full well that the time travelers were locked into their preconceived expectations of how to engage the enemy. But the coherent thought form shared by the flock of Startlings created an overpowering unified force.

The Startlings had reclaimed their Dream Zone, and now a sea of brown and white feathers dominated the landscape when only moments before Grist had most defiantly declared it as Gripp territory. There was one exception, however, in the midst of that crush of beaks and feathers, was one remaining brave Gripp soldier locked within the very center of their Dream Zone.

"Over there, in the midst of all of those birds there seems to be another Gripp. Only his head and shoulders are visible!" exclaimed Fabius.

"Yes, I see him. I can just make out the Number five on his helmet," Filloloper answered in a humorous tone of voice. "I must admit I never suspected that Stare, the engineer would be the very last to remain standing on the field of battle."

PART TWELVE

The Under-Earth

GRUBB TRIED TO ERASE any lingering thoughts about his descent into the shadowy and bizarre domain the Grundells referred to as the Under-Earth. He didn't want to think about the possibility of his imprisonment, or worse, his ultimate demise. He had no other choice but to continue following the most unusual creatures he had ever seen.

As they descended deeper into the complicated maze of caverns, Grubb was uncomfortably aware that this dark underworld offered no visible clues as to east, west, north or south. If an escape was even slightly possible, he would need to become far more knowledgeable of the inner structure of this multistoried domain.

Struggling to adjust his eyes to the ever-increasing darkness, he knew full well that the gravelly, narrow, wet ledge they were traversing offered no second chances. He must not lose his footing and fall into the vast depths of the immense, underground complex far below.

The rough, stone walls were his only support as they walked along the winding, narrow pathway. He tried to steady himself by holding onto the jagged cliffs, first to the right and then to the left of him. Many of the walls felt as though they were covered with a thick, soft moss, which did not seem to offer much support.

Only when he heard a soft squeal and could see that two, black eyes were looking at him did Grubb notice that the spongy, wall covering he thought would support him, was actually not moss at all. Instead, hanging on those walls were hundreds of giant, bat-like creatures who preferred to be left alone and unmolested.

Grubb held his breath to prevent himself from screaming out loud. His body quivered and shook with horror. He knew that this surreal, underground world must be filled with even more shocking, crawling creatures.

He looked up and became aware that ahead of him was a complex network of narrow passageways and bridges layered one over the other forming a vast three-dimensional maze stretching out as far as he could see in the dimly lit cave complex. Just as he was attempting to compose himself, he heard a voice calling to him from the trail ahead.

"Are you still there?" called Wise, not bothering to turn around to see if he was still following.

"Yes, still here!" responded Grubb in his bravest voice, trying to hide his growing terror as he was being guided deeper into the recesses of the Under-Earth by creatures, whose large, long-clawed hands and feet were at least three times larger than those of an average Gripp.

"Very well, #7 of the Exploration Team of the *Eye of Time*," Wise answered wryly with a glimmer of a smile crossing his long and narrow face. "Indeed, you must always remember to enjoy your journey. You may never know just how short it may be." Those words, even if made only in jest, served to increase Grubb's growing fear.

My life is over, he thought. *They will most certainly keep me prisoner or worse.* His feeling of panic heightened as he realized for the first time in his short Gripp life that this might be the end. He would soon be saying his final goodbye to a tortured career as a biologist in Grippland where plants were rare or almost extinct.

He had desperately tried to escape that dying world by volunteering as a mercenary explorer with the Eye of Time mission, and now he found himself in a far more desperate situation. He felt like laughing out loud at the absurdity of his misfortune, but since he had rarely experienced laughter, he spread his lips into a cynical smile.

"Are there any questions? Do you have any questions, #7? You do seem to be so preoccupied," ventured Wise, as he waited for Grubb to reach him on the narrow, damp pathway. "We are quite confident that you must have a few questions," he stated politely.

"Why, yes. Yes, of course, questions," Grubb replied nervously, trying to gain control of his growing fear as he focused on the immensity of the cave complex. And although he had a hundred questions rolling around in his head, none were available for him to form into words. "Questions, uh, do I have questions? Yes, questions," he repeated, feeling as though his words evaporated before he was able to speak.

"Your names...uh, your names?" he stuttered. "There's Bumble and Tumble, and then Stumble. Isn't that right?"

"What about our names?" replied Wise, evidently not concerned that Grubb hadn't mentioned his name?

"Well, it is strange that you have names...uh, well...that are not real names at all."

"A very excellent question."

"It is..?" replied Grubb, pleased that his attempt at appearing calm had succeeded.

"Yes, our names are won and lost and then found again! You see, I was not always Wise. In fact, being Wise is only just a simple misstep away from being called Tumble again. To fully understand Grundell names, you have to be aware of the importance of what we do and how our names reflect the manner of our actions."

Bumble interrupted to explain that all the Grundell names within a team are interchangeable. Each of the four had once been Wise. And at different times, they had also been Tumble, Bumble and Stumble. It was the nature of their work that defined their names.

Because the Grundells were continuously interacting with unique Under-Earth energies and experimenting with various plants and minerals discovered in the valley during their daily work, they sometimes stumbled, bumbled or even tumbled directly into these discoveries. Their names defined their actions and continued to be relevant as part of their teams' shared experience of exploration.

The one called Wise was the team member who was currently responsible for carrying all of the wisdom they had learned. "It's a type of a game that we find fun to play," added Tumble as he and the other Grundells smiled and jested with each other.

How can they laugh at a time like this? Thought Grubb as his own words echoed loudly within the deepest recesses of his mind. *I will never escape!*

The Grundells enthusiastically resumed their tour, and it was soon apparent to Grubb that his hosts were very delighted to show him their Under-Earth domain, pointing out the soaring ceilings of the massive cave complex.

Yet, the Grundells' delight did not allay Grubb's growing fears of being forever trapped. He certainly couldn't expect any help from his Gripp team, even if they were still alive. Most likely Grist would assume he had made his Last Grasp and would merely continue on without him.

Tumble moved closer to Grubb as they entered another vast chamber. He motioned for him to take a seat within a cavernous, theater-like setting and commented, "You are a strange and curious little creature, aren't you? I surmise that you are very far from home. Why not sit and enjoy the view?"

Grubb reluctantly sat on a bench next to the Grundells and watched the glimmering lights, which he had noticed from the trail above. The brightness of the light was growing stronger and brighter.

How is this possible? He wondered as the glow began to illuminate the immensity of the Grundells' home. In the far distance, he could see hundreds of doorways carved into the cliff face forming a honeycomb of chambers where families of Grundells were moving back and forth, carrying woven baskets over their shoulders.

"How many Grundells are here?" Grubb asked, assuming his most polite manner.

There was no response. Instead, the Grundells seemed to be meditating as the darkness magically transformed into near daylight. What appeared to be a frozen waterfall was emitting a translucent glow of golden light.

"That is Trillia Falls," explained Wise, pointing at the light source. "Over the years, we have trained the roots and vines of thousands of Trillia plants to intertwine and grow together from their water source in the Under-Earth.

"The luminescence from their roots is bright enough to light our homes, approximating daylight at least a few hours each day. In the evening, we do our preservation work with all the plants you have seen growing in the Over- Earth in The Valley of Acronos."

Grubb stared in wonder as the Trillia transmitted their radiance, creating an immense cascade of glowing vines emerging from the water far below. The Trillia enhanced their light show with a melodic humming that filled the vast complex with relaxing, undulating, rhythmic tones.

"What you are witnessing is the air, light, water, and earth connection that creates and permeates all of life. It even flows through you, Gripp #7 of the Eye of Time," explained Wise, looking over his shoulder to see if Grubb was grasping the full intent and meaning of his words.

There was nothing the biologist could say to match the beauty of this scene of natural light glimmering on the colorful rocks embedded within the massive, curving walls.

After about thirty Grippers (minutes) Tumble turned to Grubb and suggested they depart from Trillia Falls since they wanted him to see what they termed the *Inner Complex*.

"Yes, yes, an excellent idea!" agreed Bumble, Stumble, and Wise. "After all, Gripp #7 is a biologist and botanist. Perhaps he would like to offer his expertise?"

HAZARDS ON THE TRAIL

The passage leading away from Trillia Falls was far narrower than the former pathway they had traversed. Grubb became even more concerned as the Grundells led him higher and higher to yet another, adjoining chamber.

"You know Stumble, it's a long way to tumble if you stumble," smirked Grubb, attempting to jest in the face of his growing fears.

He looked down and was disturbed to see that they were at least five stories above the cave floor.

"Well, yes," replied Bumble walking just a few feet ahead of him. "You quickly learn there are some obvious hazards in the work we do. We find it is important to concentrate and not be distracted when seeking our path or any path for that matter," he mused.

"But then again, perhaps, our large feet and claws do keep us safe and secure on these slippery ledges."

Grubb glanced around and then down at the large, fur-covered paws of the Grundells equipped with long protruding claws. Even with his standard issue, Gripp boots, he wouldn't have the same advantage as these sure-footed creatures.

"So...then, Gripp #7, we do have a considerable distance to climb. Would you like to participate in creating a song or a rhyme?" Wise asked with a curious smile.

Grubb was seriously pondering his fate, and thinking that he should not be so foolish as to offend these bizarre creatures. He replied, "Well, yes! Well, I mean, sadly, we Gripps never sing or rhyme! Creative endeavors are outlawed in Grippland. High Command banned all such *amusements* many Grinds (years) ago in our history."

"Well, Gripp #7, now that you are here without your team, no one will be aware of your trip into a land where songs and rhymes are very much alive. We must insist that you participate!" suggested Wise. "Tumble, why don't you begin? We shall sing and rhyme along our way."

Without hesitating for even a moment, Tumble was humming and spontaneously singing, rhyming words that seemed to flow through him automatically:

> *Adventures bring discoveries,*
> *filling our minds with memories.*
> *Moving forward as water flows,*
> *knowing what trusting knows.*
>
> *Hidden truths are revealing,*
> *shining light on inner meaning.*
> *Does time exist, or can you go*
> *far beyond that energy flow*
> *to experience a magical instance*
> *of momentary non-existence?*
>
> *Time shifts in and out like a beam*
> *a constant, flowing, energy stream*
> *layers and layers intertwined,*
> *under and over and then aligned.*
>
> *Time is a mirror…Reflecting a mirror,*
> *shining light upon our every fear.*

Grubb relaxed with the melody. For some reason, the words seemed to flow seamlessly in his mind. Moving to one side and leaning against the wall, he turned to look back at the steep and rocky ledge on which they had been steadily climbing, only to be overwhelmed by the immensity of the Grundells' domain.

In the distance, he was able to see the full extent of Trillia Falls illuminating the lower cave complex; and there, far below, was a small winding stream he previously had not noticed. The water was slowly moving around and over sparkling gray and pink rocks covering the cave floor.

The climb upward on the twisting trail was being made even more difficult with Grubb's heavy boots weighted down with three-inch soles, and they were uncomfortably laced up nearly to his knees.

He almost fell several times on the loose rock and gravel, but his sheer will and adrenalin kept pushing him forward, fueled by the fear and also the excitement of what might lie just ahead.

The knowledge that he was all alone with these strangely shaped, bizarre creatures with their love of riddles and rhymes made him think that perhaps they were not as menacing and dangerous as they first appeared to be. But then again, there was that nagging thought that continued edging into his awareness. The Grundells seemed to be far too happy.

"Are you falling behind, #7?" questioned Tumble. "We are just about to enter the Zone of Bridges where we will be crossing over some very sheer drops. We do not want you to tumble, do we, Stumble?" mused Bumble with a slightly sinister smile crossing his lips.

"So, this is it," sighed Grubb, mumbling to himself. "Here is where it all ends! One quick push, and I will be gone! No wonder the Grundells are so happy! They have nothing to fear here in their bizarre, underground world. They nonchalantly take their visitors on a singing tour up to the drop zone, and then without warning, they simply push them off a bridge!"

Grubb tried desperately to remove negative thoughts out of his mind, but he was unable to do so. The *Gripp Manual for Total Warfare* continued to flash into his mind—Page 786, paragraph four—the most relevant section of the handbook states, "Everyone you may encounter on a mission is an enemy and a threat until they become a prisoner!"

"What have I done?" lamented Grubb, as his mind continued grinding on and on. "I have been captured by the Grundells in these dark, underground caverns. I'm following the strangest of strange creatures, and I haven't attempted to escape! Where is my Gripp Logic now?"

Apparently, the Grundell songs were amusements, and the rhymes were nothing more than cunning deceptions designed to trick his mind. *No wonder High Command banned riddles and rhymes in Grippland,* he thought as he found himself purposively lagging further and further behind.

"Come along, Number Seven of the Eye of Time Exploration Team, we do not want you to get lost or to wander off," warned Wise in a far more serious tone of voice. "The bridges are straight ahead, and the crossing will be much harder for you than it is for us. There is no turning back now!" he laughed, and then laughed again.

After carefully following still another dark and narrow trail around a jagged rock wall, Grubb caught sight of long narrow bridges extending across a vast chasm with no bottom in sight.

In front of him, a series of swinging, narrow, woven reed bridges were hanging precariously, crisscrossing the span. There was no possible way to judge the distance since the ends of the bridges disappeared into the darkness.

Grubb stood paralyzed with fear. His mind was racing as he searched his memory for any helpful hints in the *Gripp Survival Manual*, which he always carried with him. He wondered how there could ever be a solution to surviving four, possibly psychotic, fur-covered monsters who preferred to sing and rhyme while bringing their victims to the *Drop Zone*!

"Come along, Seven," repeated Wise, "You may need some help to cross the chasm and reach the inner complexes on the other side. These bridges may be dangerous without the benefit of Grundell feet," he mused. "Your fall will be quite fatal," he jested in a somber monotone.

"Right!" called out Bumble, "Well then, let the Gripp begin his rhyme."

Yes, yes, go ahead! Why not try!" Tumble called to him.

Grubb breathed deeply and pulled at his collar as if loosening it would somehow allow him to release words, which might be hiding somewhere deep within him.

Pausing for what seemed like an eternity, Grubb sang for the first time in his dreary, gray life.

> *I am a Gripp on a mission to explore.*
> *Dazed and amazed, I entered a door*
> *to witness what I desired to see.*
> *Thank you for your kind hospitality!*

Grundell Wise was closest to Grubb and could see that the words spontaneously fell away from Grubb's lips, followed by what appeared to be tears forming in his eyes.

"Excellent, Seven!" responded Wise who then added to the rhyme:

> *There Grubb stood, staring bruised and sore*
> *on the treacherous ledge above the cave floor*
> *suspended in the rhythm of our time*
> *caught within these phrases of rhyme.*

Entering our world with great dismay,
will he enjoy our sense of play?

As Grubb trudged along the dangerously steep and narrow ledge etched into the face of the cavern walls, he felt that no Grundell or Gripp could ever understand the emotions and sensations of relief that he was experiencing for the very first time in his life.

To the shock of his Grundell hosts, he was singing again:

I am Gripp #7 from a gray and dreary land.
We grab what we need and grip what we can.
I have slipped through the Eye of Time
and now find myself speaking in rhyme,
singing with words I would always hide,
revealing the real me deep inside!

On the path ahead was a long, narrow, ramp leading to the chasm edge. Upon closer inspection, Grubb was able to determine that the platform, which was cantilevered far out over the cliff, led to the suspension bridges.

It was Stumble who first made his way from the ramp onto the woven reed bridge; and upon receiving his weight, it immediately began swaying wildly back and forth.

Bumble and Tumble were next up and onto the bridge, while Wise waited patiently for Grubb to follow.

"It's…it's moving like a kite in the wind! I cannot possibly go onto that bridge! I will certainly fall!"

"Well, yes, you may fall!" responded Wise to Grubb's lament. "Would that be so terrible?" he questioned with a sly grin on his face.

Although the flimsy, suspension bridge, constructed only of reeds and vines, seemed to be structurally sound, the added weight of the three Grundells increased the severity of the motion of the bridge, rocking from side-to-side to at least six feet in both directions.

Would that be so terrible? He repeated the question over and over to himself. *It would be disastrous! It is no secret that all Gripps fear death! We have been sent on this dangerous mission by High Command specifically to seek out all possible answers to Un-Old-Age. We are attempting to postpone death. We want to stay young and healthy. I certainly don't want to experience my Last Grasp before completing this mission!*

He stopped, took a deep breath, and stated, "I cannot cross this bridge!" He held on, even more tightly to the handrail supports of the ramp. "I can go no further! I admit I am even...even, too afraid to look down!"

"How about a rhyme?" called Tumble who was swaying widely to and fro on the wobbly bridge? "Perhaps a delightful rhyme will help you regain your grip. After all, you call yourself a Gripp, do you not...?" he chided.

Is all of this just a game, a cruel hoax, a terrible plot designed to deceive me, thought Grubb. "No...no more rhymes!" he replied curtly. "I just need to concentrate. I simply need to get a grasp on the situation," He peered out over the bridge into the dark distance that now separated him from reaching the other side of the cave.

"Well, then, allow us to help you as we said we would," suggested Wise. And with that simple statement, Wise immediately picked up the trembling Gripp with his powerful, oversized paws and tossed Grubb like a limp, rag doll onto the bridge where Tumble, Bumble, and Stumble were waiting to grab him.

"Great catch, Tumble!" called out Wise, quickly making his way onto the swinging bridge.

"Certainly, you can see, Gripp Grubb, just how easy it is to move forward when you have someone to help you cross over the bridge. From time to time, we just cannot make those important, life-changing decisions on our own!" he jested as he nudged the three Grundells to keep moving.

Grubb's mind was racing so fast and projecting so many thoughts and pictures that he became dizzy and mystified that he was, indeed, still alive.

For no apparent reason, he repeated his name over and over again, "I am Gripp #7 of the Eye of Time Exploration Team. I have been sent here to explore and seek out the answers to Un-Old-Age!"

In his altered state of mind, he was not entirely aware that the Grundells had been pulling him all along the swaying walkway until they had reached the midway point on the suspension bridge.

"Here you are!" called out Stumble. "You have reached the midway point on the bridge. It is up to you to decide whether to go on or to try to make your way back from where we have come! We have important work to do since there are only so many hours of reflected light in each Grundell day."

Wise added, "It is up to you to discover what lies ahead and turn away your fears or turn back because of your fears!"

Grubb watched as the Grundells moved quickly over the swaying bridge and appeared to easily reach the other side without incident.

"We can only wait for you so long," exclaimed a voice, echoing from the darkness on the other side of the chasm. "We must go! And, of course, we must pause for tea!"

Grubb heard the words but was unable to respond. His mouth was dry and his lips were frozen. He was fixated on his fingers that were desperately clutching the flimsy railing made of vines, which was supporting him and helping him to keep his balance, preventing him from falling to his Last Grasp.

The Grundell continued speaking, "It's all up to you, Grubb. You are no longer just a member of an exploration team from Grippland. You are here to discover the real you. This is moment when you can truly determine your ultimate and final destination."

TESTING COURAGE

Grubb recognized the slow, deep, and gravely sound of the voice that was resounding through the dark void. It was Wise speaking. He was the one who supposedly possessed all the wisdom of the Grundells' discoveries.

Cautiously, Grubb released his grip ever so slightly on the swaying vines of the railing. As he tried to balance himself on the moving bridge, he was experiencing a feeling of Déjà vu. He was remembering the many times in his life when he had hoped for the best in the midst of the worst situations.

Perhaps, these furry, dark-eyed creatures were only trying to help him by leading him on to test his resolve and determine if he was truly worthy of what they termed, "encountering his final destination."

Wise called out again, "It's all your decision. You have to decide if you want to cross this bridge, Gripp Grubb. Just be careful not to stumble, bumble or tumble!"

"Yes, yes, I hear your words! I see what lies ahead!" answered Grubb, mustering up his most courageous voice. He wondered to himself, *what did the Grundell Wise mean when he said I must decide if I want to cross this bridge? I certainly didn't choose to be here!*

The words of Wise kept reverberating within his mind, '*It is up to you to discover what lies ahead and turn your back upon your fears or turn back because of your fears!*'

Grubb stood still, hesitating to move, *I guess there's always a bridge to cross somewhere. Evidently, through some cruel twist of fate, this must be my bridge at this very moment of now!*

And with that motivating thought, Grubb started moving, albeit ever so slowly, one cautious step at a time through the shadowy darkness on a bridge made from loosely twisted vines and reeds that were easily grasped by large Grundell feet and claws.

But Gripp boots were made for support with heavy soles and definitely not designed to grip onto the slick dampness of a swaying, suspension bridge. As he cautiously inched his way forward, he picked up his pace in a show of self-pride and bravado.

That is when he slipped!

Perhaps, it was his momentary lapse of attention, or maybe it was the fright of seeing the Grundells so very near to him on the ledge at the end of the bridge. Yet, there was more. Something about them had changed.

Their eyes were different. The pupils were more prominent and the color had changed. They were no longer black. Instead, their pupils had turned a deep red...the kind of red you see in the coals of a wood fire, which has reached its maximum heat.

The shock of that vision rippled through his body, and he lost his grip on the railings.

He was falling. He was falling rapidly into the darkest depths of the chasm below

He let out a barely audible scream for help that was heard by Tumble and Stumble who immediately reported to Wise that their visitor had fallen.

"He was almost a likable fellow," remarked Bumble sadly. "It is such a pity to see him tumble in this manner."

"Yes, he did seem to have potential," answered Tumble. "Too bad he had to stumble."

Wise quickly leaned over the railing, peering into the chasm to see Grubb disappearing into the mists below. In his loudest Grundell voice, he called, "Tell us, #7, and are you worthy of saving?"

The faint sound of Grubb's voice responded "Help me! Help! Help me!!"

"We shall presume that is a yes," responded the Grundells in unison, and called out, "Nets! Nets! Raise the nets!"

From the very depths of the chasm came an immediate response, "All nets up!" Grubb's fateful fall abruptly ended!

Thankfully, the nets had stopped his fall, but this was far from the end of Grubb's nightmarish experience. The very nature of the Grundells' safety nets was their extreme flexibility.

Immediately after hitting the net, Grubb bounced back like a rubber ball and found himself hurtling upwards to the level of the bridge. He was shocked when Wise quickly grabbed him out of thin air!

"What a curious fellow you are, #7, to try and take the shortcut across our bridges. Didn't we tell you that your fall could be fatal?" laughed Wise, pleased with his ability to save the falling Gripp.

Grubb gasped for breath unable to respond.

Wise placed him on the ledge and made sure he was stable enough to stand. Grateful to be alive, Grubb leaned back against the rock wall.

He suddenly remembered that it was the sudden shock of seeing the Grundells' red eyes that had caused him to lose his balance.

"It was your eyes! I saw you change! I became disorientated and lost my concentration," he stammered, trying not to look directly into the enormous, red eyes of Wise!

"Yes! Yes! Well, never mind, you are still a Gripp are you not...?" mused Wise thoughtfully. "Although, perhaps, you are slightly changed after almost making your Last Grasp, as you call it!" he grinned.

"As for our eyes...Well, yes, Grundells are very fortunate to have adapted to the darkness of our domain by developing a second set of lenses, which transform to red when the light is dimmest. It helps us to navigate these inner realms with ease.

"So then, Gripp Seven. Shall we continue our tour into the inner complex? We have so much more to show you."

A PLACE OUT OF MIND

There were reasons enough for Grubb to believe he was in a deep dream state and that his bizarre journey into the Under-Earth was nothing more than a hallucination.

However, his battered and bruised body was a constant, painful reminder that he was not in the safety of a dream but instead was living an ongoing, waking nightmare. He had apologized for his accidental intrusion into the Grundells' world and confessed why he was in Acronos, and they were polite, but in many ways, they acted as though they were not at all interested in his plight. Grubb was lost deep in another world with the most unusual creatures he had ever encountered, and now his hosts had disappeared to prepare afternoon tea.

And what is this tea the Grundells are so anxious to serve me? Why is tea time so vital to them? He wondered, shaking his head as a vision of a bridge flashed before his eyes.

This illusory bridge, however, was swaying back and forth in his mind, not beneath his feet. His thoughts and emotions were swinging from fear to curiosity to excitement and back to fear again.

As a biologist and botanist, he was also acutely aware that his descent into the Under-Earth might be an exceptional gift. It could be a very unique and rare opportunity to explore and learn much more about the many specialized plants and herbs the Grundells were growing.

Regardless, as Gripp #7 of the Eye of Time Exploration Team, he knew that survival must be his priority. He vigilantly scanned the dark perimeter surrounding him, closely watching dozens of Grundells working in the multi-level, cave complex. He wondered, and then seriously pondered the possibility of escaping to freedom.

Why had they left him alone to prepare tea? What were their real intentions? Who were these Grundells? Why weren't they at all concerned about his welfare? Didn't they think he might want to go home?

These thoughts and more were racing through Grubb's mind. His memory flashed back to paragraph four on page 136 of the *Gripp Survival Manual*, which stated: "When in doubt, always attempt escape!"

It was obvious that he had no alternative; even though if he stayed there would be the possibility of learning more about the Grundells' studies of special herbs, plants, trees, and flowers. Any one of them might provide answers to the Secret of Un-Old-Age. But what if he did not survive to deliver those precious solutions?

There would be the possibility of learning more about the Grundells' special herbs, plants, trees, and flowers, any one of which might provide answers to the Secret of Un-Old-Age.

Grubb was still lost deep in his thoughts when a sharp, tapping sensation jolted his body. Quickly turning around, poised for self-defense, he found himself encountering an even larger Grundell than those he had previously met.

"Are you ready to explore the deepest part of our domain?" the strange being questioned in a deep, raspy voice.

The shock of being tapped on the shoulder by sharp Grundell claws, coupled with a menacing tone of voice moved through Grubb like a shockwave.

"I hope you're going to enjoy your stay with us," the Grundell smiled, his mouth twisting ever so slightly into an almost sinister grin revealing sharp and jagged teeth designed for cutting and ripping.

Grubb did not respond. He could not even begin to consider the words, "…enjoy your stay with us."

"My name is Nimble. I am in charge of our seed storage and plant rejuvenation projects. I'm positive you're going to enjoy your tour, even though those heavy boots you are wearing may never make you as nimble…as Nimble!" He laughed, a strange and unusually haunting laugh that echoed off the walls of the cave.

The towering figure of Nimble cast a long, dark shadow over Grubb as he followed closely behind the monstrous Grundell into a section of the cave complex known only as the "Inner Chamber."

A blast of cool, fresh air hit Grubb as he descended several more steps into an area where massive stalagmites of every size, shape, and color stood like magnificent statues. Created by water dripping on limestone over many thousands of years, the magical formations had become towering structures reaching almost to the cave ceiling.

In the distance, beyond the sounds of rushing water from an underground cascade, Grubb caught sight of the Inner Chamber, a long, narrow, and seemingly endless corridor, where hundreds of baskets, containing seeds of every description, were stored within separate niches carved out of the cavern's rock walls.

"So, Grubb of the Eye of Time, what do your eyes behold?" asked Nimble with a dramatic tone of voice as he pointed at a multitude of baskets.

Staring off into the vast chamber, Grubb could only imagine the secrets he might discover within this treasure trove of nature. "What do you do with all of the seeds?"

"Preserve, Process, and Prepare!" Nimble replied, seemingly amused by his use of words. "We *preserve* all plant seeds in Acronos and use another *process* to create a fusion of two or more plants. Then we *prepare* those newly formed plants for replanting. That is our primary focus.

"I am certain that during your sojourn here in the Under-Earth, you will have more than enough time to learn, study, and help us to develop new ideas for preservation, processing, and planting."

Grubb nodded and continued following Nimble who was gesturing toward various storage systems, while he described in great detail how they were using all the plants and herbs for health and healing.

A moment later, Grubb's thoughts flashed back to Nimble's previous comment, "Since you have decided to join us here, you will have all the time you need to learn!"

Grubb wondered what Nimble meant by that comment. Was he expected to live in their world for the rest of his life? The Grundells had never mentioned helping him to return to the surface to reunite with his team.

It was terrifying to think that he might live out the rest of his short Gripp existence with these monstrous beings buried deep underground in this endless maze.

Indeed, as a biologist/botanist, his opportunity to gain information would be invaluable if he were ever able to return to Grippland where the only existing plants and trees were being kept alive in specialized glass domes to protect them from the heavily polluted air.

Grubb was lost in his thoughts, fearful of remaining and at the same time imagining himself as a hero returning to Grippland with hundreds of specialized seeds to help with the purification of their atmosphere.

Nimble continued speaking. He explained how the seeds were designed to store the sun's energy, gaining strength and then sending down roots, waiting patiently for their transformation into bushes, flowering and edible plants, herbs, and towering trees.

"These are the Trillia seeds," he enthused. "Certainly one of our most unusual and beneficial plant species. Not only are they luminescent, but they also serve as our First Alert

Warning System. The flowers change from white to yellow to orange, and then red when alerting us to danger.

They can also vary the vibrational rate of their humming whenever they sense any unusual changes in Acronos. Legend has it that these seeds are able to grow anywhere, even in the desert with little or no water, and they can communicate messages over vast distances.

The Trillia can also vary the vibrational rate of their humming whenever they sense any unusual changes in Acronos. Legend has it that these seeds are able to grow anywhere, even in the desert with little or no water, and they can communicate messages over vast distances.

"We are still experimenting with these Trillia vines hoping to learn much more about their natural abilities. Perhaps, as time goes by Gripp Grubb, you will be able to use your expertise to help us add to our knowledge and understanding of these plants. After all, you are a biologist or is it botanist?" Nimble leaned over Grubb, looking deeply into his narrow, gray eyes as if he was waiting for an enthusiastic reply.

Grubb was spellbound. Here within this vast chamber could very well be the answer to Un-Old-Age. "Yes, yes," he replied without thinking. "There is so much to learn." He then unconsciously grabbed a large handful of Trillia seeds and quickly stuffed them into his pocket without Nimble or the dozens of nearby Grundell workers noticing.

"Let us return to meet up with Tumble, Stumble, Bumble, and Wise. I am confident that they have prepared your most special tea by now." He grinned as his large eyes darted back-and-forth as if he were withholding a secret.

"Tea...?" asked Grubb. How could he possibly relax with a cup of tea with five, red-eyed monsters, who possessed such a bizarre sense of humor and so little regard for his welfare?

Nimble seemed to be retracing their steps back toward the Chamber of Bridges, passing by several more water cascades that were flowing down the colorful, blue-green rock walls into a winding river below.

The chamber ahead was filled with shifting shadows, making it extremely difficult to see as the angle of the sun penetrated various cracks and crevices in the cave ceiling. Wide and narrow shafts of filtered light were being projected in many directions.

"So, Gripp Grubb, we only have a few more bridges to cross, and soon we will be having tea with the others." declared Nimble in his deep resonating tone of voice. "After tea time, we will need to decide what to do with you," he laughed as he shuffled into another room.

Those were the last words Grubb could remember before he found himself running frantically through a maze of pathways and elevations, looking for a way out.

He was running for freedom, running for his life!

PART THIRTEEN

The Sphere of Fear

THERE WERE NO WORDS TO DESCRIBE Grubb's torment or the intense mental anguish he felt after facing near certain death. It was almost more than he could bear. He was cut, battered and bruised, but still alive; at least that is what he kept telling himself as the haunting images, sensations and memories of the Grundells' Under-Earth continued to pulse through him.

Yes, he had fallen into a hidden world, a place of mystery and intrigue where he had witnessed the wonder of the illuminated Trillia Falls and had followed Nimble on a tour to view the precious seeds they had collected.

He had been waiting while the four Grundells left to prepare tea when he noticed steps cut into the cliff that appeared to lead upward. Without hesitating, he ran for his life, climbing as fast as he could to escape the dark, damp depths and to hopefully once again gaze upon the open sky and fill his lungs with fresh air.

As he ran, the faces of his teammates whom he had last seen at Crystal Falls were flashing through his mind. *They must be dead!* He thought. *How could they possibly survive the Time Pool and those crystals?*

The journey had all seemed so simple at first. The team was well-equipped, experienced, and motivated to succeed.

After all, they were Gripps. They were the Eye of Time Exploration Team that had survived the devastation of their very own civilization. *They were supposed to be well prepared for anything! Anything!* He repeated.

Jumbled thoughts spiraled through Grubb's mind, as he continued to climb. He recalled the process that had led to High Command choosing him for the team. He had lied, cheated, and deceived his way into the program, but that was normal Gripp behavior. After all, that was their way.

Reaching the top of the staircase, he painfully dragged his aching body along a narrow ledge overlooking a small stream of water within the vast cave complex.

His last clear memories, before the Grundells captured him, were of being swept downstream by the intensity of a raging river. He remembered desperately struggling to grab onto rocks, trees, and bushes growing along the river bank.

In the midst of his panic, he could not remember how he had fallen so far into the Grundells' underground world and survived. Even more frightening were his haunting memories of those giant, furry beings that guided him through the Under-Earth and were amused by his presence. They had made up rhymes and songs for him that seemed to have hidden meanings.

Grubb had studied enough books to understand that he must be in a state of shock, especially after having survived Crystal Falls, but then again, perhaps none of this was real. Perhaps, he was already dead like all the others and just didn't know it...yet.

He wondered if being in a state of shock was only the preliminary state of mind before final departure into his Last Grasp. The other possibility, he mused, was that he had already entered into an alternate reality. Perhaps, all he had experienced was just a terrible, dark dream from which he refused to awaken.

The intense pain that moved through his body continued to remind him, however, that this was not a dream. He also knew that there was little chance of his escaping Acronos alive. And yet for some reason, he still found himself pulling his bruised and battered body along the jagged rocks of the cave wall, heading toward what appeared to be an opening not far ahead.

"That's right, Grubb," he said to himself. "That's exactly right. There is always something to learn." He sighed and stopped for a moment to catch his breath. "We are always seeking more information whether we are aware of it or not. We pursue the information we hope will lead to our..." his voice trailed off into silence.

Up ahead he could see bright, streaming shafts of light projecting into the shadowy darkness of the cave. The light was moving back and forth, up and down, as if looking for something or someone. *Those beams could not be from the sun*, he thought, watching the horizontal shafts of light penetrating far into the cavern.

He felt as if something was pulling him closer and closer to the opening as if an invisible force field was demanding his presence. Slowly, inching his way forward in a crouched position, he grasped the sharp, slippery rocks jutting out from the wall next to the narrow ledge for support.

Grubb felt intense fear, but his curiosity was propelling him forward to courageously encounter the unknown.

MULTICOLORED RAYS OF LIGHT

The light beams intensified and then were transformed into bright, colored rays of light, which penetrated deep into the cave. The focused beams were moving much slower, acting as if they had finally located the object of their search.

Grubb checked his utility belt. He had no weapons to defend himself. His two standard issue pistols and rifle had been stripped away by the flood even before he was swept over Crystal Falls.

Gripps don't run, he thought, *but why should I face certain death from an unseen enemy. I could retrace my steps further back into the cave and hide. I might have a chance to escape.*

The pain in his body was still unrelenting. His right leg was severely bruised and bleeding, yet he shuffled forward, a few more steps closer to the exit from the cave to see if he could catch a glimpse of the enemy.

He could only see streams of light, changing focus from wide to narrow, moving slowly through and around the cave entrance. He looked back at the ledge that had brought him to this hidden exit, then turned and peered down into the chasm.

He took a long, deep breath, realizing that any fall from this height would undoubtedly be his Last Grasp.

He had no choice. He could not run. He was not in any condition to run. And then, he remembered that he might have a weapon to defend himself. His twelve-inch survival knife that had been strapped to his shoulder harness was still in its sheath. *I am a scientist,* he thought. *I didn't sign onto this mission for combat duty!*

He grimaced in pain as he maneuvered himself to a few yards from the entrance to the cave. *So, my time has come,* he thought. *In just a short distance, I will actually meet my enemy — an enemy that I am certain has stalked our team since the first day we arrived.*

His thoughts were moving through time as he wondered who the dogs might be. *They had seemed friendly and acted as if they only wanted to guide us in our quest. They said they were the Guardians of Acronos, but what did that mean? Maybe, we should not have trusted them from the very beginning.*

A sinister grin began to creep across Grubb's face, as he stumbled out of the cave entrance with his survival knife in hand. He shouted to the sky, "I am here. I'm the one you're looking for!"

There was no reply. "Why don't you come forward? I am sure you're here! You've been stalking me! You may have killed all the others, but you haven't gotten Grubb. Not yet! No, not yet!"

Grubb's heart was racing wildly. His breathing was short and erratic as he tumbled to the ground to take cover behind a small outcropping of rocks.

He heard nothing but the pulsing of his heart and felt the movement of his chest as he breathed. He waited. There was nothing. *It was only my imagination,* he thought. *Nothing more.* But there was more. Suddenly, he felt a strange resonating vibration begin to circle him.

Grubb instinctively turned, trying to locate the source of the sound. As he stood up to get a better view, the first beam of light hit him squarely in the chest. He felt it, but the impact wasn't strong enough to knock him off his feet.

I can survive this, he thought.

Then the second and third beams hit him, one striking him directly on his forehead and the other on his torso.

He was still standing with a grin fixed on his face. He clutched the survival knife firmly, extended his arm, and began randomly swinging around as if he could attack or defend himself from this elusive enemy.

Grubb could not see the source of the light beams until a bright object in the sky, high above him, became visible and slowly descended. There, hovering in front of him, was a brilliant, translucent sphere emitting a luminescent glow. Beams of light were slowly changing shape as they spun around and around the central core.

As he struggled to peer into the recesses of the slowly descending orb, he became mesmerized by its elegance and overwhelming beauty as it showered bright colors in all directions as if it were painting abstract images in the air.

So, this is how the journey ends, he thought. *How do you fight a rotating sphere of light?* He gathered his strength and questioned, "Who are you?"

Still clutching his survival knife, Grubb moved closer to the orb, acting as if he were challenging it, even though the fear racing through him was far stronger than he had ever felt before. Trying to regain his courage, he blurted out again, "Who are you? Have you no words to speak?"

In response to his questions, the orb descended further, hovering only a few feet off the ground and positioning itself directly in front of Grubb.

The sphere was much larger than it looked when in the air. It was at least ten times the height of an average Gripp, and Grubb was certain there would be no defense against this unusual object that appeared to be indestructible.

He stood transfixed in its presence as the glowing center lights rotated slowly round and round, as if it were examining the very reason and meaning of his existence.

Filled with overwhelming awe, Grubb instantly threw his knife to the ground and stood tall and straight, rising up to his full height.

He used the only remaining weapon he had to defend himself...his words: "I am #7 of the Eye of Time Exploration Team. We are searching for the secret of Un-Old-Age. That is our mission. I mean, that is my mission," he corrected himself, remembering that most likely he was the sole survivor of the Gripp team.

"I have done nothing wrong. I mean no harm to anyone. I am a Gripp from Grippland!" he shouted at the sphere, trying not to show his overwhelming fear.

The sphere was rotating slowly, ever so slowly, and then it stopped moving and hovered silently only a few yards in front of Grubb. He stared directly into the Orb and was nearly hypnotized by the Kaleidoscope of moving shapes and colors contained within its form.

He heard a subtle voice talking slowly, methodically, and without judgment or emotion. And, yet, Grubb could not consciously hear those words. In just a few frozen moments, he felt as though he was being led through a maze of passageways where hidden doors opened before him effortlessly.

It was an exhilarating feeling he had never experienced before. And then, he found himself trapped, cornered in a room with locked doors that refused to open. He gasped and caught himself just before his knees buckled to the ground.

Can any of this be real? He wondered.

He could not see them clearly at first. They appeared only as shadowy, animated shapes that were quite tall, slender and shaped like Gripps moving toward him.

The voice droned on without hesitation. It was as if Grubb's mind was absorbing the words even though he was not entirely aware of them. And then he saw them.

"Who are you? Who are you, really?" he asked in a pleading voice while staring directly at the expressionless faces of the shadowy beings surrounding him.

"We thought you would comprehend who we are by now! We thought you would be able to recognize us!" replied one of the forms closest to him.

"Listen carefully. It may be difficult to understand," said another voice calmly, and then continued:

"We are the energy of the choices you didn't make. We are your failures and your faded hopes and all of your forgotten dreams. We are your inner reality manifesting in front of you to show you who you are."

Grubb gasped at the surreal thought of all these different forms actually being parts of himself revealing themselves for him to see.

"Look around you," spoke another luminous form standing near him. "See those shadowy figures with blank stares and expressionless faces. They should all seem very familiar to you, Gripp Grubb. Some are your fear of failure. Others are your fear of success. And some of them represent the energy of your future fears."

"You have never been alone, Grubb," said another shadowy form moving closer into view. "You have always been surrounded by all the fear you fear," it continued sadly. "Look around you. Take a very good look. These figures are your real team. They are indeed your true inner team."

"No, no! None of this is real! I must be dreaming," stammered Grubb, unable to comprehend the moment. "You are only apparitions. You are ghosts...Nothing more! None of this can be real!"

"Are your thoughts *real*, Grubb? Are your fears *real*? Think about it. What forms your *reality*?" continued the very authoritative voice.

"It was your curiosity that allowed you to experience this encounter. You had the opportunity to run; and for whatever reason, your resolve brought you forward, even though you were aware that it could be your Last Grasp.

"For that brief moment, you were willing to see beyond your wall of fear," added the voice sympathetically. "It was your willingness to learn that we found most appealing."

Grubb's heart was pounding; his breathing was deep and erratic as he watched the foreboding, ghost-like images moving around him. He was becoming hypnotized by the power and meaning of the words.

The authoritative voice continued, "Those doorways and passageways that you envisioned within the sphere represent your way out. There is still a small part of you which yearns to be free. Those dark, shadowy, fear-filled figures speak with many voices, but they are only your keepers, your controllers. You are the prison."

"Are you saying I am still alive?" asked Grubb.

"When do you want to live? That is the more appropriate question," the voice challenged. "And wanting to live can only occur when the Harmony of Love is recreated in you. You need to understand that only Love is real.

Remember, it is fear that has imprisoned you, and fear will continue to destroy your dreams and limit all future choices in your life." There was a moment of silence. "You have been given another choice, Gripp Grubb."

The voice continued, this time radiating warmth and comforting tones, "When do you want to live? Can you acknowledge love and learn to live completely from deep within your heart? Use this opportunity wisely." The voice trailed off as the forms moving around him also began slowly fading from view.

Grubb knew something was changing in him. Perhaps, it was the shock of experiencing all those shadowy beings surrounding him. As the sphere began to glow brighter and brighter, he felt compelled to stare intensely into its overwhelming, central core.

There were no words to describe what he was feeling, but as he continued to fixate upon the ever brightening orb of light, he felt himself becoming lighter and lighter.

Within a moment he fell to his knees with exhaustion and exhilaration. The power of this otherworldly experience had overwhelmed him and dramatically changed him.

The glow from the sphere continued increasing until in a flash of brilliant white light, it disappeared.

Knowing Your Heart

When you know your heart, you are resonating with the Harmony of Love and are in contact with the ultimate power of creation, rejuvenation, and transformation. The Source Energy of Universal Love animates and flows through you.

Remember, it is all the aspects of fear (hate, anger, distrust, jealousy, and depression) that paralyze and imprison you.

When you listen to your heart, you are closer to fulfilling your dreams and expanding all your future choices. Opening your heart welcomes the Light of Love to dissolve the darkness of your fears and to fully energize your life.

Knowing your heart creates a healing process, allowing you to feel young no matter how many years you have lived.

PART FOURTEEN

Mirror Mountain

W HILE THE EXPLORATION TEAM RESTED briefly on a windy plateau, Gritt, the Half-Synth, stood up and announced that shortly before the Startlings had attacked them in the meadow, he had distinctly heard an unusual sound...the sound of bells ringing from somewhere in the mountain peaks above them.

The Gripps became quiet; and then, they also heard the tolling of bells in the distance. Once again they felt hopeful that their journey was not in vain.

"Perhaps civilization truly does exist here!" exclaimed Commander Grist. "It's highly probable that there are advanced, intelligent life forms trying to contact us!"

Grist desperately wanted to believe those words... words of redemption for a former General...words which would lead them to a successful mission. Failure was not part of Grist's vocabulary, and he ordered his team to prepare to march on.

Without delay they gathered up their remaining equipment and headed toward the beckoning of the bells.

The mid-morning daylight illuminated vibrant, pink blossoms, the fallen petals of the Komarra trees, covering the pathway and forming surreal ribbons of color leading the Gripps toward the mountain peaks.

In less than a Grippon (hour) into their endless hike up the trail, large dark clouds rolled over the mountains, hiding the sun and turning the pink and golden hues of the trail and the cliffs into dull shades of gray.

The first cool drops of water, which started as a gentle sprinkle, suddenly, without warning, turned into icy sheets of rain. Grist commanded the team to take cover under an overhanging cliff and beneath the leafy branches of nearby trees to protect them from the torrential downpour.

It was quiet, except for the sounds of the pouring rain and the incessant wind rustling the trees…too quiet! The tolling of the bells had ceased.

Huddled under the protection of an overhanging cliff, Grist, Twist, and Scheme were busy discussing the odds of mission success.

"There's absolutely no reason to keep going!" exclaimed Twist who was tired of proceeding toward what was most assuredly a figment of Grist's fertile imagination.

Surprisingly, the politician had decided he would rather return to Grippland and face the consequences. Yes, the sound of bells had encouraged him to imagine there might be some form of civilization in those mountains, but those bells were no longer ringing. Perhaps, they were merely a hallucination like a wishful, waking dream.

Scheme was quick to agree and proclaimed, "We should turn back while we still have time!" Clearly, the businessman was aware that his ability as a negotiator on this mission was completely useless. Everything they had encountered on their journey indicated that this wilderness of Acronos would share no secrets nor would it harbor any advanced civilization.

After surviving the attack by the flocks of menacing Startlings, there was little enthusiasm among the team members to continue trudging up mountain trails leading them nowhere.

Grist took a deep breath, "We have nearly three Grabbons left until the Portal in Time reopens. How can you even think about quitting when we have come so far?"

The three leaders stared at each other in silent defiance as if that silence would help them to manifest their ability to make the correct decision. Having survived so many dangerous encounters, perhaps they were pushing their luck to continue onward.

Grist looked over at his weary team sheltering and shivering under the thick branches of the Komarra tree as the icy cold rain continued to punish their spirits.

Was this entire mission doomed from the beginning? He asked himself. *Am I completely delusional? Perhaps, Twist and Scheme are correct. Maybe we are chasing an illusion of successfully accomplishing our mission.*

He looked down at the medals on his jacket, took a long, deep breath and remembered, *I am still Commander Grist! I truly believe we are closer than ever to our discovery! I signed onto this mission for success, not failure!*

He cleared his throat and said enthusiastically. "Are we not Gripps? Have we forgotten who we are?"

Grist did not have to wait long for an answer. Powerful echoes reverberated down from the mountain. They were the echoes of tolling bells!

Twist and Scheme remained speechless. An expression of shock and awe froze upon their faces as they searched for words to describe their amazement. It was as if Grist had somehow commanded those beckoning bells to ring louder and stronger at just the right moment.

"We have our answer!" exclaimed Grist with great bravado. "There is no doubt that civilization is just ahead. They are calling us! Our mission quest is still alive, and so are we!"

Grist surveyed his weary team. "We may need to journey on through the night, but we will reach our objective! There is no other choice! We have the opportunity for success just ahead of us; there is no doubt, no doubt at all! This is the moment we have been waiting for, can't you see it?"

The rain had slowed to a misty drizzle, and the beleaguered explorers slowly emerged from under their protected confines to continue upward, following the rugged mountain trail. They had no choice.

The explorers continued pushing themselves far beyond their pain and physical limits as the persistent dream of freedom provided them with just enough energy, courage, and confidence to fuel their quest.

Their odyssey brought them through a forested area into a clearing, but they were shocked and unnerved to discover that the trail had led them into what appeared to be a small, enclosed canyon surrounded by high cliffs.

Grist, Twist, and Scheme immediately exchanged angry glances and started pacing back-and-forth, arguing and gesturing toward the rocky enclosure. Their loud, gruff voices created booming echoes bouncing off the massive, sheer canyon walls. Soon, other Gripps joined in, shouting words of outrage and blame, accusing one another of betrayal and deceit, all except one.

Instead of arguing, Gritt, the Half-Synth, turned his full attention toward an unusual presence, which was moving in a zig-zag pattern high above the cliffs surrounding them.

Fabius motioned for Filloloper to watch Gritt who was apparently trying to catch a glimpse of that fleeting vision.

"Do you see him?" asked Fabius.

"Yes, but what is Phelan doing here?"

The sound of a rhyme was drifting on the cool breeze and floated down into the canyon below:

> *The way it was...*
> *The way it is...*
> *The way it wants to be*
> *is the way you'll always see.*
>
> *The why it is, is the way you are.*
> *The why is neither near nor far...*
> *the why is moving round and round*
> *inside you...waiting to be found!*

Gritt could not help but gaze in wonder at the unusual creature moving back-and-forth along the top of the sheer cliffs. Although he could not see the full image of the giant bird, he heard every word of the haunting rhyme that was repeating in his mind:

> *The way it was...*
> *The way it is...*
> *The way it wants to be!*

"That strange bird is spontaneously creating riddles and rhymes," Gritt said to himself, "but, then again, perhaps, those words can only be heard by someone who is willing to listen or by those who have extra-sensory perception!" His half-synth lips turned upward, and he managed to smile.

Yes, the Gripp team was trapped again. After searching every inch of the canyon walls for a way out, they admitted conclusively that the only solution was to retrace their steps. They added a few more abusive accusations and blame for being trapped squarely on the shoulders of the lowest numbered Gripps, Nine and Ten.

At this point, Grist stepped forward to speak. "So, this is it! This dead end is where it all ends! And why does it end here? Why? Why? Why does it end here? Because we have forgotten who we are! We have become victims of an invisible enemy—a cowardly adversary who uses tricks, illusions, and schemes to trap us!"

Grist scanned the canyon walls and continued speaking in his strongest voice as if opposing, enemy forces were listening to his every word from the rocky cliffs above.

"We will never forget that we are Gripps!" Grist declared defiantly, his voice cracking with emotion. "We will never surrender even in the face of a faceless enemy!"

In past wars, Grist had sometimes felt panic, but his seasoned, military mind would never allow him to show fear or demonstrate weakness. This mission was his command. Discovering the Secret of Un-Old-Age was to be his moment of glory, and he would not stop for any reason, most especially without meeting the enemy face-to-face!

Pacing in front of his bedraggled and spiritless team, he stoically examined each of their expressions, and thought to himself: *If only I had a properly trained military unit, I wouldn't be in this predicament!*

Grist knew full well that this might be the very moment of their complete and utter defeat. He quickly lost himself in thoughts and images of past glory, denying the reality presently confronting him. In his imagination, he was not a failure; but instead, was in the midst of leading a charge as he had done in the many wars he successfully commanded.

Monitoring every move of the Gripp team below, Phelan noticed a shift in the energy field that was growing stronger and stronger.

These explorers must have triggered the energy field of the mountain, he thought as he fearfully considered all possible outcomes. *Their frustration, anger, and emotional outbursts continue to unbalance the energy of everything around them.*

The Great Kolourian Zigalot (the last of his kind) could not help but be concerned about the welfare of those on the canyon floor below, most notably his dearest friends, the Guardians of Acronos, Fabius and Filloloper.

These strangers simply do not understand that whatever they are trying to escape is usually just waiting for them to arrive, mused Phelan as he ran his zig-zag pattern along the cliff edge, observing what was happening below.

But his view had quickly become obscured by a dark, dense fog that was enveloping the entire canyon, making all those below nearly invisible. Only Grist's continued shouts and commands indicated that they were facing still another malevolent force.

"It's here!" exclaimed Grist. "This is the moment we have been waiting for!" His voice seemed to be garbled by the dense blanket of fog moving over them.

"I know they are here!" he growled defiantly. "They are moving among us, hiding somewhere within this blanket of fog! Prepare your weapons! Prepare to engage them!" he commanded defiantly, swinging his Gripp pistol around as if he could actually see his attackers moving toward him.

Fabius and Filloloper squeezed into a narrow crevice in the canyon wall, hoping to avoid any gunfire.

"It's not safe here," warned Fabius. "They truly believe an enemy has them surrounded!"

CANYON WALLS TRANSFORMING

The blanket of fog slowly lifted, leaving a rolling mist drifting through the canyon; and even though the Gripps had sought shelter, they could not escape the appearance of the sheer rock wall directly in front of them.

Suddenly, the cliff face was changing, revealing silvery patterns and forms, which moved back-and-forth, as if responding to the foreign intrusion into their hidden space.

Grist gave orders to take cover behind large boulders just below the cliffs, not realizing that what he perceived as an "enemy" was acutely aware of their presence.

The canyon wall in front of them seemed to be alive. It was magically becoming illuminated from within as its surface continued shifting and changing into different shapes and colors. It was transforming into a majestic, light show.

The undulating wall was now depicting moving images, glowing faces with blinking eyes and animated expressions. The distorted, mask-like images seemed somewhat familiar, but as soon as they became slightly recognizable, the features and shapes quickly changed again.

My teammates still cannot see what is right before their eyes, thought Gritt, the Half-Synth.

Soon, the illuminated images on the wall became undeniable. They were the mirrored faces of each member of the Gripp team that were now being arranged in a perfect circle and placed like the numbers around a clock.

Watching with shock and trepidation, Phelan could no longer contain himself and called out a rhyme:

> *Change of face, change of place,*
> *running in a never-ending race.*
> *Not knowing what is or isn't to be*
> *from those images looking back at me.*
> *Mirror of mine, mirror of mime*
> *always magically changing in time!*

Filloloper glanced over at Fabius and said, "Phelan is desperately increasing the volume of his voice. He's trying convince the Gripps that they have a choice. Mirror Mountain is seeking information by changing its formation."

"It seems to be contagious," suggested Fabius.

"What is contagious?"

Fabius replied with a smile, "You're using *Phelan Speak.* You're speaking in rhyme. Phelan cannot help himself. He's always caught somewhere between humor and disaster. After all, as the last of his kind, he believes he alone can rescue or at least warn the travelers of what might be coming!"

"Evidently, Phelan is not the only one with a sense of humor," jested Filloloper, trying to make light of a dire situation. The energy animating Mirror Mountain has placed Grist, Twist, and Scheme at the top of the clock."

The Gripps seemed incapable of confronting the adversary taunting them. They were face-to-face with the opponent they were so desperately seeking, not knowing that the enemy was, indeed, themselves.

A MOVING WALL OF LIGHT

Filloloper and Fabius became silent witnesses to an energy exchange they had never experienced in Acronos or in the *Before Time*. They were observing the stranded adventurers staring in awe and amazement at moving light forms that animated their faces to near perfection on the cliff wall.

"The canyon wall is continuously forming and reforming their images!" exclaimed Filloloper.

"They have effectively found what they were looking for," Fabius replied, carefully modulating his voice. "Mirror Mountain has its secrets, but it should be obvious to the Gripps that the more they focus on their faces on the wall, the more those images change expressions."

Indeed, the mountain had become a mirror, not only as a reflector of light and form, but also as a measure of energy. It was imitating the fluctuating, emotional expressions of each team member while delving into the depths of their souls.

As thoughts and emotions traveled through the hearts and minds of the team below, the portraits on the wall grew in size and shape, moving and changing ever so slightly. The silvery eyes of each face were watching, monitoring, and then duplicating the exact energetic patterns discovered within each of them.

Slowly, ever so slowly, the circle of images became larger and began rotating. As it moved, the Gripps were compelled to peer deeper into their own reflections. After a few minutes, all movement stopped. The *Clock of Faces* was complete.

An invisible second-hand seemed to be turning around the clock, briefly touching each image, making the face larger and then smaller, and then time traveled on to the next face while the mirrored portraits started chanting: "Tick of the Tock! Tick of the Tock!"

"They have become the clock! The Gripps are completely caught up in Time!" exclaimed Fabius.

And then *a new pattern began.* One after the other, a face moved into the center of the clock, and that animated image confessed and dramatized all the trials and burdens they experienced in their life. Like a chorus in the background, all the other faces around the clock chimed in, mimicking the words being spoken by the face in the center.

"They...they are echoing the very same words," stammered Fabius, trying to understand what was happening. "The pain and suffering of each is being shared by all."

The clock shifted again as the faces around the clock started to chant,

> *Talk...Talk...*
> *Talk about the clock!*
> *Talk about the Talk!*

It was as though the lost travelers had actually become the clock. Their full intention and attention had become locked within the moving moments of Time.

From the top of the cliff above the Clock of Faces, an echo of a distant voice drifted into the canyon below:

> *Change of face....*
> *Change of place...*
> *Winning against time*
> *they seek to erase....!*

"Phelan is still with us!" said Fabius. "How can he possibly survive this powerful energy field? It's transforming everything in the canyon!"

"He is a Great Kolourian after all!" answered Filloloper. "Even though his unique abilities allow him to feel the slightest vibrations, he possesses an amazing will to survive even in his deepest fear of fear." She enjoyed Phalen's twist on words.

Phelan was indeed back! He was overseeing the entire event from a position very near the edge of the cliff face. He was trying to warn all concerned that if the deeply penetrating vibrations continued to increase, the entire canyon could collapse without warning.

> *The face they sought*
> *was the face in the clock…!*
> *The face they came to be*
> *was the THEY…they refused to see.*
>
> *Images of emotions erasing*
> *the hidden thoughts they were chasing*
> *are facing the enemy they despise,*
> *now looking through their eyes.*

As the faces on the wall began speaking faster and faster, expressing anger and frustration about their battered lives, the Gripps on the ground became more and more agitated, desperate to escape, but where could they run? They were locked in an energy field that held them tightly in its grasp, suspending them in place and time.

ACCELERATING TIME

Standing in rapt attention, the Gripp team watched as Time changed directions. The invisible hand of the clock was moving backward into the past. The unrelenting, energetic forces were increasing and accelerating their personal voyage into the very center of who they had become.

When each image moved into the center of the clock and spoke of sadness, anger, and fear, their faces looked older. Their twisted expressions projected on the three-dimensional, *Mountain of Mirrors* showed a heart-rending display of anguish and pain.

From high on the ridge, Phelan's voice echoed again into the canyon below:

> *Words, words, words*
> *becoming thoughts,*
> *playing a timeless game,*
> *blending into all the same.*
>
> *Being faithful to the gray and grim,*
> *defines your dream-less dreams*
> *with long-forgotten words*
> *turned into endless schemes.*
>
> *How do you create a future here,*
> *there or anywhere*
> *when your imagination swirls*
> *within all those windowless worlds?*
>
> *Words, words, words*
> *leading you back again*

in perpetual motion, chasing
the end you're never facing.
Always seeking freedom's treasure
within the recesses of your mind,
searching for wondrous words,
words you can never find.

Words, words, words,
becoming thoughts playing games
becoming your reality.
Who is to blame?

Words, words, words!

Phelan stopped his rhyming as the energy of Mirror Mountain delved deeper into the Gripps' emotional memories. It was searching for who they were when they were young

Now, when each face moved into the center of the clock, it described events that happened when they were children. These were memories of pleasant experiences before they became grabbing, gripping, grinding, duty-bound citizens of Grippland. When they spoke of childhood memories, their faces appeared younger and younger.

They used forbidden, *Museum Words* such as faith and hope, joy and love, beauty and honor, inspiration and desire. They praised culture, creative expression, loving relationships, playfulness and fun. As they expressed these positive thoughts, the other faces answered chanting:

Words against the greater good,
words that never should…
never could see the light of day.
Words that Gripps cannot say.

Words that are dead and gone,
Words in the Word Museum.

Filloloper stared at the moving *Clock of Faces* and said, "The forbidden words are making them appear younger! Even the chanting of negative *Gripp Speak* isn't stopping their positive thoughts from rejuvenating the energy locked within their hearts. When they were caught in their negative thoughts, they left their youth far behind."

The energy animating Mirror Mountain continued observing and absorbing every team member into its reflective surface, and then the *Clock of Faces* quickly changed its rate of motion.

"It's spinning faster!" exclaimed Fabius as the images on the wall became a distorted blur. Within a few moments, it slowed down and stopped. The faces were gone, replaced by nine, blue lights.

The entire Gripp team on the ground remained motionless, locked into place, as they watched the brilliant pinpoints of blue light begin to spin…slowly at first, and then faster and faster until the *Clock of Faces* was transformed into a spinning wheel of vibrant, crystal blue light.

"The canyon floor is moving!" shouted Filloloper, bracing herself as the ground beneath her began to ripple in wave-like patterns flowing through the solid rock.

"We have to escape now!" shouted Fabius. "That energy shift may become a Time Warp! We don't want to be here if that happens!"

Filloloper ran after him, avoiding the rocks and debris falling from the cliff face. They paused to look back at the Gripps who were enveloped in the penetrating, brilliant blue light projecting directly from the center of the clock.

"It's over!" exclaimed Fabius, trying to maintain balance on the shifting, canyon floor. "Mirror Mountain is absorbing all of the team members, not just their reflections!"

"What does the mountain want? What is it looking for?" asked Filloloper, worried that the explorers from another world might instantly disappear.

"Mirror Mountain is trying to balance its energy field by absorbing and neutralizing the negative Gripp energy.

The dogs watched in amazement as the canyon suddenly began transforming within a cloud of moving light.

"Look," exclaimed, Fabius, attempting to see through the blue haze. "There is a something there! I think it's a pathway through the mountain!"

Where only moments before a violent, spinning, vortex of energy had filled the canyon, there was now a perfectly formed archway carved into the very center of Mirror Mountain precisely where the *Clock of Faces* had been.

In front of the arch stood all nine, time travelers slowly becoming animated again as they stumbled to regain their balance. They stared in disbelief at the enormous archway. It was difficult to comprehend that they had not only survived, but that a pathway through the mountain had also been created for them.

Filloloper was amazed to see the sheer, canyon wall transformed into a pathway to freedom. She looked up to see Phelan disappearing into the distance and asked Fabius, "Do you think this experience will change the Gripps?"

Fabius hesitated for a moment and replied, "How could they not change? Seeing themselves caught in Time and reflected in Time, they became the mirror of their former selves. When the clock began to spin backward, they described their lives as children; and as they spoke those forbidden words, their faces did become younger."

Filloloper nodded in agreement as she watched the stunned and bewildered Eye of Time explorers slowly and silently walking through Mirror Mountain. With a new resolve, they were once more following the resonant tones of the distant tolling bells.

Living in Joy and Wonder

As you let go of past programming and conditioning, you will once again feel the joy and wonder of your youth. You allow positive memories and new concepts about who you are to dissolve the negative words and thoughts that have created fearful filters influencing your world view.

By focusing on images of inspiring subjects and positive experiences, you lift your vibrational frequency and envision new possibilities for your life.

Imagine wonderful people, beautiful places, and pleasant events you desire in your life to activate intense feelings of joy and inner peace that will heal your heart and soul.

When you live in joy and wonder, you will re-experience your youthful energy, excitement, curiosity, and enthusiasm and will marvel at the miracle of life and the beauty around you.

PART FIFTEEN

The Tolling Of Bells

THE VIBRANT SOUNDS of the distant, tolling bells were compelling Grist and his team to push ever higher up the twisting, rocky mountain trail, moving ever deeper into a wilderness that offered no defense against surprise attacks.

There were always high risks involved when tracking the unknown, and Mission Commander Grist knew those perils very well. His dark gray eyes fixated upon the mountain peaks ahead, and yet his probing thoughts were elsewhere. He was questioning why he was suddenly feeling less inclined to take risks. Something within him had shifted. He wondered if his teammates were also feeling those subtle changes in their thinking and feeling nature.

He was tempted to discuss his thoughts with the others, most especially with Twist and Scheme but decided instead to monitor the team for any unusual behavior.

He turned his attention to Fabius and Filloloper and was unable to push away the nagging feeling that there was someone else controlling Acronos, and he, she or it was directing and speaking through the dogs. *Nothing is what it appears to be here. Nothing at all,* he thought.

He remembered the dogs were watching all the unbelievable events that took place at Mirror Mountain. Did they make it happen? How did a passageway suddenly appear in a canyon wall made of solid rock? Why were the dogs anxious to guide them toward the tolling of the bells, or were they? It was unusual for Grist to be considering these thoughts, and he had far more questions than answers.

As the team continued up the trail, they were also thinking about their extraordinary, life-altering experience at Mirror Mountain. With each step, they felt more out of control physically, mentally and emotionally, and that feeling was interfering with their most precious possession — their Gripp Logic.

But what exactly had shifted their perspective? They couldn't remember all the details of entering into the *Clock of Faces*, but they knew that mysterious and bewildering event was a turning point in their lives. Most of what had happened was just beyond their ability to recall, at least for the moment.

After trekking for several Grippons (hours), Grist finally ordered his beleaguered team members to stop and take refuge for the night in a small clearing just off the trail. Spreading branches of a Syracon tree with its glossy, green leaves formed a natural canopy. Large, gray boulders nearby protected them from the brisk, cold winds blowing down from the mountain.

Settling into their campsite and gazing into the welcome warmth of a crackling fire, the Gripps could see flashes of fleeting memories moving through their minds.

There were visions of forgotten moments when they were young and full of life — elusive memories of being joyful and using forbidden words. These spontaneous, illusory images of a happy childhood were silently haunting them.

Fabius and Filloloper settled into a protected area and listened to the team members as they began talking to themselves, mumbling about their past.

"They no longer seem to be in the present," observed Fabius. "They are lost deep within their thoughts as if they are trying to retrieve parts of themselves that are no longer accessible. Do you think their experience with Mirror Mountain has permanently altered them?"

Filloloper moved closer to get a better view. "Some appear to have changed, and a few look much younger than before. I think Babble seems the youngest of all."

"Yes, but she was always the youngest." Fabius, smiled, trying to make light of the situation. "But I do understand what you're saying. They are all noticeably younger-looking, except Grist, Twist, and Scheme. Those three still look the same as when they first arrived, perhaps even a little older.

"That's not surprising since, as the leaders of the team, they are impressed with their positions in life. They can't imagine altering themselves," explained Fabius. "It is very difficult for someone who is entrenched in their image to make changes to the person they have become."

CONFESSIONS BY THE FIRE

The intensity of the fire grew stronger, projecting its glow over the smooth, silver gray boulders and illuminating the tall trees surrounding the clearing.

"Look into their faces," whispered Filloloper. "They have become mesmerized by the fire."

The flames flickered and then brightened as Commander Grist spoke in a hushed, gruff voice. He was mumbling to himself but was loud enough for the others to hear him.

"There were reasons to join the military. Excellent reasons," he said while rubbing his hands together over the open fire.

"It is honorable to defend Grippland from invaders and attackers and destroy the enemy. The reason I am #1 is my willingness to engage in battle whenever and wherever the enemy comes into sight."

"What's he talking about?" asked Filloloper softly.

"He seems to be making a confession and trying to justify his way of being," Fabius replied quietly.

One by one, each team member gazed into the center of the blazing fire, speaking in nearly inaudible words about who they had been and decisions they had made.

"By a twist of fate, Twist I became. Twist is now my name. In the beginning, I was not the same. I preferred to play another game. When I joined the team, I became second in command and learned the lay of the land. I am a master politician, prepared to make our doctrine known to all those we encounter and then later own."

"Look, Twist's face is changing from older to younger and then back again," observed Filloloper.

"It appears that the moving light from the fire has hypnotized him." answered Fabius. "They are all trapped in time by *who they were then* and *who they are now*. And more importantly, they have not yet escaped from *who they may become*. Listen, #3 is speaking."

"When I was young, I always dreamed of riches to be found," mused Scheme thoughtfully. "It was never my way to enter the fray, so I was the one to make a deal. If not to bargain, then to steal."

Next to speak was Babble who was lost in thought and staring directly into the campfire that illuminated her golden hair and youthful beauty. "There were those who said my life would be free and easy since my personality was so light and breezy. But that was then, and this is now, and I became #4, the one to travel and explore, recording the gripping of our words once more." She looked up as Stare began to speak.

"I am Stare, an engineer, prepared to save the future from our fear. I confess I'm never very aware when I find myself lost within my stare."

The sad and disheveled Doctor Grouse sat stoically by the fire and said, "I am Grouse. I became a doctor hoping that I would prosper. Before I even wondered why, I saw my world passing by. Now serving as #6, there are just too many Gripps I'm supposed to fix."

Gritt also seemed mesmerized by the fire and spoke, "I am Gritt, the geologist. I should have been an ecologist. I was the one to replace my face, so that I could save Grippland from disgrace. I am the one behind the veil who thought that he would never fail."

"What does he mean...replace his face?" asked Filloloper, moving closer trying to catch a better look at Gritt. "His face hasn't changed. He appears to look the same."

Fabius didn't reply. He knew that Gritt, the Half-Synth, had changed his face and altered his fate long ago. He was designed to contain his emotions, yet it appeared that he, too, was affected by his encounter with Mirror Mountain.

A moment later, another voice joined in. "I'm Grimm, the psychologist. As #9 I was trained to stop the spinning of the mind by using words I can never find. All disruptive words are now undone and never heard outside the Word Museum."

"She does seem very grim, but in the reflected glow of the fire on her face, I can also see a sense of kindness in her past. I don't believe she was always so grim," observed Fabius, wondering what had made her so very sad and angry.

"I am Grind, the anthropologist, #10, the very last to be in command. I am a grinder for the truth, digging, digging everywhere like a sleuth, always looking past the past to find clues to a future that truly might last."

"Why are they always talking about the past?" questioned Filloloper, perplexed by all the spontaneous confessions of the Gripps.

"They are reviewing their trail of memories, all their past actions and reactions. They think that who they were is who they are now," replied Fabius sadly. "Thus, they continue to create the same story over and over again into the future. They have not learned that every moment they are born anew."

The weary explorers continued to mumble on and on about their lives while staring transfixed into the brilliance of the fire until one by-by-one they ultimately fell into a deep sleep.

"They seem to have forgotten how little time there is before the closing of the Time Portal," suggested Filloloper in her normal tone of voice, aware that the exhausted adventurers could no longer hear their conversation.

"They are obsessed with wanting to discover the Secret of Un-Old-Age," answered Fabius, "and they cannot possibly imagine returning to Grippland as failures."

"Even if it means never going home?" asked Filloloper. "They must have learned something from their experiences here in Acronos, and by now they should know much more about who they are." She stopped speaking as she caught a glimpse of something moving within the tree line just behind the sleeping Gripps.

It's nothing, she thought. *That movement is only a play of light and shadow cast by the dying embers of the campfire.*

Once Grist and the team were asleep, Babble determined this might be her last chance to write a report for High Command. She needed to update all the information before they reached the location of the bells. Hurrying to the edge of the camp, she set up her equipment behind the base of a large tree.

GRIPP LOG 4: 47646-B
TOP SECRET REPORT

I am writing this report at the end of Grabbon five with less than two Grabbons (days) remaining before we must return to the Time Portal to return.

I am codifying this report as Top Secret since it will most likely be my last opportunity to record our journey to this location now simply known as Level Seven. It is my hope that someday this recording will be found and offer some evidence of our extreme efforts to seek out a successful conclusion to our mission quest.

Most team members, at the time of this writing realize that there is very little hope in ever reaching the Portal for our scheduled departure.

We have become bruised, battered, beaten, and humiliated by unseen forces which seem to be manipulating the natural wilderness surrounding us!

We continue to be guided by the two dogs, Fabius and Filloloper who say they only desire to be our guides; but in fact, they have led us into one trap after the other! It is very possible that these innocent-looking dogs who speak perfect Grippish are either not really dogs at all or they are being animated by some unseen force.

There can be no doubt that we have been monitored ever since our arrival as our best efforts have only been met by obstacles of every kind. Madness seems to be taking over many members of our team, mostly affecting the leaders, and our psychologist, Grimm, continues to believe that everything here must be an illusion.

Time itself seems to have been chasing us ever since we first arrived in this land called Acronos. It's as though time is constantly trying to erase our very presence here.

After departing the island to seek out another shoreline, we overcame sea monsters, called Spinners; and believed that the worst was over. But then, on the mainland, three team members alerted us to the fact that Time had changed our landing zone, and all our valuable equipment had disappeared.

Since then we have had to endure a maze of hedges, the dogs named Hedora, which for some reason was able to manifest directly in front of our pathway blocking further progress.

We were later informed by our two guides that Hedora is a name for our intuition, a strange concept whereby one receives information by not knowing where the information comes from or how it comes, for that matter.

The dogs speak about the mysterious, Seven Harmonies, but we don't understand. It's something about tones and rhythm and rhyme. Who knows what that nonsense means?

There has also been constant talk of invisible pathways and doors and forests that only wish to say, "Hello!" We endured a stage performance by two gigantic singing, blue birds, simply named Bo and Ben (the Rockin' BoBens), who were babbling on about something regarding choosing to live in the past, present or future at the Crossroads of Time.

When they weren't pleased with Grist's decision not to choose, they immediately proceeded to crush us in a torrent of water that carried us into a crystal cave. We lost our memory of what happened there.

Our valuable, biologist, Grubb, is presumed dead. He became an obvious victim of the Bash Birds, when he went missing in the cave complex!

It was only a few Grippons (hours) ago that our progress was blocked by the sheer cliffs of a box canyon. There was no way to escape, so we were forced to fight an invisible enemy who somehow projected our essences onto the structure of the cliff wall.

We were then forced to endure viewing our faces forming an enormous clock, which moved back-and-forth through time. Since that encounter it is obvious that many of us have changed, some for the better some for the worse!

Commander Grist, Twist, and Scheme seem more possessed within their extreme personalities. Grist, is now leading us higher and higher into the mountains, frantically following the sound of bells, which he believes originate from an advanced civilization. He hopes this figment of his imagination can provide us with the Secret of Un-Old-Age or possibly Grold.

There is little hope of ever reaching the location of the bells. Most members of the team truly believe this is another trick to keep us imprisoned here until our very last Grasp!

This will obviously be my last report and therefore I am overlaying all records into a permanent archive status in the hope that any future missions might find this recorder, gain wisdom, and prosper from its contents! *End of Top Secret Report.*

FOLLOWING THE BELLS

Filloloper felt as though only minutes had passed when she opened her eyes and saw the golden glow of dawn moving over the campsite and watched the team members gathering their gear. Up ahead was the winding trail, beckoning them higher into the mountains.

Something had changed within each of the Travelers in Time as a result of all their overwhelming experiences. They were still rugged, determined and unrelenting, but they now seemed to be demonstrating a greater awareness of themselves and the environment.

Filloloper and Fabius could not help but admire the Gripps strength and fortitude and their persistent quest for success! Their will to succeed seemed unshakable.

The team continued moving silently up the trail in the direction of the tolling of the bells. Their eyes were fixed solely upon the looming mountain ahead as if some unseen, magnetic force was drawing them forward.

Driving rain from the night before had left deep cuts and crevices in the surface of the rocky trail, making their progress increasingly difficult. They struggled on, balancing precariously on the narrow pathway that was hanging over sharp, rocky gorges to the left and the right of them.

The sheer drop below would most certainly mean instant death, thought Fabius, as he stepped forward cautiously. He was the first to notice that hidden deep within the crevices were small flecks of dust reflecting the rising sun.

It's the Grold, their precious Grold, he thought and wondered why no one else had noticed. *They have been walking over precisely what they were searching for...their Grold.*

He remembered their chants, "With Grold, we won't grow old!" But he felt it best to remain silent about his discovery and continued to follow the Gripps in their relentless pursuit of the tolling of the bells.

Filtered sunlight penetrated a low lying fog when Grist noticed that the pathway had widened, forming a flat ridge overlooking the valley below. He called for an immediate halt and spoke in a quiet, almost inaudible voice, motioning for his team to gather closer around him so they might hear him more clearly.

"We have all been this far before, fellow Gripps. I know that sounds absurd, but it is true." He hesitated, and then spoke louder and more forcefully. "Our success has eluded us, but not this time! Our triumph lies just ahead!"

His face flushed red with excitement. "The citizens who are ringing those bells will have the answers to our quest! They are beckoning us, encouraging us to continue onward! Don't you see? There can be no doubt! No doubt at all!"

Grist turned suddenly to look up the trail, "It's there beyond that turn, fellow Gripps, just beyond that turn!"

Fabius whispered to Filloloper, "You were right about their logic. Grist seems to have lost his grip on reality. His obsession has eliminated his fears of the elusive enemy he was so very desperate to encounter."

VISIONS FROM THE PAST

Filloloper moved closer to Fabius and started to speak, but her words stopped short as she heard the resonant tones of the tolling bells begin again, echoing down the trail and bouncing off the sheer cliffs high above them.

Grist called out, "Prepare to march in two by two formation. Raise the Gripp flag!"

"Heads high!" continued Grist. "We are about to discover a new civilization. It must be so!"

But it was not so. Instead, the nine, weary, team members looked up to see two, very large, dark gray objects flying towards them just above their heads. They were the missing long rafts, each holding a ghostly crew member gesturing for the team to follow them.

Grist was not deterred by this vision and blurted out, "It is a gift! It is a gift from the civilization we are about to encounter! They are returning our rafts for our voyage back home!" He shouted out, his voice filled with emotion.

Filloloper stared in disbelief, "Doesn't Grist realize what he is seeing? Or has he blinded himself to the fact that each of those rafts contains what appears to be a member of their Eye of Time Exploration Team?"

Fabius surveyed the scene in front of him, and after hesitating for several moments spoke with a tone of wonder, "There...is even more to disbelieve." He pointed toward a ghostly image, outlined by the brilliance of the sun, waiting at the bend in the trail only a few yards ahead.

A slight half-grin passed over Gritt's face as he observed the ghost. He thought he recognized the figure but even he was beginning to doubt what he was seeing.

After careful observation, everyone realized that standing before them was #7, Grubb, whom they thought had died within the churning waters of the River of Time.

The bright sun was shining through a soft haze directly behind him, creating an intense and dramatic silhouette. There could be no doubt. The vision was indeed Grubb.

As they watched, the pale white, otherworldly image of the biologist appeared to float above the trail as he motioned for his fellow team members to follow him.

"It's the Ghost of Grubb!" declared Twist. "He was dead, and now he's here to guide us." and

Grist hesitated to remark on the vision of Grubb, and then after staring intensely at the apparition, he blurted out, "They are returning Grubb to us! It is another gift! The civilization has sent him as a messenger!" he declared joyously. "He may be dead. But here he is again!"

The other team members quickly moved to huddle around Grist, and then quietly began to mumble, "He was dead, but here he is again!"

And then they started to chant:

> *Grubb was dead, but here he is again!*
> *Grubb was dead, but here he is again!*

The image of Grubb remained motionless. Only a slight imperceptible smile crossed his lips as if he were guarding a secret, a secret he was desperate to share. His only response was the motion of his hand indicating that he wanted them to follow him.

Slowly, deliberately, Grubb moved backward without turning around and appeared to float slightly above the ground. No one seemed to notice.

PATTERNS OF DESTINY

The shock of Grubb's ghostly arrival pushed the Gripps far beyond their ability to process logical thought. They seemed to be unaware of the changes in the atmosphere and the fact that their bodies were becoming much lighter than when they were walking in the valley below.

Rather than paying attention to the changes around them, the team members were focused on Grist's enthusiastic statement, "A new civilization is just ahead, and Ghost Grubb was sent as our messenger!"

The Gripps longed to cast their eyes on a prosperous civilization—a place they were so eager and desperate to discover. They needed to believe that Grubb was, in fact, an unexpected gift from the inhabitants. It had to be so!

As they cautiously followed Grubb around a high cliff, the team stepped out onto a broad plateau with a view of the valley and distant mountains.

There, looming above the Gripps, stood three illuminated, crystalline obelisks, each containing a glowing, golden ball of light in its center. The magnificent, translucent towers stood over thirty feet tall and were set in a triangular-shaped pattern approximately fifteen feet apart. Each multifaceted crystal was glowing with light.

Staring in silent awe, mesmerized by the magical spectacle of light and form, the team failed to notice that Grubb had taken a position behind large boulders surrounding the massive crystals. He was invisible, but they could hear his words echoing against the cliffs and down into the valley.

"This is the end, you know!" announced Grubb in a deep, haunting tone. "This is the end!" he repeated solemnly and forcefully, his voice trembled ever so slightly. The sound of his words seemed to be emanating from the very center of the shimmering, crystalline formation.

Through a filmy curtain of undulating light, one could see across the valley were mountain peaks capped in gold and what appeared to be another sun shining on a different world. The Gripps were caught between two Dimensions—the pattern of reality created by Gripp logic and the improbable truth of what was confronting them.

Grubb called out loudly, "This is the end. You are at the end of this Dimension in Time and Space!"

Grist didn't understand. He cleared his throat and rubbed his face as if he were trying to wash away Grubb's words and the vision in front of him.

He hesitated momentarily before blurting out with enthusiasm, "These crystals must be markers for the civilization that lies just ahead! There is no doubt the inhabitants will possess answers to the Secret of Un-old-Age! It must be so!" He was obviously lost within his delusion of hope and anticipation.

Grubb's voice could be heard again, *"It's only about the heart!"* He repeated, "It's only about the heart!"

Grist snapped his head around, searching, hoping to catch a glimpse of Grubb who was still hiding behind a boulder.

Grubb's voice continued, "They can feel the love you hold in your heart!"

"They? They? Who's they?" questioned Grist, desperate to understand the words spoken by the hidden Ghost of Grubb. "Do you mean the leaders we are about to meet? Are they, the 'They' who feel the love in our hearts?"

The curtain of light dividing dimensions intensified as it moved closer to the edge of the cliff. The towering crystals stood silent, overlooking the valley below.

Fabius spoke quietly, "This plateau is now projecting a reverse-magnetic field. The longer we stay here, the more anti-gravity will affect us. Did you see Grubb? He is floating above the ground!"

Glittering, golden clouds of dust from the pathway swirled weightlessly around and between the three towering, glowing crystals.

"Something isn't quite right," replied Filloloper anxiously. "I have an idea of where we are, but do you think that Grubb has really become a ghost?" She turned to look at Grist who was speaking directly to the crystals.

"I know Grubb is the messenger!" exclaimed Grist, wanting desperately to believe that the crystalline forms were communication devices for the civilization just ahead.

"Our time is limited; we have only one Grabbon left before we lose our grip on this mission. We must have the secret," he implored. "Ring the bells! Ring the bells!" he repeated frantically. "Guide us to your civilization while there is still time, precious time!" He heard no reply.

Ever since his harrowing escape from the Grundells and his encounter with the *Sphere of Fear*, Grubb had obediently followed the sound of the bells with an open mind and heart. The bells had beckoned him, and he had pushed onward until eventually arriving at the mountain plateau.

Feeling a deep affinity for the glowing crystals, Grubb began asking questions and started receiving answers from the wisdom and knowledge held within their crystalline core.

Over the next few days, he had discovered he could resonate with the energy contained within the towers.

Only then, did he understand that answers had been available to him all along, but he knew his words alone would not change his fellow Gripps enough to experience what he had discovered.

Grubb watched and waited for the right moment and then floated into view as the nine dazed team members stared in disbelief at the ghost-like figure hovering slightly above the ground. He then positioned himself directly in the center of the crystalline formation.

"Listen for the bells! These are the sounds you have so courageously traveled to hear!" he said, closing his eyes and opening his heart to match the resonating tones of the illuminated crystals.

Perfectly formed, golden balls of light, shot out from the center of each crystal tower, moving into the second and then the third crystalline form, creating the powerful, haunting tones of the tolling of the bells.

Grist, Twist, and Scheme remained motionless as they watched and listened in awe and dismay, refusing to believe the scene before them.

The team was standing on a thirty-foot wide ledge overlooking the valley far below, and, in the distance were tall mountains rising sharply toward the sky.

Grist turned around, desperately hoping to see if there was something…anything more, when he realized that they had come to a dead-end. The pathway went no further. "Is this the end of the line?" he asked, looking at Grubb who was hovering amid the crystals. "Are you the one ringing the bells? Just you? This is it? T-t-this is all there is?" he stammered.

The Gripps immediately repeated the same phrases, questioning, "This is it? This is it? This is all there is?"

Without thinking, Grist and the other team leaders were unconsciously beginning to smile. The truth was beginning to dawn on them. A crooked smirk appeared on Twist's face, and a sneaky grin lifted Scheme's expression as they both became aware that Grubb's presence on this high plateau indicated the end of their journey.

All other team members were frozen in disbelief, immobilized by the stunning realization that the tolling of bells had led them to their mission's end. Their frantic, compulsive trek up the mountain had delivered only Gripp Grubb. Their only discovery was that he had been the source of the tolling bells.

"Is this all there is? Is this all there will be?" asked Stare in a bewildered tone of voice as he wiped perspiration from his forehead.

The answer was "Yes." There would be no shining city to discover, no advanced civilization, nor piles of Grold. There was no one waiting to give them the solution to their quest for Un-Old-Age. There was nothing more!

All their well-laid plans had been replaced by the unexpected. The incongruity of the situation, the actual, bizarre reality that was now facing them was definitely in opposition to their deeply ingrained Gripp logic.

Reaching the end of their journey was both a terrible disappointment and a welcome relief from all their pent-up energy. They were released from all the hoping and striving that were met only with obstacles designed to help them learn about themselves.

Babble looked around as if she had just awakened from a bad dream, and a faint smile crossed her face. "I believe we are in the midst of a massive cosmic joke!" she said, her voice containing a stifled laugh.

Scheme looked at Babble and started to chuckle, followed by Grist and Twist who both pretended to cough to hide their overwhelming disappointment, but they were also sensing the humor and the absurdity of the situation.

Soon all other team members felt a deep emotion welling up inside, and within moments they burst into laughter, releasing the extreme tension that had built up within them. Tears rolled down their cheeks, making them question if they were laughing or crying.

Gritt silently observed his team members laughing uncontrollably, and he, too, felt a Half-Synth smile forming and then slowly widening on his face. He enjoyed and appreciated the impact of humor coursing through his Half-Gripp body as the energy of laughter gave him a heightened sense of being alive.

Fabius and Filloloper were also infected with the sound of laughter and felt themselves releasing all the worry and concern that had filled their minds. In the background, they could hear the bell tones perfectly duplicating Grubb's rhythmic heartbeat.

Fabius motioned for Filloloper to follow him for a better view through an opening in the translucent curtain of light that hovered just beyond the cliff edge.

"You know, Filloloper, the Gripps refused to listen to Grubb. They thought he was the ghost in the Gripp raft who was beckoning them onward. They simply didn't understand that Grubb was trying to explain to them that they had reached the end of the trail and the end of their quest.

"These crystals are the magnetic boundary markers of Acronos. Over there, just beyond the veil dividing the two dimensions is another civilization with mountain peaks made of Grold. The time travelers had discovered it all, even though it remains just beyond their grasp. Grubb became their messenger — a messenger of the heart!"

Humor and Laughter

The energy of laughter is a spontaneous experience of moving beyond the mind into a place of suspended awareness. Humor arises when reality twists and turns just enough that you can no longer take the situation seriously.

Laughter helps to empower and unite the physical, mental and spiritual aspects of your human experience as it vibrates all parts of your being into an even, harmonious flow.

When your sense of humor is activated, you see beyond limitations that once held you bound in confusion, upset and pain.

Knowing that each moment is fleeting, you can learn to enjoy the healing energy of laughter and bond with those around you. Your heightened sense of humor can lighten your outlook on life and energize your body, mind and spirit.

PART SIXTEEN

A Vortex in Time

G RUBB, THE BIOLOGIST, WAS LOST deep in thought as he blankly gazed out from his position in the center of the triangular formation of crystals. He was unaware that the glowing curtain of light that marked the division between dimensions was intensifying and moving closer. His mind was still searching for answers as to why his best efforts to share his transformational discovery with his team members had resulted in hysterical laughter.

After nearly three Grabbons (days) of attempting to communicate with the crystalline forms, he had finally succeeded. Only when he entered the center point between the towers and aligned with the energy being emitted by the three crystals, did he become aware that the structures could duplicate the rhythm of his heart, which resulted in a sound like the tolling of bells.

How could Grist, Twist, and Scheme possibly understand that it was Grubb's unusual, personal encounter with the *Sphere of Fear* that allowed him to access the energy and purity of love? He had never before experienced such a revelation— an inner awakening—that opened his heart and enabled him to communicate directly with the energy and stored wisdom of the crystals.

He had decided to ring the bells as a beckoning call, hoping his fellow Gripps would follow the tolling sounds so they might witness for themselves what he had discovered...that the crystals marked the end of one dimension and the beginning of another.

His discovery was met with laughter and derision, even when in front of them was a shimmering curtain of light and beyond that the gleaming mountain peaks made of Grold. They couldn't see what was right before their eyes.

Grist's initial shock of seeing Grubb floating in the midst of the crystals was being transformed into total denial. He could not believe and refused to accept that their mission was over as Grubb had so emphatically declared.

"It has to be a conspiracy," Grist suggested to Twist and Scheme who were also suspicious of Grubb's intentions. "After all, Grubb was dead, and yet, here he is again. He was beckoning us to follow him."

The three Gripps quietly continued their private conversation, checking to be sure the other explorers couldn't hear them. It would not help team morale if they thought a devious, unseen force might be manipulating Ghost Grubb.

Grist was only partially right. There was a dominant unseen force that had the capability of overpowering Grubb and all the others, and it was moving towards them at an alarming rate of speed.

Grist turned and motioned for his team to gather around him and voiced his displeasure in a chiding, condescending manner. "The tolling of the bells," he laughed. "What a cruel joke to try to make us believe in failure...to attempt to convince us that our mission is over!"

He shook his head from side-to-side, his face tightened as he stared into the eyes of each Gripp assembled around him. "It's not over! It's never over until we lose our Last Grasp!" he smirked, kicking up a cloud of dust as he paced in front of his fellow team members who were still recovering from their collapse into hysterical laughter.

It's not over! It's never over
until we lose our Last Grasp!

"And so, our mission most certainly must continue!" He reiterated in a reaffirming tone. "Stare assured me that we have less than one Grabbon left before the next cycle of the Time Portal. There is no doubt; there is no confusion about our ability to succeed!

"What have we learned fellow Gripps? What have we learned? We have learned that no matter the hardships and despite an enemy who has been so extremely elusive and deceitful, we will fight to the end!"

Grist felt that he was once more in his element as Commander. He was, after all, powerful and responsible for the successful mission of the exploration team.

"Prepare to move out! We will follow that curtain of light until we find a way through it! Look, there, beyond that veil of light is Grold, fellow Gripps, shining so brilliantly on those mountain peaks. Where there is Grold, there is wealth! And where there is wealth, there must be a city hidden somewhere below those towering mountains!"

Grist raised his arms in defiance, calling out for the team to participate in another morale raising chant. The words began to echo in his head.

We grip on!
We grab on!
We grind on!
Because that is our way!

Just as Grist was visualizing in great detail the glory, honors, praise, and cheers that would ultimately greet him as a hero upon his return to Grippland, the ground quaked and shifted, causing him almost to lose his balance.

"The distortion field is activating!" exclaimed Fabius as he ran toward the edge of the cliff with Filloloper close behind. They both stopped short. There in front of them, the mysterious veil of light was becoming a twisting spiral, transforming into a powerful vortex.

A blast of cold rain rushed over the high plateau, bringing with it a strong wind that was whirling round and round as if its sole intention was to grab everyone in sight.

"The Vortex of Time has begun!" exclaimed Filloloper. "The Gripps always imagined there was an unseen force manipulating events, and this time they are right!"

"We do not have the ability to protect these explorers any longer," answered Fabius. "I'm afraid it's too late. They have simply run out of time."

THE SHIMMERING

Grubb had beckoned them with the tolling of the bells, never imagining that his discovery and their encounter with the moving veil of light would set in motion a chain of events that could not be altered. The energy field had shifted, and the Vortex was trying to correct that imbalance.

There was another being who was also very well aware that the veil between dimensions was transforming into a spinning Vortex of Time—a vortex that would soon to be absorbing everything and everyone in its path.

Gritt had been engineered to be half-Gripp and half-experimental science, a prototype for all future generations of synthetic beings. Gripp Society was at the point that information processing was the most critical element of their evolution. Gritt was their prize—the latest and most advanced version of half-Gripp and half-artificial intelligence, a Half-Synth if you will.

Indeed, there were significant unknowns in time travel. Everyone knew the risks. Since he was designed uniquely for time travel, Gritt could remain behind and continue searching and processing data and return at some future date with valuable information.

As a Half-Synth, he was programmed never to fail, equipped with a self-generating system designed to last into an indefinite future.

Yet, something had shifted deep inside the synthesis of organic and inorganic components of his body and mind. Now, there was a compelling need to help someone else survive the certain oblivion of the Time Vortex.

Gritt had felt an affinity with Babble from the very beginning of the mission. He was aware of her history as the official recorder of events for Gripp High Command.

Their first encounter was at the Central Prison, located several stories underground at Command Headquarters. No one ever officially questioned the fact that Gritt never was imprisoned like the rest of the team. They just assumed he had a criminal background like all the others.

He was also aware of Babble's special immunity status, which would be granted to her whether or not the mission was successful. He knew she was a spy for High Command and that they were relying on her Gripp Log reports.

Gritt didn't care what the reasons were for Babble's imprisonment. What was most important to him was for her to survive.

Even partially synthetic beings can learn to feel, he thought, reflecting upon the unique effect she was having on him while simultaneously processing the life-threatening scene unfolding before him.

The Vortex winds were coming closer and at a far higher rate of speed as Gritt desperately tried to locate Babble. He knew no one could endure the dynamic funnel of energy constantly pulling everything into its center.

Even with his extrasensory perception and his excellent hearing and sight, the Half-Synth found it impossible to locate the position of each team member in the midst of the fearsome force of twisting light.

After doubting Babble's chances of survival, he caught sight of a small figure sheltered behind large boulders. She was holding a monitoring device, recording every detail of the extreme violence of the Vortex now spinning ever closer to their location.

Babble could not have imagined that Gritt was watching her as part of his mission. His secret assignment was to survey and record events through his electronic eyes and process the data within his advanced processing unit.

However, something had changed. Gritt had developed feelings he had never experienced, unusual emotions that made him want to protect her from any danger to her life.

He began to run at his fastest pace to warn her to retreat immediately and to help her move as far away as possible from the swirl of light that was becoming more and more intense. But it was too late. Babble had mysteriously disappeared from her former location. He looked in all directions to see where she could have gone.

Turning his attention to the vortex, Gritt saw three figures, gesturing and shouting into the face of the violent winds now threatening their very existence. Grist, Twist, and Scheme were standing defiantly in front of the curtain of light marking the line between dimensions. They used taunting, challenging, deriding, and demeaning words, Gripp words.

"Nothing here is real!" they shouted at the Vortex. "You are no more than a pathetic light show designed by an unseen enemy to prevent us from capturing the Grold and completing our mission!" declared Grist, his eyes bulging and his voice filled with angry defiance.

Scheme in his formal role as the team's business leader had boldly stepped forward next to Grist to try to speak to the Vortex. "What is it that you want? What are you hoping to achieve? We want to negotiate. We are willing to come to some compromise."

Scheme was beginning to worry that perhaps there was no way to coerce the storm as he continued, "Why not just show yourself? What are your terms of agreement? We are always ready and willing to listen," he continued, turning to gesture a thumbs up to Grist and Twist.

There was no response. Only the continuous roar and pulsing sensation of the shimmering Vortex approaching ever closer to the Gripp's position.

Twist, the Politician, could not comprehend what he was witnessing. Without hesitation, he loudly shouted as if his words needed to penetrate deep into the center of that spinning, magnetic force field, "We are strangers here, and you have reason to be afraid, but we represent no danger, no danger to at all!" he continued with a twisted smile.

"I am certain we can find a compromise! We need to be on our way. I know we can make a deal!" Twist implored as his former grimace turned to a frown. "Let's make a deal..." His voice trailed off, swallowed by the roaring sounds of the twisting wind.

Gritt knew Babble was in immediate danger; she was standing far too close to the three defiant leaders of the team. But before he had a chance to warn her or even attempt to reach her position, he was astonished to see Grist suddenly swept away into the Vortex, followed by Twist and Scheme.

"Babble, run, now!" Gritt implored. "Save yourself! Run while you have the chance!" But Babble had no chance. Using all the speed that a Half-Synth possessed, Gritt ran to her and reached for her hand, only to feel her being pulled into a magnetic field of overwhelming power.

Gritt's mission to "survive at all costs" was pounding in his head, but he could not let her go. Conflicting emotions prevented him from allowing her to be whisked away from him, and he was clutching her hand when, within a flash, they both disappeared into the shimmering Vortex of Time.

Fabius and Filloloper were stunned in disbelief. They had witnessed the entire scene, feeling utterly helpless to intervene as the Gripps, numbers one, two, three, four, and eight were swept into the Vortex like so many leaves blown away by a sudden gust of autumn wind.

Their attention quickly turned to the last remaining team members who had taken refuge behind large boulders bordering the flat ridge, hoping that the powerful, spinning, force field of light would pass them by, unharmed.

Stare appeared to be frozen in position, blankly staring at his equipment. From time to time, he would shake his head, uttering over and over the same phrase, "There is no such thing as a Vortex of Time! How could there be?"

As an engineer, Stare was a very valuable member of the mission. He was the only one qualified to analyze any advanced technology they might encounter. He was also in charge of keeping track of time and serving as Master Keeper of the Tick of the Tock.

But Stare could only gaze in disbelief at this distortion of light manifesting before his eyes, shredding everything that he had ever learned about time. He was looking directly into the center of Time itself.

For a few brief moments, Stare, had officially become #1, but to no avail. He was analyzing his instruments when he realized there was no time left to reach the Portal. And just then, the whirling winds of the Vortex swept him away.

"Don't, don't they understand?" stammered Filloloper. "They are the ones who are creating this imbalance in the magnetic field!"

"Time seems to be catching up with them," responded Fabius. "The emotional imbalance within each Gripp has been magnified by the crystals many times over. Only Grubb who opened his heart was able to create a harmonic field of love."

"Are you saying that Grubb delayed the arrival of the Vortex? Do you think the Vortex wouldn't exist if they could have opened their hearts?" asked Filloloper sadly.

There was no time to respond. The Guardians of Acronos watched as Grubb ran toward the remaining team members, hoping he could convince them to radiate and receive the love he felt inside.

As he hurried to where Dr. Grouse had taken shelter with Grimm and Grind, he wondered if they would be able to understand what he was trying to say.

How could they possibly comprehend what happened to me? They didn't experience the Sphere of Fear, Grubb thought. *Yes, Doctor Grouse knows about medical treatments, but she was trained to cure, not prevent disease and trauma.*

The psychologist has studied the mind and the archaeologist learned about past societies. Neither discipline was designed to comprehend the opening of one's heart to a Spiritual Revelation.

Finally reaching their shelter, he found Grouse, Grimm, and Grind attempting to come up with an escape plan.

As the team psychologist, Grimm was attempting to review the multitude of theories of personality and psychological problems she had studied, thinking something she had learned might miraculously provide a solution to the horrifying situation confronting them.

Grind was also searching for answers from her vast knowledge base. As an anthropologist, she always tried to look deeper and deeper into the past for answers to problems, but with all her studies, she could not provide a solutions to their immediate danger.

Grubb was well aware that there were precious few Grippers (minutes) left for him to explain why the Vortex of Time had reached such a state of imbalance.

If he could succeed, he might be able to convince them to experience a sense of peace within themselves by opening their hearts. Then, just maybe, they would survive.

Sadly, it was not to be.

Not even Grubb whose open heart had allowed him to discover the crystals, the markers located between dimensions…not even he was able to prevent the inevitable.

Within a brilliant flash of white light, the four remaining team members disappeared into the Vortex of Time.

THE BLUE ORB

The incessant roar and violent winds generated by the powerful magnetic storm were slowly subsiding. "Is this how the journey ends?" Filloloper asked sadly, wondering if Fabius might have another explanation for the Eye of Time explorers' fateful and surprising demise. He stood silently, still trying to recover from the shock of an event that neither of them could have imagined.

As the Guardians of Acronos, they were responsible for preserving and protecting all that was Level Seven, but it was not within their ability to save the invaders from being pulled into another dimension in time.

Fabius could see tears falling down her cheeks as she turned her head from side to side as if trying to somehow shake off or stop all the emotion now flooding through her.

"We failed them," suggested Filloloper. "We didn't protect them. I am certain that if we had tried harder, we might have reached the ones who…who…" Filloloper stopped speaking. She was lost again within the fateful vision of the entire Gripp Team being swallowed alive by a force they could neither comprehend nor destroy.

Fabius moved closer and said confidently, "We did our best, and now they're gone. There was nothing more we could do. We have to understand that we were not responsible. They made their own decisions."

"I understand," replied Filloloper, her voice still choking with emotion, "but I thought...I wanted to believe that they still had enough time, perhaps just enough time to learn and understand the Seven Harmonies. I truly wanted to believe that they could somehow become aware of their inner knowing."

Fabius did not want to admit that for some reason he also had believed there was still hope and time enough for these strange interlopers to learn from all the events they had encountered on their journey. He was searching for words to answer questions he could not explain when out of the corner of his eye, he caught sight of an unusual streak of electric blue light moving across the horizon.

Quickly alerting Filloloper, Fabius watched as the beam of light made a hard right turn and accelerated at an unbelievable rate of speed. Then, it took a sharp left, heading directly toward their position on the mountain ridge.

"I've never seen anything move so fast!" exclaimed Filloloper, mesmerized by the blue light becoming larger and larger as it approached them.

"Run toward those boulders up ahead!" called Fabius as he tried avoid a collision.

Before they could gain the momentum needed to escape, they found themselves surrounded by a brilliant cloud of blue, luminous light, accompanied by the sound of echoing words:

It was perhaps the shimmering,
within that sudden glimmering

that set my mind to wandering
within its depths of wondering
when from out of the blue
I began to see images of you!

Filloloper and Fabius felt as though they were suspended in time as the sparkling, blue light was taking shape and form. Before their eyes, it became a kaleidoscope of color rotating round and round.

Stunned by the radiating light field surrounding them and still in shock from witnessing the powerful Vortex in Time sweep away the entire Eye of Time Exploration Team, the two dogs remained motionless.

They were unable to move or understand the sounds emanating from inside the expanding and contracting rainbow of iridescent colors that were washing over them, first blue and red, then green and purple, then yellow and orange, and back to blue again.

As each color passed over Fabius and Filloloper, they appeared to become larger and then smaller, and then back to their usual size repeatedly.

Fabius noted that the curtain of light hovering between dimensions was somehow preventing the energetic being at the center of the blue light from manifesting into form.

The dogs were vigorously trying to escape, but they were locked within the overwhelming power of the light field. Their only way to communicate was to send thought-forms to one another, affirming that they would endure.

The magnetic field of the boundary curtain—the veil between dimensions—was becoming stronger. At the same time, the partially formed being within the blue light was exerting even more energy to manifest into form.

Suddenly, without warning, the sheer, flowing curtain of the dimensional veil and the powerful energy of the blue light intertwined. The two force fields became intricately entangled in a web of dynamic patterns.

The combined power of both electrical fields clashed and unleashed an overwhelming burst of magnetic energy expanding through time and space.

PART SEVENTEEN

Equilibrium

THE ENTANGLEMENT BETWEEN the two energy fields was complete. Only a subtle humming could be heard emanating from the towering crystals marking the boundary between dimensions. The mountain ridge had regained its former equilibrium.

Gone were the Gripps' defiant shouts and screams; gone were the pleas for deal-making; gone were the tears of sadness and remorse.

The racing spectacle of blue light that had been transformed into a pulsing rainbow of colors had also vanished, taking with it Fabius and Filloloper as well.

The mountain ridge remained as it was before, holding its dominant position and maintaining the force field that prevented one dimension from entering another. It was guarding against all those who would attempt to trespass and test the integrity of that power.

They were gone…all of them were gone.

The Gripps had ultimately come face-to-face with time and experienced all those moments they were so desperately seeking to capture. They had received their wish. Their mission was complete, but perhaps not as they had intended.

The Guardians of Acronos found themselves enveloped in a compelling, magnetic cloud of blue light, and they too were being swept away.

Thoughts of the *Before Time* continued to race through those two entities without form. Sensations changed into perceptions and then into wild imaginings, evaporating and then reforming, attempting to regain what was before.

They felt themselves flying through a forest of tall evergreens onto a large flat field of grass. The blue cloud of light began to shift into form as rhyming words filtered through the swaying branches:

> *Formless energy manifests being*
> *within the light beams streaming.*
> *Hurtling through time and space*
> *Faceless faces soon to replace.*

Those words...those spoken words completed the transformation. "So, nice to see you again, Princess Filloperna, and you as well, Commander Fabius."

No longer on the mountain ridge, still dazed from the process of transformation, Filloloper and Fabius were not fully aware that the power of Delphos, combined with that of the distortion field had shifted and fully manifested them as their former selves.

Unaccustomed to the weight of a human body and his heavy sword and shield, Fabius momentarily lost his balance and instinctively reached out for Filloperna.

For a precious moment in time, the two warriors, Commander Fabius and Princess Filloperna, stood side-by-side, as they had done at the time of their final departure and reassignment to Level Seven.

Delphos began to sing haunting lyrics that floated through their minds.

Dare to wander.
Dare to wonder.
Dare to wander in your wondering.

Moving through all those thoughts of you,
wondering who might be tumbling through
all those windows and doors of your mind,
sense the sensation of the 'you' to find.

Through the melody playing
it will ultimately be saying
within your heart, you'll see,
you are your greatest discovery.

Is it right or is it wrong
to seek out a place to belong,
a somewhere you can truly own,
that place you call your home?

What is real? What is make-believe?
What illusion do we all perceive
from the handwriting on the wall
to that stairway down the hall?

We wander within our wondering
always tempting fate with our discovering,
no detours too far along the way,
living within our spirit of play.

Our road stretches into infinity,
our dreams are fueled by that energy,
and then it all begins again.
Searching for that special place,
to find that magical key
that truly defines you and me.

We wonder within our wandering
tempting fate with heedless conjuring,
knowing full well our guidance sees
through the darkest night with such ease.

Is it right or is it wrong
to wonder in your wandering
searching for a place you truly own
somewhere you can call your home?

The lyrics of the inspiring melody subsided while the mystical, iridescent cloud of moving blue light continued to change, forming and reforming, into a more familiar vision…the enormous fish by the name of Delphos. He had arrived just in time to carry the Guardians of Acronos safely from the imminent threat of the unstable Force Field.

Delphos appeared more than pleased with his ability to save Fabius and Princess Filloperna as well as with the performance of his spontaneous lyrics.

He was swaying from side-to-side just above them as though suspended by an invisible cord, slowly rolling over once, and then again. His eyes widened as an enormous grin crossed his face, confirming his overwhelming satisfaction.

A brief moment later, after regaining his composure from his joyous gyrations, Delphos slowly lowered his position to peer at eye level into the eyes of Fabius and Filloperna and spoke again in rhyme:

> *I am late! I almost missed the gate!*
> *I know…I am very, very late.*
> *Even though I increased my velocity*
> *while swimming through the Cosmic Sea.*
>
> *I was in the midst of dimensional shifting*
> *when I caught sight of all that glittering.*
> *Then within the recesses of my mind,*
> *I realized the trouble that I might find.*
>
> *I am late; I am late.*
> *I almost missed the gate.*
> *And I am very, very sad to know…*
> *I did, indeed, miss the show.*
>
> *But I do admit I was not too late*
> *to save you from a desperate fate*
> *of being removed to another dimension*
> *where you'd be held in strange suspension.*
>
> *It was through my amazing acceleration,*
> *which was not an easy calculation.*
> *Knowing the energy pathways to pursue,*
> *I fortunately was able to rescue you.*

Fabius and Filloperna were both dazzled and bemused by Delphos' appearance. Their fragile emotions seemed to be suspended somewhere between laughter and tears. They were grateful he had saved them from the Vortex of Time and delighted to be together as they were in the *Before Time*. And yet, they felt saddened that the ten strangers from an even stranger land had been so quickly swept away into oblivion.

Filloperna gazed lovingly into Fabius' eyes, and then turned to Delphos saying, "We are so very thankful that you were passing through!" She smiled, trying to push back the traumatic memories of witnessing the Gripps being overpowered by the Vortex.

Filloloper clutched Fabius' hand tightly when she caught sight of a bright red cloth lying twisted in the grass a few yards to the right of her. Tears were welling up in her eyes as she held Fabius' hand even tighter.

"Great courage is needed to be a warrior and to fight for what you believe, no matter whether you are right or wrong," she said, pointing at the red flag lying on the field.

"It seems like only moments ago that the Gripps were here." Racing through her mind were images of Grist leading the team in morale-raising chants on this very meadow. They tried to regain their courage and momentum by playing a game called *Gripp-War-Ball*. I am certain they did their best..." Filloperna's last statement ended with her looking directly at Delphos.

He could see that Filloperna remembered the Gripps' perseverance, and he felt her emotion moving through him. The giant fish hesitated and then replied,

> *Well, yes, I imagine you could say*
> *that they really had their day*
> *and you may kindly lament them*
> *never finding their momentum,*
> *but now they are simply dead and gone.*

Fabius stepped forward and said, "It's not easy to die, especially on the field of battle." He took a deep breath and continued, "Filloperna is saying that in their way, the Gripps just never gave up. We did our best to guide them, hoping to make them aware that the real war was inside of them, not in front of them."

Delphos listened silently and then began to sway back-and-forth, mumbling to himself before replying.

> *Hmmm...well, yes, yes, yes!*
> *Allow me a moment to guess.*
> *You are attempting to justify*
> *any reasons which might apply*
> *to support some bizarre conclusions,*
> *which might end their strange delusions.*
> *But sadly, there is no one left to blame!*
> *They have merely left the game!*

Fabius glanced at Filloperna, and then moved closer to Delphos and said, "I know that as the Guardians of Acronos, we were privileged to have received this assignment. We are grateful to feel free again and experiencing life. Filloperna truly believes in her heart that the Seven Harmonies could possibly add clarity and understanding to the Gripps' never-ending quest for Un-Old-Age."

Delphos performed a small, half-roll from side-to-side, and then gained altitude, circling slowly over the two Guardians. He was lost deep in thought within his multidimensional mind, calculating all reasonable probabilities in space-time.

After hesitating for a moment, Delphos began to glow with a transparency that Fabius and Filloperna had experienced once before in the Crystal Cave. He spoke slowly, the tone of his voice tinged with a touch of sadness as he was fading from view.

> *Well, you know,*
> *a show is just a show.*
> *And as you may recall,*
> *I believe I've said it all.*
>
> *Now it's time to find the door,*
> *to explore another distant shore.*
> *So, I must bid you a fond farewell,*
> *unless you find a less sad story to tell....!"*

Filloperna could not contain herself, realizing that within a blink of an eye Delphos could disappear like so much cosmic dust. "Wait, please wait!" she pleaded. "Your song, remember your most lovely song. You must recall the words." Moving her awareness into the center of her heart, she began to sing. Her melodious voice was filled with tender emotion.

> *Dare to wander.*
> *Dare to wonder.*
> *Dare to wander in your wondering.*
>
> *Moving through all those thoughts of you*
> *wondering who might be tumbling through*
> *all those windows and doors of your mind,*
> *sense the sensation of the 'you,' you might find.*
>
> *Through the melody playing*
> *it will ultimately be saying*

within your heart, you'll see,
you are your greatest discovery.

Delphos was touched by the soft lilting, heartfelt sound of Filloperna's voice as it resonated through every part of his being. He attempted to reply, and then stopped to turn away so that neither Fabius nor Filloperna could see the emotion moving through him.

He slowly made a half-turn, and then gently swayed directly in front of her saying, "I have never heard anyone sing my songs back to me. In some ways, perhaps in many ways, those words become much more meaningful." Delphos' voice cracked, and his eyes filled with tears. "Filloperna, your voice is wonderful. You are a true warrior on so many levels!"

Filloperna appreciated Delphos' reaction and was surprised to hear him answer in such a sincere and emotional tone of voice. She was not aware that he had already calculated the possibilities of rescuing the ten strange beings swept away by the Vortex of Time.

Filled with emotion, Delphos was still not willing to admit that her haunting performance had affected him so profoundly. He tried to evade her request to save the ten explorers by saying:

Their inevitable is regrettable,
but now they are so forgettable.
Their lack of learning is a crime,
always running, they ran out of time,
never finding their rhythm or rhyme.

They never discovered their inner tone
or any identity they could truly own.

So, they are finally dead and gone,
twisting and spiraling in the far beyond!

Fabius and Filloperna noticed that slowly, ever so slowly, Delphos had one more time fully materialized. They knew there was only one chance to convince this brilliant and stubborn multidimensional being that it was worthwhile to consider the impossible…to try attempt an improbable rescue.

They clung to the hope that perhaps within the bizarre nature of the Universe, these pushy, brazen beings from another world who were struggling so diligently to survive, could somehow still be saved.

THE DREAM ZONE

A strong, chilly wind was blowing through the tall, Sycanion trees and across the broad, flat, grassy field, which the Startlings called their *Dream Zone*.

Fabius and Filloperna were standing where Grist had determined that this field was actually a military training ground to prepare to fight an enemy, any enemy. He had decided this was a perfect place to get his team in shape, since, he was worried they were losing their ability to grab on, grip on and grind on.

He had divided the eight Gripps into two teams, a red team and a blue team, to play a game called *Gripp-War-Ball*. Grist was so desperate to find their elusive foe that he ordered the Gripps to play against each other, attempting to activate their fighting spirit to battle the real enemy they might soon encounter.

Fabius and Princess Filloperna were also warriors. It was impossible for them to deny that their thought processes held a similar dynamic—an unyielding steadfastness that would never allow them to walk away from a commitment or a field of battle.

As warriors, they had been trained since childhood to develop a strong body combined with a keen intellect. The two guardians held an unwavering belief that an unseen, spiritual force was always present to assist them and were confident that even against overwhelming odds, they would possess the courage and personal fortitude necessary to achieve victory.

And yet, the Guardians of Acronos knew that in this very moment, they were facing an enormous, iridescent fish with unusual powers and a strange sense of humor who preferred to communicate in song and rhyme.

Filloperna was the first to speak to Delphos, taking full advantage of the fact that he was still emotionally impressed with her ability to sing the words of a song that he had spontaneously composed.

Those words continued to resonate within Delphos, and Filloperna knew that she had only one chance to convince him to help save the tortured Gripps, and it had to be now! She was also aware that the righteous spirit moving through her warrior form would not settle for defeat without entering the field of battle.

She turned to Fabius and instantly transferred her thought-forms to him, wondering if those same images and feelings lived within his heart.

Fabius squeezed her hand tightly; and with that loving acknowledgment, Filloperna gazed up at Delphos and entreated, "If you believe we have enough time, we want to try to save the Gripps once more!"

Delphos wiped his eyes with one enormous blue fin as if to gesture his reply. He did not want to use the words he was thinking to himself: *Please don't ask the impossible!* But indeed, that is precisely what she had asked.

The Guardians watched as Delphos was rocked back-and-forth like a gigantic child suspended in an invisible rocking chair, as he spoke,

> *I rescued the two of you,*
> *and now you wish to say*
> *that for these wayward Gripps,*
> *I should also save the day.*

Delphos could not help but be both amused and emotionally moved by the beautiful, young warriors standing in front of him with such firm resolve and pure hearts.

I am a most ephemeral being, he thought, *but then again, perhaps I have been far too spoiled by my present incarnation. I certainly have not experienced the drama and the passion that these brave souls represent.*

Delphos would not allow himself to admit that he wanted to help. But then again, just by being Delphos, he also loved his mischievous way of testing people or any other entity for that matter. So, instead of agreeing with Filloperna and Fabius, he replied:

> *They were always such a bore*
> *ever since they washed ashore.*
> *It came as neither shock nor surprise,*
> *when they became crystallized.*

Indeed, I saved them once before,
and now as your words do implore
that if by some miracle they did survive,
they would be grateful and not contrive
to always seek out glory and fame
to proudly attach to their name!

Extraordinarily pleased with his immediate, rhyming reply to their request, Delphos went into a full roll over and then started swimming back-and-forth slowly in front of Filloperna and Fabius, as if taunting them to respond with a reply even half as unique and witty as his own.

Filloperna cleared her throat and responded:

It was always a war
they were looking for,
but all they could find
was the prison of their mind.

Fabius and I can do no more
to help them find freedom's shore.
The key lies in your ability
to provide the faintest possibility
that when we open that prison door,
their souls may now be allowed to soar!

A huge smile spread across Delphos' face, and he responded by immediately executing a double roll over, and then began to float around Fabius and Filloperna at such a rate of speed that they almost fell into each other.

"So, you really reached for it, didn't you, Filloperna! That was a wonderful rhyme, indeed! But then, perhaps I underestimated your resolve. I seem to forget from time to time when I visit Acronos that this is most certainly Level Seven!"

With a twinkle in his enormous eyes, he announced, "Whenever you're ready! There's no time to waste!" He smiled ever so slightly at his play on words.

DARE TO WANDER

Without further hesitation, a bright, luminous, blue cloud was surrounding Fabius and Filloperna, accompanied by Delphos' last-minute instructions and solemn admonitions. "You do understand that we may not be capable of finding the Gripps' location within the Vortex of Time...in time?" he jested and then said in rhyme:

> *Stay close behind the gleam*
> *of my magnetic stream.*
> *I will attempt to provide*
> *a window and a door*
> *to contact them as before.*

Additional instructions continued as the bright, blue cloud slowly lifted away from The Startlings' *Dream Zone*.

Delphos made it clear that the Guardians would not be traveling in their familiar forms, either as warriors from the *Before Time*, nor as Fabius and Filloloper, but instead as two, luminous balls of golden light.

If they were able to reach the Gripps within the Vortex of Time, their voices alone would activate the Gripps' ability to see them as they were before. They would not appear as balls of light, but as the two dogs who were known to them only as the Guardians of Acronos.

Delphos did not wait for a response. He was gaining altitude and speed and thought to himself:

> *Should I be admitting*
> *that I am enjoying my exemption*
> *from any rules of prevention*

of my travels through time and space?
Should I not explore the possibilities
of all my future potentialities,
reveling in the concept of the chase?

Delphos did understand that it was his keen sense of adventure, as well as the possibility of learning more about the mysteries of the Universe that continued to drive his never-ending curiosity.

Within less than a few Grippings (seconds) three balls of light, one brilliant blue and two glowing with an intense golden color, could be seen streaking high in the sky above Acronos before disappearing altogether.

There was no doubt that Delphos was once again testing his boasting words, "Should I not explore the possibilities of all my future potentialities!"

Yet, after many detours and several changes in altitude and course corrections, Delphos reluctantly came to the sad conclusion that although he had tried, the Vortex of Time had disappeared within itself.

How could he possibly confess to his fellow travelers that he had failed! Instinctively, the giant, radiant fish in the form of a large, blue ball of light spontaneously began to chant as he continued to search the horizon, gazing far out into the Cosmos for any sign of the Vortex.

Out of sight and out of mind,
A Vortex of Time I must quickly find!

Delphos increased his altitude dramatically while attempting to construct a plausible excuse he could use to explain why he could not find the Gripps.

At that moment, he heard Filloperna shout out, "I can hear them! I can hear their cries!"

"Hmm...out of sight out of mind...?" Delphos questioned himself. He had relied on his cosmic sight and had neglected his ability to hear distinctly.

Who would have guessed that the combined senses of Filloloper and Filloperna provided a special ability to hear that allowed her to discover the missing explorers?

Indeed, they could now see the ten Gripps tumbling and spiraling around and around. Their tortured faces were distorted in pain and confusion as they struggled against the grasp of the ever-spinning Vortex.

There appeared to be no way to escape the magnetic field, and these explorers from another land could no longer beg, borrow, steal or even make a deal with this incredible force that was pulling them ever closer to its center.

How ironic it was that these ten bold and courageous members of the Eye of Time Exploration Team found themselves caught within the Eye of Time! Delphos was more than well aware that to stray anywhere near the magnetic center of the Time Vortex would be disastrous for all concerned.

Realizing that it was far too late to save the Gripps, Fabius suggested to Filloperna that it was time to say goodbye to these strangers who possessed the strength and will to try to survive, but apparently, could not or would not learn from their experiences.

---

*How ironic it was that these ten bold and courageous
members of the Eye of Time Exploration Team found
themselves caught within the Eye of Time!*

Filloperna listened to Fabius' words as she witnessed the
power of the Vortex pulling apart the very essence of its
captives. Her unwavering bravery as a warrior in the *Before
Time* combined with her sense of justice would not allow her
to stop. She felt compelled to attempt one last try and urged
Delphos to bring them closer to the Vortex center, nearer the
Gripps who were calling out in fear and pain.

The giant fish disguised as a massive ball of blue light
didn't seem to hear Filloperna's request to bring them closer to
the Gripps. He was lost within his multidimensional mind,
calculating the overwhelming odds of rescuing the tormented
beings versus the extreme risk of being absorbed and
devoured by the Vortex. The Guardians were surprised when
Delphos did not respond.

After several moments had passed, he answered the only
way he could, which was to speak in rhyme:

> *It is my simple observation*
> *that the Gripps lack imagination.*
> *Caught in an endless conversation*
> *never grasping the information.*
>
> *Always victims of statements*
> *they can never forgive,*
> *they are captives of words,*
> *which they'll never outlive.*

Repeating memories of memories,
their future is bound.
Without vision or curiosity,
youthful freedom's not found.

Listening intently to Delphos' melancholy rhyme, Filloperna thought that perhaps he was right; maybe there was no hope. Within her mind, she caught flashes of memories, reflections of the adventures she shared with Fabius and the Gripps who had dominated their time and space.

Gone were the orders and the constant chorus of parading Gripps chanting in cadence: *We grab on! We grip on! We grind on! Because that is Our Way!* Gone were the shouts and commands to find the enemy!

Filloperna's memories revealed vibrant scenes unfolding before her. She remembered watching Gritt in the Forest of Tones rushing to Babble's side, holding her tightly when she had been shot and looking into her eyes with such loving care and concern.

How could Filloperna possibly forget the confusion and frustration of the Gripps when they were incapable of escaping the Hedges of Hedora or their stunned silence when the Bash Birds performed and tried to teach them about rhythm and rhyme at the Crossroads of Time? And then, there was Delphos who freed them when they were crystallized in the cave at Crystal Falls. All these images and more continued to flood through her memory as she realized that the Gripps' struggle to find the secret of Un-Old-Age was finally over.

And yet, she remained bewildered as to why they were so obsessed with Un-Old-Age; and at the same time, they willfully ignored and did not even question the meaning of the Seven Harmonies. Why could they not understand how the Harmonies were linked directly to all their personal experiences in Acronos and the ability to maintain their feeling of youth?

Filloperna was continued reviewing the scenes from their journey when, suddenly, a massive shockwave from the very center of the Vortex rolled over her, bringing with it the sounds of obsessive chanting by the tormented Gripps whose voices were repeating over and over again, "Grab, grasp, grip, and grind! Grab, grasp, grip, and grind!"

They were in the midst of experiencing time crossing over time, bringing the power of their words back to them in a never-ending spiral.

Their negative words and beliefs were creating erratic emotions that were generating a series of interweaving, electromagnetic waves. Those waves were being magnified many times over by the Vortex.

The Gripps were experiencing time crossing over time, bringing the power of their words back to them in a never-ending spiral.

Delphos knew that if the Vortex pulled the trapped explorers into the center of its magnetic intensity, the energy of the Gripps' emotional imbalance could set off a hazardous, chain reaction.

"There is still time!" promised Filloperna, hoping that the Gripps could ultimately forgive and let go of all their devastating beliefs, words, emotions, and actions initially designed for self-defense, control and conquest.

They needed to release their deeply held concepts that based in fear and to eliminate the words and beliefs that were creating feelings of hate, which led to conflict and war. Somehow they must erase the past experiences that were controlling them and bringing them ever closer to oblivion.

The Gripps' intense energy of anger and fear was feeding the Vortex, and now that very same imbalance was pulling them deeper into the center of that spiraling light. They desperately needed to forgive and let go of their past anger and pain, which was holding them suspended in the swirling Vortex of Time.

They desperately needed to forgive and let go of
the past that was holding them suspended
in the swirling Vortex of Time.

Delphos hesitated to mention to Filloperna and Fabius how very futile their attempts were to save these strange beings from another land. He thought that perhaps speaking in rhythm and rhyme would be the most appropriate way of wishing them a final goodbye.

You must surely agree
it's now too late, far too late.
The Gripps' words and deeds
have delivered their fate.

In the beginning,
when I was just cruising through,
I had no idea that a Vortex
was endangering you.

I was only searching for lyrics that rhyme
and here I am chasing a Vortex in Time.
But now, I must say goodbye and adieu.
As a fond farewell, I'll write a song or two
to those disappearing without a trace
into the depths of never-ending space.

Filloperna and Fabius could not hear Delphos, and so he watched and waited as they moved closer to the Vortex in Time. There was no up or down, in or out, over or under in the surging energy of the Vortex, and yet they could see and feel direction. They used their intention and intuition to find the explorers who were hopelessly entangled in words and beliefs, which had endangered the entire society of Grippland by creating constant conflict, thus aging them prematurely.

Their words had become their mantras, ultimately shutting down their ability to see, hear or accept a future with life-enhancing possibilities.

The explorers were hopelessly entangled in words
and beliefs that had endangered the entire society of
Grippland by creating constant conflict,
thus aging them prematurely.

LOST IN TIME

Intent upon rescuing the prisoners caught in the *Time Spiral*, Princess Filloperna and Commander Fabius were preparing to rebalance the Gripps' negative energy, which was empowering the *Vortex of Time*.

Fabius' mind was flooded with scenes from his warrior past when so many times he had faced overwhelming odds. In his very last battle, he had saved Princess Filloperna, but in so doing he had sacrificed his own life. He wondered what sacrifices they would need to make this time.

Was there something deep inside each of them that was encouraging and pushing them to fight against adversity? Was history about to repeat itself? What could be the reason for the overwhelming compulsion driving Filloperna's and his own attempt to save these uninvited explorers?

Fabius could not help but remember how often he had held his ground in battle, standing fast, and never retreating. He could sense the same inner strength, power and determination was moving through Filloperna. What Spiritual force was propelling them besides their moral compass and a benevolent inclination to save these ungrateful strangers?

Were these Gripps even worthy of saving? Questioned Fabius, knowing full well how menacing they were and how they refused to learn, thus relying only upon information from their past experiences.

And now there was to be a duel in the sky over Acronos. Fabius felt this was one of those moments in which he was compelled to act without being fully aware of any particular justification or understanding as to the reason why.

It seemed as though his actions were being compelled and guided by an *Intuitive Force Field*. But there was no time left for conjecture as to the 'what if' and 'why for' or 'should he' enter into battle.

And then, the energy of the Vortex shifted again. As far as Fabius could see into the distance, there was nothing! The Vortex of Time had disappeared from view, and with it the captured Gripps as well. He breathed a sigh of relief. Perhaps this meant that the real threat to Acronos was over, and they could restore the delicate balance and equilibrium of nature.

How ephemeral we are, thought Fabius, as he attempted to communicate silently with Filloperna, but the intensity of the magnetic stream created by Delphos made it almost impossible to send thoughts through the atmosphere.

I am so glad it is over! He thought. But within that very same thought, Fabius also realized that it was not over.

Delphos dramatically accelerated his speed and lowered his altitude to bring into view the Vortex of Time that was moving just above Acronos, altering everything in its path. Before their eyes, the hills, valleys, and streams they had known so well were being replaced by different fields and woods of a mysterious origin.

Filloperna was obviously right. Not only had she felt compelled to save the Gripps, but her very own *Spiritual Force Field* had made her aware of all other possibilities, including the possible destruction of Acronos.

Delphos lowered his altitude, cautiously following the path of destruction and re-creation that the Time Vortex was leaving in its wake.

The Acronos of the past was now the Acronos of the future, thought Delphos as he viewed the rocky hillsides overlooking the shoreline being replaced by vast fields covered in a variety of colorful flowers. It was evident that the longer the Vortex continued to maintain its current path, everything and everyone that they knew and loved could very well disappear, leaving behind an entirely new landscape.

The Vortex of Time was indeed a wheel within a wheel— two ever-spinning wheels, one of time and the other consisting of energy, each desperately trying to rebalance and establish an equilibrium.

Nothing could possibly survive within that spinning force of Time! Thought Delphos. He was confident that they would not survive, but then again, he had witnessed far stranger phenomena in his long and varied lifetimes in the Cosmos.

He accelerated his flight pattern and followed the Vortex at the safest possible distance, watching the enormous power of Time contained within and forcefully moving that swirl of luminous light.

It continued onward, cutting a path of transformation along the coastline of Achronos before heading out to sea. And then, it disappeared!

The emotional trauma of that moment startled Filloperna and Fabius as dramatically as the physical shockwave vibrating around and through them. Before their eyes, the past, present, and future of Acronos had been altered in a brief moment in time.

Forgiving and Letting Go

To forgive is giving for-ward to begin a new life. Forgiving and letting go provides an opportunity to consciously create a future free from the negative aspects of the past.

Letting go of the negative beliefs, thoughts, words, events, emotions, and people that caused you upset and pain will allow the release of energy that has trapped you to another time and place.

Time tumbles each of us in the flowing stream of life until we thoroughly understand the enormous, hidden power within our beliefs. Those beliefs become our thoughts, activating emotions that generate words, which form our habits and behaviors.

Through this process of manifestation, beliefs create, manifest and maintain your personal reality. By forgiving and letting go of past heartaches and negative experiences, you can consciously create a renewed life of harmony, joy, and peace.

PART EIGHTEEN

Visions in Rhythm

SOARING HIGH ABOVE THE TREETOPS, Delphos, Filloperna, and Fabius followed closely in the wake of the massive energy Vortex, which only moments before had distorted all of time and space in its path.

Just below them, Acronos displayed an altered, glowing landscape that gave the impression of a magical star-field covering the ground. Energy auras of radiant light sparkled around newly formed forests and over cascading rivers and streams, creating a three-dimensional light show, glowing brilliantly in the afternoon sun.

Each leaf, branch, flower and every blade of grass shimmered with colors of every description, revealing the immediacy of creation formed in the wake of the spinning, vortex that had transformed all it touched from what it *was* into what it *was to be*!

And now it was gone! Only the sound of a faint, magnetic crackling and humming remained in the atmosphere. The three, intrepid, camouflaged beings of light followed the path of destruction and recreation until reaching the shoreline where the Vortex had suddenly changed course and disappeared out to sea.

The rolling hills above the beach had become a bright yellow field of blooming flowers, which replaced the rocky hillsides that had first greeted the travelers from another time and place. All traces of the Gripps' arrival and exploration of Acronos were eliminated. But why?

Delphos was fully aware that the disappearance of the intense energy field was not random and this realization led him to ponder what other reason could have caused the Vortex's abrupt departure.

A sly smile of knowingness crossed his lips as he raised his altitude to peer far out to sea. There, in a rolling bank of dense fog were traces of streaming, multicolored lights shifting back-and-forth on a trajectory directly on course to the island of Acronos.

Nothing is born before its perfected time, Delphos mused. *It's always about time! And if my suspicions are correct, Time will be chasing Time to arrive right on time. There is usually a reason, and yes, perhaps, even a rhyme!*

A CLOSER VIEW

The three bold travelers, cloaked as blue and golden balls of light, changed course to head out to sea and increased their altitude as they cautiously approached the dense bank of rolling, illuminated fog that was covering the island. Flashes of lightning coupled with deep, resonant, sounds of thunder rolled overhead. But was it really thunder?

There were no signs of a raging storm, only the intermittent flashes of light moving within the fog. There were also distant echoes of what sounded like chanting, a strange, rhythmic chanting that seemed to be beckoning them: "Na...Nanana...Na... Nanana...Na!"

Concerned about the danger of moving directly over the island, Delphos quickly lowered his altitude dramatically and began to hover just above the shoreline. His ever-present curiosity, however, brought him closer than initially intended.

Shockingly, he could see shadowy creatures of an unknown origin moving within the density of the fog. He cautiously maneuvered to get a better view when the chanting and beating sounds of thunder became louder.

The dense fog was slowly lifting, and it soon became apparent that those powerful flashes, appearing as lightning, were light streams emanating from the three, illuminated, crystal towers on the island.

The Portal in Time was now being charged and recharged by the beams of light. A strange dance of energy was moving across the island — a dance of balance and imbalance within the Portal and far beyond.

As the fog dissipated, the thunder sounded more like a drum, and a brilliant blue light was moving back and forth in perfect synchrony with the rhythm of the beat, echoing far beyond the island and out to sea.

And the chanting, that strange rhythmic chanting, began repeating. Only this time both the tone and the beat were more intense as if there was music being played to create a trance-like state in all those with the ability to hear. It seemed to be calling forth those illusory creatures from the very depths of that rolling fog, "Na...Nanana...Na... Nanana...Na!"

Perhaps it was synchronicity or just by chance that the haunting, rhythmic beat compelled the shadowy forms to approach the pulsating lights. There, barely visible within the density of the thick fog, emerged Stare and Babble, the first of the ten, stunned Gripps.

Stare stumbled a few steps forward and then stopped to look back at his teammates slowly gathering together. He had no recollection as to how they had miraculously escaped from the raging, Time Vortex or why they had been deposited back at the three crystals marking the Portal in Time on Acronos Island, nor did he wish to know.

Everyone on the team had miraculously survived, but according to Stare's previous calculations, he knew, even in his state of disorientation, that the critical departure date for their return to Grippland had long past.

Babble was also adrift in a trance-like state as she robotically recorded images of the team assembling in a semi-circle around Commander Grist.

"We....we have succeeded!" he mumbled in a less than convincing voice. "We have once more emerged victor..." His words of victory were cut short, interrupted by the overpowering sounds emanating from a platform next to the Portal.

The Synchronicity of Time crossing time was taking center stage. Flashes of brilliant light were moving mysteriously within the fog, slowly forming into recognizable shapes accompanied by the hard-driving rhythmic beats and sounds of chanting repeating over and over again:

> *Na...Nanana...Na... Nanana...Na!*
> *Na...Nanana...Na... Nanana...Na!*

For a moment, there was only silence until a very familiar voice rang out, "Welcome! Welcome! I am Bo, and this is Ben! As you may remember, we are the Rockin' BoBens! We are here to entertain you with exciting new compositions created just for you!"

Bo Bash continued, "Welcome to our stage, which happens to be strategically located directly upon the Crossroads of Time! You have arrived *just in time* for our first performance of the day!" With that simple introduction, the Bash Birds began to sing a powerful, rhythmic, beat-driven song.

RUNNING OUT OF TIME!

You gotta get that harmony,
You gotta get that rhyme,
You gotta get that curiosity,
You're running out of time.

You've lost that youthful spirit.
There's nothing left to chase.
Right or left, your words inhibit,
and now you're lost in space.

Locked within your hesitations,
looking for that then of when
following your deviant deviations,
look at you…you're back again.

Never using words that rhyme,
you're always running out of time!

Na…Nanana…Na… Nanana…Na!
Na…Nanana…Na… Nanana…Na!

Still searching for that youthful glow,
you hope your logic will discover.

Yet, you won't forgive and let go
so hopeful dreams you can't recover.

Here you are back again...
Still searching for that then of when.
Never using words that rhyme.
Always running out of time!

Na...Nanana...Na... Nanana...Na!
Na...Nanana...Na... Nanana...Na!

Locked within all your powers,
losing all those precious hours,
never feeling joy and wonders,
watching clocks with all those numbers.

Here you are back again.
Running your same old game.
Never trusting your intuition.
Now, ain't that a shame!

Level Seven Harmony
was a secret never found.
Though you kept looking...
looking all around!

Here you are back again
running your same old game.
Seeking Grold to grow Un-Old.
You have no one else to blame!

Na...Nanana...Na... Nanana...Na!
Na...Nanana...Na... Nanana...Na!

You gotta find your rhythm!
You gotta find your tone!
You gotta escape what's hidden
within all those words that drone!

Here you are back again
running your same old game.
Now, ain't that a shame!

Here you are back again...
Still searching for that then of when.
Still searching for that then of when!

The Rockin' BoBens had delivered a special tune, a brilliant performance, dancing and singing their way across the stage while beating out an incredible rhythm designed to resonate deep within the hearts of those in their audience.

The Gripps were more than well aware that the song, "Running out of Time!" had been written specifically for them, and this time rather than being disturbed, they seemed emotionally moved by the penetrating and challenging lyrics.

Babble finished recording the song and thought to herself: *If my reports survive, perhaps in the distant future, someone will review them and decipher the full meaning of all of our experiences here in Acronos.*

The heavy fog surrounding the Time Portal was being replaced by a soft, glowing mist, illuminated by the towering crystals. A moving veil of light was forming a curtain, which would soon reveal to all those present why the Vortex of Time had taken such a sudden turn away from Acronos to head out to sea in the direction of the island.

The Guardians, now visible as dogs were delighted to experience such a lively, upbeat performance presented by Bo and Ben who were so fashionably dressed in their tuxedos of brilliant, blue feathers. The Guardians were even more surprised when the Brothers Bash introduced the second song in their repertoire.

Delphos was discretely observing the show a short distance away. He wondered what unexpected synchronicity the Bash Birds might weave into their next song that would undoubtedly illustrate their amazing *Visions in Rhythm*.

He was reluctant to admit how much the lyrics had impressed him. The words kept repeating over and over in his head...most especially: "Here you are back again, running your same old game. Ain't that a shame?"

This multidimensional, cosmic traveler was well aware that the *Vortex of Time* had been playing a game, a game of balance and imbalance. The Force activating the Vortex was attempting to correct an anomaly in space and time, created by the Gripps' unintentional arrival on Level 7.

It was not by chance that the Vortex took a sudden right turn out to sea to transport the explorers from another world back to the Portal precisely on time.

Delphos thought to himself, *Perhaps all crucial moments in time are actually related to Synchronicity — the simultaneous collision of events that seem to fit together perfectly, yet also appear to occur at random.*

The Time Portal answered his question when it began to re-activate spontaneously.

Everything seemed to be changing, even unexpected variations were reflected in the appearance of the Gripps. The once self-determined and cunning Grist, Twist, and Scheme seemed to be far less consumed by their self-importance. Instead, they appeared more focused on other team members.

Babble, Stare, and Dr. Grouse seemed to have awakened from a dream. They were more alert, open and alive. Grubb, as well as Gritt, the Half-Synth, were displaying increased determination and clarity in their behavior and appearance. They had all been changed in some way, perhaps none more than Grimm and Grind who seemed far more confident and ready for what might come next in their lives.

There is more to survival than just staying alive, thought Filloloper. *Survival without purpose and learning would never be enough! The Vortex of Time was a cruel teacher, but it may also have been a benevolent Master!*

Fabius and Filloloper were reflecting upon all the events, which had led them to this very moment when they, too, felt changes in their anatomy. The crystals forming the Time Portal were radiating all the colors of the rainbow. The energized and transformative energy field was affecting everything and everyone on the island.

Feeling the dynamic, pulsing energy surging through his body, Stare shockingly surmised that the impossible had happened. For some reason, the Time Portal was opening.

"How can this happen?" he questioned. "We were very late. We had missed the opportunity to reach the Portal, and we had run out of time! There were no Grabbons (days) left to grab onto!"

And then, he fully understood that they were, indeed, actually on time! The Vortex of Time had *erased time* to bring them back *in time*…to be *on time*!

Stare could not contain his amusement and smiled broadly at this amazing turn of events.

He quickly urged his fellow teammates to enter the Portal immediately, guiding the nine valiant members of the Exploration Team to assemble in the very center between the three beaming crystals.

Indeed, as Masters of Synchronicity, the Bash Birds had appeared on the Crossroads of Time once before, but this time it was to say their final goodbye to those intrepid *Explorers in Time* whose lives were dedicated to *chasing time.*

THERE'S STILL TIME

As the first powerful sensations of the Portal began to penetrate every fiber of their being, the Bash Birds took center stage and in perfect harmony and synchronicity launched into their final song.

Gritt, the Half-Synth, spontaneously reached for Babble's hand as he heard the first, lilting lyrics.

> *There's still time…*
> *Time enough to shine*
> *through all that darkness,*
> *which always kept you blind*
> *to the memory of your words*
> *now repeating in your mind.*
>
> *There's still time…*
> *Time enough to shine!*
>
> *There's still time enough to feel*
> *with an aching heart to heal*
> *time enough to know*
> *all you need to grow.*

Let those dark clouds rain.
You don't need to feel the pain.

There's still time...
Time enough to shine!

Escape, escape from being
trapped within your fears.
Escape those false beliefs
gathered through the years.
Embrace joy and happiness
until sunshine reappears.

There's still time...
Time enough to shine!

There's time enough to recover
from the twisting of your schemes
to realize the potential
of all your hidden dreams
and finally discover the true
Rhythm of your Rhyme.

There's still time...
Time enough to shine!

Know the real you is waiting
somewhere deep inside
for your heart to escape
from the fear you always hide,
remembering the reasons
you continued on and tried.

There's still time...
Time enough to shine!

Your future is in you.
Fate has long been waiting there
for your courage to grow stronger
thus allowing you to care
to open your mind and heart
for the wisdom you can share.

There's still time...
Time enough to shine!

Bo and Ben bowed to their audience. They were extremely pleased to have presented a truly memorable performance of their heartfelt composition, which was designed to inspire hope within these bold, but beleaguered explorers from another world.

Fortunately, they had magically appeared once again to meet the Gripps at the *Crossroads of Time*, and it was at this moment that the synchronicity was in alignment and ready to take the *Eye of Time Explorers* home.

The pulsating crystals were glowing even more brilliantly. With only a few precious moments remaining, the Guardians of Acronos rushed toward the Portal to say farewell.

As they approached the Portal, they could feel the power of the intense energy that was now penetrating everything and everyone on the island, especially those within its very center.

The powerful streams of rainbow light flowed through each member of the Gripp Exploration Team. Their bodies were vibrating at an extremely high frequency until they became more and more translucent.

Huddling closer together within the center of the Portal, the team members were comforting each other, resigned to their fateful departure from the Land of Acronos.

Reaching the perimeter of the Time Portal, Fabius and Filloloper could immediately feel the effects of the force field sending a resonating wave of energy washing over them, changing every cell in their body.

The Portal was reaching its maximum force as the Guardians witnessed the entire team becoming more and more transparent, almost ghostlike in their appearance. Some had tears in their eyes, while others displayed expressions of shock and sadness.

"It's time!" declared Fabius. "The Gripps are on their way home, if they are fortunate enough to arrive safely."

Filloloper drew closer, standing only a few feet away from the Portal that was in the process of reaching its maximum brilliance. From the edge of the perimeter, she made her presence known to the departing Eye of Time Explorers to bid her last farewell.

Standing close behind her, Fabius was also affected by the energy flow and felt his deepest emotions rising within him. He watched the bold explorers transforming into translucent light forms as they slowly began to disappear.

The changes in the time travelers were dramatic but no more obvious than the shift within Fabius and Filloloper. As they experienced the potent power surging through them, the Guardians became aware that they were once again being transformed into Commander Fabius and Princess Filloperna.

Watching with amazement, the Gripps were overwhelmed when for the first time they beheld the ancient identities of their Guardian hosts—two proud and mighty, young warriors from the past.

With the light streaming intensely through him, Grubb stretched out his arms as if he were trying to reach beyond that powerful veil of light to touch Fabius and Filloperna. He opened his hands and resting on his palms were the Trillia seeds he had taken with him from the Under-Earth. It was his final gesture of goodbye and with it a message of hope for future communications with Acronos.

Babble and Gritt were still tightly clutching each other's hands as they began to disappear within the brilliance of the Portal. Each Gripp in their own way was attempting to say goodbye, most with tears in their eyes, still others with more hopeful expressions on their face.

But there was one remaining Gripp who was still struggling against that powerful, magnetic field to move forward. Using all of his force, he managed a final step.

He ceremoniously clasped his hands together and held them close against his chest and then extended his clasped hands outward, pointing directly toward the two warriors standing before him.

It was #1, Grist, the Commander, who was demonstrating his acknowledgement of the Guardians of Acronos and the journey they had experienced together. Demonstrating the official Gripp Salute was his way of honoring their presence and bidding them farewell.

With that simple gesture and in that final moment, Fabius and Filloperna felt deep within their hearts the emotional impact of the many life-changing events their journey with the Gripps had provided for each of them.

And in one brilliant flash, they were gone!

The Portal in Time closed instantly, taking with it those ten intrepid souls from another world whose destiny would remain unknown.

Awestruck and emotionally shaken by the Gripps' departure, neither Fabius nor Filloperna were aware of another powerful presence hovering over them. Only the rhyming words floating effortlessly through the air provided his identity as he sang one last song.

> *A spectacular sight it was indeed*
> *to see those who were finally freed*
> *to escape back through time and space*
> *filled with memories so hard to erase.*

> *Little did they understand or contemplate*
> *such a compelling journey that was their fate.*
> *I hope their hearts will open, and they may find*
> *Love and harmony with peace of mind.*

The interdimensional traveler, known as Delphos had briefly manifested and was swaying back-and-forth just above the two warriors, enveloping them in a glowing, blue orb of light. Delphos smiled broadly, his bright, black eyes reflecting the sun's golden glow, showering them with love.

Fabius and Princess Filloperna could not help but wonder if something had also shifted within each of them. The overwhelming presence of Delphos as an Oracle and intermediary in Time was always awe-inspiring, and yet they felt another transformation taking place. Indeed, the time-traveling warriors were now manifesting as the two dogs, Fabius and Filloloper, the Guardians of Acronos.

Delphos executed a quick roll over, and in a blaze of brilliant light, he, too, vanished into the *Nothingness.* The Portal in time was closed. Its bright, pulsating light was becoming a soft glow emanating from the core of each of the three crystals.

"Do you think they will remember?" asked Fabius, gazing out at the distant horizon.

"What do you mean, remember," replied Filloloper.

"Do you think the Gripps will remember their experiences here, or will it seem as though it was only a dream?"

Filloloper turned to Fabius and looked deeply into his eyes for several moments and then replied, "We remembered each other after so many centuries, didn't we?"

Fabius returned her gaze, his voice full of emotion, "How could I ever forget you?"

Filloloper simply nodded her silent reply, then brushed her head against his, sharing his deep-felt emotion. "Life is really about what you cherish...what you hold dear in your heart. Hopefully, those time travelers will remember. After all, opening your heart and loving each moment might be the only way anyone ever experiences time standing still."

---

*After all, opening your heart and loving each
moment might be the only way anyone ever
experiences time standing still.*

She paused and looked up at the towering crystals. "How many Portals in Time do you suppose there are?"

"More than we will ever know," replied Fabius, staring into the depths of the still glowing, crystalline forms. "Far more than we will ever know."

"There are many mysteries and riddles in life," responded Filloloper. "Perhaps, one day, we will experience even more answers to these questions we hold so dear to us. The Bash Birds certainly had something to say about life and time. For some reason, I continue to hear those haunting lyrics repeating in my head." Filloloper began to sing:

> *Your future is in you.*
> *Fate has long been waiting there*
> *for your courage to grow stronger*
> *thus allowing you to care*
> *to open your mind and heart*
> *for the wisdom you can share.*
>
> *There's still time.*
> *Time enough to shine!*

"You sing those words so beautifully!" commented Fabius. "The Bash Birds were always trying to present their wisdom the only way they knew how. We can hope the Eye of Time Explorers will be able to open up their hearts and minds," Fabius responded softly with just a hint of sadness in his voice.

"Most certainly those are lessons we all can share," Filloloper replied while watching the afternoon sun casting a golden glow over the island as soft, white clouds drifted overhead. "You know, it is going to be extremely quiet here now that the Gripps are gone; but then again, perhaps, we do need a rest from all the stress of the emotional and physical journey we experienced over the past few days."

Fabius nodded and was about to say a few words when out of the corner of his eye, he saw something moving very fast across the water. "Do you see it? It's over there moving parallel to the coastline! No, now it seems to be moving in another direction. Do you see it?"

Filloloper immediately turned her attention toward the Bay of Acronos and witnessed a strange object skimming across the water, heading directly toward them.

Catching the beams of light and casting a shadow on the gentle waves was a figure traveling at an incredible rate of speed, sending sprays of water in all directions. It was definitely on a direct course to the island, quickly coming closer and closer.

"Can you make out what it is?" asked Fabius pretending he could not comprehend what he was seeing.

Filloloper did not reply; and when Fabius turned to look at her for an answer, he saw her wiping the tears rolling down her cheeks.

She had recognized the very unusual and yet familiar, zigzag pattern of the speeding phenomenon coming toward them, partially flying and partially running across the water.

It was none other than their friend, the Great Kolourian Zigalot named Phelan.

ABOUT THE AUTHOR

JOHN TERESSI, a native Californian, began his exploration into higher consciousness through the study of psychology and metaphysics. In his twenties, he experienced a transformational, spiritual event—a moment suspended in time—when walking through a forest on the Monterey Peninsula, CA.

This memorable event led him on a quest to explore many *Power Places* throughout Europe and Mexico, always seeking more answers to satisfy his ever-questioning mind.

The wisdom derived from his extensive travels, led by intense curiosity and guided by intuition, inspired this lyrical adventure that was written to uplift your soul and empower your heart.

EDITOR AND PUBLISHER

VERLAINE CRAWFORD is honored to have been part of the development of this delightful and fantastical journey through time that will entertain and inspire you.

Verlaine is author of the books, *Ending the Battle Within: How to Create a Harmonious Life Working with Your Sub-Personalities* and a book of poetry: *Daughter of God: Angelic Messages of Wisdom and Love.*

ACKNOWLEDGEMENTS

I would like to thank all those who have inspired and encouraged me to write and complete this book, "Portals in Time: The Quest for Un-Old-Age." It has been a meaningful, illuminating, and challenging journey. The story and its many characters seemed to take on a life of their own.

I would particularly like to thank Verlaine Crawford, my editor, for her inspiration and extreme patience. Without her countless hours dedicated to intense discussions, revisions, and editing, there would be no book.

For all the late-night conversations about other dimensions and life here and beyond this experience on Planet Earth, I send my love and appreciation to my dear friend and mentor, Hubert Gilchrist. We spent countless hours discussing the origin and meaning of words and how they can become controllers and or liberators in our lives. I am saddened by his departure to another realm in 2017, before I could present this final version to him.

I also wish to extend my gratitude to Dirk Wagenaar, Jr. who was my friend since childhood for his enthusiastic response to my stories. Over the years, it was my pleasure to enjoy his wry sense of humor and enthusiasm for life, poetry and the written word.

I would like to thank my father Joseph for being the ultimate example of Un-Old-Age (He was always much younger than I.), and my loving mother, Mary, for her kindness, support, wisdom and understanding.

And I send gratitude to my grandparents, Fortunato and Anna Tripodi, whose youthful outlook on life (even beyond their seventieth wedding anniversary and into their nineties) served as a powerful reminder and example that age is definitely not a number.

Lastly, I would like to thank all those dear friends in England, France and Spain whose optimism and enthusiasm have motivated me to continue on as a writer.

THE SEVEN HARMONIES

When you embrace the Seven Harmonies, you hold the keys to unlock the Secret of Un-Old-Age. You will soon realize that there is no such thing as "old energy" since the Universal Life Force is moving through all of creation at every moment.

The wisdom of the Harmonies assists you in releasing blocked energy thus allowing you to feel younger, more vibrant, and full of life.

Just as you can enjoy the harmony of beautiful music, you can experience your unique tone and individual rhythm and rhyme. You will be able to trust your intuition, know your heart, live in joy and wonder with humor and laughter, and learn to forgive and let go of negative concepts and memories.

You will enjoy a feeling of at-Oneness and renewed peacefulness with yourself and the world around you.

HARMONY #1

Your Inner Tone

Your inner tone reflects your dominant feeling nature and acts as a resonant, guiding beacon that can indicate which events and circumstances are in harmony with your life.

Just as there are no two fingerprints or snowflakes exactly alike, this unique vibrational frequency signifies your true nature, character and manner of being that define personal motivations and the decisions that are most beneficial for you.

Your ever-present, inner tone influences your responses, attitude, and interactions with people and events. When you are aware of your inner tone, you will be able to make choices that are more in Harmony with your heart and soul.

HARMONY #2

Rhythm and Rhyme

Rhythm and Rhyme are your heart, mind and body connection creating the musical harmony you feel inside. This harmony enables you to make the very best choices every moment at the Crossroads of Time and serves as your harmonic guide to those events which most closely match your true identity.

Rhythm is your inner tempo or beat that helps form and define how you relate to the world. Do you feel comfortable in upbeat, high stress situations or are you more productive in low stress environments?

Rhyme is the melody, the flow of your feeling nature, which is alert to all matching events, people and activities that will create the desired harmony in your life.

Acknowledging your life's unique Rhythm and Rhyme helps to determine the tone, tempo and flow of your natural rhythm, which frees your mind and heart to become the true you in all aspects of life.

HARMONY #3

Intuition and Trust

Intuition is your inner knowingness. It is an instinctive feeling, which protects and enhances your life experiences. Your inner guidance comes through quiet words, dreams, visions or feelings.

Monitoring all aspects of life, intuition is your sixth sense alerting you to events in the present as well as in the future, providing information that is beyond your conscious reasoning.

As you begin to hear, sense or feel your inner guidance, you will develop trust in the information. When that trust grows stronger, you will be able to respond immediately to warnings of danger and also to follow specific pathways to your success.

Using your intuition, you will become more aware of people, places and experiences, and you will expand your ability to perceive information beyond the physical world around you.

HARMONY #4

Knowing Your Heart

When you know your heart, you are resonating with the Harmony of Love and are in contact with the ultimate power of creation, rejuvenation, and transformation. The Source Energy of Universal Love animates and flows through you.

Remember, it is all the aspects of fear (hate, anger, distrust, jealousy, and depression) that paralyze and imprison you.

When you listen to your heart, you are closer to fulfilling your dreams and expanding all your future choices. Opening your heart welcomes the Light of Love to dissolve the darkness of your fears and to fully energize your life.

Knowing your heart creates a healing process, allowing you to feel young no matter how many years you have lived.

HARMONY #5

Living in Joy and Wonder

As you let go of past programming and conditioning, you will once again feel the joy and wonder of your youth. You allow positive memories and new concepts about who you are to dissolve the negative words and thoughts that have created fearful filters influencing your world view.

By focusing on images of inspiring subjects and positive experiences, you lift your vibrational frequency and envision new possibilities for your life.

Imagine wonderful people, beautiful places, and pleasant events you desire in your life to activate intense feelings of joy and inner peace that will heal your heart and soul.

When you live in joy and wonder, you will re-experience your youthful energy, excitement, curiosity, and enthusiasm and will marvel at the miracle of life and the beauty around you.

HARMONY #6

Humor and Laughter

The energy of laughter is a spontaneous experience of moving beyond the mind into a place of suspended awareness. Humor arises when reality twists and turns just enough that you can no longer take the situation seriously.

Laughter helps to empower and unite the physical, mental and spiritual aspects of your human experience as it vibrates all parts of your being into an even, harmonious flow.

When your sense of humor is activated, you see beyond limitations that once held you bound in confusion, upset and pain.

Knowing that each moment is fleeting, you can learn to enjoy the healing energy of laughter and bond with those around you. Your heightened sense of humor can lighten your outlook on life and energize your body, mind and spirit.

HARMONY #7

Forgiving and Letting Go

To forgive is giving for-ward to begin a new life. Forgiving and letting go provides an opportunity to consciously create a future free from the negative aspects of the past.

Letting go of the negative beliefs, thoughts, words, events, emotions, and people that caused you upset and pain will allow the release of energy that has trapped you to another time and place.

Time tumbles each of us in the flowing stream of life until we thoroughly understand the enormous, hidden power within our beliefs. Those beliefs become our thoughts, activating emotions that generate words, which form our habits and behaviors.

Through this process of manifestation, beliefs create, manifest and maintain your personal reality. By forgiving and letting go of past heartaches and negative experiences, you can consciously create a renewed life of harmony, joy, and peace.

THE GRIPPS
EYE OF TIME EXPLORATION TEAM

An assembly of ten Gripps who were imprisoned for crimes against Grippland are granted the opportunity to receive amnesty if they volunteer for a time travel expedition to find the Secret of Un-Old-Age.

GRIPP #1, COMMANDER GRIST

Grist is a stern and hardened veteran of many Gripp wars, yet he is optimistic and ready to grind on. Suspicious by nature, he is always searching for an enemy and on guard for surprise attacks. He lives in a constant state of agitation since time is running out for their mission quest. He was imprisoned for disobeying orders even though he had successfully directed his troops to win the battle.

GRIPP #2, TWIST,
THE CORRUPT POLITICIAN

Twist is charismatic and energetic with a ready smile. He was chosen to negotiate treaties or to find ways to take over any territory or resources they might discover. He usually succeeds at tricking his opponents and has successfully constructed his life with words, and the meticulous twisting of all those words. He was prosecuted for accepting bribery.

GRIPP #3, SCHEME, THE SCANDALOUS BUSINESSMAN

Scheme is a large-bodied, round-faced businessman and deal-maker who is known for his greed (he was prosecuted for fraud). He is a master manipulator and was chosen by High Command to make deals with business leaders if they found a civilization. In truth, he is looking for Grold.

GRIPP #4, BABBLE, THE PUBLICIST

Babble is a young, attractive woman with a background as a publicist who was imprisoned for possessing classified information. She was chosen by High Command to report on the mission and to spy on the other team members.

GRIPP #5, STARE, THE ENGINEER

Stare is a tall, thin, narrow-faced, brilliant introvert who is obsessed by time and is the *Keeper of the Tock*. He designed power plants as an engineer and followed orders to change calculations that resulted in an explosion.

GRIPP #6, GROUSE, THE DOCTOR

Dr. Grouse is an older, angry and intelligent female, medical researcher who hopes to gain riches by finding a way to stop the aging process. She was arrested for fraud and her company closed when a cure she developed didn't work.

GRIPP #7, GRUBB, THE BIOLOGIST

Grubb is strong of will and body and a vigorous explorer of nature. He was chosen to work closely with Dr. Grouse to identify any plants, which could be the answer to Un-Old-Age. He was imprisoned for creating dangerous substances.

GRIPP #8, GRITT, THE GEOLOGIST

Gritt is tall and handsome by Gripp standards and a Half-Synth who was chosen to be an observer and protector to ensure the Mission's success. His job was to search for minerals, most especially Grold. He also holds a secret yet untold.

GRIPP #9, GRIMM, THE PSYCHOLOGIST

Grimm is tall and thin-faced with deep-set eyes. Her job is to monitor the psychological fitness of the team. She became grim when arrested for using positive and uplifting words, *forbidden words,* to help her patients.

GRIPP #10, GRIND, THE ARCHAEOLOGIST

Grind is a researcher who loves learning. She was imprisoned for studying and hoarding hundreds of *forbidden books* and was chosen for her knowledge to assist in communicating with any tribes or civilization they might encounter.

TIME AND MONEY IN GRIPPLAND

Time in Grippland is measured in a variety of ways, such as: **Half-Grippings, Grippings, Grippers, Grippons, Grabbons and Grinds.**

A *Half-Gripping* = equals a half-second.

A full *Gripping* = one second.

A *Gripper* = one minute (60 *Grippings*)

A *Grippon* = one hour (*60 Grippers*)

A *Grabbon* = one day (24 *Grippons*)

A **Grind** = one year (365 *Grabbons*)

An entire Gripp lifetime = a *Grasp*.
When a Gripp dies, it is called their *Last Grasp.*

Money in Grippland = Grippars

50 Grippars = ½ Grabb

100 Grippars = A Grabb

1,000 Grippars = A Full Grabb

10,000 Grippars = A Complete Grabb

THE WORD MUSEUM

High Command had decided to pass laws against forbidden thoughts and thus created the *Word Museum*, which was established to lock away all personal expression.

It was considered treasonous to speak or write words such as *honor, dignity, gallantry, trust, harmony, hope, joy* and *love* were certainly treasonous and forbidden. Those words endangered the overall survival of the "Greater Order of Grippland" (*Greater Control* by High Command). Therefore, most positive and uplifting words were labeled as ephemeral words—simple platitudes without purpose, substance, or order.

Instead, words such as *Duty, Obedience, Obligation,* and *Sacrifice* replaced all words expressing personal desires. No one knew why the hidden words were treasonous, only that they were. They were considered unacceptable concepts from another time and place.

Few of the citizens questioned the establishment of the Word Museum. To object would mean going to trial. And a trial guaranteed that you would be declared guilty since everyone was considered to be guilty until proven un-guilty, which was always impossible.

— Chapter: Eye of Time Exploration Team

QUOTES

Part 1: The Eye of Time Exploration Team

*He was immersed in silence, suspended in a pause
within the very framework of Time itself.*

*What enemy slips and slides within the tides
and within itself is now beckoning
us to enter and explore?*

*The most significant threat is when you do not know
where or when the next danger
will surround you.*

Part 2: The Valley of Acronos

*Is time a spiral a simple thread of energy wound
round and round itself?*

*He could hear distant whispers of the past moving
within the winds of time.*

Part 3: Is This a Dream?

*The words began to echo in his mind, sweeping over
him like the warm embrace of power.*

*He looked into the mirrored surfaces, which were
angled in such a way that they reflected into one
another like an ever-expanding collage of images.*

You are on a much higher level of existence now. The clash of armies, the destruction of cultures, the wasting of lives is all behind you

Remember your words…and remember to breathe, Fabius. Breathe deeply! Let that fire in you become vibrant again! Know that the Harmonies will be there for you! And remember to enjoy the adventure!

Life is always about the Now and not the Then of When. Power is ONLY available at each moment and all those extended moments, becoming more moments, ultimately becoming the Powerful Momentum of Time moving through all things!

Every being has a different walk. We all speak in a variety of ways, and we carry ourselves in our particular manner. It's the way we interpret the space around us. – The Tower Tree

Part 5: The Forest of Tones

When the trees match your tonal frequency, your unique signature, the forest will be able to communicate with you.

There are subtle energies everywhere, waiting to communicate without the benefit of using words.

Altogether in unison, the entire Forest of Tones was creating beautiful music – a harmonic resonance that

perfectly matched the majestic,
tonal quality of the Universe.

Part 6: The Crossroads of Time

*Acronos had always been a place of refuge, a
transition destination for those who had progressed
beyond the need for confrontation and aggressive
action.*

*Being spontaneous is the only way you can catch the
real you in Time.*

*Time is what you wish to explore. Time is
always presenting a door, an opening to here or there,
to now or then, or even before.*

Part 7: Crystal Falls

*You mean those who refuse to listen and learn will
experience the 'Time Spiral' bringing forth similar
and possibly even more shocking events?*

*Fear replaced trust; and as a result, discord
replaced harmony. Their words betrayed them, and
their thoughts secretly and
irretrievably stole their future.*

Part 9: Hedges of Hedora

*You must learn to trust entirely to understand the
truth completely. Trust is one of the keys to living
your life in harmony.*

*You can only hear, sense or feel Hedora by tapping
into the flow of synchronicity. Then you can move
with her effortlessly. It is all part of the
process of learning the Seven Harmonies.*

*It is always easier to believe that what you know is all
you need to know. Lessons learned
are lessons earned.*

*Hedora isn't a person. Hedora is your Intuition. She
is your inner guidance system.*

Part 11: The Under-Earth

*There would be the possibility of learning more about
the Grundells' special herbs, plants, trees, and flowers,
any one of which might provide answers to the Secret
of Un-Old-Age.*

*Trillia can vary their vibrational rate of humming
when they sense unusual changes in Acronos. Legend
says they can grow anywhere and can
communicate messages over vast distances.*

*We are the energy of the choices you didn't make. We
are your failures and your faded hopes and all of your
forgotten dreams. We are your inner reality
manifesting in front of you to show you who you
are. — The Sphere of Fear*

*It's not over! It's never over until we lose
our Last Grasp! — A Vortex in Time*

Part 16: Equilibrium

The Gripps were experiencing time crossing over time, bringing the power of their words back to them in a never-ending spiral.

How ironic it was that these ten bold and courageous members of the Eye of Time Exploration Team now found themselves caught within the Eye of Time!

They needed to release deeply held concepts based in fear and eliminate words and beliefs that created feelings of hate, which led to conflict, subjugation, and war. Somehow, they must erase past experiences that were controlling them and bringing them ever closer to oblivion.

They desperately needed to forgive and let go of the past that was holding them suspended in the swirling Vortex of Time.

The lost *explorers were hopelessly entangled in words and beliefs, which had endangered the entire society of Grippland by creating constant conflict, thus aging them prematurely.*

Part 17: Visions in Rhythm

*Your future is in you. Fate has long been waiting
there for your courage to grow stronger thus
allowing you to care to open your mind and heart
for the wisdom you can share.*

*There's still time...
Time enough to shine!*

*After all, opening your heart and loving each
moment might be the only way anyone ever
experiences time standing still.*

WE HOPE YOU ENJOYED
"PORTALS IN TIME:
THE QUEST FOR UN-OLD-AGE!"

If you found this adventure thought-provoking
and entertaining, please feel free to post a review
at "Portals in Time" at Amazon.com.

You may contact us at
HighCastlePublishing@gmail.com

Follow us on Facebook at
www.Facebook.com/PortalsinTime

www.ingramcontent.com/pod-product-compliance
Lightning Source LLC
Chambersburg PA
CBHW030801260626
47169CB00001B/148